To Rahel.

with best wishes

from

Rhamin

Coming soon by Bryce Thomas

Lucy Lockhart: The Awakening

The first Lucy Lockhart adventure

Rhamin

by
Bryce Thomas

THOMAS HAMILTON & CO.

First published in Great Britain 2010
by Thomas Hamilton & Co Publishers
80 Warham Road, Harrow. HA3 7HZ

Cover artwork by Neil Booth

A CIP catalogue record of this book is
available from The British Library

ISBN: 978-1-907696-02-2

Printed and bound in the UK
by CPI Mackays, Chatham ME5 8TD

FIRST PAPERBACK EDITION

www.thomashamilton.co.uk

To my wife June

I am indebted to my wife June for all her hours of patient reading and checking of grammar; and to my son Bryce Jnr. and daughter Helena for all their help and advice.

PART 1

FIRST CONTACT

CHAPTER ONE

The plan was flawed.

From the very beginning Zelda had warned them. But hunger drives all living creatures to take unfathomed risks. And they were all hungry.

It was a plan Rhamin had considered more than once. But men were deadly creatures. He remembered only too vividly how his mother had died. It seemed a long time ago now, but no amount of passing years would lessen the memory he carried with him. Solin hadn't been born so he didn't know. He didn't recall the days when their father, Anval, and his pack were hunted down by men.

The pack had killed an animal, one of six or more in a herd, which belonged to men. But it was far away from the enclosures that men built for mile upon mile with sharp, metal wire strung between thick wooden posts. Somehow, they had escaped their open cages. Rhamin remembered at least six cattle roaming through the long dry tussock grass of the plain that was bordered at one side by woodland where they lived and at the other by the rocky base of the foothills.

It seemed too easy really. The pack, with their long teeth, could have killed all the creatures, but they only hunted what they needed to eat. 'You stay here,' Dori, Rhamin's mother, had commanded, leading her young cubs to the shelter of a rocky outcrop that straggled alongside the woodland. From there the youngsters could watch the hunt and learn how the pack worked as one, overtaking their quarry and killing it. Only if it ran did the wolves give chase. It was a necessary part of the hunting game and it was essential to show the youngsters how to bring down a fleeing animal.

The cattle seemed totally witless. They possessed little sense of danger and had no idea how to cope with it when it presented itself. The wolves circled the herd time and time again until eventually the dumb creatures started to become aware that there was something amiss. Rhamin watched, fascinated, as the cattle became more and more unsettled and began milling about in a circle, kicking up dust from beneath their feet as they trampled the dry grass. Still the wolves did nothing, until suddenly one of the animals broke loose from the herd and began to run.

Rhamin thought it had escaped, but he was learning that it was only the beginning of the hunt. Yet it was over all too quickly. The beast was caught by Silvah, one of the faster female wolves. Females tend to be smaller and more lightly built than males and this makes them faster in a short sprint. Silvah was there at the front of the animal, trying to bring it down before any of the rest of the pack. Eventually, slowed by the weight of Silvah on its throat, and the lack of air passing through its crushed wind pipe, the other wolves caught up and brought it down by grabbing onto its back end. It was what Rhamin would always remember as a classic hunt and kill procedure used for big animals.

And Rhamin remembered the feast they all had. There had been more than enough for them. The rocks would give them shelter, and a nearby brook would provide water for days while they rested and fed on the remains. He didn't remember just how long they had stayed there; perhaps five days, possibly more. He had enjoyed being taught how to hunt by his father and learning the tricks of self defence while play fighting with his brothers and sister. In the woodland, his mother had pointed out the fungi that were not to be eaten and those from which, if they were really hungry, they could get good sustenance. It had seemed an ideal world.

But suddenly it had all changed. They had decided to move on and locate that stray herd again. Only a few white tufts of cloud cushioned the horizon from the starkness of the clear blue sky as the wolves meandered along the edge of the plain, following the animals' tracks. With the breeze behind them Anval had wanted to circle around the cattle to hunt them from up wind but Dori said that the animals were so stupid they would not panic even when they smelt the wolf pack approaching. But as things turned out they had no time to locate them and carry out an attack. Anval had stopped and turned his head from side to side, ears pricked, straining to pick up the low frequency noise he thought he had heard. The others did the same.

'What is it?' Dori asked.

But it was too late to answer. The noise suddenly became much louder. As it thundered towards them, there was a moment of indecision. Then, without any further warning, five men on horseback burst from the woodland that lay ahead and to the right.

The horses still seemed a long way off but it didn't stop the long reach of the men's loud firing sticks hitting two of the pack, sending them crashing head over tails into the long, brittle grass. The rest of the pack ran. There was only one option; to flee back along the plain and try to reach the cover of the trees. The wolves were agile and fast but, with four small cubs, they were losing ground rapidly as the horsemen cut across to intercept them. Anval barked an order for them to split up. 'I'll take two cubs and you take two,' he barked and, without waiting, grabbed Seth and Powla in his mouth and set off to the trees. Dori picked up the other two, but they were big now and she was smaller than Anval, and as she ran, she kept dropping Rhamin. Silvah came to her rescue and picked him up, her teeth firmly around his shoulders as they bounded into the cover of the trees.

But the horsemen hardly slowed. Their horses crashed through the brittle undergrowth now only yards behind Dori. Rhamin heard a loud crack and a yelp. He wasn't sure what was happening but Silvah just panted, and kept on running. Now she was alone with Rhamin hanging, wet with saliva from her mouth. For a while Rhamin thought they were clear of their hunters, but then, just as Silvah was going towards a rocky overhang under the roots of a massive oak tree, he heard another crack and, almost at the same moment, a rush of burning air above made Silvah drop him. There was a whining sound as sparks flew up from the base of the rock spitting hot particles into the parched grass which lay further ahead. Silvah yelped. The invisible point of death had nicked her face, and Rhamin, feeling her jaws relax, had fallen helplessly to the ground with a thud. Silvah spun around, jerked to one side as another invisible missile whined off the rocky ground beside her and came running back towards him. She swept him up with two teeth sunk deep into the loose skin of his neck, and hurdled a fallen tree. She spun around again and, quickly pushing the cub into a hollow beneath the tree trunk, she left him there as she sped off and veered to the right.

Rhamin crouched down, petrified. The drumming sound of the horses' feet deafened him as they thundered after Silvah. Black shadows engulfed him as the animals and their riders sailed over his head, blocking out the light. The riders hadn't seen him huddled beneath them as they hurtled past, but he was sure that one of the horses had spotted him. But, not slowing, it seemed to be driven on, mindless of quarry or danger, only doing the man's bidding. Its eyes were wide, almost frantic, its nostrils flared as its chest heaved to suck air into its huge lungs. As it landed far beyond Rhamin's hiding place, he watched as the legs of the man kicked into its sides, driving it on, urging it not to lose any of its speed or momentum.

Rhamin began shivering with fright as the sound of horses and men, crashing through the brush and undergrowth, subsided into the distance. He buried his face in his tail, not daring to even lift his nose to see whether the hunters were near. His body was wet and steaming with saliva from Silvah's mouth. He felt dizzy and rested for a moment trying to think what to do. There was an unfamiliar smell in the air. It frightened him; he had never smelt it before. In moments less than he could count, a dark grey, choking, acrid cloud enveloped him. All he could do was hug the bare ground hoping it would pass, but it wasn't to be. Instead, he heard a crackling sound, every second getting closer and closer. Hardly able to breathe, he sucked at the pocket of air beneath his belly and tried to hold the breath in his lungs as long as he could. The crackle suddenly got louder and then, hot, orange and yellow flames like tongues of a thousand wild creatures broke through the dense cloud and crashed about him, consuming the brittle grass and eating up the dry ivy that hung above his head. The flames licked at his wet fur. He could smell it singeing with the heat. And then he felt a searing pain. The dry fur on his ears melted and curled as the ivy that had dangled above his head, combusted. He cried out in agony but nobody heard him.

The flames passed as suddenly as they had appeared and, with their departure, brought in new and cleaner air that enabled Rhamin to breathe again. There was still some smoke but now it was a lighter grey and becoming wispy, gradually dying as each scorched stem of grass dropped to the ground as a string of black dust. His eyes running with tears, he lay there, sneezing and coughing and shaking his head in pain. Eventually he cleared his streaming nose. He listened for long seconds and then sniffed at the air. The danger seemed to have gone. He waited and listened again for what seemed forever, but the hunters did not return and, eventually, he fell into a fitful sleep.

It was dark when he awoke. All around him the stench of charred wood and grass filled his nostrils. Gradually, he gathered his senses and, piece by piece, remembered what had happened. He thought about the other wolves, wondering if any of them had escaped the horsemen. He wasn't sure about his mother; her yell was still ringing in his ears. His ears! They hurt. They were burned. His black fur was grey with ash, and under the ash his coat was a scorched and dirty brown. His eyes were still smarting with the effect of the smoke and dust. Apart from the memory, still thundering inside his head, everything around him was silent. It was as if the world had suddenly come to an end and he was left there alone in a dark hinterland, between death and the place his mother had told him all wolves go when they grow old and die. He struggled to his feet and coughed and sneezed, but with every breath he sucked in more dust. When he eventually stopped retching, his nose and mouth were dripping with black streaked mucus. He licked it away but the taste was too bitter. It made him retch again. He rested for a while, trying to sniff the air but his nose just wasn't working. Slowly, pulling himself out of the hollow and now caring little whether the hunters were still around, he shouted for his mother. It was a short howl, not unlike the first one he had ever made, only this one didn't surprise him as much as the first. He listened for a response but heard nothing. Everything around him was silent. Even the birds and the insects were muted. They had all disappeared. He was lost in this blackened, deserted wood.

He racked his memory to try and remember if his mother or father had told him what to do if they ever got separated. It was hard to remember anything. He felt cold and began to shiver. There was no sign of the dark clouds that had engulfed him and, once again, the star studded night sky was clear. What had his father said about the stars? Was there some way to find your way home by following them? He couldn't remember; and anyway, where was home? They had been travelling and camping in different sites. He couldn't recall his mother or father saying that any place in particular was their permanent place of abode. He sighed and, kicking up a mini dust cloud as his oversized feet padded in the thick layer of ash, he plodded to the outskirts of the wood. The ground around him on the plain was no different to what he had left behind in the wood. It was black and dusty and smelled the same. A tear came to his eye. There was nobody about; none of his kin, nor even any other wild creatures. A thin, sickle moon gave a dim grey light to the plain, making it even blacker, and the dark woodland cast a murky, waving shadow towards him. He sat down and began to sob. In his short life he had never known such silence. He watched and listened and waited. Nobody came. After what seemed like forever, slowly and stiff with fatigue, he curled up, twined his tail around his face and fell back into a dreamless sleep.

He didn't know how long he had slept. He woke to the sound of a wolf's voice in the distance. He listened again and then, after a moment or two he heard the voice again, only this time it sounded a little closer. He sprang to his feet and began to run towards it, and then he remembered. He stopped, raised his head into the air, took a deep, deep breath, so deep that he thought his raw lungs would burst, and then he howled. That is what the pack did to call each other together; they howled. They did it every night to call and guide the rest of the pack back home. Suddenly he recognised the deep howl of his father. He howled back again and now another voice filled the night air. It was Silvah. He would know her voice anywhere. It was a triumphant howl, which filled the whole night sky and beyond, resounding and echoing back from the rocky hillside. Rhamin howled again… and again… and again, until the next thing he knew was that his father and Silvah were there licking him and wagging their tails as they danced around him with delight.

Yes, Rhamin remembered man and what he was capable of doing. He remembered the guns that cracked like thunder and sent out hot, invisible teeth amidst a coat of flame, and the way men sat on their horses and drove them forward with their feet. He remembered the smell and the sound of the creatures, sweating and panting, and the lingering sickly-sweet smell of their hooves. And he remembered the sound of the men's voices as they scented blood and chased for the kill. His father, Anval, had escaped to the hills with two of the cubs, but the hunters had killed his mother and the cub she carried with her. They had killed two other members of the pack as well that day, and now, four years later, he had to explain why hunting the animals that were enclosed by man, was not something they should do.

Solin was a year younger than Rhamin. After the death of Rhamin's mother, his father had taken a determined and ambitious young wolf, Rhiana as his mate and the following season Solin had been first born male of six cubs. Then, two years later, Anval had been mortally wounded when he was trampled by a buffalo. It was the nature of being a wolf. Very few wolves ever survived without some serious injury such as a broken leg or fractured skull or cracked ribs. Anval's injuries were just too great to overcome and on his demise, Rhamin, who was by far the biggest and strongest contender for leadership became leader of the pack unchallenged except for a half hearted attempt by Solin.

Rhiana was replaced as the alpha female by the younger and, by now, stronger and faster Yeltsa. She was one of three females from another decimated pack, hunted down by men, not on horses this time, but by men on noisy metal creatures with glaring lights and wheels that trampled everything in their path. Those creatures smelt of death before they even got close. Those wolves of the Bardin pack had their own story to tell of fear and death and man. They supported Rhamin, knowing what hunting men's animals would mean. They had seen men standing aloft on the back of the metal creatures and had seen them direct the beams of sunlight at their quarry so that there was nowhere to hide in the darkness. They had seen the men point their guns at the wolves as they ran to escape from the spotlights, and how their fellow creature would, with the crack of thunder rushing through the air, and pain thrusting through their bodies, simply roll over and die.

All the wolves in Rhamin's pack, and in many other packs which he had encountered, had made an uneasy and unspoken truce with the man kind. Never attack man and, by some unspoken law, man, in the last three years, at least, had not attacked the wolves. And "attacking men" included their animals which were penned in enclosures.

Zelda told stories, passed down through generations, of how at one time wolves and man fought for the same prey. She was not only the oldest wolf in the pack; she was older than any other wolf living. Rhamin couldn't even remember what relation Zelda was to him or the rest of the pack. She had been there for ever. Her face was dished and white with age, her bulging eyes seeing nothing but blurred shadows in daylight and nothing at all at night. Her coat was scraggy; a dark grey all over and there were tufts of last season's under coat poking out from beneath her latest growth of guard hairs; she shed them like a dandelion sheds its seeds, pieces wafting about on the floor of the camp in the eddies of dry air. Her legs were bent, and she had but few good teeth. She relied on the regurgitated food of the younger wolves to survive. Yet they kept her and guarded her safely. No wolf knew as much as Zelda. She knew many things about the past but she also had some way of knowing what was going to happen in the future. And she had warned against this plan even before Solin had suggested it. 'The plan is flawed,' she had said in her sleep. Silvah had heard her say it many times. But now it was no dream.

Solin's eyes gradually travelled round the whole circle of

wolves and finally settled on the eyes of Rhamin. If it was a challenge to the leader, Rhamin had to put it to one side. The very survival of his pack depended on harmony amongst its members. 'We have no alternative,' argued Solin. 'Unless we take some of his food then we will all perish. At least this way some of us will survive.'

'The plan is flawed,' croaked Zelda.

'Oh shut up you withered old dog,' Solin snapped. 'You of all people should be in favour of this idea; you who depend on all the rest of the pack for your pre-digested food. And anyway, I haven't told you any plan yet!'

'The plan is flawed!' croaked Zelda again, flinching as Solin jumped towards her.

'Leave her be,' commanded Rhamin. 'We all have a right to speak in this circle. I allow it. Otherwise why are you speaking?'

'Huh,' Solin snarled, 'I suppose you are going to listen to her then?'

'I am listening to all of you,' Rhamin countered. 'So say your piece and get it over with.'

'Yes, get it over with,' Solin parroted in a squeaky unnatural and skitting voice. 'Well,' he said, now in his most adversarial tone, 'I will get on with it and I will say what none of you cowards dare to hear.'

Rhamin just glared at him. Solin paused to make sure he had everybody's attention. 'It is a risk we will have to take. If we do not attack the men's compound then we have only two choices: move north now and seek out our usual prey, or…' He looked at the two sisters, Charka and Fayli of the Bardin pack, staring them straight in the eyes. 'Or we sit here and die. Die, I said. That is the option. All our food has migrated and we have been left behind because our beloved Rhamin has decreed that the rains will return. Well they haven't returned and we are all dying. Not today perhaps, but soon.'

He was right of course. They were slowly starving to death. It hadn't always been so. But the season had changed. The mild spring with its gusty winds, warming sunshine and sustaining rainfall that nurtures all young life, from the sprouting cone seed to the foetal young inside a creature's womb, had turned into a prolonged and scorching sun baked hell. All the food that had been abundant in years past had now disappeared; or even worse it had not developed. Seedlings had pushed up under the first, warm rays of spring and, as the soil had dried, they had pushed their primary roots down deeper into the soil and their primary leaf shoots up towards the sky. But the heavy beads of night dew alone could not sustain them through the scorching heat of the day. Now, the old vegetation from last year that had been grazed down to the roots was not growing back; nor was it being replaced by new life, which, if not still born, had suffered a premature demise.

That was not an end to it of course. It was just the beginning. The animals that grazed on the natural resources of the earth were no longer there. They had moved in pace with the weather or perished. And the animals that preyed on those creatures in a natural balance of nature had to follow them or die.

Rhamin had chosen not do that. His mate, Yeltsa, was already overdue to give birth to her babies. It was too late to embark upon the long and hazardous trek to the north. And even if they did, neither he nor any of the pack could say if they would reach a promised land. Each day that passed, the returning members of the pack brought back less and less food. There was nothing big; a rat here and a vole there; nothing that would sustain a pack of fourteen wolves. Rhamin worked hard to keep the pack together, but every day it became a little harder. The younger members of the pack were restless. Until recently, their loyalty had been flawless, and even now, none of them resented having to bring back their spoils to share. Rhamin had maintained the rule. It was a rule of survival passed down from leader to leader, from generation to generation. Every wolf had the right to share his pack-mates' quarry and when they themselves caught food then they had the same duty to bring it back for all. In times of plenty the strongest never ate first. Wolves are not like other predatory animals. When feeding on a kill, the whole pack shares. And those wolves or young that are unable to travel to the kill are fed with meat brought back or with regurgitated food from any or all of the hunters when the pack returns to the den. But maintaining pack morale by sharing didn't dispel disappointment.

In the hierarchy of the pack, Solin was second only to his leader. It was his dream to take over but Rhamin was too strong. He stood almost a head taller than all the other males. Rhamin was king of the pack and there was never any mistake about that. He was a giant among wolves, his size and his white ears and black coat distinguishing him from not only all the members of his own pack, but from any other wolf they had ever encountered. None dared speak against Rhamin but when he called a meeting of the pack all voices were heard.

It was early in the night. What clouds there were in the sky were wispy and scarcely veiled the moon when they drifted across its face. The air was still dry but cooler now. Solin sniffed it, his nose pointing upwards as if searching for some scent carried on the still night air. Slowly, he strolled around the inside of the circle, looking each wolf in the eyes, as if challenging any of them to argue with him. 'We have to raid the farm.'

'The plan is flawed. Death dog!' murmured Zelda, hardly audible; but Solin heard.

'What are you chuntering about? Without the food we bring back to you you'd be dead long ago you old stiff!' Solin grunted as he turned to address the circle again. 'And who's going to feed Yeltsa and her cubs when they are born? We are all slowly starving to death.'

'I notice *you* never manage to bring anything back for those in the camp,' Natan, a young male barked at him. Solin glared back at him and bared his teeth. Natan laid back his ears and backed away submissively. He was neither old enough nor brave enough to take on Solin. But he respected Rhamin and thought that anything Solin suggested automatically sucked.

'And just what is your plan,' Rhamin demanded.

Solin sniggered, barring his teeth defiantly. 'The man's animals are just food. They kill them and eat them. All I'm suggesting is that in this time of hardship, we take a small share to eat. How bad can that be? After all, I don't see us hunting men down when they kill one of our buffalo or hunt our deer!'

'Bad enough for us to have to move far away,' a voice came from the crowd.

'The man's enclosures are over sixty miles away. He'll be lucky to find us. Our Darin is well hidden. It is the best hidden den in the whole country. No other pack is as well hidden as we are. Nor does any other pack take such care as we do to leave no trace of our whereabouts.'

Rhamin pondered the remark. It was true; they had the very best den that any wolf pack could have found. It was a cave complex with an opening behind a wall of rock. To get to the mouth of the cave they had to climb up a slope and then descend behind the rock to the opening. From there, a tunnel, about the height of a wolf, sloped gently up to a cavern. There were passages and caverns beyond that, some small, some big, but no wolf had ever found the end of the underground complex. Even with their keen eyes and sense of smell, the darkness was so impenetrable that discovery of what lay beyond was never an issue. They had other dens that they used on their travels, but they always returned to this one. This they called their Darin, a fortress of a home. If they left to travel north in search of food they might have to travel for many days. They could travel fifty miles at a gentle lope in one night. Their long slender legs give them the appearance of floating over the ground as their four large feet just seem to flick them along. But the journey would take them across the territory of other wolf packs, and they might never return.

'So you want to start a war with the man?' Rhamin said, almost under his breath. Solin heard.

'My plan is for seven or eight of us to go into the man's enclosure, take one small sheep or a cow's calf each and disappear before he even sees who has taken them. He won't even know who was responsible He might not even know they are missing. We can get in and out in less time than it takes to travel a tenth of the way.'

Rhamin glanced at Zelda. Her eyes were closed and she was rocking backwards and forwards, and murmuring quietly. Somehow she sensed him looking at her and, suddenly, her eyes flashed open and she jumped in the air as if she had been stung on the backside by a scorpion. For several moments her sightless eyes locked on his and then, as if looking beyond him, quietly she spoke. 'The man will see you.' She swayed from side to side and then flopped down where she had been lying. 'He will see you!' she said in a resigned and fading whisper, and turning towards Solin, 'And you!' she snapped.

'Huggh!' Solin gave out a disgusted growl. 'You are too old to know what you are talking about. 'We'll be in and out and gone before he knows any of his precious creatures are missing.'

Rhamin had to admit that the plan seemed straight forward and simple. He had passed the man's farmstead several times recently and it was as Solin had just described. In essence the plan to raid the farm seemed simple and reasonably safe for the participants. At worst they could leave empty handed and high tail it out of the compound if they were seen.

'We're all very hungry,' a voice called from back of the circle.

'Isn't it worth a try?' another young wolf put forward.

Solin grinned. 'So what about it Rhamin?' he said, adding in a derisory tone, 'Oh great leader!'

'I'll think about it,' Rhamin said, his voice calm and even.

'That's right, you think while we all starve!' Solin snapped.

Rhamin glared at him. Then turning to the pack he said, 'I'll let you all know my decision by the morning.' He walked past Zelda, who was murmuring to her front paws and shaking her head.

'A wolf with no ears!' she chanted over and over again, 'A wolf with no ears!'

'I have heard,' Rhamin stated. His coat was black. But for the fire that burned his ears when he was a cub, and left them white when the fur grew back, he would have been a totally black wolf. In the winter, against a snowy background, he often looked like a black shadow without any ears. 'You've had your say; now be quiet!' Zelda's voice dropped to a whisper that Rhamin couldn't make out. 'That's better.' He walked back to the mouth of the cave and disappeared into its blackness.

CHAPTER TWO

Morning came early but Rhamin hadn't hunted for long before the sun cleared the horizon. He had caught two lizards and then, towards sun rise, had happened upon a weak and skinny rabbit which he had pounced on with his two front feet and carried back to the den. Some of the other pack members had already returned when he arrived. He dropped the rabbit by the base of the rock at the mouth of the cave and climbed up to his position on top of it. A long loud harmonic howl made sure that all the wolves inside the cave and any that might not yet have returned from their night's hunting, heard it and came to assembly below. To his surprise, Solin was one of the last to arrive. He sloped along giving the impression that the decision, over which Rhamin had pondered all night, would be going against him. He had already decided to leave. None of the females had, so far, said that they would go with him but last night's speeches might have changed his luck. He had always planned to take over from Rhamin, but now he felt he would be better off as a single male than a browbeaten heir apparent. He had always lived in Rhamin's shadow. His coat was a dark shade of grey with a couple of white tufts at the bottom of his chest. He was a good head shorter in height but that was not because he was a small wolf, Rhamin was just big; too big for Solin's liking. True, Rhamin's size held great advantage when he used that and his strength to drag down a fully grown buffalo, but Solin was slim and sleek and could outrun any male wolf both in a sprint and over massive distances. Only a few of the sleek and slender females could outrun him, and that was only in the shorter sprints. Solin despised the other wolves for not being as fast as him. If only Rhamin hadn't been so big and strong.

It wasn't long before all the pack was assembled below the rock. 'Listen, everybody,' Rhamin began, 'I'll make this brief.' He didn't want to leave any time for Solin to start arguing this morning; the wolf was always so adversarial. Anyway, he was in no mood to put up with Solin's insolence; it was going to be a long hard day. 'My decision is yes.' There was a gasp from the gathered pack. 'Yes, we will invade the man's territory,' he followed on. 'Yes we will take some of his food, so get prepared. We set off when I come down from this rock.'

'So you've seen sense at last,' called Solin.

'I've made a decision. That is all. None of us should be pleased about it. It is the most dangerous hunt we are ever likely to undertake, because we are probably going to end up being the hunted. That will be no fun, mark my words. Man will spare us no mercy. If they hunt and find us, we will die as sure as the sun comes up in the morning.'

'But what about what you said last night?' Rowan, a young female asked. Her eyes were wide with fear.

'For once Solin is right, we eat or die. There could well be losses but we will just have to take all precautions to prevent them.' He glanced around and settled his eyes on Solin.

Solin's eyes were strange. His face showed more than just the pleased look of getting one over on the ruler of the pack. Rhamin tilted his head and, with an inquisitive gesture, waited for a comment from his half brother. 'It will be easy,' Solin bragged. 'Straight in and straight out. No messing. We'll take one small sheep each and disappear into the night. Are we all ready to go?' he called out.

'I haven't finished,' Rhamin proclaimed before anyone could answer. 'We have to prepare for the worst.'

'That isn't necessary,' shouted Solin. 'It will be easy peasy.'

Rhamin glared at him. 'If you're not going to follow orders then leave.'

Solin scowled and visibly restrained himself from answering back. He wanted to be in at the kill and it was just like Rhamin to leave him on guard duty. It wouldn't be the first time. Rhamin continued. First he looked around at the faces of his pack. Some looked wide eyed with fear, some wide eyed with anticipation; he could tell the difference. 'I will take eight of our best hunters.'

'That counts you out then Solin,' shouted Natan. Rhamin could see him being a challenge to Solin when he was a mature wolf. Solin just snarled.

'That isn't so,' Rhamin insisted. 'Solin is one of the best. He is one of the fastest in the pack. He can bring down a buffalo on his own.' He paused and looked at Natan intently. Solin grunted his acknowledgement of the tribute. Natan reluctantly nodded. 'But you are also one of my best hunters. During this drought you have brought back more small prey than any other. It shows ability, cunning and thought. We will need that.' Natan smiled broadly, his tongue lolloping out of the side of his mouth as it always tended to do as he panted with pride. 'I will also take Fayli and Charka for not only are they strong but they know what it is like to be hunted by men and that will bring caution into our group.' The two sisters of Bardin looked at each other surprised, but noticeably proud to be chosen. They had always hunted together and now was not the time to split them up.

'I also choose Seth and Powla for they too know as surely as I do what man is like.' They were the brother and sister that escaped the hunt by men when Rhamin was saved by Silvah. 'I take Rasci for he is as strong as any wolf here,' he continued.

'And an idiot!' Solin snapped. He had never liked Rasci, but then, the feeling was entirely mutual. Rasci was the same age as Solin. Raised by Zelda and Silvah as an orphan pup he was now the pack jester. But he hunted as well as any other wolf.

'And finally, I choose Silvah who is no less brave and strong.' Silvah was now the second female only to Yeltsa. She beamed. There was no time she loved more than when hunting with Rhamin. She had loved him and cared for him since the day he was born and, although Rhamin never looked at her as anything other than a surrogate mother, she had once hoped he would notice her as a potential mother for his cubs. She was the most mature female of the pack – excluding old Zelda. She too was a dark grey colour and she had a thin white bib running from her chin to her chest. She was always sure to keep herself clean and smart for her leader, and would spend hours cleaning her face after the pack had been feasting. She knew all the water holes and never missed a chance to bathe in them. She had found that a great advantage during this hard dry summer. Not only was her coat kept free of old fur but she found it cooling and refreshing. Many of the other wolves thought she was a little eccentric. Rhamin thought she set a good example to the youngsters.

Rhamin continued, 'When we leave the compound where we hope to get our prey, we must not return straight home. We will no doubt be split up and so it is imperative that we all take a round about route. I know those back at the Darin will be hungry, but Yeltsa's safety is paramount. We must not lead the men to our home. We will place guards not just outside the mouth of the cave but two or three miles away as well. The guards will practice their warning calls so that there will be no mistake that it is a warning and not a call to bring us together. As a last resort, two guards will remain at the Darin, and it will be their task to distract the hunters and divert them from their path if they are coming near our home and becoming a threat to Yeltsa. Does everyone understand?'

Every wolf barked their confirmation and Rhamin bounded down. He looked around and his team was already behind him.

The group followed him to the water hole at the back of the first big cave and, like Rhamin, took their fill. When he saw everyone was ready, he trotted out of the cave into the bright morning sunlight climbed over the facing rock and set off at a steady lope, his long thin legs eating up the ground as he gazed at the dark line of mountains on the distant horizon. The air was stirred by a light breeze, sending up the dust in eddies that travelled along in front of them. The sun was behind them at first and their long shadows danced ahead of them on the surface of the bare dusty ground; but as the sun rose higher and higher in the sky, with every stride and every heartbeat, their shadows shortened beneath them, becoming black spots, magic carpets of darkness transporting them effortlessly, through the blistering sunlight, to their destination.

For half the day they kept up the pace and still the distant line of mountains appeared no nearer. There was a river nearby where they intended to stop and rest for a short while. But when they arrived at its bank the river bed was dry and cracked as far as the eye could see. They split up and wandered along the dry depression looking for any sign of wetness but the surface was hot and as solid as rock. 'Okay,' Rhamin stated. 'That just means we have to find and take on water before we invade the compound. None of us will have time to stop afterwards.' With that, they regrouped and resumed their loping trek towards the mountains.

It was late in the day and an hour after sunset when they arrived at the sharp metal strands of fencing that formed the outer perimeter of the farm. The mountains to the northeast were still no bigger, yet they had travelled more than sixty miles towards them. They all lay down and panted, sniffing the air to obtain as much information as they could about their surroundings. There was a faint smell of water on the breeze but it was towards the centre of the farm compound, possibly another three miles ahead. There was no sign of cattle, calves or sheep.

Silvah looked along the fence. It seemed endless but she noticed that it was not impenetrable. With her sharp eyes she had spotted a patch that had been repaired. They ambled towards it. 'Looks like a good place to go through,' she said as she squeezed under the bottom wire. The others followed without a sound, although Seth gave out a faint squeal as his ear was slashed by a spike on the wire that was as sharp as a mountain lion's claw. Powla licked it clean and silently nudged him for being so careless. When all were through the fence Rhamin silently set off again loping gently on ahead. Without a sound, the others followed in single file. They all knew how important it was to be totally quiet. Their big feet made almost no noise at all, and despite the long journey their breathing was still easy and unlaboured. They crossed another line of fencing within sight of the farm stead. This fence was less difficult to traverse, being only three strands of sharply barbed metal. Yet there was still no sign of any animals. Rhamin looked at the others. Even Solin looked puzzled, though he didn't say a word.

'I smell water,' Natan declared in a whisper. They all stopped and lifted their heads. Instantly they realised that they were within a few hundred yards of the farm troughs, containers that men used for putting water in for their animals; and despite the strong smell of sheep mixed with the scent of various other animals, there was clearly water close by.

Moving on, they would soon see now that the troughs were inside a third line of fencing, this time made from tall posts and rails of wood and covered with a strong metal net. Rhamin sat and studied for a while. There was a farm house in the centre of the complex half hidden behind a large man made shelter. There was a similar large man-made construction on the opposite side, forming and completing the square. They were big but got even bigger as they headed towards the first trough. Jumping easily over the fence Rhamin took a drink from it. The others followed suit. It was warm water, heated by the day's bright sunlight, but it was refreshing. 'Take your time,' he whispered. Daylight had now faded into darkness. There was no cloud cover and the moon was dark, but starlight would be adequate for their keen eyesight. He signalled for Fayli and Charka to go around the fence to the right and for Seth, Rasci and Natan to circle round to the left. They all knew what they were looking for. Rhamin nodded to Solin, Powla and Silvah to follow him. He was taking the direct route straight to the centre of the farmstead. Soon the four were up against the walls of the large structure. It was even higher than they had expected, its black form towering into the night sky above them. Slowly, they edged around the perimeter of the building to an open end facing the house; inside was darker than the night. It took him only a moment to realise there were no animals there. It smelled of old dirt and stale fodder.

Then suddenly they heard it; the sound of a sheep bleating. The silence was so great that the sound, small as it was, made them jump. Their ears pricked up and zoned in on the silence where the sound had been only a fraction of a second before. There were, no doubt, animals penned up at the opposite side of the farmstead.

'Come, let's head round by the water troughs,' Rhamin whispered, turning to head back the way they had come.

'What? For goodness sake!' Solin protested.

'Quiet!' Rhamin was angry. On a still night such as this any sound carries for miles. He turned and headed away from the farmstead, looking for the other two teams. But when he got to the fence he realised that Solin had not followed.

'Damn' Rhamin cursed. His eyes strained into the distance but Solin was nowhere to be seen. 'I'm going back for him,' he growled. 'You two see if you can regroup and get around to the enclosure at the other side of those buildings.' With that he loped quietly back towards the opening between the house and the building. He stopped at the corner. He could hear voices inside the house. A dog barked and then there was more talking by a man. 'Where is Solin?' he thought to himself. Surely he hasn't gone straight through the farm yard. Once again he stopped and waited, listening for any sound. Suddenly a light beam shot out from the peak of one of the three buildings, drowning the far side of the yard in light. The dog barked again, only this time it didn't stop. Rhamin stayed in the shadows, concealed by the corner of the building. He peered into the floodlit area, wishing the dog would shut up. It was warning the men folk. Even at that distance he could hear the dog saying that there were intruders in the yard. The farmer was yelling back at the dog with commands that Rhamin did not understand. Solin was nowhere to be seen but he must have done something that had caused the shaft of light to appear. They will see you, he recalled what Zelda had said. The light beam must have picked out Solin. But still Rhamin did not know what to do. With Solin in there somewhere, the farmer was bound to see him now.

And then, suddenly the dog stopped barking and the lights went out.

It was a false hope that the farmer was going to settle down for the night. The silence lasted all of two seconds. Suddenly, a door opened and a broad shaft of light sprang across the back yard and onward to the adjacent field. Then, a shadow broke the light beam and behind it there was a man with a long pointed stick in one hand and a shorter, thicker stick in the other. Suddenly the short stick lit up, sending a beam of light where there had previously been darkness. Wherever he turned the stick, the light beam followed, totally under his control as he swung it around in the darkness looking for the intruders. Then, without warning, the dog pushed past him and headed for the paddock at the far side of the house. The dog was big and, from where Rhamin stood, looked as if it had no ears. As it spun around in the beam of light, he realised that it had soft floppy ears, in his mind, not much good for hearing directionally. It had a broad face with correspondingly floppy jowls, a thin smooth coat and a tail no longer than the tip of its nose. It was at least as big as a wolf, even as big as Rhamin, and much heavier ; it was wider and, by the looks of it, much stronger. It looked like a solid block of muscle. Beneath the dog swung its pendulous udders. It was thin in the waist. Obviously it had recently given birth to a litter of pups and Rhamin supposed she was still feeding them. For an instance he thought of Yeltsa and her babies. They were overdue, but birthing was a cherished time for every wolf in the pack. All would take a part in helping to rear them. It was an activity that bonded every member of the pack to every other. Most of the time.

The torch light flashed towards Rhamin but he kept well down. As the light beam panned past him he watched as the man shone it in the opposite direction and headed towards the far enclosure. The sound of bleating sheep could be heard clearly now, coming from the far side of the farm. They were not calling for their offspring as the calls heard earlier no doubt had been. The sounds now were noises of fear and panic. The other wolves were already attacking. The man shouted something and the dog veered off in the direction of the light beam and the crying sheep.

Rhamin knew he had no time to make his way around the perimeter of the building. Instead he sprang up and raced across the yard, sheltering from the man and his light behind the corner of the house. He could see it all happening from there. The farmer shone his light at Seth who was holding down a sheep by the throat. The light beam startled Seth, and instantly, realising he was in danger, he let go of the sheep and began to run. But swerve as he did, he could not shake off the light beam. The manoeuvring slowed him down and within seconds the dog had intercepted him. They shouted something at each other and then the dog's jaws clenched tightly on Seth's shoulder. There was a fight unlike Rhamin had seen for many a year. There was snarling and growling and teeth snapping and tearing. Then suddenly the man, who had been running and closing in on them, shouted and the dog let go and dropped to the ground like a stone. The man lifted his pointed weapon. There was a crack like thunder; a flash of flame from the tip of the gun; and Seth fell over. He didn't move. The man took only a second to contemplate the dead wolf before swinging the torch onto Fayli who was carrying off a dead sheep. She kept hold of it as she ran but it was impossible to outrun a dog with such a heavy payload. The dog soon caught up to her and, as Fayli dropped her prey, she sunk her long canine teeth into the jowls of the enraged attacker. Once again, there was an almighty scrap. Blood spurted from the dog's face as Fayli wrenched at it with her iron jaws, refusing to let it go or be shaken off. For a moment Rhamin thought that Fayli was going to win the fight. He felt so proud of her as the dog tore itself free from her clenched teeth. But then, suddenly, seeing his dog free, the farmer shouted and once again it dropped like a stone. A sound of thunder, a flash of fire, the smell of something burning and Fayli fell over with a yelp.

Rhamin stood there helpless. He just had no idea how to get around to the other side to help his comrades. He did not have time to circumvent the farmstead's massive buildings, and going straight through the yard would just take him within yards of the farmer and his deadly device. He just watched and hoped that the others had fled. They were getting killed and the only way to end the carnage was to get everyone out. But the light beam swung in a wide arc across the paddock. Sure enough there were two more wolves attempting to carry off a sheep. The man shouted a command, the dog bounded towards the wolves and the man ran after it. He was a long way off them and it was obvious he needed to get closer to do the manoeuvre that was to kill them. Rhamin had no time to waste. He had to distract the dog and the man somehow. He howled at the top of his voice. The dog spun around, but the man commanded and the dog set off again after the two wolves that were, perhaps, two hundred and fifty yards away. They had seen the dog and had dropped the sheep. They were running and swerving, trying to escape from the sticky grip of the light beam.

The open door of the house was only fifteen or twenty paces away and Rhamin was heading past it. With the intention of distracting the dog, he called out again, spurring the farmer to swivel the light beam around, blinding Rhamin for an instance. But then, suddenly, from out of the black shadows, Solin raced past Rhamin's shoulder and went through the open door and straight into the interior of the dwelling. At first Rhamin thought he was imagining it. His pack was being slaughtered and Solin goes into their killer's home! Without thinking, he followed close on Solin's heals. Solin had stopped. There, in the corner of the room were two young children; and behind them lay a basket with a mound of heaving puppies.

'We have to kill them to distract the man,' Solin barked.

The two children stood, huddled together, their saucer eyes transfixed by the salivering jowls of the big grey wolf that confronted them. As Solin paused, Rhamin could see he was deciding whether to take the larger or the smaller of the two.

'No!' Rhamin commanded as he lunged towards Solin from the middle of the room, but Solin was taking no notice. Somewhere there was a scream. Solin's teeth flashed as he lunged at the little boy, but he didn't know what had hit him. Rhamin's feet landed on Solin's side, knocking him off balance and making him slide on his side towards another door. There was a woman standing there that, in the heat of the moment, neither of the wolves had seen. She lowered her hand from her mouth and screamed again.

'Get out now,' Rhamin said to Solin. 'If you don't, then I'll kill you.'

'You fool; you want to have the pleasure of killing them yourself.'

'Out!' Rhamin repeated and went for Solin's throat.

Solin was fast. He side stepped and caught Rhamin on the side of the head with his long teeth as the black wolf slid past on the slippery floor. As Rhamin swung around, Solin, once again, was between him and the children. Keeping his eyes locked on Solin's, head down, slowly, Rhamin circled around him so that yet again he formed a barrier through which he knew Solin would, this time, not attempt to break.

'You're a fool.' Solin turned to the door. 'I hope he kills you,' he snapped and then lurched out into the cool breeze.

Rhamin looked up at the woman. She was quiet now but still holding her hand to her mouth. He looked at the children. Their eyes seemed even wider now. The bundle of puppies still squirmed in the basket behind them, oblivious to any danger. Without wasting another second he pushed past the little boy whose tiny hands pressed against the wolf's thick black pelage. The little boy had reacted automatically; fearlessly trying to push the animal away from his sister and himself. But Rhamin felt nothing as he reached into the basket and grabbed two of the sightless dog pups. They didn't move. They didn't even make a sound. He turned, looked once more directly at the little boy, their eyes locking as they exchanged glances. The boy's big eyes didn't show fear anymore. They revealed a child's courage as he, mouth pursed with determination, once again pushed with both hands against the shoulder of the giant wolf. And then, letting out a grunt of admiration, a sound possibly not understood by his tiny adversary, Rhamin bounded out of the door and headed towards the shadows at the other side of the yard.

The man was heading back. He had heard his wife scream, but he was still a good hundred yards away. He had shouted a command to the dog and she was on her way to attack Solin and delay him until the man could get near enough to get a clear shot with his weapon. Solin took the dog head on. He was going to sort it out once and for all. But it had a weight advantage and when they collided he went bouncing off heavily to one side like a rubber ball. The farmer was closing now as the dog intercepted Solin again. Rhamin could see what was going to happen. He thought he should leave Solin to his fate but then he put down the puppies and howled at the top of his lungs, 'See what I have got, you big ugly prairie rat!' The dog spun around only to see Rhamin pick up the two puppies again and head off towards the fence. He knew the dog was after him, guessing that her puppies meant more to her than the man's stupid sheep. He knew she would be upon him soon if he didn't clear the fence first time. He did. His long legs streaked over it and he landed on his big cushion feet and sped off into the darkness. He felt a rush of air as a piece of hot metal passed between his ears and whined as it skimmed the rock hard ground. A cold shiver snaked along his back as he recalled the horrible memory of a similar piece of hot metal that skimmed past Silvah when they were being hunted that first time by men. Another tiny but deadly missile went way over his head, but he didn't stop to look round; he could hear the panting dog in close pursuit. She was gaining on him.

They must have been half way to the outer perimeter fence before the big dog barked. Sheer determination driving her on, she was now only a few strides behind him. Hardly slowing, Rhamin dropped one of his prey and kept on running. He thought the dog would stop to attend to that one puppy but he was wrong. With one less puppy to carry, he could breathe easier now, but he was still losing ground. He figured that if he dropped this one she would still keep after him. No, he had no choice. He ran. Then, from behind he heard Natan barking at the dog. The young wolf was heading towards the puppy that Rhamin had dropped. The dog slowed and then stopped. She saw another wolf coming up behind Natan, and they were going to kill her baby. She raced back towards it, picked it up and stood there, puppy in her mouth, chest heaving, and growling at her two attackers as they veered off and followed Rhamin into the night.

CHAPTER THREE

The shadowy forms of Natan and Charka emerged out of the distance as they cut across towards Rhamin.

'You okay?' he asked them as they slowed to a trot.

'You were right,' Natan said, his tongue lolloping out at the side of his mouth as he panted. 'Men's animals are not as easy prey as they look! And men kind are deadly!'

'Old Zelda was right,' Rhamin replied. 'Our plan was about as useful as a ten day old corpse in a hot summer.' He sat down dejected. 'What have I done?' he groaned. 'We've gained no food and lost two of our family into the bargain.' He looked at Charka. 'I am so sorry about your sister, Charka,' he said, and went over to her. He licked her face where a tear had left a dark stain down her muzzle. 'I am so sorry.'

She nodded. 'Fayli was a brave wolf. But she died in a fight, and that's the way she would have wanted it to be. She was never one to want to grow old gracefully. I mean, look at Zelda for goodness sake!'

The attempt to lighten his mood was in vain. Rhamin shook his head and sighed deeply.

'Death is part of our lives, Rhamin, you know that. When we look the buffalo in the eye it is he that decides to run or make a stand. It is he that decides it is the time to die. They must know that if they stand their ground we won't attack, not because we cannot kill them if they do, but because it is not their time to die. But we never give in to death like other animals. We live life to the full and death takes us where it may, looking it in the face and saying, "Not today thank you!" And if it does take us, then we haven't spent any of our time worrying about it.'

Natan brushed against her neck consolingly. 'Who would have expected that to happen; a stupid dog of all things! I reckon Fayli died by trickery, that's what! Men and dogs; men and horses. It'll be men and wolves next!' As he stopped speaking, his tongue lolloped out again, and he turned to Rhamin. 'And what're we going to do with that?' he asked, pointing his nose at a dark curled up fur ball on the ground.

'Huh. Well I took that to get the dog's attention.' Rhamin paused and looked down at it. 'It's something I suppose. Don't reckon it'll hurt to take it with us.'

'A tasty morsel for Yeltsa when we get home then,' Natan suggested.

'We'd better find the others,' Rhamin said, suddenly raising his nose and sniffing the air. He picked up the night's pathetically small catch and headed towards the dark and distant mountains.

Rhamin's instructions to travel away from the farmstead towards the mountains before heading back home was a simple precaution for if the men folk responded immediately by getting on their horses, or worse their creatures of metal and wheels, to pursue them, they would carry on in the direction in which they had started, expecting to overtake the wolves. The plain was flat and crossed by fences that became natural barriers, so there was little chance of looking across at the farm, in the dim starlight, even with his keen eyes, to see what activity the pack had stirred up. There was a slight breeze blowing, but that was against them heading across the farmstead and homeward, so he couldn't even pick up any scent of activity on the wind.

Neither Natan nor Charka complained about the trek away from their home. They followed his command unquestioningly. Then suddenly, Charka let out a quiet bark. A wolf's bark is not like that of a dog, it is a 'woof' that comes up from deep in their chest. The rest of the group stopped in their tracks and, pricking up their ears, they strained to hear what Charka had heard.

Gifted with hearing through a very wide range that would include the ultra sound of a bat – which helps them hunt out mice and small game under grass and snow – and the deep vibrations of the lowly buffalo and elk whose almost sub-sonic rumbling tones wolves can hear from many miles away, the silence seemed unnatural. Even the crickets were in respite. The long drought had caused most of the natural prey and wildlife to move from the plain, apart from the insects that is. Those creatures gathered around carcasses and occasional piles of dung. But there was little other micro life left there to bother making mating sounds or calling boundaries. Without essential moisture, their eggs and pupa remained dormant.

Everyone looked at Charka. She stood stone still. She was the wolf that had always had exceptional hearing, more sensitive to sound vibrations that any wolf Rhamin had ever met. She stood silently listening and then, she woofed again, louder this time. A few seconds later Rhamin heard a reply. It was Silvah. She was due west of the farmstead. 'Silvah, Solin and Powla are heading towards us now,' she said quietly. She looked at Rhamin for confirmation that they should remain there. Rhamin just nodded. He knew intuitively what she was asking without her opening her mouth. He dropped his prey at his feet and lay down. The other two followed suit and settled down.

It wasn't long before they heard the sound of Solin's voice barking out orders to his two companions. Rhamin couldn't make out what he was saying. He looked at Charka, and after a moment or two, Charka turned her head to him and said, quietly, 'Solin is trying to persuade them to leave the pack with him. I can hear him telling them that they should be following him instead of heading back to "the great Rhamin!"'

'Huh,' Rhamin said quietly. 'We have already lost two of our best tonight.'

'Do you think he is serious about leaving?' Natan joined in. 'It would be no great loss.'

'It would if he split the pack,' Rhamin said angrily. 'He might be less edgy if you didn't bait him all the time.'

Natan dropped his ears. 'Sorry boss.'

Rhamin thought about how close Solin had been to killing the man's children back at the farmstead. If I hadn't stopped him, he thought, the man would have already been hunting us down. 'He is very dangerous,' he said, almost but not quite, under his breath.

Natan heard. He looked at Rhamin in surprise. 'He's no match for you boss,' he said truthfully.

'I didn't mean it like that, Natan. Yes, I know I am bigger and stronger. I hope I always will be, for the benefit of the pack.' He looked at Natan. 'Promise me something.'

'Anything boss, you know that.'

Rhamin went up close to Natan and licked him on the ear. 'You are a good wolf, Natan. Promise me…' He paused.

'Promise me that if anything happens to me you will not challenge Solin to a fight.'

'I'm not afraid of him,' Natan boasted a little too eagerly.

'You have a lot of growing to do yet. When you are big enough.' He held his head up to stop Natan from speaking again. 'But, I'd expect you to take as many of the pack away with you at the first opportunity. He is a dangerous wolf, not just because he is still bigger than you, but because of the dangers he would bring upon the pack.'

Natan was about to say something in reply, but then, out of the darkness, Silvah came bounding up to them.

'Where are the others?' Rhamin asked her.

'They're coming up behind but they have two sheep and they are not small ones. Powla and I saw the commotion at the farm house and we snuck in and took the two sheep that had been worried already while the man and his dog were distracted. The one I was dragging was much larger than the other. Solin offered to carry it for me.'

'Did he now?' Rhamin half asked, half exclaimed. 'So what treason was he inciting on the way over here then, if he had his mouth full?'

'No, I was still carrying the sheep then. He was saying we should eat the smaller one and take the other away to the mountains with us.'

'I see.'

'I'm sorry,' said Silvah, 'I didn't mean to upset you.'

'You haven't,' Rhamin said softly, and before he could say anything else to reassure her, Solin arrived with the sheep. His mouth was around its throat and his head was tilted down and to one side as he dragged the creature along the ground. Its blood was no longer dripping off its short fleece, but congealing into a black mass around Solin's mouth. He put the sheep down and licked his lips as Powla panted up out of the darkness, dragging the other dead animal in a trail of rising dust.

'Seems like I got a decent meal for every one,' he boasted and at the same time pointedly glanced down at the catch that Rhamin had at his feet. 'You had better eat that before the rest of the pack back home see what a useless catch you've got.'

Rhamin saw the hair on the back of Silvah's neck bristle. 'Your catch?! You…'

Rhamin broke in quickly. 'What we've caught tonight belongs to the whole pack; not you, not me, not any of us here, but every member of our pack when we get it back to the Darin.' He looked Silvah in the eye. It was a consoling look. It was a look that told her he believed her side of the story, a look that melted her anger; the same look that he sometimes gave to her, that turned her long legs to spring water.

'You can't stand anybody being better than you, can you?' Solin snapped. He was going to go on but Rhamin growled and barred his teeth. It was a warning.

'We are still a wolf down,' Rhamin stated. 'So, instead if bickering, can anyone tell me where Rasci is?' The wolves all shook their heads. He was reluctant to head off home without the full compliment but he dare not call out to find the missing member of the pack.

'Has any one seen what happened to him?' Once again they all shook their heads. 'Okay. Let's get this food back to the Darin,' he ordered. 'We'll look for him later.'

Although the losses were hard to bear, the night's work would see the whole pack through the next week or more. Seeing that his members had succeeded in getting some prey, he had made up his mind what he was going to do next. But he wasn't going to tell any of them yet.

'We'll take it in turns at carrying the prey,' Rhamin decreed. 'We have a long journey home and I intend having this food back at the Darin before mid day. We are all going to eat heartily.' He looked directly at Solin. 'You can carry that a little longer, but when you start falling behind, then your shift will have ended.' He turned to the rest of the pack. 'And that goes for all of us.'

Rhamin was careful to gage the trek home so that all had a spell at carrying the sheep. They couldn't have been more than half way back to the Darin when, through the semi light of night, they spotted a lone figure of a wolf bobbing up and down as it trudged heavily onwards ahead of them. As they gained on the wolf they realised it was Rasci struggling with another large sheep. They soon overtook him. Before they could say anything, Rasci spoke. 'There's no way I was going to carry this in the opposite direction,' he stated, dropping his heavy load and sinking down onto the ground beside it. It was the biggest of all the captured prey.

Rhamin said nothing except, 'We're taking it in turns at carrying the food. You need some help?' Exhausted, Rasci just nodded.

Rhamin handed the dog pup to Rasci and took over the work of carrying the large sheep. They all changed around several times, Solin actually taking another shift with a sheep rather than be seen carrying the small, almost worthless prey that Rhamin had grabbed. They tracked hard and long through the cool cloudless night and saw the thin, faint light of day creep along the horizon long before he headed the tired, panting and dusty hunting pack into camp.

Rowan, one of the guards had already gone on ahead to tell the pack the news and when the hunters arrived there was a cheer from all, followed by a communal wagging of tails and the greeting of friends.

Yeltsa glanced over at Rhamin who was now, once again, carrying the dog pup. He looked back at her with adoring eyes, suddenly noticing something different about her. She was much thinner and her breasts were engorged and heavy with milk. As she ran towards him, they swung from side to side, heavily beneath her. He dropped his prey from his mouth and licked her face affectionately. You've had your babies!' he exclaimed.

She licked his face and said, 'At last! I thought they were never going to come out!' It had been a long pregnancy. The normal gestation period for the grey wolf is sixty three days. Yeltsa had seen the sixty eighth day come and go before the hunting pack had departed. Rhamin had considered migrating north to where the white tailed deer were likely to have found pasture, but it meant many days trekking and, in her condition, Yeltsa would never have been able to stand the heat and the lack of food and water for more than two days. No one could have known that the rains would not be coming. His decision to stay and wait out the drought had been solely to ensure the safety of his mate and her unborn offspring.

'How many have we had?' he asked.

'Five born but one was still born. The first was too big and it took almost the whole day to get its head clear. After that he slid into the world, complaining before I had even had time to lick him dry. But the last born must have waited too long. He died before he could take a breath.'

'Never mind my love,' he said softly. 'Four is just fine.'

Yeltsa was about to speak again when she noticed the prey that Rhamin had dropped at her feet. It was moving. It was still alive. She sniffed at it curiously. 'What on earth!'

'Oh, it's a dog pup,' Solin barked from across the camp. 'It's all he could manage.' Rhamin ignored him. There was plenty of time to make Solin sorry but now was not it.

'A dog pup,' Rhamin repeated. 'You can eat it if you want. It should be tasty.'

Yeltsa sniffed it again and then licked it. It stirred and whimpered thinking that its mother had returned to feed it. Yeltsa's face changed. She had been hungry for too long and she had babies to feed every few hours. Suddenly her engorged breasts began to drip milk. She needed her babies to relieve them. She closed her mouth around the dog pup's body and picked it up, and as she lifted her head, she looked at the rest of the pack and growled. The dog pup squeaked, suddenly afraid. It had realised that this wasn't its mother. Turning, Yeltsa gave out another growl, deeper and louder this time. It was the growl of the dominant female asserting her right to take the first pickings. Solin might have thought that the offering was worthless but Yeltsa was quite obviously not of the same opinion. Rhamin watched her, puzzled as she paced slowly at first, head held high, and then, springing on her toes, bounded deep into the cave.

It was mid afternoon when Yeltsa emerged and went over to the place where the rest of the pack had been feasting on the prey. There was plenty left, though some of the best bits had disappeared. All the pack was resting around lazily except for Silvah who was busy feeding Zelda. Rhamin watched as Yeltsa trotted over to the carcass of the biggest sheep and began to eat. He knew that after she had whelped, she would have eaten the afterbirth and even the still born baby, but now he realised that she would have to eat almost constantly for the next few days to recover her strength and to make the milk she needed to keep and feed her four babies. Often, wolves refrain from breeding during a drought or even lose their young prematurely if it seems likely that there will be no food to maintain them when they are born. But the early drought had caught them out. It was never expected to last, and every day Zelda had said that rain would come in time. But the skies were still clear and cloudless, the days scorching hot and the pickings of prey now totally inadequate.

When she had eventually had her fill, Yeltsa looked up. Rhamin was lying facing her, watching over her as he always did. He had explained about Fayli and Seth and she had taken the losses rather more casually than he had expected. The rest of the pack was asleep except for Rasci who had been sent up to the top of the rocky outcrop to sit out the hot day in the shadow of a rock on guard duty, and Silvah, who, Rhamin knew, had gone down to the drinking hole in the back of the caves to wash. She never liked being seen with blood on her face and coat. The task of washing, however, was getting harder. Even the water hole in the caves was turning shallow, the source stream now subsided to a trickle. They had never known it dry up, but Rhamin was worried this year that the water would disappear before Yeltsa could give birth to her pups. At least it had lasted that long. She wandered over to him, gave him an affectionate lick on the ears and said, 'Best be getting back to the babies.'

Rhamin licked her muzzle. 'Get as much to eat as you can from now on. In two days we will prepare to move out.'

'Oh, dear,' she gasped. She looked into his eyes with that 'do we really have to?' look.

'Don't worry, the pups will be safe. We will carry them. But you do understand, don't you? You could not have travelled and given birth to them on the move. We had to wait it out.'

Yeltsa nodded. She did understand. She also knew that Rhamin would make sure that she got a good fair share of the food before it was all eaten. With their tremendously strong jaws, by the time the sheep had been eaten, there would be nothing left but the fleeces. Wolves' jaws are capable of splintering the bones of a buffalo. Sheep were succulent morsels by comparison. As she turned and headed back into the cave, Rhamin watched her every move with admiration. His mate had done well.

The next morning, Yeltsa emerged once again from the cave, her body leaner and showing signs of the heavy toll feeding the babies was taking on her. Rhamin had saved the sheep on which she had fed the day before. The rest of the pack understood. Their job, once the second sheep had been completely devoured, was to go out hunting again. During the day there was to be little respite from the gruelling sun, so hunting began in earnest again during the cool calm hours of darkness.

The following day, shortly after the sun had reached its highest point in the sky, Rhamin howled and called the pack together. After making sure all his pack was around him he looked towards the north and said, 'You all know what is planned, but for those with any doubts, let me make it quite clear, we all have to be prepared for a trek lasting at least ten days.'

'And just how do we propose to live?' Solin demanded. 'I say we should return to the farmer's pens and eat our fill.' He looked around to see if any of the other wolves were nodding in agreement. They all stood still, waiting for Rhamin to answer.

'We will hunt on the way and we will seek water from the many rivers and streams which cover our territory. But if we find none, there will be no turning back.' He paused to make sure that Solin was not going to interrupt. 'And more serious still is the fact that our journey will, inevitably, take us beyond our own territory, vast as it is. We will be travelling within the boundaries of other wolf packs.'

'But isn't that risking being attacked?' Bamar, a young male asked. 'I hear that the packs to the north are dangerous, especially one belonging to a wolf called Pagin.'

'We have successfully protected our territory from all other packs,' explained Rhamin, 'because we have had the advantage of numbers. That is why I have fought to keep our pack together,' he continued, giving Solin a rocky glance. 'As we stand, even with the loss of Seth and Fayli, we are still a formidable force. Of course, numbers are not going to be our only deterrent from attack, we will have to be prepared to fight, and fight we will; but most importantly, we must be determined not to be turned back. If we are lucky, the other packs to the north will have moved on the same as us but they may only just have made their move as we are doing, and in that case they will fight to keep whatever right they claim to their hunting grounds while we are moving through them.'

'Are we ever going to return to our beloved cave?' Silvah asked.

'When the rains return, so will our prey. But until then, remaining here means certain death to us all. If we attack the man's animals again, not only will we lose more of our pack, but as surely as the rains will come eventually, the man will hunt us until we are either all dead or have moved to a place beyond his reach. Then we will never be able to return home.'

There was a dreadful silence from the members of the pack. Not one of them spoke. All watched and waited for Rhamin to give further instructions. 'From now on,' he continued, 'we will follow our prey. Never again will we be caught out by such a freak summer. We will remain a big pack and we will fight for the right to hunt and eat wherever we are. We will return to our precious home only when the hunting is good again.'

Eventually, Solin spoke. 'So when are we setting off on this epic walk?'

'We eat and take our fill of water now,' Rhamin replied. 'We gather up any food we have left, take the babies in our mouths and we set off in time to travel a good distance before sun set.'

During the whole of the meeting, Zelda had remained totally silent, her sightless eyes wet with tears. Rhamin hadn't failed to notice. He knew that the old wolf was afraid that she was to be left behind. Without the pack she would perish within days. 'Zelda,' he called. Her head lifted and her sightless eyes looked straight at him. Sad as she was, she, like all the other members of the pack, responded instantly to his call. 'I hope that you have fed as well as the rest of us over the past three days.'

'Yes,' she said in a quiet tone. 'Silvah and Rasci have fed me well. They have done their duty by me. I do understand that I will remain here.'

'Oh you do, do you?' Silvah asked, her head tilting and her eyebrows raised. 'And who said so?' She looked towards Rhamin.

All eyes swung to Rhamin. He shook his head. 'Not me!' he said lightly with a shrug. But his eyes showed concern. 'As I said, Zelda, we are a big pack and size gives us an advantage not only in hunting but in deterring our enemies.'

'And what use is a withered old scroat like me then?' she said.

'The same use you have always been Zelda the wise.' He saw a noticeable rise in her stature; her head became more upright and her chest puffed out.

'I don't recall anyone taking any notice of my wisdom lately,' she countered.

'Well there you are wrong old thing. Perhaps we didn't take enough notice of you, but we certainly knew you had warned us and with that we took more care than we might otherwise have done.'

'But the rains are coming,' she said gazing blankly ahead of her. 'I know it. We could all stay and wait for them.'

'You don't have to say that, Zelda. We are not going to leave you behind.'

'It's true,' she insisted. 'And, if you think I won't slow you down then I suspect your eyes are as bad as mine.'

'Oh I have good enough eyes to see that you do not have the teeth to hunt with us any more but you travel quickly, even if your speed isn't as fast as the rest of us. You have travelled to our different rendezvous camps with us over the years. This will just be a longer trip, that's all.'

Zelda closed her eyes. 'I don't know what to say,' she sobbed.

Rhamin licked her affectionately on the muzzle. 'If you have nothing to say then we know our journey must succeed,' he stated bluntly. 'Have you warned us against this journey?'

'Well, no, but…'

'And why not?'

'Well I haven't seen anything! I haven't seen a long journey, I've seen rain, and Corvak the Raven returning and…'

'You never see anything Zelda,' Rasci quipped. 'That's what happens when you go blind. You just dream and fart a lot.'

'Oh shut up you young tyrant,' Zelda scolded. 'You're not too old to get a good bite from me.'

'Or a nasty suck!'

'I'm warning you, young whippet!'

'Sorry Gran!' Rasci had always found it difficult to be serious about anything. He always cheered up the old wolf with his comical but candid repartee. In return for her telling him stories of long ago, he spent much of his time with her, telling her about his hunting experiences; for instance telling her about the time he had been overpowered by a hare, when in fact it simply played dead and when he put it down it got up and ran off. But the detail he put into the story made it all very convincing. He knew that Zelda never took him totally seriously. He adored the old wolf, and took it as being a duty to feed her whenever he caught anything. But Silvah understood why this young male comedian with his silver and brown streaked coat and his small white bib under his chin was so fond of Zelda. More than any of the other wolves, together they had protected him when he was a baby.

'So, I'm coming with you then?' Zelda asked tentatively.

'Zelda! Why do you think we are still here?' Rhamin asked her. 'We're waiting for you!'

'And I've been waiting for you, for goodness sake! Well, really, I don't know. Tut.' She paused as all the other wolves had a hearty giggle. Even Solin grinned. 'Well, I'm ready.

Who else are we waiting for?'

'Just me,' Yeltsa answered. 'I'll get the babies.'

'Oh, can I carry one for a while?' Zelda asked. 'I promise I won't bite!'

'As I said, more of a suck really,' commented Rasci. Then he added, 'I'll carry one.'

'And me,' Silvah came in quickly.

'Right,' said Rhamin. 'It doesn't seem like I can have any fatherly duties at the present then?'

Yeltsa turned to him and rubbed up against him. 'Darling,' she whispered.

'What is it my love?'

'You can carry the biggest.'

'Oh, okay then,' he said pleased with the result of the conversation. 'It'll do you good to have a rest, anyway.'

'Surprise! It's a surprise,' whispered Zelda.

As Yeltsa turned he followed her into the cave. Rasci and Silvah did the same.

At the back of the first cave, in a dark corner and up a slight gradient away from any direct beam of daylight, there was a small passage that lead three or four paces further on to a chamber about the height of a standing male wolf. Not the height of Rhamin, of course, for he was much bigger than the average male wolf, standing a head higher than any of his contemporaries. No one knew who or what had made this cave complex, but the designer had most certainly been a wolf.

Yeltsa stood over her brood and quietly picked one up and handed it to Silvah. It was the smallest of the litter and was all grey. 'I have named her Depni,' she said. 'Take that one for Zelda will you please?'

'Oh, she's adorable!' Yeltsa could hear Zelda exclaim as

Silvah passed her the pup.

'And you can take Floss,' She said to Rasci. 'Carry her gently.'

'I will, don't worry about that,' he said with a grin that couldn't be seen in the darkness of the cave.

'And I named this one Ramusan, after you,' She said to Rhamin. 'It means son of Rhamin, because he is big and is going to be huge like his father.' Rhamin nodded and bent forward to take him. 'Not so fast! Yeltsa said quickly.

Rhamin lifted his head back up to face her. 'What do you mean?' he asked.

'I mean that Silvah is to carry this one.' Silvah had returned, 'Silvah, take care of him as you did Rhamin when he was a baby,'

'You can be sure of it,' Silvah said proudly.

'I know. I am,' said Yeltsa. Then she picked up another pup and handed it to Rhamin. 'This is yours, I believe. Her name is Lexa,' she said and waited for a response from her mate.

Rhamin sniffed at the baby and felt it with the tip of his nose as he fitted his mouth around it. It was much bigger than any of the others, it smelt of the others and it smelt of Yeltsa's milk. He popped it down at his feet so that he could speak. 'I can't believe she is only three days old,' he exclaimed.

'Darling,' Yeltsa whispered in his ear. 'She isn't.'

'What? How do you mean?' He stood there trying to work it out. 'How could she have a baby older and bigger… Huh! You didn't! Yeltsa, please tell me you didn't keep that dog thing!'

'Darling,' she said again, licking his nose. 'You told me to keep it. You said it was for me.'

'Yes, but I meant…' He bent his head down to the furry mass that now squeaked and smelt just the same as the other pups.

'Tell me then,' Yeltsa said, licking his face now, 'Why didn't you kill it?'

'Well I... I... I'm not really sure to be honest. I mean, it didn't fight back or anything.'

'Not that it was likely to!'

'It didn't even move or make a noise until you grabbed a hold of it.'

'Exactly, you coward. You expected me to kill the little thing. They aren't so much unlike us as you think, you know.'

'Tell me about it!' Rhamin said, recalling the dog that had confronted them on the farm. He let out a huge sigh. 'Oh well,' he said after seemingly gathering his strength, 'goodness knows what gip I'm going to get from that bunch now! Especially that dog of a wolf Solin!'

'Careful now my Rhamin. You use the word 'dog' as a swear word. You'll have to stop doing that now. We have a dog in our pack!'

'Oh, for goodness sake,' he said stooping to pick up Lexa. 'Come on then you dog!' He couldn't see Yeltsa's expression but he could sense it. He picked up the pup. 'Goodness knows what they'll say!' he chuntered unintelligibly through the soft folds of Lexa's skin and waited for Yeltsa. She got the gist of his complaint.

'Oh, and by the way,' she said with a noticeable chuckle in her voice, 'This last one, which I'll be carrying, is Fatz. I call him that because he is a chubby little fellow.'

Rhamin couldn't speak anymore with his mouth full. Perhaps it was just as well.

CHAPTER FOUR

Rhamin was right of course. All the wolves had a good laugh at his expense. Yeltsa had adopted Lexa, because Rhamin had spared her life, and by doing so he had started the adoption procedure. Yeltsa had just completed the formality of taking her into her family. Now Lexa was as much a wolf as all the rest of the pups. She smelt the same, cried the same and she drank twice as much milk. Yeltsa still reckoned that Lexa was only a week older than her siblings; her eyes were still closed and would remain so for another week. But Lexa was almost twice the size of her adoptive brothers and sisters. 'What kind of dog was her natural mother?' she asked when they had stopped in the early evening, well before sun-set. It was the first time they had rested that day, since leaving the Darin. At this early stage in the lives of new born pups she would have to stop every three hours or so in order to feed them and give them a chance to rest together. The pups, or cubs as they are called as they become a little older, would fall into deep mists of sleep even as they were being carried but Yeltsa was concerned. She didn't like the fact that they were not together. Baby animals do not easily regulate their temperatures like older members of the species. They don't pant, and wolves do not sweat. The days were still scorching hot and the starry cloudless nights drew in a cool breeze. She had no doubt that the babies needed to be nurtured in their nest away from the daytime sun and the cold of the night.

The pack had dropped the pups in a heap in the centre of the circle of wolves. Yeltsa's question had brought all eyes around to examine the babies. There were distinct similarities between Lexa and her brothers and sisters. But she was different.

Eventually Rhamin replied. 'A massive ugly bitch,' he snapped rather too quickly.

'Now, now,' Yeltsa consoled. 'You're using that word as a swear word now!'

'No, seriously,' Rhamin explained for all to hear, 'the others that were there will back me up on this.' He glanced around at his companions. They had all winced and, all but one, were noticeably trying to avoid getting drawn into the conversation. The other, Solin, just grinned triumphantly. Rhamin went on, 'Come on guys, back me up on this!'

'I have to admit,' said Solin, remembering how the big animal had body-checked him in the farm yard, knocking him sideways, 'she was big.' He paused and then said, 'And ugly! Fellas, was she ugly or what?!'

'Sure was,' confirmed Charka.

'Oh yes?' retorted Yeltsa.

'Useless flopped down ears, face as broad as a Zelda's backside and muscles in all the wrong places. Ugh!' joined in Natan, his tongue hanging out as usual, half way down to the ground.

'I see you're all enjoying this, I can tell,' mused Rhamin. 'At last I've managed to do something right! I've brightened up your day!'

'Wish I hadn't asked now!' Yeltsa said rather less dejectedly than she tried to appear. It was obvious to all the wolves, and not just Rhamin, that she was besotted will all five of her new babies. But she really did want to know what kind of dog Lexa would grow up to be. Sure, she would be a wolf in nature. She would eat like a wolf, howl like a wolf, hunt like a wolf, but she would always be unmistakable if she looked, as the hunting pack had described, like her natural mother.

While they rested, they saw that Corvak the raven had landed near to Zelda. It had been a long time since they had seen him. She was no doubt telling him about their planned trek. The old wolf and the raven chatted for a long time before, eventually, her friend took off to the sky again. She lay sightlessly pondering their conversation for a long while, until, eventually, she fell into a deep sleep, twitching and contorting uncontrollably. She passed wind a couple of times, almost awakening herself with the sound, and then lapsed back into blankness. Rasci and Silvah, who had been lying next to her, casually stood up, stretched as if restless, and moved to the up wind side of the old wolf. 'It's a good job there aren't a lot of animals that prey on wolves,' Rasci commented as he settled down on a soft patch of dusty earth. 'She'd be a dead give away.'

'Don't speak too soon,' said Charka a moment later. Her head was up and her ears pricked forward. She suddenly gave out a warning bark; a quiet 'woof'. Rasci jumped in alarm, sprang to his feet and spun around, ears and head rotating, listening for the sound of danger. All in the pack stood up silently and strained their ears in anticipation. 'It's down wind,' Charka whispered in a low tone.

'What is?' Rhamin said close to her ear.

'I'm not sure, but I've sensed this danger before, not too long ago,' she said almost inaudibly. Rhamin could see that she was half talking to him and half talking to herself. 'But then I could smell it as well as hear it; it was coming to us from upwind that time. I was sure danger was somewhere out there, but it was several miles away. Now its sound is much nearer.'

Rhamin gestured to Natan and Solin for them to circle around and take a look to see what was approaching them. They could all hear now what Charka had heard. There was movement through the dry grass, and a sound of suppressed breathing. Obviously the maker didn't want Rhamin and his pack to hear. It sounded like a big animal, but not an elk or deer.

Suddenly Zelda awoke with a squeal. 'Run!' She yelped.

'What is it? Zelda,' asked Rhamin.

'Heh?' Zelda looked confused. 'I… I was dreaming,' she said, her voice trailing off as she thought more about the question. She gazed sightlessly towards the darkening cloudless horizon. Rhamin could hear the sounds getting closer but he waited for Zelda to continue.

Then, from up in the sky, way up, from a speck floating in the breeze, came the caw-caw of Corvak the raven's rasping voice. 'Yes!' Zelda cried suddenly. She stood up shakily and bounded stiffly towards the bundle of puppies. 'We must get them back to our home,' she said, picking up the top most, black bundle from the pile of sleeping babies. She looked around sightlessly, waiting for the other wolves to follow suit and then lead her away. But they all looked at her, unable to understand her mood.

'What is it, Zelda?' Rhamin asked her again.

She put the puppy down at her feet. 'Run!' she woofed. 'We must run. We can out run them.' With that last warning, she picked up Lexa and bounded off down the trail they had all left earlier, blindly crashing through brush and thicket.

'After her!' Rhamin yelled, gathering up the next baby. Yeltsa followed suit, and within seconds, the pack, all except the two scouts, were bounding after Zelda.

Corvak the raven cawed again, nearer this time. When the warning from the scouts came, they were sharp yaps in quick succession, warnings of imminent danger. By this time the pack had overtaken Zelda and, telling her to follow close, they guided her the way she had wanted to go. It wasn't directly away from the danger, more at right angles to the sound of running and heavy breathing. They could hear the sound of heavy creatures crashing through the brush to intercept them. The voices of Natan and Solin yapped incessantly. Zelda was falling behind. Bamar the yearling male noticed first. He circled back to find her standing panting, mouth dripping with saliva as she gasped for air past the small motionless puppy. 'Come, give me that bundle,' he said standing in front of her so that she could not pass. Obediently she put Lexa down on the ground and Bamar picked her up. Then, stepping to one side, he waited for Zelda to run along beside him. 'Run!' she gasped. 'Leave me. Save the baby!'

Bamar stood his ground. 'That isn't an option,' he stated as the sound of crashing feet and heavy breathing seemed almost upon them. Bamar could see clearly now what the chase was about. Looming up from the dried stubble of vegetation, a huge brown head bobbed up and down as huge paws ate up the ground beneath it; a large snout with a wet black nose, which seemed half the length of its face, curled back to reveal the fangs of a bear. He had heard of this bear before; it was a mean and vicious old male called Bortag. And Bortag was probably no less hungry than the wolves. He was preparing to attack.

'You know what you have to do Zelda!' Bamar yapped as he dropped Lexa and ran forward. By now his attacker was only paces away. Once again, Zelda picked up the dog pup and ran, though in which direction she knew not, except that it was directly away from the crashing sound and imminent danger. Bamar bounded towards the bear, seemingly intent on meeting it head on. The huge creature opened its mouth ready to grab him but in his last stride before lunging, Bamar twisted his body, and sinking his teeth into the front paw of the bear, he veered off to the left. The momentum of Bamar's body swung the bear around, flailing and slashing with its other arm. As Bamar swung at the end of the bleeding paw, he was spun around like a lifeless fish. He let go somewhere in an arc as he circled the bear and suddenly started to glide backwards, legs splayed and tail spinning, ready to land. He sailed through the hot windless air in a straight line away from the bear but still facing the enemy. It paused only momentarily to see him land awkwardly amidst a pile of drift wood and then, seeing the wolf at a disadvantage, the bear resumed its pursuit. Bamar yelped as his back legs hit the wood first, sending him somersaulting backwards into the dust and then landing with a heavy thump with his back against a rock. He had less than a second to get his bearings, but he was winded and dazed. The bear was relentless, teeth barred ready to grab him. Pain shot through his whole body as the bear bounded closer.

Then, as Bamar shook himself to clear his vision, suddenly,

from nowhere, four wolves, all as if synchronised, floated through the air, Rhamin slightly ahead, landing his huge front paws on the shoulder of the bear, sinking his long canine fangs into its face. One by one, the others seemingly in slow motion landed upon the quarry, Natan on its back tearing at its thick fur along the bottom of its spine; Powla grabbed its back foot and Silvah hit the top of its left arm as she grabbed for its throat.

When attacking a large animal, wolves attack by ripping and tearing at their prey, then they leave go and attack again until, eventually they wear down the creature and expose it to a final and fatal attack. There was no way to do that with a bear. They have thick, almost impenetrable coats and are only really exposed on their faces and their feet which are, inevitably, well protected by teeth and claws. As each one of the wolves ripped and then let go, they knew that one blow from the long claws or one bite from the jaws of their enemy would be fatal. The bear's claws could rip open their sides like breaking the surface of a still pond. Its jaws could crush their bones or their skulls in a single gnashing lunge. Only Rhamin kept his grip on the animal. With his feet braced against the giant body, and with his long teeth sunk deep into the animal's eye, the skin on its face began to tear as he hung there, shaking and twisting at the loosening flesh beneath its lower eyelid. The warm dust laden air vibrated with the sound of the bear as it let out a tremendous growl that boomed into the evening sky. Enraged and now injured, the bear stood upright, and made an upward swing with its injured paw. Rhamin thought of letting go but he would have fallen at the feet of this giant animal where, if he landed off balance, he would have been slain immediately. There was nothing he could do but hold on until, eventually, he was knocked off the bear's shoulder by the upward force of its paw. Rhamin's teeth, clenched by the force of his powerful jaws, ripped right through the skin of Bortag's face as he was thrown clear, rotating through the air, his tail spinning and legs splayed to stabilise his flight. He landed on all fours amidst a cloud of dust and flying grit. He recovered his balance immediately, and joining the others, he began to circle the attacker the way they would do when hunting their prey. The bear swung wildly at them with its claws as each wolf snapped and withdrew with practiced locomotion, circling it, ripping at its heels, tiring it and making it dizzy.

And then, as suddenly as they had attacked, they followed Rhamin's lead and disappeared towards the spot where they had last seen Zelda. She had howled. It was a cry for help. It took less than five seconds to reach sight of her, and there, in a flurry of dust, saliva and clamour, she stood in front of a second bear, equally as big, snapping and snarling like none of the pack had ever seen her. Zelda's one existing long tooth was slashing and cutting at the air in front of the bear's huge black nose. Behind her was the dog puppy, covered in dust and flying grit, motionless and totally oblivious to the danger amidst the turmoil. To one side, Rasci, as wolves do, was slashing at the attacker and turning and bounding away time and time again, each time, his rebound synchronised to avoid the motor reaction of the swiping arm and claws of the bear.

Like wolves, bears often prey on weak or elderly animals or the very young. In nature, in the wild such predation leaves the herds of the hunted stronger and regulates their numbers. It was no coincidence that the bears had sought out Zelda. She was clearly at a disadvantage. And the baby she was carrying was totally helpless. But Zelda wasn't ready to leave this world. Perhaps her instinct to protect the young contributed to that drive to survive. And to her all the pack was young. It was clear now, that in her prime, back in forgotten history, Zelda must have been a formidable hunter and fighter. She stood her ground, sensing the swinging arms of the huge bear and somehow, miraculously swayed and swerved out of the sweeping path of its claws.

Then, once again, the pack descended on the creature, running, floating and hitting their target, tearing and leaving in one smooth practised action. From the corner of his eye, Rhamin saw Zelda pick up Lexa and scamper away as they circled and tormented the bear. Soon it was joined by Bortag, his face wet with blood, his right eye closed completely. Together the pack attacked and withdrew, worrying, snapping, slashing with their teeth, constantly moving; not giving either of the bears any chance to organise any tactical retaliation upon them. Eventually, when they were sure Zelda had got clear, they circled off in single file, leaving the bears panting and disheartened.

It was only a short while before they caught up with Yeltsa, Charka and young Rowan. Each was carrying one of the puppies. Bamar had joined them, limping badly, his left back leg suspended from touching the ground. He carried a fourth youngster. But old Zelda was nowhere to be seen.

Rhamin looked back. There was still a flurry of dust in the background. 'Come!' he ordered and headed back with all the unburdened wolves at his heels. Zelda was isolated and carrying a baby, and there was no time to lose as they raced back towards the dust cloud. But his concern was unnecessary. There, trotting along side the old wolf, and carrying Lexa was Solin. There was no sign now of the bears, just the raven cawing overhead. As the pack appeared, Solin stopped abruptly. He spat out the youngster which tumbled over the dusty ground.

'We could have decoyed them with that thing,' he said spitting in disgust. 'But instead, we end up in a scrap to save it!'

'They were after Zelda,' Rhamin stated. 'Didn't you notice that wherever she was the bears were?'

'As a matter of fact, no,' Solin snarled.

'Well, you were conspicuous by your absence,' Rhamin stated bluntly. 'We heard you but what fighting did you do?'

Solin scowled and barred his teeth. 'I happened to be busy with the third bear,' he growled.

'Oh, really?' Rhamin said, sceptically.

'No, it's true,' Natan interjected. 'There were three of them. I saw them too.'

'And I kept one of them busy while you dealt with the rest,' Solin hissed. 'They were all spread out, closing in on the pack from three sides.'

'You took on the smaller one, then,' quipped Natan.

'I didn't see you taking one on by yourself,' Solin recalled, 'whatever the size.'

'All right,' Rhamin said in a conciliatory tone. He paused for a second or two and then, looking from one to the other, said, 'We did well, all of us.' With that he licked Zelda's nose and squeaked as wolves do to the pack members they admire. 'Come on then, let's join the others.'

'Er...' said Solin, standing his ground. 'I only carried that thing to get the old fool to move. Don't think I'm going to carry it now!' He cuffed the wet, round black bundle with his huge paw, making it roll over with a squeak. Zelda's hackles rose as she stepped past Lexa and faced Solin nose to nose.

'Don't get me cross,' she said quite seriously.

'Oh you and your stupid dog pup!' Solin grumbled. 'It was because of you I've been seen carrying it!' He faced the others. 'If I hadn't got her to shift, the bears would have still been on her ragged tail. I don't know why I bothered!'

'I'm sure you know exactly why you bothered and I'm also sure you know she's grateful,' Rhamin consoled. 'But you do have a way of upsetting everybody.'

'Me? You don't think perhaps some younger members of our pack would do better to keep their mouths shut?' he half asked, half stated, looking directly at Natan.

Rhamin smiled. Despite his aching body, he needed to remain in firm control. 'Come,' he said. He picked up Lexa ready to lead the way.

'And just where is it we're supposed to be going?' asked Solin.

'Home,' Zelda stated.

'But what about the drought?' Solin asked. 'We are still short of game to hunt.'

Zelda looked at Rhamin with her glazed eyes. Looking back at her, Rhamin asked, 'Well?'

'The rains are coming, I promise,' Zelda stated matter of factly.

'And until then?' asked Solin, looking towards Rhamin. 'Are we to hunt the man's stock as he hunts ours?'

'It shouldn't be necessary,' Zelda said confidently. 'The rains are here and I know where there are six buffalo.'

'And how do you know that?' Solin sniped. 'Another of your farty dreams I suppose.'

'Corvak told me.'

'A raven! That stupid bird that played at pulling your tail last winter!'

'A raven,' confirmed the old wolf. 'You know very well that he and his mate used to follow us to our prey. Well he often told me where to find it in the first place. We share our food with him because he helps us.'

'You never told me that,' Solin complained. 'You always made out that you had some kind of ability to foresee things you old fraud.'

'I don't need to explain my methods to you, Solin. I said they *sometimes* talk to me.'

'That doesn't mean Corvak or whatever you call him gave you any information about rain.'

'I'm not answering that,' Zelda said angrily.

'It might help all of us if you did,' Rhamin said in arbitration.

Zelda sighed. 'Well, you know Corvak can travel a hundred times faster and further than we can in a day,' she said, still panting heavily. 'Well, he tells me he has seen the rain coming this way.'

'Huh, well I hope it gets here soon then,' Solin quipped, as he started off in the direction of the rest of the pack and the Darin. 'Because if it doesn't, we are all bear food.'

'We certainly gave those bears a good whupping, though!' Rasci boasted, noticeably lightening the mood as he skipped on behind, tossing a dry stick in the air playfully.

'Yes, I think we did,' Rhamin said with a chuckle as he took the lead.

Towards midnight the pack stopped once again to give Yeltsa time to feed her litter. It was good that she was returning them to the safety of the Darin. The pups were looking noticeably stressed. She knew there was little chance that they would have survived a ten day journey.

But they had started on the trek because the pack had to survive. Although everything in a wolf pack centres around the new litter and their mother, in times of dire hardship the survival of the adults takes precedence and in such circumstances, wolves have been known to leave the young to die or to even kill them. But Yeltsa and Rhamin knew that their pack would do everything in their power to protect the babies and prevent the death of any of the offspring. Now, if the rains were coming and they could find food for a few more weeks, all the game would return to the hills, the forests and the plains.

'The buffalo are beside the dry lake, two day's travel away, towards the rising sun,' Zelda explained to the assembled pack. 'They have travelled along the rivers down stream to the lake following the water from the rains in the mountains to the north. The water is flowing much faster than the rains are travelling, and the cracks in the dried up lake bed have already started to fill.'

'I supposed this will be another wild profitless escapade,' Solin grunted. 'And you will expect us to carry a buffalo back for your dinner!'

'Only if I'm right,' Zelda retorted.

'Well, I've got to admit, you're not just an ugly old wolf,' Solin said sarcastically. 'If you're right then I take back everything I have said about you!'

'And what is that exactly, as if I didn't know already?'

'Nobody ever listens to him,' Natan cut in, 'so don't you bother to listen to him either!'

Solin raised himself up on his toes and looked down at Natan. 'You should know better than to mock your betters,' he stated threateningly.

'Didn't know I was doing,' Natan replied undaunted and

standing on tip toe, eyes burning into Solin. 'It was just you I was getting at.'

'You can both calm down,' Rhamin said, standing up and stepping between them. 'We have hunting to do and we have to see our young and elderly safely back to the Darin before we go. I'm not prepared to leave them at any risk out here. If the bears are tracking us, another attack from them will be fatal if we have split up. Zelda, Yeltsa and the babies must be returned safely tonight.'

CHAPTER FIVE

It was no surprise, even to the sceptic Solin that Zelda had been right. The hunting pack located the small herd of buffalo by mid day two days after leaving the Darin. Zelda had instructed Rhamin to follow Corvak and his mate, Corvus. They had been good guides. Rhamin looked down towards the animals from a small ridge that ran along the chain of hills and rises that formed a long barrier between the plains and the steep upper banks of the lake. The upper banks were just a brown dusty extension of the hilly slopes, bone dry and showing little sign of ever having been submerged in water. Further down, the site became flatter, stretching for what seemed an endless distance into the horizon, with cracks so wide that even the big paws of the wolves would not span them. Over to their left the pack could see a broken silver line reflecting the sunlight as it twisted and turned and snaked its way far into the distance like an umbilical chord connecting the embryo of a new and freshly growing lake to the dark clouds of its remote mother source. It wasn't possible to say whether the buffalo had yet visited the gathering waters which the pack could just distinguish as a silver patch far, far away, but their tracks indicated that they had followed the path of the newly replenished river. The water had raced down to the lake ahead of the rains because so little of it had been absorbed by the baked river beds and the parched ground far away in the mountains. It had nowhere to go but to run off down the dry streams and rivers, channelling and cascading its way over the rocks and pebbles and, gathering speed and collecting dirt, it drove along, pulling out dead branches and trees and any other debris in its path. It raced down hill, faster and faster, nothing able to impede its progress until, released from the confines of the steep mountain valleys, it spread out like a blanket, soaking into the cracks of the plain and the dry lake bed. But once the surface had been given time to absorb the water the land adjacent to the old river bed had begun to soak up the water like a dry sponge, diminishing the torrent to a trickling stream as most of the liquid disappeared into the ground. And as if by magic, the resilient grasses were reappearing, sending up new shoots that gave the landscape along the side of the silver ribbon a welcome green hue. The buffalo had been following the new green growth, nipping off every new grassy leaf tip.

When the pack got close to the herd, the animals appeared much thinner than they should have been for the time of year, for they too had suffered severely from the drought. There were no young calves with them as there would have been in a normal year. They had either died from lack of food or they had been preyed upon by other hungry predators. But these adult animals were healthy. Rhamin selected a young bull to take, leaving a mature bull and his females to breed. Rhamin knew that in the long term it would benefit them to allow all of the hunted animals in their area to multiply, especially after such a deadly dry spring and early summer. If there had been a disabled or a diseased animal, despite the desperate need of the pack, he would have taken that rather than a healthy one and for no other reason but to preserve the stock number. Wolves are quite capable of taking large healthy animals but when they perform their style of husbandry, it is usually dismissed by humans as the wolves' inability to bring down the larger animals. That just isn't so. As it was, Rhamin left the females and their mature male for they were the important ones needed to increase the stock in the next breeding season. In fact, Rhamin knew that they would probably be already in calf for next spring.

Zelda who had stubs of teeth and needed pre-digested food, Bamar who had a broken leg and Yeltsa who was nursing her young, all stayed at the Darin. The rest had travelled with Rhamin and they all fed well that afternoon. They lay in a circle around the carcass resting and sleeping as they digested their huge meals. Corvak and his mate Corvus had been joined by several vultures, but Rhamin lay close enough to the carcass to keep them at bay whist the ravens dined.

Wolves can eat a third of their own body weight in meat at one go, washed down by ample supplies of water, in this case from the newly replenished streams tumbling towards the lake. But their digestive systems can work remarkably fast, and by sun-down, Rhamin's pack were tucking into the carcass once again, taking their fill this time ready for their journey home during the cool hours of the night.

While the rest of the pack rested and Silvah bathed in the fast flowing stream, Rasci joined Rhamin to say farewell to Corvak. The huge black raven cawed and Rasci gave a low woof as if to say that he understood. Rhamin looked at him quizzically. 'Do you understand him?' he asked, suddenly shocked by the revelation.

'A bit,' Rasci replied as he woofed at Corvak again.

'And does he understand you?'

'Oh yes,' Rasci said proudly. 'He knows what we are all saying.'

'But how do you know their language?' Rhamin enquired, his curiosity all consuming.

'Well, Zelda, of course. She knows many languages. She knows the sounds of animals but she also understands the other languages of their minds and their bodies. When I sit with her she teaches me as best she can. But there is too much to learn. I fear I shall never be able to carry her knowledge on. Not all of it, anyway. Often she tells me tales of wolves many years ago, stories passed down to her from her elders when she was young.'

'Of course,' Rhamin nodded that he understood. 'I think she is hoping you will be able to pass it all on when she has gone.'

Rasci sighed. It was hard to think that one day the old wolf would no longer be with them. 'She can go on for years yet,' he said, a sadness passing a veil over his eyes. Zelda was so old, nobody knew if she was even related to them. She was at least five generations older than Rhamin.

'You and Silvah do a good job of keeping her well.'

'We're working on it,' Rasci smiled, showing his rows of new white teeth. 'She carries in her head such wisdom.'

'She is a valuable member of our pack,' said Rhamin.

Rasci's eyes suddenly lit up. 'And did you see her seeing that bear off!' he exclaimed proudly.

As their mood lightened, a cooler breeze blew from the west, a sure sign of a change in the weather. Thick cumulus nimbus clouds were piling up on the skyline causing the sun to disappear suddenly and without trace for the last time that day. 'We had better be making a start,' Rhamin said, as darkness engulfed them. Turning to the rest of the pack, he said, 'We each need to carry some food with us. Those back at the Darin are relying on us to return soon.'

'Perhaps, tomorrow, we can keep on travelling through the day. If the weather is changing,' Natan suggested, 'it is likely to be much cooler.'

'I agree,' said Rhamin. 'We'll all have time to rest once they have been fed.'

And so, after gathering up as many huge haunches of the carcass as was possible, under the first cloud filled starless sky they had seen for many moons they set out for home, leaving Corvak cawing softly in the darkness to his mate.

The pack travelled well during the night, heading towards a storm. Behind the far distant horizon, sharp daggers of light lit up the sky every few seconds. They all felt good, loping through the darkness with a spring in their legs such as they had't had for a long time. They were well fed, well rested, and heading to their favourite home, their Darin. It wasn't long before the distant rumble of thunder could be heard from way ahead of them, and before dawn broke, the first heavy droplets of rain plopped onto their thick coats and onto the parched ground around them, each heavy droplet sending up a plume of dust like a tiny explosion. As the night passed and daylight began to force its way through the greyness of the sky, the crashing sound of thunder grew closer and closer and the flashing blades of light in the sky began to cut over their heads. At times it was so close that the static electricity in the air made the guard hairs in their thick coats stand on end.

But wolves have two coats. The bottom fleecy soft coat

is a thick thermal layer. Above that the guard hairs, as the top coat layers are called, act as a waterproof barrier better than any plastic raincoat that humans wear. The rain was cool and refreshing. The pack stopped several times, not to rest, but to put down their food supplies and lift their heads up into the air to feel the water running over their faces. They opened their mouths and let the heavy rain wash onto their tongues and over their teeth and gums. Nature had had its bad spell and now it was telling them that life giving water was here once again. It was back and, hopefully, it was here to stay. Water gathered in puddles on the dry dusty ground, which would take hours to become porous again. Only slowly over the coming days would the land sponge up the rain. Rasci and Natan danced around in the water, biting and snapping at it as it was splashed up by their plate-like feet.

It wasn't long before the pack was, once again, loping homeward, and by late evening, as the rain abated and as the face of the moon peeped though a break in the clouds, they arrived within five miles of the Darin. Here, they stopped and together they howled, calling to the waiting wolves to tell them that they were near, and they in turn returned the call. As they reached the Darin, Yeltsa was the first to greet them, tail sticking upright, nose pushing into Rhamin's fur, squeaking and smiling with her mouth wide with excitement. No exhilaration is greater than the mood of the pack reunited. Zelda was next out of the cave, placing her head over Rasci's shoulder and he doing the same with her as they walked jubilantly side by side. And then Bamar limped into the open, tail wagging as he balanced expertly on three legs. He seemed to be suffering pain. His leg hung loosely from the knee joint, but it did not lessen his happiness to see his pack return, not just safely, but with food to last them all for days.

After the tail wagging and excitement had died down, Silvah went over to Zelda and fed her. Rhamin left a large slab of meat at Yeltsa's feet and Rasci did the same with a whole buffalo leg for Bamar.

Yeltsa looked thin. 'Is everything all right?' Rhamin asked her, peering beyond her to the mouth of the cave.

'It is now,' she replied as she began to eat. 'But the pups are really dragging me down. I need food regularly if we are going to prevent them from suffering any permanent damage from their ordeal the other day.'

'We'll be fine now,' Rhamin reassured her, resting his chin on her back as she ate. He remained there, close by her side, for some time, and then, tiredness overtaking him, he joined the rest of his hunting pack, and lay down amongst them to let sleep wash over him.

The drought had not just affected wolves, of course. Animals throughout the land were washing in the rain, celebrating the return of life giving plant growth and slowly heading homeward to their summer habitat. A sense of calm permeated the world as they saw it. In the days following the rain, blades of grass sprung miraculously from nowhere painting the landscape in hundreds of shades of green. The evergreen trees of the forest seemed to breathe a sigh of relief as their huge trunks channelled up water to their needles. The deciduous trees were slower to respond. They had grown new leaves in the spring and those leaves had survived only because the trees found water supplies deep beneath their tap roots. But many younger trees had lost their leaves and, as the drought continued, closing their systems down into a state of hibernation just like in winter, they had become bare and lifeless. Some had died and those that had survived were going to take all the rest of the year to recover, sending out only a few new shoots to stimulate life before hibernating once again in the fall. With the resilience of nature, however, things were gradually returning to normal and because of the perseverance of the pack, the baby wolves and Lexa all survived.

Male wolf pups grow quicker than their female siblings. A female will generally gain two and a half pounds a week in their first three months after being born, but a male will gain between three and three and a half pounds per week. At four weeks old, Ramusan was showing signs of growing up to be a giant wolf like his father and he was closing the gap between himself and his foster sister Lexa who, up till that time, had remained considerably bigger than the rest of the pups.

However, as the cubs steadily developed their shapes as wolves with long noses and large feet, Lexa's nose remained blunt and her ears didn't start to become erect but remained folded over like loose curtains. And as time progressed, Yeltsa resigned herself to the fact that Lexa would never look like the other wolves in the pack. By the age of eight weeks wolves are already covered in an adult–like hair, but it was obvious to the pack that Lexa was never going to grow a long coat like the rest of them. Whilst the dark coats of the wolf cubs began to lighten to silvery grey, Lexa's coat remained dark. Her face and muzzle remained black, but her jowls and her eyebrows, began to lighten, matching the tan on her forelegs, and as the wolf cubs' eyes began to change from blue to amber, Lexa's eyes began to go dark brown. And most unusual, where the other wolves had bushy tails, Lexa had merely a stump. But no-one in the pack seemed to take a lot of notice. To them, the cubs, including Lexa, were just the next generation.

Ramusan was going to grow up to be the dominant cub, except for Lexa. Yeltsa often had to separate the two of them from their fighting game when Lexa refused to leave go of Ramusan's fur. She knew that wolves had formidable jaw strength with a biting pressure double that of most of the domestic dogs the pack was ever likely to encounter. Even the German shepherd dog that looks similar to a wolf has only half the strength that a wolf has in its jaw. But Lexa was different. Her jaw was short and from three weeks old, she, like her siblings, had baby canine and pre-molar teeth. But her bite always matched that of Ramusan and over a period of time, as the two play fought and strived for dominance, the rivalry between the pair left the other three cubs in a separate and less dominant group.

As the season progressed and the cubs started to develop into young adults, Yeltsa enjoyed taking them on hunting trips with Rhamin. They moved their camp outside into the open, where, along with Bamar, who was still unable to travel far, and Rasci, Silvah and Zelda, they could start the long training period of the newest generation. The cubs had always used any wolf available to pounce upon in their play fighting, but now, as the serious training began, Rhamin taught them the rules of collaboration when attacking a large animal. At first they used Zelda as their "prey". Being a relatively inactive member of the pack, she was only too pleased to be a useful part of their training. For their first hunting lesson with the old wolf he showed them how to split up and create a pincer movement to drive prey into the path of those wolves that had circled around ready to trap the fleeing creature. 'Run!' he shouted to Zelda as he and the pups set out on their attack. Zelda picked herself up and began to trot steadily away.

'Is this fast enough?' she shouted behind her, but got no reply. Suddenly, without warning, Lexa landed on Zelda's head from the left as Ramusan came up on the opposite side and tugged at the thick coat on her shoulder. 'Umph! Obviously not!' she grunted as they floored her.

'Well done guys,' Rhamin shouted as he monitored the hunt and the remainder of the pack of yapping cubs as they joined in and jumped on Zelda. They all had a tug at the tufts of old under coat that stuck out through her guard hairs, and finally they alighted from her, shaking their heads, spitting and blowing to get the fluff out of their mouths.

Eventually, of course, as the teaching progressed and the cubs got stronger and faster, it was a relief to Zelda that the other wolves took over the her role as prey, and in turn, she reverted to her permanent task of teaching the young wolves all about those other creatures in the world that would inevitably become part of their lives.

And Corvak was one. He often visited the pack, and late one afternoon, after a rather longer period away than normal, the old raven flew in. This time, however, as well as bringing his mate Corvus, the pair was accompanied by two young ravens.

'My young ones,' Corvak proudly stated as he stood next to Zelda. The two young ravens landed beside him and after an explanation to the cubs from Rasci that not just Corvak but all his family were considered to be members of the pack, Lexa immediately went about chasing them, panting and grinning with her mouth wide and tongue flapping wildly, skidding and turning, and eventually sliding to a halt at Zelda's feet only inches away from Corvak. The old raven was totally unfazed by her behaviour. It was just Lexa's playful way, always full of energy, always attacking the other cubs, and in turn being attacked by them.

'It is good that she and her brothers and sisters know we are friends,' remarked Corvak, as he looked on proudly, 'and that friends need not be afraid of those whose closeness is essential in times of hardship.'

'Yes, it's good to have friends,' Lexa panted, her tongue hanging out and showering streams of saliva onto Crufus and Betrix, the two young ravens who had hopped up to her nose. Crufus pecked at one of her short whiskers making her tongue retract suddenly as she nudged him out of the way. 'Ouch!' she called and then bounced up on all fours and did another circuit of the camp site closely pursued by her two young feathered friends.

'Settle down,' Yeltsa ordered as Lexa disturbed the other resting cubs. 'It's time for you all to get some rest.'

'Then can we have a story?' asked Lexa, her brown eyes pleading.

'Tomorrow perhaps. I think Zelda has a story to tell you, about three bears.'

'Huh! Don't remind me,' Zelda said with a shiver. 'I still have bad dreams about that.'

CHAPTER SIX

To contact the rest of the pack, each night the young wolves joined their parents and howled, sometimes for a little while, sometimes for much longer. Rhamin liked to know where all his wolves were, even if they were not returning to the camp regularly. But after several weeks of hearing nothing from a number of the older wolves, Rhamin began to get a little concerned. Silvah, in particular, was not a wolf to take her leave lightly, yet she had been away for weeks. Nor had Rhamin heard recently from Powla and Charka who had travelled to the opposite side of the territory. However, he was used to the fact that they were not so bothered about calling back to base so regularly. That left Solin and Rowan. Rhamin hadn't heard from them for at least two moons.

It wasn't just Rhamin that was becoming unsettled. Zelda, too, had been restless. For some reason, she had not been her usual happy self. Instead, she had spent much of her time some distance away from the rest of the pack, sleeping restlessly, dreaming as she did when things were on her mind.

Rhamin didn't like a fragmented pack; it was not easily controlled and it left each faction vulnerable, so he decided to make sure every member of the pack was safe and well by calling them all back to camp. There would be a night of happiness and celebration, and then when the merriment abated, he would lay down the law. No longer was he going to allow this sloppy do-as-you-like behaviour. It was worrying to him and it was disconcerting for those other non alpha pack members that needed to have the assurance that, with total co-operation and proper co-ordination, they were never to become vulnerable in any way. It was time now, anyway, to re-unite the pack ready for the winter months.

Climbing onto his rock and lifting his muzzle to the star studded sky, he called out. The call was the loudest and longest Lexa had ever heard. It was meant to reach as far as sound could travel, to reach as many of the pack as possible. After several minutes, his voice tailed off and he stood there on the rock like a statue, silhouetted by the moon, motionless all but for his ears which rotated and adjusted their angle of reception in order to detect any faint response from far away.

'Still no word from Silvah,' he said to the young pup as he turned and listened.

'Maybe she's too far away,' Lexa suggested.

'Probably. But it's not like her,' Rhamin explained, and then, 'No, it's not like her at all.' A couple of minutes later he heard faint sounds from Powla and Charka, and with that, Rhamin seemed to relax a little. But, Lexa could see in his eyes that he was still unsettled as he climbed down from his podium. 'Come young Lexa, it's time you rejoined the others.'

He remained silent the whole of the time that they were walking back to the camp. Lexa followed in his footsteps silently, waiting for her leader to speak again, but he uttered no sound. It wasn't until he reached the camp that his depression lifted.

'Are they all coming then?' Yeltsa asked him as he appeared from the darkness.

'I'm not sure,' he answered. He went up to her and muzzled her beneath her ear. 'I don't know what to think,' he went on eventually. 'I'm getting worried.' He turned towards Zelda. 'What do you think old girl?' he asked as Zelda lifted her head towards him.

Zelda thought for a moment and then she stood up, a little unsteadily, Rhamin thought, and shook herself awake. She almost lost her balance as the shake rippled though her whole body to the end of her shaggy tail. Bits of old fluffy hair floated off her into the distance, carried by a cool westerly breeze. 'I am a bit concerned, too,' she said eventually.

'About what?' asked Rhamin.

'I'm not sure.' She thought for quite some time and then said, 'You are going to have to follow your instincts.'

'Meaning what exactly?'

'You're the leader,' she stated bluntly.

Rhamin looked at her curiously. 'What is it, Zelda? What are you trying to tell me?'

'You're the leader,' Zelda said once again, her eyes staring blankly past Rhamin, and into the darkness. Suddenly she jerked as if awakened from a trance. She turned her head to him and faced him sightlessly. 'You are a good leader,' she said quietly.

'I'm flattered, but it isn't helping, Zelda. Haven't you anything you can tell me?'

'I... I mean,' she paused and thought again. Rhamin just waited patiently. He knew Zelda was struggling to either see something or say something. She wasn't given to stating the obvious, especially when she was concentrating on her sight into the other dimensions. When she spoke under those circumstances, everything had a clear meaning. The trouble is, it was never clear what she meant immediately. Eventually, just as Rhamin was about to give up and quietly walk away from the transcending old wolf, she woofed. 'We must assemble the pack,' she stated as if suddenly enlightened. 'We can defend ourselves then.'

'Defend? From what Zelda?'

'The other pack,' she replied and then slumped down on her belly, exhausted.

Yeltsa shook her head in disbelief. 'The other pack? What is she talking about?'

'I don't know,' Rhamin said with a sigh. 'All I know is that we haven't heard from Silvah or Natan for far too long. It could spell trouble.'

'But we haven't heard any other packs calling in our territory, have we?'

'No,' Rhamin replied. 'Nor have any of our wolves called in to say they have seen any other packs about.'

That evening, Rhamin gathered the wolves at the camp around him and explained that he thought there may be trouble brewing – although he knew not what. He announced that they were going to stay at the rendezvous point and wait for all the other wolves to join them. Until then, no one was going to go too far to call. To reach the Darin it was two or more days trek, travelling day and night in the direction of Charka and Powla and he knew that Silvah and Natan were somewhere in the opposite direction. There was hunting to do, the cubs needed to keep their food intake up to maintain their growth rate, and there was Zelda to consider. She needed feeding and she wasn't up to travelling without rest for days. But despite being offered plenty of food, the rest of the travellers could not induce Zelda to eat much. She seemed constantly agitated. The cubs were giving the old story-teller a wide birth. She snapped at them whenever they went near her and she ignored them if they spoke to her. 'Leave me alone,' she would yap, getting up and moving further from the gathered pack. It created a feeling of gloom that gradually cast a cloud over all of them.

'Well,' Yeltsa said the following day as two more of the straying wolves arrived at the camp. 'We are gathering the pack here. What else do you advise?'

'Advise? Advise? What do you mean,' came Zelda's sharp reply.

'Oh, for goodness sake, Gran!' Rasci, who was lying nearby, exclaimed exasperatedly. 'It was your idea to stay here!'

'Well all I can say, is that you should know,' she reprimanded the youngster.

Rasci shook his head and sighed. 'Will she ever make sense?' he whispered to Rhamin.

Zelda also sighed. 'My sight might be crap but I can hear perfectly well you young whelp!'

'But you aren't making sense,' Rasci objected.

'So who's going to take my place? Don't tell me I have been wasting my time on you? Why does it always have to be me?' she called angrily.

Rasci studied the face of the old wolf for several minutes while she seemed to get distracted by a mosquito that had landed on her paw. She licked the top of her foot where it had been parked. He was about to speak but Zelda beat him to it. 'What do you see?' she asked.

'Nothing!' Rasci answered honestly.

'Then what do you feel for goodness sake!'

Rasci was going to give her the same reply when he suddenly stopped himself from speaking. He looked at Zelda and then, remembering what she had taught him, he began to relax, letting his eyes go out of focus, seeing nothing in his normal three dimensional world, but instead, seeing the pictures in his mind.

'What do you see?' Zelda urged him again.

Rasci still stood in front of her, motionless, gazing through her into some far distant landscape.

'Well?'

'Don't rush me Gran!' came his reply in a soft tone, indicating that she should let him concentrate and not disturb his train of thought. So Zelda waited patiently.

Eventually, he spoke. 'I see many wolves.'

'Well, hooooray!!'

'They're not our wolves,' he stated.'

'Really!' Her sarcasm was pointedly obvious.

'No.' He concentrated again, quite unaware of her manner. 'I… I can't tell if I am imagining this or seeing something,' he said, afraid to go on.

'You must say what you see,' Zelda instructed.

'I see Rhamin fighting with two… three… many of them!' he said, eyes widening in disbelief as he concentrated on what was in front of him as if it were happening there and then.

'Yes!!' Zelda woofed. 'Yes, I knew it!'

'Knew it? Knew what?'

'I… I knew I wasn't just dreaming,' Zelda cried out, the tone of relief in her voice clearly noticeable.

'But I thought you always saw things in your dreams, Gran'

Her voice lowered from excitement to absolute seriousness. 'Yes my little prodigy, but sometimes we begin to doubt ourselves. We begin to think that if the members of our pack are worried then we should worry. But that is a mistake. A mistake I tell you. *We* must never worry, because if we do, we let ourselves down and we let the pack down. If we worry, then our minds conjure up all the wrong answers to the questions that worrying raises.'

'I don't think you are making sense.'

'What I am saying, young Rasci is that I was worried. I was imagining the worst!'

'And?'

'And, I'm telling you, you must not imagine, my little joker! You must not worry because you must not imagine the results of that worry. You must keep a clear and objective view of things… of everything. You must remain completely detached.'

'But when you are part of a pack you worry about your friends!'

'But you mustn't,' Zelda continued to instruct. 'You mustn't.'

'It isn't so easy to clear my mind?' stated Rasci.

'Well obviously not!' the old wolf panted, her mouth opening in a wide smile of missing and worn down teeth. 'Obviously not! Where your loved ones are concerned there is nothing harder than being totally detached and objective.'

Yeltsa had been listening to the conversation, transfixed by what was being said. At this moment she thought it opportune to break into the discussion. 'So you saw Rhamin fighting?' she posed.

'Yes!' Zelda and Rasci answered as one.

'So we must go back to the Darin and prepare to defend ourselves,' Yeltsa continued.

'That won't be necessary,' Rasci stated. There was a pause while the others waited for him to continue. 'We will be going to them!'

Rasci looked towards Zelda, who returned his glance.

'What do you think, Gran?'

'I'm asking you.'

With a shrug, Rasci tilted his head towards his leader. Up till now, Rhamin had remained totally silent, letting Zelda do what she needed to. Zelda had been ill, if not in body, then, to some extent, she had been ill in her mind. It had been five or more days since she had communicated with any of them in any tangible way and now she was talking, she was well on her way to getting herself better. She was explaining it in her own way that she had not been able to detach herself from her pack because she was worrying. She had been unable to sort out fact from fiction created by a troubled mind. She had entered a cloud of confusion, and needed young Rasci to help her through it. Now she was well on her way to reaching the other side.

Rhamin didn't seem to be in the least surprised with what Zelda and Rasci had told him. Their curious looks eventually triggered a response. 'I saw Corvak on my travels yesterday evening.' He admitted.

'And what did he tell you?' Zelda asked eagerly. Suddenly, the cloud had dissipated. She was rapidly returning to her usual self.

'Well you know I can only read his body language, but he was extremely agitated. He kept flying around in circles and then taking off towards the east. He did it time after time. I knew he wanted me to follow him, but I dare not for if I went in that direction I would soon be too far away from the pack to respond if there were any emergency. I acknowledged his warning though. I think he understood me.'

'And what do you reckon is going on?' Yeltsa asked as she licked his muzzle.

'I still don't know,' he said. 'I honestly do not have any idea.' He licked Yeltsa back on her nose and then said, 'But I am going to do something about it, all the same.'

'Which is?'

'First, I am going to go look for Silvah.' He looked into Yeltsa's orange-yellow eyes. 'Don't worry,' he comforted her. 'I'll be all right. But I want you to keep every other wolf on alert. And you must call me if there is the slightest threat of trouble.'

Rhamin explained to Rasci that he had to look after Yeltsa and the pack whilst he himself was setting off immediately first to the north and then, following the mountains in the east, he would search for those wolves who had not arrived back at the camp. Charka and Powla were on their way to join them from the west and they would be back in the next day or so. The pack could then follow on after him. With that in mind, and sensing that time was now of greatest importance, he set off at a loping stride towards the great mountain range that fed the rivers into the eastern lakes.

For six days and six nights he travelled, sleeping only a little and hunting on the way, catching mainly hares and ground fowl and stopping only to take time to eat them and find water with which to wash down the food. Each evening he would rest for a few hours after calling out and then listening for a response. He listened for a reply from his pack, but he knew he was now out of earshot. Then he strained his ears towards the mountains in the east, waiting and hoping that he would receive a reply. He called several times, at regular intervals, quietly listening in between for some sort of answer. But each time he called, no sound of wolves came to his ears.

On the seventh night of his travels, however, his heart

was lightened. He had sent out his usual call but when he heard nothing in return, he lay down and quietly listened to the sounds of the night. He got to his feet ready to call out once again and then, suddenly, from the south-east he detected a noise, a far and remote whisper. It was the faint call of a wolf. Muted by distance, it was muffled and unclear, but he knew it was Silvah's call. He would have known her voice in a chorus of wolves. But then, there was silence. No more calls followed. Or if they did, he couldn't hear them. The brief communication had ended. At first he began to doubt himself. Had he heard Silvah calling to him, or was it only what he wanted to hear? Was he so tired that he was imagining her voice, coming to him from somewhere in space? Nevertheless, his spirits had already been lifted. With strength flowing back into his weary body, he sniffed the air, looked at the stars to get his bearings and set out towards the mountain forests and his lost friend.

The going wasn't easy. The country was uneven and in places steep cliffs of impassable rock blocked his path. Making his way around them and regaining his direction by watching the stars, he loped on through the night. It was early morning when he reached the edge of a forest that, by his calculation was near the spot where Silvah had been when he had heard her. He knew the trees would have muffled the sound of her call, and now, as a grey daylight broke through the dark clouds, he stood up tall and howled once more. Patiently he waited, but no reply came his way. Once again he called out and once again the early morning air remained silent except for the call of awakening birds and for a cold stiff breeze that whistled through the branches towards him. He called a third time only to get the same soundless response.

Dejectedly, he started off through the first tree line of the forest, but he had gone only a few yards when something on the breeze stopped him in his tracks. He lifted his nose to the wind and sniffed it carefully. He had made no mistake. His senses had picked up the scent of another pack of wolves, their scent marks probably somewhere close at the edge of the forest. Alerted to the danger, he paced carefully forward, listening, looking and sniffing to gain any advantage he could. He knew the unfamiliar wolf scent was that of another pack, and he knew that the pack would not be friendly. He carefully considered what Rasci had told him. Rasci and Zelda would no doubt be right. He was going to meet an enemy and he needed every advantage he could muster. He was travelling up wind, so his enemies would not be able to hear or smell him as quickly as he would detect them. But he had been calling out so they would know he was coming.

Careful not to break from the cover of the trees, he made short bursts forward and then, stopping suddenly, he lay down as close to the ground as he could. Each time he stopped he sniffed the air and listened. He was in no doubt that the pack would have heard him. They would have heard Silvah last night. But where was she? He lifted his body off the ground and darted forward another few hundred yards. Once again he flattened himself against the ground in the soft pine needles. He was in no hurry. He waited, watched and smelt the air. Eventually, he heard noises, not of voices but of movement. It was a muffled sound, softened by a wall of trees and the bed of pine needles, but he knew it was footsteps that he could hear, and they were coming towards him, slowly, carefully, deliberately. Still he waited, biding his time, letting the danger come to him. Quietly he burrowed himself into the pine needles. The shuffling sounds stopped and started more times than he could count. At first he estimated that they were coming from deep in the forest, but eventually, he tensed his whole body as the sound came so close that he felt he could reach out and touch it. He knew now that he could attack and strike within seconds. All he needed was to be able to see his target. The trees formed a thick barrier, allowing no straight line of vision for more than ten or fifteen yards, and they slowed the breeze down to a standstill. He held his breath, sniffing the air, and gave out a low squeak. He was sure the air carried the scent of Silvah, but not the Silvah he knew. This Silvah was unwashed. And there was something else about the scent that disturbed him deeply.

Still motionless, he waited and watched the trees ahead. The scent was coming closer and as it did so, it became stronger. Now, he was in no doubt that Silvah wasn't well. But he dare not move. He knew there were other wolves about. What was strange though, was that he had not once, despite getting closer to them every day, heard any of them calling out. As time slowly passed he eventually caught sight of movement in the trees. Slowly and deliberately something was moving towards him, trying not to be heard, and keeping close to the ground. He waited.

Whatever it was, Rhamin was prepared to wait until it was right upon him before he gave his position away. Still it smelled like Silvah, but not like her in another way. And then, he caught a glimpse of her. It *was* Silvah. She looked to be moving slowly, stopping and glancing behind her every few seconds. Then she would move forward past another few trees and stop and repeat her actions. Rhamin felt like jumping up and greeting her as he would greet any returning pack member, but he knew that would be unwise. Something about her behaviour warned him to stay where he was. Something was very wrong here. There was unseen danger, something menacing and malevolent.

Eventually, Silvah moved within ten yards of him, heading past, not detecting his presence. As she went by, he could tell she was injured. She moved forward in bursts, first on her toes and then with her belly on the ground. Creeping forward slowly, foot by foot, yard by yard she went by. Still, her behaviour was unsettling. She was close enough now for Rhamin to see that she had a wound on her shoulder, not a new wound, but one that was festering and weeping, sending a stream of discharged, foul smelling liquid down her coat, staining it dark against her silver guard hairs.

Unsure why she was behaving as she was, he slowly raised himself up and squeaked very softly; no louder than a mouse. Silvah stopped dead in her tracks, standing up a little shakily, but otherwise, remaining motionless. Rhamin squeaked again, no louder than the first call. This time, Silvah turned her head and, seeing her leader, lowered her ears and gave a slight wag of her tail. Still she did not greet him. Instead, trying not to acknowledge him, she stood up tall, looked straight ahead and circled around him, heading off at an angle. Rhamin settled back down on his belly, deep into the bed of pine needles and watched as now, Silvah, on her toes, and moving faster, headed past towards the edge of the forest.

And then Rhamin could smell it. It was the smell of danger; the scent of unknown strange wolves. He knew Silvah was leading them to him but at the same time she was leading them past him. As they came into sight, Rhamin counted three, then a fourth some distance away. Soon, the nearest two were almost upon him but yet, they were so intent on watching and tracking Silvah, following her every move, that they did not see him. When he was sure that he had counted all that were there, and as the nearest wolf trod only feet away, Rhamin raised himself out of the needles, stood to full height and growled. He barred his teeth, laid back his white ears, and startling the wolf which had spun around to see what had made the noise, he lunged forward and grabbed it by the throat. As he did so, from the corner of his eyes he could see the other three wolves spin around, hackles raised and heading towards him.

A quick twist of his powerful jaws, and a more powerful whiplashing shake with his head, dispatched his victim. He let it fall to the ground, and stepped to one side to take the two nearest wolves head on. They were on him in no more than a second, bounding towards him, shoulder to shoulder. Rhamin stood his ground, snarled, stood up once again to full height and met them square on. He parried as if he was going to grab the one on the left, but then, as that wolf faltered, suspecting he would be caught like the first wolf, in Rhamin's powerful jaws, Rhamin swung his broad head to the right instead, sunk his long teeth into the shoulder of the other one, and let its momentum roll him backwards. They tumbled through the soft mulch, the attacker snarling and lashing with his teeth to try and get a hold of Rhamin. But Rhamin kept his hold on its shoulder and, eventually as they rolled to a stand still, and using his superior weight, he ended up straddled over his combatant. Just then the third wolf, teeth gnashing, came at him from the side so Rhamin let go of his quarry and turned to meet the attacker, both rising up on their back legs as they lashed out and snapped at each other, each one trying to gain the first hold. Rhamin suddenly bounced around, landing to one side, giving himself a full view of the remaining three attackers. The one he had tumbled with was regaining its feet, the second was preparing to attack again and the third, which had been some way away when Rhamin had sprung his surprise attack, was now quickly closing the distance between them. It was this wolf that Rhamin set his eyes upon. The other two were a little disparaged, firstly by their failure to get to grips with him, but also because of his size.

The third remaining wolf had yet to experience Rhamin's weight and height advantage. He bounded away from the other two and met the last wolf in mid air as they both jumped at each other. The attacker fell backwards as Rhamin's front paws hit it in the chest. He continued to travel forward, and as his enemy struggled to try and keep on its feet, Rhamin grabbed the back of its neck and, using his momentum, jerked it backwards. They both landed several yards further away from their point of collision, Rhamin splaying his legs to stay upright, his victim on its side, yelping to the others for help. The others had not been slow to respond and, as all wolves do when attacking, they tried to co-ordinate their movements. Two wolves bore down on him now, while he was still holding their comrade. Rhamin jerked his head upwards, lifting his quarry up and swinging him towards the two oncoming wolves. As he did so, from the corner of his eye, he saw Silvah gliding through the air. She had run towards them and had jumped and taken off from the ground just yards away. Her jaws squarely hit one of Rhamin's attackers on the side of the face, teeth sinking into its jowls. Taking the advantage, and almost simultaneously, Rhamin stopped the other wolf in its tracks as it hit its companion in mid air. As the two fell to the ground, Rhamin was upon them, killing one instantly with his huge jaws crushing its throat. The other turned on its back in submission, but Rhamin did not spare it. Somehow, he knew that these wolves were responsible for Silvah's condition. Not only had they invaded his territory, they had waged war. These were not innocent wolves passing through; they were soldiers in an army that gave no quarter. Towering over the prostrate, yelping wolf, he grabbed it and, shaking it like a toy, snapped its neck. When he turned, he saw Silvah through the trees battling with the remaining wolf under a fallen tree. His vision was impaired by the branches and tree trunks, and as he bounded towards the two snarling wolves, he saw Silvah dispatch her opponent by hanging onto its throat, crushing its windpipe until it could no longer breathe.

'That will teach you,' Silvah said through her teeth as life passed from her defeated opponent. Rhamin saw its eyes acknowledge the fact as it passed from this world.

'You can leave go now,' Rhamin said to his friend, some time later. 'Come on, Silvah, leave go!'

Silvah sank down on her belly, leaving go of the deceased and spitting its fur from her mouth. 'Hello my young Rhamin,' she said, now almost too weak to speak.

Rhamin went over to her and pushed his muzzle into the thick coat of her neck. 'You had me worried,' he said eventually.

Silvah seemed tired. 'You have good cause to be,' she stated in a weary voice. 'They,' she said, nodding to the dead wolves, 'are only part of our problem.'

CHAPTER SEVEN

Silvah was very weak, for despite her strength being sheared up by the presence of her leader, she had been systematically starved. The first thing Rhamin did was feed her. He had eaten well that evening, and now, regurgitating some of his meal, he let Silvah eat. With food, strength seemed to flow back into her body quickly. Rhamin, still concerned that there was a likelihood of another attack, walked over to the gap in the trees from where Silvah had come, and lay down keeping his ears strained for any sound from beyond the small clearing. He watched her, letting her take her time, not asking her to answer any questions. Eventually, she stood up straight, shook herself from her head to the tip of her tail and, only a little unsteadily now, she walked over to him.

Despite the fact that Rhamin was all alone, Silvah felt safe. She had nurtured him when he was a pup and she had loved him as her leader. She would die for him without any question, but she knew that Rhamin would do the same, not just for her, but for any of his pack. That is what made him so special. And that is why, his pack stayed so closely bonded to him.

Now, settling down beside him, she could tell him what

had happened to her and why she had not been able to come home. Wolves have been known to go for seventeen days without food, but, although she had been allowed to eat a little, Silvah had been deliberately kept short of food. 'We have to go back,' she said, pointing her nose towards the interior of the forest.

'I take it that there are more where they came from,' Rhamin said, looking at one of the dead wolves.

'Oh yes,' Silvah confirmed with a nod. 'Fifteen more to be precise, including…' She paused, unclear as to how Rhamin would take it.

'Phew, that's a big pack,' Rhamin panted. 'Including?'

'Solin,' Silvah began to explain. 'It's his pack.'

'Solin!' Rhamin stared towards the thickest part of the forest, his eyes cutting through the trees as he visualised his half brother. 'Well! I knew he wasn't content in my pack.'

'No, he wasn't.'

'So what happened?' Rhamin began to lick her coat where the wound had wept.

Silvah moved forward a little on her belly, so that Rhamin could reach it properly. Patiently, he let her take her time to explain. He was in no hurry. She was safe now, or at least as safe as she could be with a pack of fifteen renegade wolves possibly hunting for her and their missing scouts. But it was important to get the full picture and, at the same time, it was equally important to give Silvah time to fully regain her strength for he knew that, despite his size and strength, in a fight he would not be able to take on fifteen wolves alone. Shortly, he and Silvah would have to run for their lives.

'Well,' Silvah began, 'it started several moons ago when we all went on our territorial expeditions. Solin had gone north. He went way beyond our boundaries and eventually he tracked down some members of the Pagin mountain pack. They too were split up and travelling around their territory. According to his bragging, he kept a low profile, keeping out of sight and watching them, and getting to know who was who. He said he had travelled up north as far as that the year before and had narrowly missed being caught by the whole pack. It seems like he met up with some young males that had left the pack and he had been able to get a great deal of information from them. This year he went back there and waited until their leader was out on his own, and then he ambushed him and killed him. As Solin tells it, it was a great battle, but I doubt if he took any risks with his own life.'

'No, but he's a pretty tough nut, Silvah, I think you know that.'

Silvah growled a begrudging acknowledgement. She sighed. 'Hmm, well, I hate him,' she gesticulated, barring her teeth at the thought of him. 'He was always trying to persuade the members of our pack to leave you. You know that, don't you?'

'Oh, yes,' Rhamin said and then, 'But in every large pack you can expect some dissention.'

'As I was saying,' Silvah endeavoured to explain, 'Solin defeated the leader of the northern pack and then he intercepted each of their pack members and told them so. He challenged any of them for leadership and only one accepted. It seems like he defeated that wolf in a fight to the death, but then spared him at the last minute. By doing so, he gained an ally and that wolf gathered in the rest of the pack, all except for Pagin's mate and this year's pups who refused to join him. They went on the run so that Solin and the pack couldn't find them.'

'So what is Solin doing down here at the far corner of our territory if he has taken over the northern territory?'

'Well, he didn't want that as badly as he wanted to take yours.'

'So it's personal,' Rhamin said sadly.

'Oh yes! Very personal,' Silvah confirmed. 'He has hated you ever since you took over as leader.'

'I always put it down to sibling rivalry.'

Silvah shook her head. 'Oh Rhamin, you can be so naive sometimes! You always see the best in your wolves, don't you?'

'I am proud to say I do. The Rhamin pack is the best. Some of them may be new blood from other packs, and some are direct family, but they are all worthy wolves.'

'Not all of them, Rhamin. You are going to have to face up to the facts. Solin is your enemy.'

'And what about Natan and Rowan? Where are they?'

'Natan and I met up with Rowan one night and we were celebrating our reunion when Solin burst upon us with his new pack. He must have been watching us for some time because I can't think it was just by accident that he caught us all together. Well, you know that Natan has never got on with Solin, and when Solin and his pack surrounded us, Natan told him where to get off.'

Rhamin grinned proudly. 'I'm sure I can guess just how he put it!'

'And more!' Silvah said proudly. 'He challenged Solin but Solin had the backing of the rest of the pack. It was never a fair contest. As they fought, the others kept nipping at Natan from behind, and pushing him off balance and doing things like that.' Silvah's voice became sad. She sniffed back a tear. 'Eventually Solin got the better of him and I knew he would kill him. So I shouted for Solin to stop.'

'And did he?'

'He stopped when I shouted a second time. He turned to me and said I was going to be the next to die. I said there would be no need for that if he spared Natan. I told him that I would join his pack so long as Natan was in it. Rowan barked that she would do the same.'

'And of course, he couldn't resist the offer!' Rhamin stated, nodding his understanding. 'So he gained three members of our pack. Quite a coup. He could brag about it for years to come!'

'Well I think that was his reasoning to start with,' Silvah agreed. 'But as the days passed, and as he turned matters over in his own mind, he decided we would be better as lures to get you to come looking for us. He has travelled close to our pack several times, but he gave strict instructions that none of his pack should use calls to each other by way of communication because he didn't want to give his position or any other advantage away.'

'And on top of that, by forcing you to stay with his pack, he had hostages if by any chance I began to get the better of him.'

'That's right. But he's changed. He's not the wolf who you knew as your brother. He's become bitter. He flies into a temper if any other wolf disobeys him. For the past couple of weeks he has treated me like a prisoner, and the other two had to go along with his behaviour for my sake. He has forced them and me into submission. And the only howling he allowed was for us to lure you to come out here. He seemed to know you'd be on your own or at least, poorly backed up.'

'He was right there!' Rhamin contemplated his own vanity. Breaking out of what was becoming a depressing train of thought, he continued, 'So where is he now?'

'He is still in his camp. He expected those four pitiful examples there to kill you on their own.' Silvah sighed. 'But he'll know different soon. He'll also know I have joined you.' She paused and then said, 'He knows we're going to have to make a run for it.'

'That is what he'll expect, Silvah, but when he finds those dead wolves, he is likely to take his revenge out on his captives.'

Silvah looked into Rhamin's amber eyes. 'You mean…?'

'Yes, I mean I am going to get Natan and Rowan if it's the last thing I do, and I'll have to do it fast. Soon those scout wolves will be missed. And then he'll realise you are missing too. You've broken the original contract, Silvah. Natan and Rowan were his lever on you.'

'Either way, run or fight, he's got numbers on his side, Rhamin. Can we possibly do it?'

'Well, I wasn't thinking of we.'

Silvah looked her leader directly in the eyes. 'Huh, you'd better believe it!'

'Well then,' Rhamin said decisively, 'if he thinks we are going to make a run for it, then we had better not disappoint him.' With that final thought, the two wolves headed away from the forest in the direction of home.

By mid morning, in a clearing beneath a cloudless sky, Silvah spotted a pair of deer. One was limping badly, supporting its hind leg off the ground. Despite their urgency the lame deer was an opportunity not to be missed, and on a hillside overlooking the clearing they attacked it and brought it down. They fed well on it, watched from on high by a gathering circle of vultures, sailing on a thermal, watching and waiting for their opportunity to feast on the remains.

Birds of prey have exceptional eyesight and as the

vultures watched and waited high up in the sky, so they in turn were spotted by a number of other birds, with equally good eyesight, many miles away. As those birds flew closer they recognised their wolf friends Silvah and Rhamin. Corvak and Corvus, accompanied by their young offspring, flew in low beneath the circle of vultures and landed beside the two wolves. One of the vultures saw the cue and began a long silent descent, but as it stretched out its long bony legs in preparation for its landing, it was sharply dispatched by Rhamin, flapping wildly to reverse its descent as it struggled to take back to the air.

'Hi there,' Corvak said cheerily as Rhamin looked around.

Silvah replied first for she, like Rasci had spent much time with Zelda and was able to converse easily with her black feathered friends. 'Oh, Corvak, how good to hear your cheery voice!'

'You look like you've been fighting,' he observed as he pecked a fly off the wound on her shoulder.

'It's an old wound,' she said dismissively. 'But no doubt I shall get a few more cuts and scrapes very soon.'

'Oh!' Corvak squawked; his body wrung with apprehension. 'And just where would that be?'

As Silvah explained what had happened to her and her friends, Corvak cawed and bobbed up and down in an agitated manner. He was noticeably distressed by the news. 'I must help you,' he said boldly. 'Yes! I must help you!'

'That's very good of you,' Silvah replied, 'but there is little you can do to reduce the odds against us. I know how brave you are, but you would have no chance against any of Solin's savage pack.'

'Ah,' Corvak cawed, 'but he cannot reach me! I can torment him; I can sweep in and attack from the air. Whoosh; hit;

and away!' He enthusiastically feinted several attacks on Silvah's tail. 'I'm going to be unstoppable! Yes! I can see air power being an invaluable asset now I've invented it! '

'That's a wonderful offer my small friend,' said Silvah, trying not to burst Corvak's bubble of enthusiasm. 'I know you are brave and courageous, but the problem is,' she went on, to try and dissuade him from doing anything he or she would regret, 'we are not sure just how we are going to face them. We have no time to fetch the rest of our pack so we are outnumbered seven to one.'

'Hmm, long odds even for your brave leader,' Corvak commended.

'Too long,' said Silvah.

'Well,' Corvak squawked; his enthusiasm in no way diminished. 'I can be your eyes in the deep forest. I can scout for you and they will never be able to reach me. They might see me but they will not suspect a thing. I'll be a spy! Yes, a spy! That's the way to defeat the enemy!' he said, eyes glazed, looking upward into a visionary bubble.

'That's a much better idea,' Silvah said. 'Rhamin could use a spy to great advantage. It would help him break into the pack, knowing just where they all are and what their plans are.'

'Well that's settled then!' Corvak agreed, coming back to reality with a jerk.

Silvah licked her friend on the wing. 'It's a brilliant idea,' she said, as Corvak responded by ballooning out his chest with pride.

'We'll, explain to Rhamin what you have suggested. I am sure he can use your skills to lessen the numbers against us.'

Rhamin had been listening, picking up on bits of the conversation. Eventually, Silvah explained what Corvak had said.

'Well, one thing I do know, Solin will know where we are by now. If Corvak spotted the vultures then his pack will not have missed them. So they will either be on our trail or they will think we are fleeing back to the Darin.'

'I can find out what they are doing,' Corvak suggested eagerly. And with that, instructing his family to stay and feed, he took flight and disappeared into the distance.

Solin's camp was not permanent, but it was a base, a fixed point from which he could carry out his plans. What he didn't want to do was to have a battle with Rhamin's pack when it was at full strength. His plan was to split the wolves up and preferably get Rhamin on his own as indeed his scout wolves had found him. Unfortunately for Solin, there had not been enough of them to defeat the giant wolf. And he hadn't suspected nor anticipated Silvah's help. However, the camp was pretty well defended. It was an open, rock strewn patch in the thickest part of the forest and inaccessible to any intruder, who would be spotted by the scouts long before reaching the clearing. On three sides there were several well worn trails reaching out through the forest, like spokes in a wheel. At the rear of the camp, however was a steep sided gorge with a rocky pathway snaking down from the forest to a gravel strewn shore beside flat water. A high waterfall fed into the patch of calmer water from the north, and to the south, the water ran quickly into white water rapids that carried the river on its journey down the steep sided ravine. The rocky path down to the river was only a few hundred yards from Solin's camp. It was at that point that the wolves made their way down the steep path to a pebble strewn bank where they drank after feeding. From their watering hole they could look across the rapids to the sheer walls of rock opposite. It was the one side of Solin's camp that was unguarded.

Silvah had only seen the watering hole a few times as she and her companion captives were given little food. With his deliberate action to keep them weak and defenceless, Solin never left his hostages alone. Five or six fit, well fed guards were the normal detachment left with them at all times. All this, Rhamin knew from what Silvah had told him. What he didn't know, until Corvak had happened along, was that, each day, the remainder of the wolves of Solin's pack would spread out in a fan-like formation as they headed away from the camp, thus explaining the many trails converging on the camp. By spreading out like that, the wolves could make sure that they spotted any approaching creature and could warn the guards at the camp by howling back to them.

Corvak was an excellent spy. He not only saw what was happening in Solin's camp, but from branches high above the pack, he could listen to what was being said. Rhamin needed to know if Solin and the members of his pack believed that he and Silvah had returned to the Darin. He knew that Solin would be hoping that he would not give up on his friends but if he wasn't to be seen anywhere, then it could bode well for Rhamin's plan. Corvak's reconnaissance answered his question. Solin had, indeed, seen the spiral of vultures off to the south east and, keeping his wolves back, was not allowing any of them to hunt alone. It appeared to Corvak that Solin was preparing to wait for Rhamin to return with reinforcements, rather than split his pack and head off in pursuit. Rhamin knew that Solin was sure he had superior numbers and Solin's pack consisted of fully mature wolves. Corvak could see how confident Solin was, and he was sure Solin expected to win any battle brought to him on what was now familiar ground.

After another short rest, whilst they waited for Corvak to return, Rhamin and Silvah, circling wide, swung back through the forest and travelled north until they eventually reached the rapidly flowing river. There, they turned south. Now, once again guided by Corvak, they were able to make sure that there were none of Solin's wolves nearby to see them. Only once did Corvak warn them of a scout heading out to the edge of the forest. When they were sure that the scout had turned south and was travelling away from them, slowly, and guided by Corvak, they followed the steep slope of the river along the top of the ravine. Eventually, they came to the edge of a cliff which overlooked Solin's camp. To the left was the waterfall that dropped into the bubbling pool of water that flattened out towards the watering hole, and to the right, a thin trail led back down towards the camp. Silvah pointed out a clump of scrub bush. 'That's where Natan and Rowan are,' she explained. She pointed to an overhanging slab of bedrock that, about eighty feet beneath them, ran out from the base of the cliff towards the middle of the camp. 'The rest of the wolves should be beneath that.'

They watched as Corvak circled above and then swooped in and made a perfect landing in a tree beside them. The black raven confirmed what Silvah had said. Rhamin pulled back from the edge of the cliff, settled down on his belly and spoke quietly to Silvah. Eventually, watched by Corvak who seemed distracted for a while as he groomed his feathers under his left wing, Silvah stood up and, taking the raven with her, headed back down the narrow track into the forest. Rhamin waited a while and then followed her, scent marking the thin trail as he went. After half an hour or so, he turned back up the track to the top of the cliff where he remained, lying down, closing his eyes, and for a while, resting and waiting.

There could not have been more than half an hour's daylight remaining when Corvak returned and called gently to Rhamin, who stood up and walked over to the edge of the cliff. Taking a deep breath, he turned his head up to the sky and howled as loud as he had ever called. The sound eerily broke the silence, reverberating through the forest and sending echoes bouncing from side to side off the steep gorge and over the white water in the distance. Nothing could have prepared him for the reaction from the pack below. There was a chorus of barking and yapping as the pack suddenly sprang into a frenzy of activity, scurrying around, looking for the source of the sound, racing from one side of the camp to the other. It was a scene of total surprised panic. Rhamin pulled back from the edge, watching from the cover of a low, thickly cloaked branch of a pine tree. Over the din and chaos, he heard Solin barking out orders. He was telling them to stop running about and to calm down. But it didn't seem to be working.

'Obviously, they have seen what you did to the front guard,' Corvak whispered in Rhamin's ear. His head swivelled around as he pecked confidently at the bark on the tree. 'They are afraid! It's obvious!'

Rhamin just nodded his acknowledgement of the statement, not sure what Corvak had said, but he knew what Corvak knew. He could see that the pack below were racing about, trying to discover from which side the attack was coming, for clearly, they looked as if they believed Rhamin had somehow returned with an army of wolves. Once again, moving further down the edge of the cliff, Rhamin let out the loudest howl he could muster, and once again, as it echoed from one side of the ravine to the other, it sent the pack into a frenzy of yapping and racing about. Some of them joined together and headed down one of the paths into the forest. Another group led by Solin headed down another track, firmly believing that the sound had come from that direction. Another five ran down the track towards the ravine and watering hole. Solin snapped out orders but no one took any notice as the remaining three wolves ran up the narrow track towards the top of the cliff. Now Rhamin remained silent. He didn't want to give any of the splintered pack a clue as to which group was chasing in the right direction. Quietly, he headed back the way he had come, to the north and along the narrow winding path that would eventually take him deep into the dark forest.

Far behind he could hear Solin howling to the rest of his pack while Rhamin, loping gently on led the three renegade wolves along the lonely track. He could hear them barking and panting heavily as they followed his scent marks and raced to gain ground on him. When he thought he had travelled far enough away from the rest of Solin's wolves he stopped beside a clump of mature oaks. He settled in the thick patch of bracken next to one of his scent marks, where he knew they would hesitate a moment before rushing on along the path. Only seconds passed before the first wolf raced up the track. He faltered slightly as his nose picked up the scent mark and then raced on, following the trail. The next wolf was only twenty yards behind and in an effort to catch up with the leader, it didn't slow. Rhamin could hear a third wolf somewhere not too far behind. Bracing himself on his back legs and raising his body off the ground he waited, only for a second and then, as the wolf came by he pounced. It didn't have a chance. He had taken it completely unawares. Rhamin grabbed it by the neck and with a whiplash shake of his head he killed it before it could make any retaliatory or defensive manoeuvre. With a high squeak and a gurgle, it fell to the ground at his feet.

The two wolves ahead heard the sound and slid to a halt. Barking ferociously they turned on their prey, only they were not side by side. On the narrow path between two mature oaks they could only attack in single file. As Rhamin met the nearest wolf in mid air his weight snapped its head backwards as it plummeted back, bouncing firstly off him and then off solid wood and into the path of its comrade. Rhamin's momentum carried him onto the top of the chasing wolf. He grabbed its throat and shook and shook again until all life had left its limp body. With a final angry growl of satisfaction, he tossed it into the bracken.

Another three down and twelve to go. Rhamin knew he had evened the odds a little, but he also knew that Solin would soon have realised that he was chasing the wrong way when he heard the wolves barking excitedly in pursuit of Rhamin. Solin had bounded up the narrow path and it was clear from the scent marks that, although Rhamin was not alone the only other wolf's footprints his powerful scent glands could detect was the weak and sickly Silvah. But despite all his calling he was having difficulty gathering his pack behind him. 'Come on you cowards,' he was shouting. 'He is only one wolf!' The first four casualties must have been discovered by now, and they were four of Solin's best. Clearly, Rhamin's reputation had preceded him for not all the wolves seemed intent on pursuit.

Rhamin's problem was that he wasn't sure at that moment which scent Solin had picked up. Was it just the scent of Silvah? In that case his plan had failed. Or was he following Rhamin's carefully scent marked trail? Either way, heading back to see what Solin was up to, was a bad idea. Solin still had a twelve wolf pack, too many for Rhamin to fight at once. He decided to put some more distance between himself and his enemy.

Steadily he loped along, conserving his energy. As darkness fell and the canopy of the forest blacked out all but a straying star beam there was a sudden silent stillness. What was Solin doing now, he wondered? There was nothing Rhamin could do now but keep going. Corvak could not help him for ravens are not nocturnal birds. Until daylight, Rhamin would be all alone. The canopy sheltered the forest floor from any wind or breeze, and without sound or scent he had no idea where the enemy was. Oh how he could have used Charka's extraordinary sense of hearing now! If Only! But at least there was no advantage given to his enemy. There was just one thing Rhamin knew in his own mind for sure: Solin's pack may have been looking for him, trying to locate him. But, in their eyes he was the hunter now, not the hunted.

High, high above the forest, riding on the first sunbeams of the day, long before the same light had reached the ground beneath the canopy of the forest, Corvus's incredible eyes soon detected movement. She hovered and circled until the figure below crossed a clearing. 'Found him!' she chuntered to herself, beginning a spiralling, downward dive. Lower down, still in the twilight of the morning, she glided over the treetops, scanning for any other movement. When eventually she located Rhamin again, dawn had reached ground level.

In the blackness of the dense overhead canopy Rhamin had used his keen eyesight and his intense sense of smell to backtrack along his original path. More able to pick up the scent of Silvah's footprints than his own, he was now grateful he had had her beside him on the journey into the forest. He had instructed Corvak to join Silvah when day broke, so when he heard Corvus caw as he broke out into the open, he felt a sheer sense of relief that he was no longer alone. His only worry now was that his plan might have failed. He didn't know if Silvah had succeeded in leading Natan and Rowan to safety. All he knew was that she had had a better chance to escape with the pack chasing after him.

As the sun began to cast a long shadow behind him, Rhamin climbed an escarpment that ran along the base of the mountains like a ripple around a lake of water. From the top he looked back to the edge of the steeply rising forest. He saw no wolves on his trail. Neither could any movement be seen in the thinner patches of forest. His heart sank as he thought now his plan had failed. If Solin had not followed him then he must have gone after Silvah, and alone or even with her two friends, he would certainly have killed them by now.

With a heavy heart he lay down in a hollow that afforded him a clear view of the path along which he had just come. He rested his chin on his paws and, with a tired sigh, watched and waited. As the sun climbed in the morning sky and the beams of radiant heat began to warm his coat, his body began to feel the effects of long days and nights of travelling with little rest or sleep. For a short while his eyes closed and his mind began to wander between semi-sleep and consciousness, only prevented from falling into a deep sleep when he flicked his ears to shake off a group of pestering flies. Then, suddenly, from behind him a voice broke the silence.

'Well done, Rhamin,' Corvus said as she alighted beside him. 'It's worked.'

At first Rhamin could not understand what she had said. He stood up and shook himself to make sure he wasn't dreaming and then looked at the black raven intensely, waiting for her to speak again. She bobbed up and down excitedly. Rhamin studied her and, by her manner, he was now able to understand her a little better, more from her behaviour than her language. He knew the ravens could understand him for Corvak had insisted on making Corvus learn the language of wolves when talking with Zelda during the long cool evenings. 'Have Silvah, Natan and Rowan escaped?' he asked.

Corvus nodded excitedly and cawed and danced about. 'Yes!' she was calling, 'Yes! Yes!'

Rhamin sighed with relief. That much he could understand. He looked up over the crest of the escarpment and thought for a moment. 'So where is Solin and his pack?'

Corvus cawed again, and pointed with her wing towards the tree line on the mountain side. 'They are coming after you.' She shouted the last words as if shouting made it easier for Rhamin to understand. 'But Solin has had a bit of trouble getting his wolves to follow in the dark forest,' Corvus carried on, mimicking the movements of a wolf trying to get his pack to follow him by walking forward and then stopping and waving an imaginary pack on with her wing.

'They have taken their time because they were afraid,' she explained by cowering and looking around furtively. 'They were afraid you were lying waiting to ambush them.' She pounced forward to illustrate.

Rhamin was beginning to regret not taking the time to sit with Zelda, as Rasci and Silvah had done, to learn how to talk to the ravens more fluently.

'If they are to fight you,' Corvus went on, shouting the key words and once again gesticulating an attack on Rhamin by waving her wings and pouncing forward, 'they are going to do it in the daylight.' She pointed at the sun. 'When they can see you properly.' She put her wings over her eyes as if peering at Rhamin from a distance. He wasn't sure he understood every word but from the antics of his friend he managed to gather the bare bones of the conversation, even if they were lacking in meat.

He smiled, as wolves do, panting with satisfaction, his forty two white teeth gleaming against his black face. 'And what about Silvah, Natan and Rowan? Where are they now?'

Corvus pointed over to the north east side of the forest. 'They are heading back to your Darin,' she said, pointing to the south confidently. 'Don't worry, Corvak is watching out for them. He'll let us know if there is any problem. I left him at first light to come and tell you.'

Once again, from studying her actions rather than her words, Rhamin managed to understand her. 'In that case,' Rhamin concluded, 'I think I'll leave Solin and his bunch of nomads to chase their tails. They can have me if they can catch me!' And with that, he stood up. 'Thank you dearly my good friend,' he said, putting his nose close to the old raven. The sun glistened in a myriad of iridescent colours on her shining black feathers as she leaned forward and pecked him affectionately on the muzzle. Lighter of heart now, and refreshed by the good news, he began to glide in his effortless loping stride in the direction of home.

However, only minutes into his journey, Rhamin spotted two specs in the sky above the horizon, and stopping to get a better view, he soon made out two birds approaching. He heard Corvus cawing from behind him, and was soon aware that she was calling to the birds. It was Crufus and Betrix. They took less than two minutes to reach Rhamin and their mother.

Excitedly, the young ravens fluttered to a perfect landing by his side. They were fully grown now, and experts at aeronautics. 'They are coming!' Betrix exclaimed, pointing with her wing back from where they had come.

Corvus cawed and nodded excitedly to Rhamin. 'Good, good!!' she shouted at him to make sure he understood.

Rhamin sensed that their happiness and excitement and the direction from which they had flown meant only one thing; his own pack was coming to find him. A few more parrying of words, where Rhamin asked the questions and Corvus nodded or shook her head to say if he was on the right track, confirmed what had been explained by the youngsters. So, once again, led by the three ravens, he set off homeward bound and it wasn't long before, on the distant horizon, he spotted a grey line of wolves snaking their way through the contours of the land and heading to meet him. Above them he could see Corvak. Everybody was there including Silvah, Natan and Rowan. Pointed in the right direction by Corvak, they had met the approaching pack during the night and, at first light, Corvak had caught them up again and had taken over guiding them towards their leader.

Eventually, once the excitement had died down, Rhamin

was told that, Powla and Charka had returned soon after he had departed, and the pack then set off to find Rhamin and the missing wolves.

Rhamin knew that, with the help of his feathered friends, Solin had little chance of catching him or outflanking him, but he knew he would have to deal with Solin sometime. He considered if now was the right time. Including Solin there were twelve wolves left in his pack, none younger than a year and a half old, whereas Rhamin had fourteen wolves, but that included toothless old Zelda, Bamar who was still favouring his healing leg, and the five cubs. He was not prepared to risk the lives of his youngsters who, despite the training they had been given were relatively inexperienced at serious fighting. They were still growing, soon to begin their slower period of growth towards adulthood and they had only just had their second set of teeth. Getting into a fight with them and Zelda involved would seriously compromise the way the battle went because much effort would be expended protecting the young and the old, and he knew Solin would work on that weakness. But he knew that although he could keep ahead of Solin and his pack, running away was only going to make the renegade pack more confident and eager to fight. Now that Silvah had told him word for word what Corvus had tried to explain earlier, he knew that Solin's followers were in no way confident of victory.

Standing in the centre of a circle of wolves Rhamin explained the situation to them. Natan, Silvah and Rowan, although not fully recovered from their ordeal, had been well fed by the rest of the pack when they met up. They, more than any of the pack, were angered by Solin's treachery. He had not just wanted to lead a pack of his own. He had made it personal and taken hostages. In their opinion, it was time things were put right.

The other adults agreed that fleeing was not an option. The cubs listened intently to the discussion. Lexa and Ramusan, although not fully grown were as big as the rest of the adult wolves in the pack and slightly bigger than the female wolves. They were excited. Play fighting with each other was getting a little boring.

'Let's do it dad!' Ramusan barked eagerly. 'Let's show them!'

Lexa barked. 'We're not afraid father!' she said, snarling and showing the razor sharp teeth in her short, thick set jowls.

Rhamin grinned proudly. It was now that he saw how he was going to approach the matter. For some time he explained his plan to them all and then, taking the lead, he followed a trail up the escarpment back in the direction of the forest. Behind the crest of the slope, Rhamin let his pack rest while he and Yeltsa watched and waited. It wasn't long before Solin's renegade pack came into full view. Even then, Rhamin still waited until he was sure that all of Solin's wolves would be able to see and hear him clearly. Then he stepped over the crest of the escarpment. 'You misguided wolves down there!' he howled at the top of his voice.

All of Solin's followers stopped dead in their tracks as Rhamin's voice echoed down to the valley bottom. A few of them barked, startled by the sudden sight and sound of their enemy. They were not sure what to make of his actions and stood there waiting for leadership from Solin. Solin just snarled, arched his back ready to commence a chase. The rest, triggered by Solin's cue, did the same.

'Before you attack me,' Rhamin barked, 'you had better know that I will spare only those wolves that remain where they are now.' He could see many of them falter in their step. They looked up at the figure of the black wolf against the skyline, his size magnified by the starkness against the clear blue sky. 'And those that follow Solin,' Rhamin continued, transfixing all the wolves beneath him, 'will watch as I dispatch their leader to the next world. Then,' he continued, deliberately speaking slowly and looking at each of them directly. 'Then, you will look on as I dispatch each of you in turn.'

'Your time is up!' Solin howled back as he started to slink forward.

With that, Rhamin turned and nodded to Natan. Slowly and deliberately he brought the line of wolves up to the crest of the hill so that from down in the valley the skyline seemed to be sprouting wolves. With the light behind them and silhouetted against the skyline, they all, including the cubs, looked enormous. They outnumbered Solin's pack. Solin had eleven followers. From the hill top, Rhamin was displaying fourteen combatants. The wolves from the northern territory had long ago heard of the giant Black Wolf as they knew him. They had seen the results of his meeting four of their front guard and three others were missing.

'Half of them are babies,' Solin scoffed as he began to bound forward. But only six wolves, pre-battle adrenalin pumping through their arteries, bounced up along side him.

'Babies, heh?' Rhamin said with a wide grin. He turned his head and nodded to Lexa. With that signal she let out the loudest bark she could push from the base of her chest. The sound echoed down the valley and rung from hillside to hillside. It was uncanny and unsettling.

'It's only a dog pup for goodness sake!' barked Solin, as he noticed his most loyal troops hesitate.

Lexa barked again. Another ripple of hesitation shook the wolves below. Wolves and dogs are old enemies. Ordinary dogs are often killed by packs of wolves, but some of Solin's pack had seen wolf hounds, had seen how big they were, and had been chased and hunted by them. They knew that big dogs were dangerous and they only had Solin's bravado to dispel any fear.

Rhamin strode forward alone, his posture showing total confidence, his direction straight towards Solin.

Sensing that the remainder of their pack had faltered, the six loyal followers behind Solin hesitated too, slowing in their stride and leaving Solin bounding forward ahead of them alone. Rhamin strutted steadily down the slope towards them. Now Solin, sensing that the resolve of his pack had withered, began to slow down. Still, Rhamin walked slowly and deliberately down towards him.

Suddenly, Solin stopped; his ears went back and he turned his head away. 'You cowards!' he barked down the hill as he turned and trotted down towards his broken pack. Then to save face, 'Come on you miserable lot, we'll wait until we have better odds.'

Rhamin stopped and smiled. He watched as Solin led his pack away, remaining silent in his bloodless victory. He had no argument with the wolves that Solin had persuaded to follow him. His only argument was against their combined wish to move out of their own territory and take over Rhamin's homeland on the basis of Solin's hatred. Rhamin had no doubt, however, that the day would come when Solin would bring his prejudices back to haunt him. But for the moment, he had left them in no doubt that this was, and would remain, Rhamin's territory.

As Solin and his pack turned back towards the forest, Rhamin turned back to the crest of the escarpment. He didn't have to say anything; the look on the faces of all his pack was that of immense pride in their leader. Silently, and with their heads held up high, they all gathered behind their gallant leader and headed home.

CHAPTER EIGHT

The next day bloomed with a sunrise that Rhamin would never forget. Golden shafts broke from the hub of light sending wide spokes through the distant dark rain clouds. The prize of success had bolstered the whole pack. They were alive, they were happy and they were heading back to their Darin.

Gradually, but with no sense of urgency they headed south, taking a circular route towards their home. On their way they descended onto the plains where the cubs were able to try their new skills hunting a deer without the help of the adult wolves. The going was easy again, and Zelda wanted to use the time to explain more about men. Recently, the attitude of men had seemingly abated somewhat, often ignoring wolves when they encountered them. She explained, as they travelled, that perhaps, during the drought, the man who shot at and killed two of their pack only did so because he also was in dire straits. He too would have been struggling to keep his tame animals alive, to find food or grazing for them, and struggling to keep his family. Despite the loss of Fayli and Seth, she persuaded Rhamin that he should not consider that particular man a permanent enemy. After all, he had acted no differently to a wolf pack guarding its own territory.

'The man will know,' Zelda said, once again not making the context of her statement at all clear.

'I'm sure he did know we were all starving,' Rhamin accepted. 'But we did invade his den and Solin did threaten to kill his man cubs.'

'Yes, but you stopped that stupid wolf, didn't you?' Silvah argued.

'All the same, I can't see him offering us an easy amnesty.'

'Well believe me, he will,' Zelda stated bluntly.

'Well, I hope I live to see that!' Rhamin said, in a manner meant to patronise the old wolf.

'Puhh,' Zelda replied. 'When will you ever listen to me *before* I'm proven right?'

'Just being careful my dear old girl. Just being careful!'

'Well, let me tell you something.' Zelda stood up and signalled for all the wolves to circle around her. 'I'm going to tell you a true story,' she said, speaking to Rhamin as if he were just one of the cubs. 'So sit down now and listen.'

Rhamin did as he was told and made sure the rest of the wolves came closer and obeyed the old wolf as well.

'There was once a young female wolf who left her pack in the hope of finding a mate,' Zelda commenced. 'Because the wolf pack system only encourages the mating of the two most dominant wolves, the alpha male and female, any young female has to leave the pack if she wants to find a mate.

'She was a strong young female, and when she was travelling across the dry and arid land she saw a man on a horse. He was alone, and was steadily making his way towards the greener land still many miles ahead. This was a time when men had made hard tracks through the land and travelled on the metal creatures with round feet. But men were often seen on horseback between those trails.

'The man spotted the wolf but, whether he was hungry or not, he never so much as gave her a second glance. He had with him one of those long fire sticks, but never once did he point it at the young wolf who, by this time, had crisscrossed his path several times in her exploration of the territory.

'Eventually, he began to follow the wolf, for he knew that the wolf would lead him and his horse to water, and lo and behold, that is exactly what happened. The wolf travelled slowly so that he could follow without exhausting the horse, which was, by this time, beginning to look very tired and very thirsty.

'After that, the wolf drank and went on her way, only to pass, at quite a distance, a group of men on horses riding towards the waterhole. But there was something about them that made the young wolf wary. Every time she spotted them her hackles rose and she had shivers down her spine. The next day, while the sun was at its hottest and she sheltered under a rocky overhang, she fell asleep and dreamt that these men were not friendly like the lone man she had led to water. These men not only killed wolves, they were so evil that they even killed other men. She dreamt that they were so dangerous that, on waking, she never intended to go near them again.

'Well, several days later, as she circled back to the water hole, she saw a number of vultures circling high in the sky. Thinking that there was going to be some easy prey, possibly a fallen buffalo or the like, she headed towards them. They were so far away that, by the time she reached the spot where they were circling, the vultures were very close to the ground and coming to land almost as she got there. But what she found was not a fallen animal. She came upon the first man, only this time, he was not on his horse. He had been tied down with thongs of skin and staked to the ground. He was struggling to free himself, but the bonds were too strong. He was not weak enough for the vultures to start their meal but it wouldn't have been long before they realised that he was helpless. So the young wolf sent them off, chasing them and snapping at their tails until they took to flight again. Of course, they continued to glide and circle in the sky up above because they, as they usually do, were quite prepared to wait until the wolf had had her fill.'

Zelda heard some gasps from the listening pack, but only paused long enough for good effect. 'Well, the man spoke in his language to the wolf and, although the wolf could not translate the words, she could tell by his voice that he was greeting her in a friendly tone. He showed no fear of her and she felt none of him. He continued to talk to her as she went up close and, strangely, she seemed to be able to see what was happening in his mind. He seemed totally surprised when she began to gnaw through the thong that tied one of his hands, not understanding how she knew what he was thinking. It took no time at all to free his arm and then he quickly untied the remaining bands on his other hand and on both his feet.

'The man stood up shakily and stretched and then, talking softly to the wolf, began to walk in the direction of the water hole. Having been robbed of his foot covering, he trod gingerly on the ground. Curious, the wolf trailed along behind him. One night, however, the man, who was by this time looking very weary and suffering from thirst, sat down on the ground to rest, and while he slept, the wolf caught a hare, then left it beside him.

'When he awoke, he found the hare and managed to eat

most of its soft flesh, although he didn't eat as much as a wolf would have eaten. Feeling refreshed he continued and eventually reached the water hole. There, the wolf brought him more food.

'It was then that the female wolf spotted another wolf approaching. As it came closer, the man watched and he became a little agitated. He didn't know this wolf and wasn't sure what it would do. However, the wolf was not interested in the man. It took a wide path around him and barked gently at the female. The female woofed back and then, a certain amount of squeaking and other noises followed the likes of which you will all appreciate between young couples.'

The attentive audience all giggled. Zelda smiled to herself as she went on with her story. 'The male wolf was called Romax, and he explained to her that he had seen the same group of men that she had seen, and that he had also seen them attack the single man at night while he slept. They took everything that belonged to the man and left him tied to the ground. However, Romax admitted that he had not trusted the man enough to go to try and help him, and he had no idea how he could do so, for unlike the female wolf, he had no ability to see inside the man's mind.

'With the female as company, however, Romax was happy to trust her instincts and so he joined her in accompanying the man as he travelled back to his own kind many miles away.

'After a while, the pack of bad men, now travelling in the opposite direction, came upon the lone man's trail. They had seen the wolf tracks, but had expected the wolves to have killed him or eaten him after he had died in the desert, but at no time did they expect the wolves and the man to have befriended each other. They eventually spotted the man walking on his own, not barefoot any longer but wearing the skins of hares on his feet. This time they did not wait until dark when the man stopped for rest. They were not afraid of him and intended to finish off their murderous act. Now, the female wolf could see clearly in her mind that the men were afraid that he would reach safety and return with other men to hunt them down. They closed in on him in broad daylight, no longer afraid that he might be able to defend himself, but had not taken into account the wolves.' Zelda's eyes glistened with excitement as she told this part of the story. 'As the riders approached the man in a final charge, whooping and shouting like victorious hunters, the wolves emerged from some brush wood and took down the first two of them off their horses. One of the fallen men was the leader and once the others had seen him killed, they fled.

'Eventually, the friendly man having regained some clothes and some hard covering for his feet, gathered up one of the bad men's horses, and travelled safely back to his own place of abode. The two wolves escorted him to the edge of the inhabited buildings of his camp and left him.

'Over that time in the scrub land, the wolves had hunted for the man and shared their food with him, often eating together as wolves do. They were both rather saddened when they left him. Knowing he was safe, they thought they would never see him again, men being men and wolves being wolves.'

'But did they?' a voice came from the back of the pack. Silvah was always one for a happy ending.

'Well,' Zelda said, thinking for a moment as if recalling the facts in a way that she could relate them as a conclusion to her tale. 'Well, it's like this,' she said eventually. 'That was about the time when men began to stop hunting wolves.

I know the wolves never saw the man in person again, but the female wolf had many visions of him, and in those visions she saw him fighting the cause of wolves and telling people his story.

'So there we are,' Zelda concluded. 'There are good men and there are bad men, just as there are good wolves and bad wolves. Don't look at them all with the same eye. See them each for what they are.'

'What a remarkable story,' Yeltsa said when she was sure Zelda had reached the end of her tale.

'What I don't understand,' Lexa said, 'is that you told us the name of Romax, but what was the female wolf's name. You never mentioned that once.'

Zelda smiled. 'No I didn't,' she said, her mind gliding off into the past. She sighed. 'I was young once you know,' she said eventually.

CHAPTER NINE

Since the drought, Rhamin's pack had eaten well, gained weight and, with the escapades of the season, their bonding, emotional and social grouping had become very firm. The cubs, however, although almost having reached their full height, had not yet reached full size and, as all wolves of that age, they were not able, unlike their elders, to gain the necessary weight and store energy reserves. So, as many of the larger animals, upon which the wolves preyed, migrated, Rhamin's pack now grew closer together, hunting in well formed groups rather than individually or in pairs, and they began to use the Darin as their main rendezvous site more often than using the outlying camps.

Just as the beginning of the summer had been nothing like a normal year, the winter played its role completely out of character. As the nights became longer and the days shorter, as expected, there were long spells of heavy persistent rain, interspersed with warm, hanging mists carried on warm south easterly winds. But after two full cycles of the moon, and at least a moon before the shortest day, the weather changed again, this time to arctic winds from the north east bringing hard frost that made the ground, even in the forests, as solid as the rock walls of the cave. Now, as each day progressed, the temperatures plummeted far below those of a normal winter. Once again, the extreme weather drew the pack closer together and hunting took every moment of their time.

Wolves cope well with extremes, especially in cold winter months, but as the weather changed, Rhamin realised that Lexa's behaviour was beginning to change also. Where she had once been a happy, self confident and sociable pack member, she now began to be withdrawn, spending most of her time in the cave with Zelda. It wasn't just Rhamin that had noticed the change in Lexa. All the other wolves had commented on how she had begun to drift away from the pack. She was restless and solitary. She didn't go on long hunting trips and rarely hunted with the pack at all. Instead she travelled on her own near to the Darin, hunting for smaller prey, chasing ground squirrels and foxes. She only hunted during the day when often the rest of the pack had returned with food that they would have gladly shared with her. Rhamin had watched her over the days and weeks as her broad chest began to reveal ridges where her ribs pressed against her smooth coat. That too was changing. Where it had been sleek and shiny; now her coat stood out, all starey and dull. But Rhamin had no answers.

One bitter cold morning after returning with food from a successful hunt, Rhamin decided to consult his aged seer. He had waited and waited for Lexa to say something to him, to tell him what was ailing her, or to tell him why she was unhappy, but she had not so much as spoken a dozen words to him in the last two weeks. Now, he had to ask Zelda. If she didn't know the answer to his questions then he was afraid that the pack was going to lose Lexa, one way or another.

'Are you awake old thing?' He asked as he approached

the curled up mass of fur that more and more resembled just another rough boulder in the dark depths of the cave.

The soft boulder expanded slightly as Zelda took in a deep breath, and then a nose poked out from beneath a thick brushy tail. 'I am, young wolf,' she said quietly. 'I don't sleep all the time. Sometimes I just think and sometimes I just daydream. Sometimes…'

'Well that's good,' Rhamin cut in. He saw his opportunity now. 'What's wrong with Lexa?' he asked. A straight question to get a straight answer for once.

'Well, she's not like us,' Zelda stated matter of factly. 'Haven't you noticed?'

Rhamin blew out his breath in a long cloud of water vapour. 'Of course I have noticed she's different,' he said, once again not knowing just what Zelda was getting at. 'Isn't there ever a definitive answer to any of my questions?'

'Oh yes my young master. However, for such simple answers you need to ask simple questions.'

'Oh, for goodness sake, Zelda!'

Zelda could detect a hint of annoyance creeping into Rhamin's voice.

'You just see her as another wolf, don't you Rhamin? You don't really see her as anything other than one of our pack. We all look different in some way and she is no exception. That's it, isn't it?'

'Well, she is one of the pack!' Rhamin protested. 'She was brought up as one of us and always will be one of us.'

'Oh yes, she's one of us all right, I grant you that, but you don't see it do you?'

'Don't see what for goodness sake? You always speak in riddles Zelda. When are you ever going to tell me it as it is, instead of making me have to work out what you mean?'

Zelda wrapped her tail around her legs and sighed. 'Oh Rhamin my child, you are a wonderful wolf. You care for your pack like no other I have ever known, but you can be so thick sometimes!'

'Well thanks for that vote of allegiance! I was beginning to wonder if it was just my size that made the pack follow me!'

'Don't be silly! For heaven's sake! You know what I mean.' She shuffled herself into a position so that, as she curled her tail around her feet, she looked like a thick grey woollen mat with a protruding black nose. 'Oh yes you are a giant among wolves, but that is not why the pack follow you. They don't follow you through fear. They follow you because they respect you. You would die for any of them, and you treat them like your own family, even those that have joined from other packs. They want to be with you, don't you see?' She buried her nose in her fur and closed her eyes, sighing.

'Well, yes, of course.' He looked at Zelda and waited for her to carry on talking. He knew that if he just stood there, she would eventually continue the conversation. Slowly she opened her eyes and lifted her nose from her fur again.

'I'm old and I do not move about a lot,' she began. That's why, when you are all outside, totally immune to the bitter icy wind, I stay in the shelter of the cave.'

'Right,' Rhamin said, still waiting for her to speak plainly. 'So you feel the cold!'

'Well haven't you noticed that Lexa has no thick coat, no impenetrable undercoat like wolves? She is a wolf at heart but she was born... a dog. She was born in a man's world where they keep dogs in their homes and do silly things like cutting off the tails of the young pups. They are bred to be companions to men not to wolves.'

Rhamin nodded, finally realising what she meant. 'Sorry Zelda, I *am* being thick!' He lay down beside the old wolf, wondering just how many more winters the ancient old wolf could survive.

'I know what you're thinking young Rhamin, and I expect that I'll not see many more years in your pack, but you will be all right. There are others who will replace me.' Before he could ask who, she went on. 'Lexa is feeling the cold. She sleeps close up to me and when she's not with me I have seen her snuggling in between Ramusan and Depni, or any other two that happen to be lying conveniently close together.'

'But she could have said something!'

'She doesn't say anything because she's a wolf. She doesn't see herself as any different to the rest of us. Okay, she has seen a reflection of her face in the still water of the lake but it isn't the same as seeing herself like we see her. She sees that she has smaller paws and most of all she realises she has no brush tail to wrap around herself to keep her warm. But since we have all taken her in as one of us, even the others including you don't notice any difference. She's just one of us, don't you see?'

'Well now I do! But she could have told us she was suffering from the cold.'

'It's not as easy as that, Rhamin. She suddenly feels cold but sees the rest of the pack carrying on as normal. She thinks she is ill so she comes to the cave and snuggles up to me. She goes hunting on her own and keeps herself out of the way of the pack because she doesn't want to be a liability.'

'But she could have talked to me about it,' Rhamin said, rather upset now that Lexa had not seen fit to confide in him.

'Stupid cub,' Zelda scolded. 'She no more wanted you to know than she was prepared to accept the fact herself. She still hasn't accepted the fact that she's different. She's just working her way through the problem in her own way.'

'Right,' Rhamin said softly. He thought for a moment. This time Zelda didn't speak as she would normally do when he fell silent. She just looked at him and waited. She let him work out what he was going to do and then he spoke again. 'I'm going to have a talk with her,' he said eventually. He looked at Zelda with compassionate eyes. 'Thanks, Zelda. I... I...'

'Pooh,' Zelda broke in, 'talking won't help much.' She buried her face in her thick tail and closed her eyes as if to sleep. Rhamin knew the sign and, frowning to himself, quietly left her in peace.

Rhamin watched Lexa closely. He could see now how easily she would suffer from the cold. During the coldest weather, when she emerged from the Darin, if she stopped moving about for any length of time, she would begin to shiver uncontrollably until she moved again. On the rare occasion she joined them on the hunt, sighting the prey was the climax to her day. She joined in the chase, playing her part as one of the pack and, with the exertion, raised her body temperature once again. She was fine while the pack kept moving, but when they stopped, she would just keep scouting around, never stopping until tiredness forced her to rest. Then, her body would take over once again, shaking shivers racking her body, creating heat the only way it could.

Rhamin had not spoken about her coat to Lexa. Instead, he spoke to the rest of the pack. They, too, had seen her strange behaviour and when Rhamin explained what had brought about the change in Lexa, they all understood immediately. It was as if a blindfold had suddenly been taken off their eyes. They now saw Lexa for what she actually was, a dear member of the pack, but a dog! And, as the other wolves realised that their adopted pack member was going to need help to keep warm they acted accordingly, not saying anything at all to their trusted friend, just acting differently. All were instructed not to speak of it to Lexa. But a plan was hatched.

From that day on, during the extremely cold wintry periods, Lexa was given the task of guarding the Darin and looking after Zelda, along with one volunteer, Silvah. Rhamin explained the instruction by stating that he could not leave the old wolf unguarded as he suspected that Solin, although many miles away, had still not departed from the territory. With this simple instruction, Lexa's face changed noticeably. She carried her ears forward and a light returned to her eyes that had almost been extinguished. It was the light of responsibility, a light of belonging, of feeling to be one of the pack; the light of love of, and by, her family. Her instructions were clear. She was to remain in or about the Darin guarding Zelda, and Silvah was to remain close at hand. And although travelling further out into the forest and onto the plain in the warmer spells, she was to remain with the other two wolves at times of extreme cold, and especially at night when the temperatures plummeted, making sure that Lexa had two warm coats lying close beside her at all times. Lexa gradually regained the weight that had left her so suddenly. For an animal without an extra thick coat of fur, fat is the next best insulator.

Winter is not always cold, however. Even with snow on the ground, days can be warm and sunny, and on those days, Zelda as well as Lexa emerged from the safety of their den and joined the others in the play activities that would soon become essential to the survival of the whole pack.

CHAPTER TEN

Many human beings have a new year that, in the Northern Hemisphere, curiously starts in the darkest, wildest month when the true winter weather, as humans and wolves alike know it, is just about to take its cold, icy grip on the more northerly regions. The new year for wolves, and almost all other animals and plants is springtime, the time of new growth and regeneration; the time when plants and trees display their blossom for pollination; the time when the winter berries are ripe for picking so that the seeds within the fruits can be passed through digestive tracts, stratified, dispersed and given new life in pastures, and crevices, growing from within their newly deposited and fertile eco-compost.

Once again, scarcity of food meant maintaining their large territory and protecting it from habitation by other packs of wolves which, if discovered on their patch, would be dispatched by any means available. It is at times like these that wolves will kill wolves of other packs. If the insurgents do not flee, then their fate will be decided by the dominant pack leader. And this came to pass.

It was at a well used rendezvous point, a days travel

away from the Darin, that the whole pack settled down to sleep after feeding on a buffalo brought down in the early hours of the spring morning. Once again, their old friend, Corvak, had given them news that the small herd was travelling down to the plain. The sun was already warming the ground and, sated on their feast, the pack lay resting and sleeping in the shade of a straggling skeleton of a wood next to a small, winding river.

There was, somewhere in the distance, a rumbling sound, an indefinable drone. Natan heard it first. He pricked up his ears and, lifting his head off the ground, gave an involuntary woof, a reaction triggered by a subconscious need in all animals to alert, to warn, when danger is sensed, whether it be real or imagined. The action instantly triggered alert in all the other wolves and, seconds later, they were on their feet and racing towards the edge of the river. From there, out of the way of the trees, they could see along the plain and into the distance. With ears pricked and rotating to locate the exact direction from which the noise was coming, they listened, looked and waited. First it was a cloud of dust in the distance that appeared like the beginning of a grass fire. Then, as the distant rumbling sound became louder, turning into a defined mechanical sound that the wolves had all heard before, the wheeled vehicles emerged. The sun glinted off the glass as the charging vehicles twisted and turned through the tussock grass. There were no man made tracks. The men's mechanical horses had to weave in and out of the rocks and the fallen trees. Despite their inherent speed, they were reduced to travelling no faster than the running wolves that now, Rhamin and his pack could plainly see, were fleeing their pursuers, and heading for the cover of the trees that formed the beginning of the up hill rise of the rocky and forested foothills. There were four of them, swerving around rocks, jumping fallen trees, as dust sprang up around them and at their heels. Then the sound of the men's fire sticks, like tiny cracks of thunder arrived at the ears of Rhamin's pack long after the consequence of their use had passed.

There were two of the men's carriages. They bounced about like pine cones on a white river as they crossed ruts and hit stones, swerved to avoid holes and trees and corrected their course to continue their pursuit. The wolves were running for their lives; the men, with a sense of sheer desperate determination, were intent on taking that from them.

Rhamin drew his pack into a hollow behind the deep bank of the river. The water was running fiercely, but the level was lower than it had been in the winter rains. Lower down, the bank was shaded by a clump of bog willow. It was an adequate hideout, giving cool shade beside the tumbling water. Patiently, the wolves watched and waited. Rhamin made it quite clear that no one was to move or give away their position. The men could not know that the wolves of Rhamin were there. For the time being, at least, they were safe. It was a matter of waiting to see what was happening without panicking and giving away their position, a position which, had they broken their cover, would have been almost impossible to flee without the vehicles being able to give chase, for the men's carriages were now between the wolves and the safety of the forest.

As Rhamin suspected, the vehicles headed past them with little attempt to search the river bank. Perhaps one of the passengers had glanced over in their direction, but from their watching post beneath the shade of the blooming willows, Rhamin was sure nothing and no one had been seen. The men's hunting party kept up a steady, relentless pace, until it disappeared into the tree line on the horizon. Hardly slowing, the vehicles could be seen weaving in and out of the sparse growth until, eventually, the tree cover hid them completely.

We'll head in the opposite direction tonight, Rhamin stated. There was no sense in heading towards danger, and vehicles like those, driven with such purpose, were likely to be big trouble. The wolves settled back in the shade and slept the day out.

Then Rhamin heard it; a howl, but it was not a call from one of their own pack because all Rhamin's family were there beside him. Even old Zelda was travelling with them. She had no suggestions as to where the men and their vehicles were heading. But the howl was not just a wolf trying to locate his band. It was a wolf desperate to warn someone. Both Silvah and Zelda knew what the howl meant. They looked at each other and then Silvah spoke. 'That is one of Solin's pack,' she said pensively. 'She is calling to Solin, warning him, telling him to run. But I can't understand whether he is being warned to run for his life or he is being warned for something else.'

'Solin?' Rhamin asked. 'I thought he might have left to take over the Northern Territory by now. What is he still doing so far south?'

'He never left,' Zelda said curtly. 'He still wants your skin sun bleached on a rocky, river bank. He is obviously going to challenge you again.'

'Well he has a funny way of going about it,' Rhamin said dismissively. 'He doesn't have the backbone to challenge me alone. And he can't think all his pack will stand and fight for something that they don't believe in. They know where they belong. It's only Solin that doesn't belong in the north. But he doesn't seem to have got his head round that yet.'

'But what does it all mean?' asked Ramusan. 'Why are those people after Solin?'

'I hate to think,' Silvah answered for her master. 'But we could go and find out.'

'Now just wait a minute,' Rhamin said angrily. 'If you think I am going to endanger a single wolf in my pack just to find out what Solin has got himself into, then you can think again. Solin is his own worst enemy. I really have no interest in what he is doing apart from why he is still in my territory.'

'But that's just it,' Silvah replied. 'We can only find that out if we go and investigate. I am sure that there is a connection here.'

Zelda had remained quiet for some time. As the conversation waned, she stood up and walked to the centre of the gathering. 'I think Silvah is right,' she said quietly to Rhamin. 'Something tells me that Solin and you are inextricably linked in some way.'

'Not as far as I am concerned,' Rhamin said firmly. 'Unless, I am destined to kill him at some stage in his murky life.'

'That might be so. But we need to find out, I am sure of it.'

Rhamin lay down and folded his paws one on top of the other. It was inevitable that he would have to see what Solin was up to sooner or later. But had it got to be just now, while men in wheeled vehicles were hunting all around him? 'Perhaps they aren't after Solin,' he said eventually. 'Perhaps it is just a coincidence. The men are heading his way and one wolf in his pack is just warning him to get out of the way.' But the supposition seemed weak even to Rhamin. All he wanted was peace and quiet. He had always had to fight young male wolves because he was the one to beat. He was bigger than any other wolf. Whereas an average wolf would weigh forty to fifty kilograms, Rhamin weighed nearer ninety. He was taller, longer and stronger than any wolf around at that time. It was imperative for would-be pack leaders and lone male wolves to challenge the giant black wolf. But, despite the fact that they were no match for Rhamin, he had never killed a lone challenger. Rhamin wanted wolves to live in peace. He breathed out a big sigh, got up and went over to the river bank, and settled down in the river washed gravel. He waited and thought. No other wolf had any better suggestions, and at this particular moment, waiting seemed good.

No time at all seemed to have passed before Corvak glided into a faultless landing on the upper most branch of the tallest willow. Rhamin looked up as Zelda went over and sat beneath the old raven. There was an exchange of noises between them. Clicking and cawing, the two old friends were oblivious to the watching audience. 'I don't believe it,' Silvah said suddenly. Rhamin knew that Silvah could understand them. But it wasn't just Silvah.

Rasci nodded. 'They are discussing Solin,' he stated proudly. He clearly took great pride at being able to translate for his master. 'Solin has been causing trouble with the men,' he continued. 'But,' he said with a curious scowl, 'Solin has been trying to make the man at the farm think you were responsible for the trouble.'

'That sounds like Solin,' Rhamin agreed with a nod. 'And just how is he doing that?'

Rasci shook his head. 'I can't make out what Corvak is saying,' he said apologetically. He is speaking too fast and using sounds I do not understand.'

'Then relax and open your mind,' came a scolding voice from beneath the tree. Zelda had been listening with one ear.

'But is it serious?' asked Rasci.

She turned to the gathered wolves. 'You are all going to act fast,' she said. 'Solin is going to bring death to us unless we take it to him. We have to rid ourselves of him once and for all. If he won't leave then he must be killed. That's how serious it is.' There was some more discourse between the old raven and the ancient wolf, and when it was clear that the conversation was finished, Rhamin spoke.

'Well then,' he said, 'what's the damage this time?'

'You might well ask,' said the old wolf. 'Solin is trying to get you blamed for killing the man's four young dog pups.'

'I haven't been near them!'

'No, but he may well think so. Corvak has told me how Solin has been travelling to an outcrop of white soft rock and, by rubbing the top of his head on a rocky overhang, he is able to make his ears white. The man from the farm is looking for a wolf with white ears, Rhamin. Don't you understand? That rogue of a wolf is passing himself off as you and at the same time attacking those creatures that will inevitably make the man so angry that he will come looking for the perpetrator. In this case, that's you. You are the only wolf with white ears, the only wolf daring enough to take him on, or so he believes.'

'So Solin has been back to the farm, causing trouble, eh?'

'That's what I am told,' Zelda confirmed.

'Thank you Corvak,' Rhamin said to the creature that was now preening itself in the treetop. Corvak cawed. 'So where do we find Solin now?'

Corvak gabbled again to Zelda. 'The men are heading in the wrong direction,' Zelda said eventually. 'They think they are heading towards us, but they have missed us. They think we are cowering in the foothills, hiding from them.'

'So Solin is where exactly?'

'Heading back to the farm again.'

'Again!' Rhamin nodded. 'I see.' Once again he stood and thought, but not for long. 'Then we must go there straight away.'

The farm was about half a day's travel away. 'If we set off now,' Silvah stated, 'then we should be there before nightfall.'

'If you leave me behind,' stated Zelda. 'I cannot keep up with you when you travel at full speed.'

'Then you will remain here with Rasci and Silvah to look after you,' ordered Rhamin. 'The rest of us have to go and go now'.

'No,' Zelda stated firmly. 'You must take Silvah. Corvak will take you straight to Solin and Silvah will be your interpreter. You can leave young Rasci to protect me.'

'All right, but on one condition.'

'And that is?'

'As we travel into the sun, you travel towards the Great Forest. There, you will be untraceable. We'll meet you at our usual rendezvous site near the mountain lake. Wait for our call.'

The warm sun shone on the outer coats of the wolves as they raced through the hot afternoon. Their thick undercoat, now thinning for the summer months, still acted as insulation. Just as the cold weather and bitter cold winds could not penetrate their thick wadge of fur, neither could the sun.

Corvak remained with them, chattering away in the sky above Silvah, urging them on. Eventually, Silvah explained that Corvak had watched the renegade pack of wolves flee from the outskirts of the farm. He had seen Solin with them and, not long ago, he and six other wolves had suddenly split from the pack and had hidden in a hole that seemed specially dug out for the purpose, whilst the four young decoys led the men folk away into the woods.'

'So does anybody know what his plan is?' Rhamin asked, as he urged the pack to go faster. There was a renewed sense of urgency. Now he knew that unless he stopped Solin then not only would he, Rhamin, be in danger, but all wolves in the territory would have retribution brought down upon them. For what, he knew not, but he knew now that this particular moment in time was going to be a matter of destiny, a particle in the lives of wolves that would settle in the bedrock of their history. It was no longer a feeling of foreboding, it was sure knowledge. Solin was so determined to settle his score with Rhamin he was prepared to do anything. And that anything had to be something that would result in revenge by the man and his kind. It was the only way Solin could get the better of his half brother. He couldn't defeat Rhamin. But men could.

The pack raced on, stopping only once to take on cool, refreshing liquid from a small, meandering stream. They were hot and panting heavily when, not long before nightfall, they arrived at the outer ring fence of the farm. Corvak gave some instructions to Silvah and then flew off to the farmstead to reconnoitre before the daylight failed him altogether, for after darkness fell, he would no longer be of any help to his friends.

There was a sense of foreboding moving through the pack as the wolves that had travelled this route last summer crossed the fences and headed in the same direction. They raced on, led by Rhamin. In the distance he could hear several wolves howling, calling out, over and over again. Now he was running as fast as he could. Before they had crossed the inner ring fence, Corvak returned. Another exchange of sounds and Silvah reported that Solin had started indiscriminately killing cattle in one of the paddocks. Corvak had given directions and Rhamin bounded on ahead. Yeltsa, Silvah, Charka and Rowan were beside him when he spotted the carnage. Solin and his hunting pack had killed three cattle already. The herd was clustered together in one corner of the paddock, milling about, trying to defend itself as a group, the bigger, older animals facing outwards to attack the worrying wolves.

Usually, a wolf will not attack an animal that stands up to it. It will wait for the animal to panic and then attack only when it turns and runs. But Solin was impatient to do his work. He intended to kill as many of the cattle as he could in as short a time. His motive wasn't hunger. It wasn't greed. It was revenge, revenge on Rhamin, for now, as he ran closer, Rhamin could see what Corvak had been saying was true. Solin had white ears. He was impersonating Rhamin and he was killing the cattle with only one purpose; he wanted the farmer to hunt down his enemy for him. And he was succeeding in creating disturbance at the farmstead. He and his pack had called out in order to do just that. They wanted to be seen.

A young bull was standing his ground courageously. Already he had tossed one of the rogue wolves over his head. It landed in the midst of the herd and was instantly trampled in a melee of panicking beasts. But Solin was not discouraged. The wolves of his pack were dispensable. If he succeeded in getting rid of Rhamin then he would gather the biggest ever pack around him. A few casualties were inevitable in war, and he was taking the longer view. His bid for power had begun in earnest.

Just then, a hundred yards or more away, a woman ran into the paddock, her hair flowing behind her as she raced through the failing light towards the chaos. She raised a fire stick and instantly Rhamin saw a puff of smoke eject from the barrel, followed shortly afterwards by a loud crack. None of the remaining five wolves of the Solin pack went down. Clearly, the woman was either not as skilled with the implement or the light was getting too poor for her to see properly. On top of that, she was hindered by the fact that the wolves were between her and the herd of milling cattle. Solin had realised that she could not safely kill his hunters without risk of killing the cattle. He ordered them to keep on attacking, snapping and tearing at the faces and chests of the animals, who in response, kept their heads down butting and tossing at the air.

But Solin didn't join in. For a moment he stood and watched them, making sure they carried out his orders. Then, turning towards the woman, he snarled and lowered his head. It wasn't easy to see what she was doing, for Rhamin was a good hundred yards away and behind her. But she was clearly having difficulty with the fire stick in some way. Rhamin was not the only one to have seen this. Solin had seen her struggling and he had seen his opportunity. Rhamin could almost read his mind. What better way to get the farmer to hunt down the wolf with white ears. His woman, his mate would testify to the description of the wolf that had mauled her. He wouldn't kill her; no, that would defeat the purpose. But he would do her a serious injury. He would make sure that Rhamin was hunted down to the end of the earth if necessary. There would be no hiding place, no sanctuary, and no mercy for the wolf with white ears. Solin loped towards the woman, teeth barred and head down. He took his time, wanting her to see his ears, to know exactly who was attacking her. No, he was in no hurry now. But he hadn't seen Rhamin or his companions. His delay was to Rhamin's advantage, for as Solin took one last lunge towards his prey, Rhamin appeared from behind her. He took off with a leap that carried him past the woman's shoulder, landing his huge paws against Solin's chest as, only inches from the woman, he sunk his long canine teeth deep into the face of her attacker. The woman froze. She knew that she had been attacked from the wolf in front of her, but she didn't see Rhamin before he glided past her. Neither did she know why there was now a bloody fight taking place at her feet. She could still make out enough detail to see that both wolves had white ears, but in the increasing darkness, she could tell that only one looked and moved like a snarling, black shadow. Rhamin took no notice of the woman or her reaction. His task was already laid out before him: Solin lay on his side, blood pouring from his face as Rhamin stood over him. He grabbed the wounded wolf by the throat, but Solin managed to get his paw up in front of him, preventing Rhamin from crushing his wind pipe. Rhamin swung up his strong neck and carried his foe towards the centre of the paddock. When he dropped Solin, he noticed that Yeltsa, Rowan, Silvah and Charka had been joined by Lexa and Ramusan, and they were fighting fiercely with the four Solin wolves. Soon, they were joined by Natan and Bamar, and then by Floss, Depni and Fatz who were determined not to be left out.

'Spare me,' Solin gasped as he watched the remainder of his pack being torn down. 'I'll work with you, I promise!'

Rhamin ignored him. He stood with his huge paw on Solin's neck, watching his pack, making sure that nothing happened that he could prevent if he had to. But his wolves were courageous in their work and skilled at fighting. The youngsters were no less brave. They outnumbered the enemy, but none were afraid to be the ones to go in for the kill.

Although it seemed like time stood still, it took less than a few minutes to end Solin's treachery. What Rhamin didn't see was the woman as she departed the way she had come. The sound of the door shutting behind her brought Rhamin's head around, only to find that the courageous woman, left shaken and frightened, had disappeared back to the safety of her den. Rhamin's pack loped around, checking for any other insurgents. There were none. 'What are you going to do with that gutless calf?' Natan asked, pointing his nose at Solin.

Rhamin did not answer. He pricked up his ears and looked to the north. Lights and the sound of the men's carriages returning from their hunt suddenly rose above the sound of bellowing cattle. The animals were still bunched in a corner, waving their heads threateningly at the surrounding wolves, which in turn, just ignored them.

'Time to go,' Rhamin called quickly. 'Everybody out. Now! I'll follow. Don't stop for anything.'

With that, the pack exited quietly and quickly in the opposite direction to the approaching vehicles. Rhamin took little time catching them up, and silently and as fast as they could run, together, they disappeared into the night.

CHAPTER ELEVEN

No one asked what Rhamin had done when he was left alone with Solin. One thing they knew for sure was that Rhamin had to stop Solin from impersonating him again. Immediately, Rhamin concentrated on regrouping his pack at the waterfall in the forest. There, they rested and slept off the fatigue of the last day's events. Because of what Solin had done, they had never faced danger so great as they did now. All they could do was to stay in the forest and lie low until they knew that the danger from the man was over.

But, would the danger ever really be over? Rhamin had done his best to show the man that he was not to blame for the deeds of the rogue wolf Solin. But he could only guess what the farmer was going to think when he saw the results of Solin's evil work. On top of that, once again, Solin had attacked one of the man's family. And once again it had been Rhamin that had stopped him only with seconds to spare. The whole affair had been a disastrous turn of events. And it was only with Corvak's help that he had been able to avert an even more precipitous catastrophe. Without the help of the old raven, Rhamin would never have arrived at the farmstead in time. Without the help of Corvak, all hope would, by now, have been lost.

It was with that in mind that Rhamin told Silvah and Zelda to invite Corvak and his family to the camp so that he could thank him personally for all his help. The old raven had been seen high in the sky above them before the battle, heading towards some trees where he would no doubt spend the night. But, in the days that followed, Corvak had not come to the pack either to tell of the presence of game nor had he come to share the food that Rhamin and his pack had caught.

One evening, Rhamin went to the top of a rocky outcrop that looked out over the great wooded valley below. The half moon was already rising, even though it was over an hour to go to sunset. To his right, far away, a dark cloud of rooks were flying to their rookery somewhere in the distance, filling the early evening air with a chorus of their communicative chatter. In the opposite direction, distant specs on the skyline could have been Corvak and his family, but he wasn't sure, and unless the raven wanted to come and visit the pack, Rhamin had no way of asking the old bird to visit. Sadly, he climbed down and made his way back through the trees to his camp site. Sitting next to Zelda, he pulled at a tuft of old undercoat that was sticking out of her side. It was instantly caught by a breeze and wafted off into the air on a rising current. He watched it disappear over the tree tops, chased by a robin that was looking for just the right thing for lining her nest, and then he asked, 'Can you suggest how we can contact Corvak?'

Zelda looked tired. Her face had long been white with age and now, with every day that passed, her natural grey coat turned even lighter. Her unseeing eyes bulged as she thought for a moment and then replied. 'He's an old bird, you know. He may have gone away, but so long as he's all right, he'll turn up when he wants to.' She paused to think again. 'I do know that his mate Corvus died during the winter. I wasn't going to tell you. He asked me not to. But I don't think anything has happened to him.'

Rhamin felt saddened by the news. True, birds and wolves alike grow old and eventually, they die as do all living things. But he hadn't had the chance to thank Corvus, properly for her help last year. 'I wish I had known,' Rhamin said despondently.

'But it was a hard winter, Rhamin. Even we were lucky to get through it without losing any of our pack. Look how ill Lexa became. And me! Pooh, I'm on borrowed time, that's for sure!'

Rhamin settled down on his belly next to the old wolf, wrapping his thick tail around his feet. Yeltsa was not best company at the moment. She was nearing the end of her gestation period and was pestering Rhamin to return to the cave ready for her to give birth. Wolves have few predators. Apart from man, those that are seriously dangerous are bears on the ground and eagles from the air. Despite having used their cave as their Darin since before he could remember, Rhamin was now sure that safety lay in the depths of the thick expanse of forest, covered by the canopy of new growth, hidden from natural predators and most of all, from the tendrils of man and his kind. He wondered if Corvak would be able to find them under the cover of the trees, but then Corvak would call if he was searching for them and, since all the wolves in the pack knew him, one of them would answer him if they were within earshot.

And so it was. Yeltsa dug a deep hole beneath the roots of a huge redwood tree, and there she prepared herself a den ready for having her next litter of pups. For the next nine days they lived and hunted in the mountain forests, each day, watching from lookout points on the mountain sides, listening to every sound that travelled across the plains and the valleys. It was on the tenth day that two of Rhamin's young scouts raced up to their camp. They had been sent out to look for deer, but they returned with news that they had seen four unknown wolves heading towards Rhamin's new den. Rhamin suspected that these were the four wolves that Solin used as decoys, the ones chased and shot at by the men. They were without a leader now, unless they had formed a new pack of their own. They were obviously doing the same as Rhamin and his pack, lying low, keeping out of sight, waiting until the danger passed. But, whatever their reasons for being there, this was still Rhamin's territory and no other wolves, alone or in packs, were allowed to trespass. Most of the pack was present when the two youngsters arrived. All the wolves volunteered to go and check out the strays, but Rhamin urged caution. What he didn't want, was to attract any attention to the pack's whereabouts, for although they had looked out for approaching men, there may well be one or many more within hearing range. Sound travels for miles in the mountains, bouncing off cliffs and echoing down the steep banked river valleys. Rhamin had forbidden any communication between pack members by howling and the sound of fighting wolves could be just what some man was waiting to hear. There was going to be a better solution.

Leaving only Yeltsa and Zelda behind, and led by the two young scouts, Rhamin and his pack headed towards the point where the lone wolves had last been seen. But it wasn't long before Silvah picked up the scent. She stood and listened for a moment or two and then, taking the lead with Rhamin, and instructing all the wolves to travel quietly, she headed down a steep bank towards a fast flowing river. There, lying on the shingle bank, and oblivious to any approaching danger because of the noise of the tumbling rapids, three wolves rested next to the carcass of a young deer. The fourth was lapping at the water on the river's edge. There was no doubt that these were the wolves that had been pursued by the men. One of the resting wolves sported a wound on the top of its shoulder where it was likely that one of the men's firing sticks had hurled its deadly load. But none looked too ill to travel, and were well fed and clearly not distressed by their circumstances.

Rhamin whispered to his followers. 'Stay here. You know what to do if they decide to fight. But only come down if that is the only option.'

With that he worked his way through the branches and the briars towards the unsuspecting group. When he was about fifteen yards away, he stood and waited, watching the single wolf that had just finished drinking. It shook itself vigorously and then, picking up a short stick between its teeth, threw it in the air and began to prance around catching it and tossing it about until the game grew stale and, as the stick landed for the last time, walked past its toy and joined the others. It acted as if it didn't have a care in the world, but Rhamin knew better. Carefully moderating his voice, he gave out a low bark. The playful wolf stiffened and swivelled its head. Still, the other three wolves rested, unaware of any danger. The nearer they were to the rapid flowing water, the louder was the noise to mask all other noises. The standing wolf looked around and then, spotting Rhamin standing alone in the cover of the undergrowth like a black shadow, it responded with hackles up and letting out a sharp warning yap.

Instantly the other three wolves were on their feet, the coats on their backs bristled; their lips curled back to show their teeth as they searched for the danger. They spread out in a semicircle, a deliberate manoeuvre to place them in the best position to defend themselves if Rhamin attacked. They knew instantly who he was, the giant black wolf that had confronted Solin before the winter, but Rhamin didn't recognise any of them. He hadn't taken any particular notice of the pack that Solin had gathered to support him, apart from that fact that their number were remarkably consistent in their grey colour. Wolves often vary in colour and markings. But these four wolves, in particular, were surprisingly alike. They were young, only in their second year, Rhamin suspected; they were fit and obviously they were well fed. But they were only average sized wolves. Two slightly larger males, two smaller females.

Rhamin moved forward slowly, making no outward sign of aggression. It made them relax a little, though they remained alert and on their toes. Their hackles slowly smoothed, but their teeth remained barred. When he reached a point four or five yards from the centre of the semicircle, and in line with the two outer wolves, Rhamin barred his teeth. The reaction was instant. Three of the four wolves lowered their bodies and laid their ears back against their heads. They tucked their tails between their back legs and tilted their heads slightly to one side. The fourth didn't move. He remained bristle coated, on tip toe, eyes wide, teeth barred and still ready to defend himself.

'You were the ones that helped Solin.' Rhamin stated. 'Why are you in my territory?'

The four wolves glanced at each other. They were looking to see who was going to answer Rhamin's question. Time seemed to slow as they waited for each other to respond. Rhamin had seen the submissive reaction of three of the wolves, so turned his head to the one wolf that remained aggressive. 'You!' he barked. 'Answer me!'

Somehow the aggressive wolf seemed less threatening. He raised his head, relaxed onto his feet and replied in a confident voice. 'We're passing through,' he stated as if Rhamin would condone his presence.

'You never left,' Rhamin scolded. 'You have been sucking up to that rogue Solin.'

'We're on the way out,' one of the females came in, 'but we didn't know you were around here. We didn't hear any of your pack.' She looked around curious at what she had just stated. 'Are you on your own?'

'Fancy your chances, then do you?'

The female remained submissive. 'No, it's just that…'

'You seem a long way from where we thought you were,' the aggressive male butted in.

'So you don't intend to fight me for my territory then?'

There was a short silence. 'We would prefer to leave you in peace,' the aggressive one stated. 'But we are not afraid to defend ourselves.'

'Glad to hear it,' Rhamin said lightly. 'I can't stand cowards.'

'Neither can we.'

'In that case, what were you doing with that slug Solin? He hardly sticks in my mind as being the bravest of the brave, letting you do all his dirty work.'

'A regrettable decision, that.' The young grey wolf was becoming more relaxed now. The aggression was abating.

Rhamin smiled. 'So you know what happened then?'

'I went back alone. I saw what had been done.'

'But there were more of you before the winter,' Rhamin

observed.

'Oh, the others went back north.' He shook his head. 'We should have gone with them. The trouble was there was no clear leader. The oldest was not the strongest and the strongest was no leader.'

'Aren't you strong enough?' Rhamin asked.

'I wasn't then,' the wolf replied candidly. 'And now, who knows who has taken over? It's not all that easy to start a good pack. Any wolf can lead a rabble.'

'What are you going to do?' the submissive female asked.

'Me? I have a mind to teach you what a good pack is like.'

'Is that a threat?' the young male said, once again rising on his toes.

'No, it's an offer.'

'An offer?'

'Well, you have three choices,' Rhamin said, glancing at each wolf in turn. 'First you can fight, but you may not like that option.'

'Or?' asked the female.

'Or you can leave my territory in peace, so long as you never set foot in it again.'

'Or?'

'Or you can join my pack. You are young, you are new blood, and no doubt you will have some knowledge that will benefit the rest of us. And more than likely, you can throw some light on the extent of the damage that that dog Solin has done.'

The wolves looked one to the other. Each seemed to be confirming what the other was thinking. After a long wait, the now not so aggressive male nodded his head. 'We can live with that,' he said politely. He thought for a moment and then spoke again. 'We all know who you are. Your reputation is famous throughout not just your own territory, but wherever wolves might travel. But allow me to tell you our names.'

Vela, Goma, Jual and Tula joined the pack without any comment from the rest of Rhamin's followers. They all had history and it was Rhamin that welded them together as a single active unit. Even when they were not together, the objectives of the pack were the same, all for one and one for all. And to give the newcomers their due, they were happy to be members. The next day, three of them went hunting with Charka and Bamar. Tula remained at the rendezvous point with Zelda. Her shoulder had an open wound on it and Rhamin had decided that it was better that she stayed out of action until it had healed. An open wound can fester, and in doing so, can kill the creature concerned. And even when not fatal, the smell can draw in other predators, or at least alert the prey it is hunting. Wolves' saliva contains antibodies and enzymes that prevent bleeding and promote healing so with rest and help from Zelda who licked the wound regularly, Tula's shoulder would heal cleanly within a week.

As spring forged forward, because food was not as plentiful as in springs gone by, the pack split up to hunt in groups. The devastatingly dry early summer followed by the harsh winter had left none of the usual wild berries on the bushes that were the early springtime food for many smaller species in the mountain forests. Wildlife was depleted and, without help from Corvak, inevitably, Rhamin's hunter groups had to split up and go out in different directions to find food. Had they not done so then Rasci may never have discovered what the farmer was doing.

CHAPTER TWELVE

Rasci raced towards the camp, calling to the other members of the pack. His tongue hung out like a dead snake, flapping about wildly as he ran and panted. He stopped and tried to get his breath.

Rhamin greeted his young comedian with a smile. 'What wasp has got inside your fur,' he laughed as Rasci's chest heaved uncontrollably. Although he tried to gasp out some unintelligible words, it took a good long minute before Rasci could speak. Eventually, after replenishing the muscles in his legs with oxygen, he took a good deep breath and then spoke. 'The man is in the foothills beyond the Great Forest,' he panted, licking his face with his long tongue.

'The man? What man?'

'The man with the sheep!'

'With his sheep!'

'No, not *with* his sheep!'

'You mean the man whose sheep we stole is in the foothills?'

Rasci nodded. 'Right.'

'The man whose family Solin put in great danger?'

Rasci nodded again.

Rhamin thought for a moment. 'So what is he doing here?'

Rasci looked perplexed. 'What is he doing here?' he parroted.

'Rasci! For goodness sake be sensible can't you?'

'No, I am being sensible. Honest Rhamin.'

'So what is the man whose sheep we stole, doing in the foothills?'

'I didn't think to ask him!' Rasci said with a broad grin, his rows of white teeth gleaming against his pink gums.

Rhamin shook his head. 'I really don't know why I bother sometimes, do you know that?'

'No, seriously Rhamin, I really don't know what he's doing. He's with another man and heading up through the forest. That's all I can say.'

Rhamin nodded. 'He's heading up to the mountains then,' he stated as if he had got a full answer to his question. This was, indeed, an intriguing piece of information. Now, why would a flatland domesticated livestock farmer be heading to a wilderness? There seemed only one answer.

Later that day, more wolves returned to the rendezvous camp. Rhamin instructed them to stay close. He couldn't call out to any of his pack. To do so would surely give their positions away. Like Rasci, some had travelled many miles away and by the evening he only managed to gather the youngsters, Ramusan, Depni, Floss and Fatz, along with Natan who had been on a hunting trip with them, teaching and training them. Silvah was at the new camp, for she looked after Zelda, returning there every day; and Lexa had been accompanying Rhamin and Yeltsa on their own expedition locally, because Yeltsa was, by now, heavily pregnant. The four newcomers from the north were out with Charka and Bamar. So, without the use of wolf calls, which were still banned by Rhamin, there was no way of gathering the whole pack together at short notice.

The meeting was preceded by the usual greetings that underlay the bonding between wolves, and then Rhamin got down to the business of the day. Simply, he wanted to know whether the pack agreed with him. The territory was crossed by hard tracks, roads laid down by man, and there was always some awareness of the presence of the cars and trucks that travelled along them as well as the people in them. Wolves adapted to those changes over the generations just as the other animals of the hills, forests and plains had done. But he was curious as to what the farmer was up to. This was the man his pack had crossed. This was a man from whom he had stolen Lexa, albeit as a diversion to stop the man's dog attacking more of the pack within reach of the man's weapon. The wolves seemed open minded about the man's intention, except for Rasci, who seemed particularly agitated. But he still couldn't explain why. He had simply observed the man travelling first in a wheeled vehicle and then, on reaching the point where the road changed into a track, he had stopped the vehicle and, with one other man and his dog, set out on foot up through the trees into the rugged mountains. Once again, without a positive decision, Rhamin consulted Zelda.

Zelda shook her head. 'I don't see any danger,' she said, closing her eyes and concentrating. Then, she turned to Rasci. 'You, young wolf, what do you feel?'

'Me? I… well I just felt it was important,' he stated, not sure what else to say. 'I was coming down from the mountains and was curious at first. So when I saw who was in the vehicle, I followed it. It wasn't long before he stopped in a clearing, got out, and with another man and that big dog that looks like…'

'Like Lexa,' Rhamin put in.

'Er, well yes,' Rasci said, glancing at Lexa whose ears were forward and whose face showed that she was more than curious as to what they were talking about. 'Well, they set off on foot up towards the mountain.'

'Men folk do that,' Yeltsa stated. 'They go hunting just like we do.'

'But this was the sheep man,' Rasci replied, his eyes questioning what Yeltsa had just said. 'It just seemed…'

'Strange?' asked Silvah.

Rasci thought for a moment. 'Well no, not really. I just thought we should be there, you know.' He looked at Zelda but she just watched him, her head slightly tilted to one side as if to ask him to elaborate on his thinking process. He sighed. 'I can't really explain it,' he said finally, with a shrug. 'I just felt I should tell you, and that you would all want to find out what he was doing, that's all.'

'And rightly so,' Rhamin said reassuringly. He could see there was something bothering Rasci, something not unlike the feelings that Zelda often got when she was uneasy about something, something that had happened or was about to happen. 'But you don't think he was looking for us then?'

'I didn't want to show myself and find out,' replied Rasci.

Rhamin decided to take the able bodied members of his pack, or at least the ones that were available, in search of the man. It was important to find out what he was doing in the mountain forests and no amount of debate would give them an answer.

Gradually, over a period of about three hours, Rasci led the pack back to where he had seen the man. Sure enough, the vehicle was still parked where the track became too narrow to permit its passage. From there, the wolves had no difficulty tracking the men and their dog by scent, as they took the same path through clearings, along narrow animal trails and deeper into the thickly wooded mountains. It wasn't long before they were able to hear the men brushing past branches and softly treading on the thick bed of leaf mould and fern. It occurred to Rhamin that perhaps the men were tracking another creature in the same way. He discussed it with his companions. It was unlikely that the men were hunting wolves. They all agreed, therefore, that if they were not looking for wolves, then they must be hunting deer, and only a few minutes later, their assumption was confirmed. First they heard the loud crack made by the fire spitting weapon the men were carrying. There was a commotion as birds set to flight, amidst much squawking and flapping of wings against branches and leaves, in a desperate effort to flee. Then, the soft sound of life passing from a creature as it breathed out its last breath, followed by a crumpling of leaves and branches as it fell, told the wolves that it was, indeed, a deer that the men were hunting.

They had come to the edge of a bare rocky clearing. Around it, the tree cover was thick, and as they looked on from beneath a canopy of broad leaves, they could see, at the other end of the clearing, beneath a long overhanging branch of a tall redwood tree, two men examining the body of their prize. There was some chatter as the men discussed it and then a little laughter. The farmer was explaining something to the other man. As he talked, he drew out a knife and began to demonstrate how to clean the animal of all its innards ready for carrying back down the mountain side. That was a good thing for Rhamin, because wolves find the insides of animals just as nutritious as the meat and the bone. They would have a good feast later.

The man who was watching the farmer, eventually stood upright, leaving the farmer to get on with his task. He had taken out a leather thong and attached it to the dog by a collar around its neck. He was keeping the dog away from the carcass. Rhamin recognised the dog immediately. It was the same animal that had attacked Seth and Fayli the day they had been killed by the man's fire stick, the one that had chased him when he had stolen two of its pups. That dog was Lexa's mother.

It was the dog that saw Rhamin first. She suddenly stood up, and with her flopped ears pushed forward at either side of a creased forehead, she barred her teeth and barked. The suddenness of it made both the men swivel around, the farmer reaching instinctively for his gun. The accomplice struggled to hold the dog firm. The farmer shouted a command and she lay down as suddenly as she had done all those months ago when she was caught up in the battle with Rhamin's wolves. They both glanced around, searching for the object of the dog's warning. Then, the accomplice spotted Rhamin who was ahead of and slightly above the other wolves. The hard, uneven, rocky floor of the clearing gave adequate cover to all. Rhamin had inched forward to see what the men were doing, and in doing so had exposed himself in the open. The dog had seen him. He knew she had recognised him also. Her teeth remained barred in a face that was, despite Rhamin being used to seeing Lexa play fighting and hunting, in every way as ugly as he remembered it the night they rustled the farmer's sheep. But somehow, it was the dog itself that made the face so fearsome. It crossed his mind that he never saw Lexa in the same light, although now, if the two dogs had been standing together, he would have had difficulty telling them apart.

Lexa was younger of course, and had still got some growing to do. But the similarity was hypnotic. Rhamin just stood and stared.

The accomplice bent down and picked up his gun. There was a clicking sound as he moved the bolt out, back and then forward again. All the time, the gun was being raised to his shoulder. As if in slow motion, the contraption lifted in the air, its open point eventually being all Rhamin could see in front of the man's face. The rest of the pack was peering through the still, thick leaves that hung heavily down to the ground. Although they could see into the clearing, they were out of sight and almost totally sheltered from danger behind the crest of rock. They had been watching as well, and they too seemed just as mesmerised by what was going on.

The gun fired. The sound echoed through the forest, repeating itself as it bounced from mountain wall to solid bedrock, from trees and back again. Birds, that not long before had settled nearby after the sound made by the same contraption, scattered once again in a crescendo of beating wings and vocal surprise. As the noise came from the open end of the gun, and the flame sped outwards from it, it seemed to be arcing upwards. Something hot and deadly passed over Rhamin's head and splattered through twigs, leaves and branches behind him, showering the pack with broken dead wood. He flinched, but his amber eyes were still fixed on the men in front of him. He realised he hadn't done what he had told the rest of the pack they must do if man ever pointed anything towards them. For some reason that he couldn't explain even to himself, he remained on the spot, transfixed. It had all happened, seemingly in slow motion, something, some feeling or sense had told him that he should remain there, still and silent. He had seen the farmer rising from his crouching position, arm arching upwards in slow motion, his hand contacting with the gun as it fired. And, as the deafening sound died down, he heard the accomplice shout something that seemed to be an angry declaration, but the farmer said nothing. Then, after letting the accomplice settle a little, calmly, he spoke again, first to his dog that was becoming restless, rising to its feet, waiting for instructions. It settled back down, all its body tense and taut like a coiled spring waiting to be released. Then, just as calmly, he spoke to the other man. The man's face altered as the discourse progressed. He shook his head. The farmer pointed to Rhamin who, heart calming slightly now, was still watching and waiting. There was more discourse. And then, the farmer smiled. Not at the companion. It was a smile aimed directly at Rhamin. The farmer said something to the black wolf, but it made no sense to him, and then the man gave him a wave; a sort of acknowledgement wave; a wave that Rhamin could comprehend. Rhamin lifted his head slightly as if to let the farmer know that he had understood. There was a long silence as both looked into each other's eyes, then, still held in the farmer's gaze, Rhamin turned slowly, hopped down from the ledge and disappeared into the cover of the dark undergrowth.

So Rhamin knew now that the farmer had forgiven him for stealing his sheep. He knew, as well, that Solin's evil plan had not worked. He knew that the farmer's wife or the children must have told him what had happened in their house when Rhamin stopped Solin from killing the man's young ones. Perhaps she had been able to understand also, Rhamin's actions on the night he dispatched Solin and his band of rogue wolves. Whatever happened after those events, Rhamin was sure that the farmer knew that the black wolf and his pack wanted to live in peace with him. It was with a sigh of relief and a much lighter heart that he and his pack departed from the clearing. For the first time in weeks, Rhamin let out a howl. He was free again in his own territory; he could communicate freely with his pack. As if released from beneath an invisible, heavy, suffocating cloud, one by one, and then together, the wolves began to howl.

The rejoicing didn't last long though. Rhamin calmed down his wolves eventually, for although their achievement today would have been worth starving for a month, they had unfinished business. Back in the clearing, once the men descended the mountain with their catch, the wolves could return for the remainder of the deer. Waste not, want not. Rhamin had let the wolves that were still away, and within earshot, know his position. And by doing so, he had alerted them to the fact that the all clear had been given as regards the danger they had so greatly feared.

Patiently, and with much playfulness, the pack waited, and eventually, as the day passed they began to head slowly back to the rocky clearing.

The men had made themselves a little camp fire and were sitting chatting and laughing as they cooked meat on a stick and ate. Although not yet in sight, the smell was quite appetizing, even to wolves that preferred raw meat. But the men seemed in no hurry, and so the wolves, from a distance, silently waited and watched for the men's departure.

It was a calm warm afternoon, too calm for Rasci. He liked to act the fool and bounce about playfully. But now he was constrained to wolf-like behaviour. He had to be quiet and wait. But, wait as he may, he still fidgeted uneasily. A couple of times, Rhamin reprimanded him for his restlessness, but Rasci couldn't explain it. He was a clown of a wolf, but nevertheless, he was a wolf at heart, and patience is inbred to all wolves. But Rasci wandered about restlessly, muttering under his breath, shaking his head, then settling down and sighing heavily. While all the other wolves rested, he out of them all remained alert to any slight noise from the forest.

Except Lexa. She had been thinking about the dog she had seen. She also had things on her mind. And when the noise came, she was awake and alert. She heard the sound but it was one she didn't know, or at least it was a sound she could not remember. But Rasci knew what it was. He had heard it before. Lexa's ears were forward. She was about to bark but Rasci checked her. 'Shh' he said quickly; and then quietly, 'Rhamin! Rhamin, are you awake.' It was almost a whisper.

Rhamin stirred from a deep sleep. He had relaxed this day more than he had done for months. A heavy cloud had seemed to have been miraculously lifted off his shoulders. Today, he was happy. It was one of the best days in his life. 'What is it, Rasci?' he said, taking in a deep breath to revive himself to consciousness.

'Master, we have trouble.'

Rhamin sprang to his feet. 'In what way?'

'Rhamin, I hear the bears. I am not mistaken. They are coming down the mountain.'

'Where are they heading, can you tell?'

'They are only just above the clearing, if I am not mistaken. I suspect that they have smelt the men and their food.'

And Rasci was right. As Rhamin stirred the rest of the

wolves into action, there was another sound of the man's gun, but this time amidst a greater commotion than they had heard in a long time. It took little effort to work out what was happening. Bears hibernate over the winter months, losing up to one third of their body weight as they sleep. The winter had been long and hard. The fat reserves that bears build up before hibernating run out eventually and, come what may, they have to wake up and find food. Only, the food that bears depend on most when they first awake is the wild berries, rich in sugars and high in energy. But they need fifteen kilograms of berries a day to build up their strength and start to gain weight. This spring they were not likely to achieve that target. The wild berries were just not there. They had either not been produced in large enough numbers during the unusually dry summer, or they had been consumed by the other smaller creatures who themselves had to survive the winter. Those creatures too, after the long winter, had to build up their strength once again. They too had families to rear if their species were to survive. This year's salmon had not yet commenced their run up the rapids of the mountain rivers after their three years at sea. That part of the food chain was due soon, but was still to come. In the meantime, the bears were starving. Now they were prepared to attack and kill anything including humans for food. There were two men and a dog. But more than that, there was a dead deer. All told, there was meat enough for a feast. The two men were no longer at the top of the food chain. As far as the starving bears were concerned the men, their dog and the deer were definitely *in* the food chain.

Rhamin's ears took in the sounds as, in his mind, he pictured what was happening. 'I can't let the bears do this!'

he exclaimed, uncertain why this particular man was worth getting into a fight for. 'I must go and see what I can do.' He looked around at his followers. 'I'm not asking any of you to follow me. You make your own mind up. But I know, for me, it was meant to be.'

'Me too,' said Rasci, surprisingly serious this time.

Rhamin smiled at his young companion. Saying not another word, he turned and bounded up towards the clearing. It took less than a minute to reach the spot from where they had watched the men and as he travelled, he heard sounds that made his coat hairs stand on end. There was the sound of a dog, not barking but snarling and yapping and then yelping. There was shouting by one of the men and another gun shot, followed by a clattering sound as the gun fell onto a hard rock floor. Then there was the sound of a man yelling in pain and growling.

And then Rhamin broke into the clearing, silently running towards Bortag, the biggest of three bears that he could now clearly see.

Bortag hadn't seen Rhamin; the lens of his right eye was white and coated in an opaque glaze. Rhamin knew the bear would not forgive him for that. But one of Bortag's companions, a female, did see the black wolf bounding towards the mêlée. It was only slightly smaller than Bortag, but both bears were thin. This bear was standing over one of the men. There was blood on its jowls. As it saw Rhamin it spun around to face him. Rhamin kept on going. He was heading directly towards Bortag and was not going to be distracted by the other bear as he took off. He landed squarely against the shoulders of the big bear, sinking his teeth into the thick coat on its neck. Now, Rhamin could see the farmer beneath Bortag, stabbing with a knife at the bear's carpeted underbelly. It stumbled forward, off balance, away to one side of its victim. The farmer, like his companion, was covered in blood, but immediately, freed from the bear, he scrambled to his feet and ran to a crevice in the rocks where his gun had fallen. But Bortag just turned and, regardless of Rhamin, shook him off and went after the man again. Rhamin knew that the big bear had not really understood what had hit him in the back. Bortag had only one thing on his mind and, with single minded determination, nothing was going to stop him.

Before Rhamin could recover his balance and attack Bortag again, the other bear was upon him, but at that moment, Rasci sailed through the air, grabbed the female bear by the cheek and, with the momentum of his weight, and with teeth clenched on the bears face, he spun its head around. Rasci had taken it totally by surprise, knocking it off balance and wrenching its gnashing teeth away from Rhamin. It fell awkwardly in a sitting position and then, effortlessly, it rolled back onto all four feet.

More wolves came into the attack. Vela, Jual and Goma appeared from nowhere. They must have heard the wolf calls earlier and now they had found the pack in full battle mode. They seemed to work as one as they, with Rasci set out a well rehearsed system of bite, tear and leave go, none getting in the other's way, all returning time and time again with such ferocity that the female bear had no chance to take on Rhamin. Once again, the big male bear was almost upon the farmer who had failed to recover his weapon which was now securely wedged down a crack in the rocks. He turned to face the oncoming bear and was knocked off balance by the force of a huge swinging paw that hit him squarely on the side of the head. Huge jaws closed only inches from his chest as the bear snapped at the tumbling victim. Rhamin grabbed the offending limb, but despite his weight, the bear shook him off like a loose branch. It was Ramusan that made the decisive move. He had circled around the bear, and getting the full attention of the huge animal, who could now see him through his one good eye, the young wolf went for the one vulnerable spot. The bear desperately tried to protect its eye as Ramusan snapped his strong jaws onto Bortag's upper eyelid, ripping with all his weight behind his leap, and then letting go before the bear's savage jaws could swing around to catch him. As Bortag's head swung round in pursuit of Ramusan, Lexa closed her jaws on the bear's windpipe, throwing it off balance. To stop it hitting Lexa with the full force of its paw, Rhamin grabbed the bear's right arm and, as it went over on its side, Natan and Depni grabbed the bear's left arm and shook and tugged at it with their powerful jaws. Lexa remained clamped on the bear's windpipe, slowly starving the big creature of the vital oxygen it needed to remain conscious. Now the bear was fighting for its life. It had to get the pack of wolves off it and to do so it fell forward on its belly and began to roll over and over on the hard rock floor. Lexa had to let go of her hold on the animal's throat as its weight landed squarely on top of her; but instead of crushing her, it pressed her into a hollow crevice. Likewise, the others had to get out of the way of three hundred kilograms of rolling bear. Had the bear been at full weight and without a thick coat, Lexa would surely have been crushed to death, but luckily, the bear's neck and not its solid chest landed across her body as it spun over her. Freed from clinging wolves, Bortag got up, shook himself as if he had just been for an afternoon swim and roared as he set off into the thickest part of the forest. The female bear had already given up the fight with the rest of the pack and had been swinging wildly and defensively at her attackers until she saw Bortag take his leave. With a final roar of defiance, she followed her mate and disappeared out of the clearing.

The third younger bear, had fled as soon as Rhamin appeared, but Rhamin only realised why it had not stayed to fight when Charka and Bamar appeared, panting heavily, grinning with satisfaction. What Rhamin had noticed through the corner of his eye as he pounded towards Bortag was the man's dog repeatedly attacking and retreating from that other female bear. Now, Charka and Bamar explained how they had joined in to attack that bear and, with the farmer's dog, chased it off into the forest. The bear had been wounded by the second man's weapon, not fatally. But the wound had tempered its enthusiasm to fight, and with the help of the wolves, the dog had seen it off. The dog, however had refused to join them on the way back to the clearing, but had made its own way back to its master where she now lay guarding him, not sure what the next move would be by the wolves. She was clearly perplexed. She only knew the wolves as her and her master's enemy, and her only thought now was for the safety of her master.

The farmer was bleeding badly from his left leg. As he sat against a tree, legs stretched out straight in front of him, he reached for his knife and cut a strip of material off his badly torn shirt. Padding it against the gaping wound on his leg he took off a belt from around his waist, wrapped it around the top of his leg and tightened it.

As the wolves milled about after the heat of battle, clearly excited by their victory, Lexa suddenly struggled free from the hollow on the rocky ledge. She jumped up and barked as loud as Rhamin had ever heard her bark. It resounded around the valley until, fading away, silence returned as all eyes turned towards her. She barked again, this time not loudly, but to tell her pack that she had found the second man. He had fallen off the ledge when the bears attacked, but remarkably, he was practically unscathed. A gash on his shoulder, a few scrapes and grazes on his hands and face bore witness to his fleeting encounter with death, but otherwise, he remained intact. Remarkable as well was the fact that he seemed oblivious to the presence of the wolves. The one he seemed to notice was Lexa, who was similarly, singularly interested in the man. Stiffly, the man walked over to his hunting companion and, giving the farmer's dog a pat on the shoulder, he knelt beside its master and began to help to dress his wound.

Rhamin looked on with deep interest. He had never had such a close encounter with man kind. As the farmer began to recover from the trauma of his injury, and was regaining some of his spent energy, he noticed Lexa milling about in the excited pack of wolves. He turned his head and looked down to make sure his dog was beside him and then looked back up again at Lexa. Rhamin watched his face. He was recalling what happened at the farm when he stole the farmer's pups and the farmer was obviously recalling the same moment. The farmer smiled, and despite being in obvious pain, he shook his head and began to chuckle. His companion tried to calm him, thinking that the wounded man was becoming light headed from loss of blood, but the farmer spoke to him in reassuring tones. He was wounded, but he was happy. He could return to his farm with a story for his wife and two young children. Somehow, Rhamin could sense the joy and relief in the man's manner. They both had a story to tell. But little did either of them know that it was only the beginning.

PART 2

NO MORE THE FOOL

CHAPTER THIRTEEN

Apart from a pestering bluebottle, there was no sound.

Rasci slept soundly in the shadow cast by the laden branches of the big willow. The fly landed on his ear which he flicked in an auto-response, still fast asleep. The pestering insect buzzed off towards the remains of the deer that he had killed in the early hours of the morning. Now in his fifth year, Rasci was a mature member of the Rhamin pack, and for the last three days he had been hunting alone. During the night, he would head back to the Darin with a full stomach and a haunch of meat for Zelda. Her age was finally telling on her and she travelled very little with the other wolves now. He would, as usual, have to chew the food up for her first. It was the least he could do for the frail old wolf that had taught him so much.

Raymond Rozalski slept too. He was still recovering from the wounds that he had received from a bear, whilst hunting deer in the mountain forests. It was mid afternoon and he was resting with one leg on an elm rocking chair whilst reclining along a stout bench in the shade of the veranda of his farmhouse. In the background there were noises; his wife, giving a farm worker instructions what to do; their four year old daughter, Margo, singing and playing in the kitchen, experimenting at mixing some flour with water and dog biscuits and watching the resulting gooey substance cling stubbornly to her fingers. Somewhere in the distance Ben, their five year old son, could be heard calling to Smokey. They were all the usual noises of life; youngsters playing, birds singing, insects flying by or scurrying past.

The subsonic vibrations from far away were inaudible; at least, to a human ear.

Rasci was having a dream. In his mind, somewhere, miles away, he was watching Ben and his dog chasing a rabbit through some long grass, in a small man made enclosure, at the side of the farmhouse. He had seen this boy in his dreams several times before. He didn't know why. He had never met him; only the dog. He knew the dog's name. He had heard Raymond Rozalski calling for Smokey on the mountain, when they fought the bears, but then he had not understood what he had said. But now, in his mind, he could see Ben calling her. 'Smokey, Smokey! Over here!' If Rasci had been there, what he was seeing and hearing would have been no clearer. In fact, in his dream, somehow the boy was speaking a language Rasci could understand. It was better than being there.

Ben was running bandy-legged as he tried to skip over the long grass. 'Over here Smokey!' he cried. But the dog had found its own trail to follow. Suddenly, Ben was distracted by a shadow at the edge of his vision. He stopped and listened. He looked up at the sky and then, his head slowly dipping, he seemed to study a long shaft of grass by his feet. But he wasn't seeing it. He was in another world of childish daydreams and far away places. Rasci watched him standing there in front of him, transfixed, eyes wide and staring. The boy stood there for what seemed like an age, and then, nudged by Smokey who had lost interest in her quarry without her comrade, the child blinked back to consciousness. His head swivelled. 'Smokey!' he exclaimed. He put his arm over the big dog's shoulder and, abandoning the hunt, together they ran back to the farmhouse.

Rasci slept on, but he was restless now. Something was breaking into his dream. He could hear a voice speaking to him far away in the background. 'Some birds don't land in trees,' it was calling.

'What?' he was talking aloud but his eyes were still closed. The noise was louder. Low frequency vibrations, that hardly moved the air, were travelling over a vast distance, and the sound that those vibrations made was getting nearer. It was like flapping wings; only it wasn't wings.

Raymond Rozalski jumped as the sound engulfed him. Rasci saw it clearly. The noise cracked the quiet tranquillity of the summer's day. A helicopter in the middle of nowhere, when it appears, on a baking, sun washed afternoon, when nature is at its most subdued, is alien to all around, even humans. Why it had to fly directly over the farmstead, suddenly scaring man, sheep and cattle alike, was a mystery to Raymond. It could well have detoured a little to the north or the south as it travelled westward. It wobbled as it went over and then, for some reason known only to the occupants, it turned and did another pass, this time banking to one side as if the pilot was looking for something. Then, as suddenly as it had appeared, it sped off towards the west and the plains that ran up to the foothills and the mountain forests.

'Some birds don't land in trees.'

'What?' Rasci was suddenly awake. His head jerked up and his ears rotated to get the best directional reception.

He had heard something. The flies on the meat buzzed excitedly, but it wasn't that noise that had bothered him; that was the sound of nature. There was something else, something alien, still a long way off.

Travelling at two hundred knots, the helicopter had passed over the Darin within another twenty minutes. The pilot didn't know the Darin was there, of course. No human being did. That's why it was such a good den for Rhamin and his pack. Old Zelda was there, asleep in the cool shade of the cave. From the air, there was no sign of an opening to the cavern. It was just one of many tree scattered, rocky outcrops in the undulating landscape. The ancient old wolf had heard the beating noise of the rotor blades. She, too, had been dreaming when the sound first reached her ears. But she was soon awakened as it approached directly.

Rasci had only seen the helicopter in his dream. He was twenty miles to the south of the Darin. But the sound was loud enough to be able to identify it. He wondered where it was heading. He had seen helicopters before, passing close by, but they were part of life, as were all the trappings of man. He knew about the hard surfaces men built and called roads and the vehicles that travelled along them; he knew about the collections of abodes, built from rock and wood, which men call houses, and which were gathered into townships. Wherever a wolf went in the world, men kind left an imprint. Man was almost everywhere at some time; in the forests, on the plains, in their enclosures they call farms and, far, far in the distance, there were distinctive rock buildings that belched out smoke and gave out chemicals that, even if not sensed by humans, were disturbing to the sensory glands of other creatures. And he knew that the factories, as humans know them, were scrunched in between huge gatherings of houses and other man made structures that make up what men kind know as cities. He had never seen a city or a factory, but Corvak, the wise, old raven had. He had told Rasci about them. Forests of buildings, Corvak called them, 'stretching as far as the eye can see, even from the air!' That had impressed Rasci. Even from the air! Where he lived, in the territory of his leader, Rhamin, there were no such forests; only forests of trees.

He made a mental note to discuss the helicopter with Rhamin when they gathered together. Tonight he would call out and see if any other wolves from the pack were returning. He was looking forward to getting back to Zelda anyway because he needed to discuss his dreams.

'Hello Gran,' Rasci said. He dropped the meat he'd been carrying, on the floor by the mouth of the cave. Zelda was the wisest wolf Rasci had ever known. She was the only wolf he knew that could foretell what was going to happen in the future, and it was because of her gift that she was so regularly consulted by Rhamin. She was loved by the whole pack who would hunt for her and even fight for her, as they did a year ago when they fought the bears. Rasci loved her most of all for teaching him everything she knew. He couldn't remember a time when Zelda wasn't old. The last year of extremes in the weather had taken its toll more than age itself and now she walked very little and staggered unsteadily whenever she had to go outside the cave. Five years ago, when Rasci was a baby, she had been able to see him. She was very old even then. But she remembered his grey coat and thin, silver bib. He wasn't her cub nor was she his mother, but he felt he was related to her in some way and, affectionately, he always called her "Gran". He was only sorry she couldn't see him now that he was full sized and mature. She would have been so proud of him. Now fully grown, he was as big as any other wolf in the pack except for Rhamin.

Rasci had the same father as Rhamin, but he was the result of an illicit meeting between his father, Anval, and a young beta female called Celion who died soon after giving birth. He had inherited some of the size that his half brother Rhamin possessed and, like Rhamin, he was strong and fast.

But Zelda knew Rasci well enough. She knew he was the clown of the pack, with never a bad word to say about anybody unless they deserved it. He was her source of news, and with it he brought humour as well as food. To Zelda's mind, he was more like their leader Rhamin than Rasci realised. 'What is it?' Zelda asked, sensing Rasci was a little unsettled. She could hear him sighing and moving about restlessly by the mouth of the cave. He stood there, watching the last shaft of sunlight explode through a gap in a distant clump of trees as the sun fell silently from the sky.

'It will soon be dark.' He continued to gaze after the sun. 'No moon tonight, Gran,' he said as he contemplated what was on his mind.

'Starlight is fine for your young eyes.' She tilted her head, searching for some input from her carer. 'Are you all right?'

'Oh, I'm fine, Gran, don't you worry.' He broke his gaze from the fading sunset and turned towards her. 'I'll not be hunting tonight.' With that, he went outside and climbed to the top of the rock that Rhamin used as a podium to address his pack. He lifted his head and howled.

Moments later he heard a far-off call from Silvah. Her voice seemed strained, somehow. Then he heard another call from even further away. It was hardly perceptible, but he knew it was Natan. Natan would, most likely, be answering Silvah's call. Rasci howled again, trying his best to convey his meaning. He needed the rest of the pack right now. He wasn't sure in his mind why. It was just a feeling. Some of the wolves would be alone, and some in groups. He wondered where Rhamin was. He usually called in the evening. Perhaps he was too far away to call tonight. Perhaps the other wolves had heard him.

Quietly, and with a sense of foreboding, he climbed back down from the rock and went back to the cave. Zelda had moved just inside.

'Well then? Tell me, what's the matter?'

'Sorry, old girl. I don't know what's wrong with me.' He came and flopped down beside her and rested his chin on his front paws. He'd come home intending to discuss his dreams with her, but now he was back at the Darin he felt uneasy. 'I must be tired,' He said, with a quiet sigh.

'But you always have something to tell me.' Zelda gazed at him sightlessly, but he said no more. As the last light faded in the cave, Rasci closed his eyes and sunk into a troubled sleep.

It was Zelda's barking that awoke Rasci. At first he didn't know if it was part of his dream, but slowly, as the old wolf's bark got louder, he fought off the clinging, overpowering tentacles of sleep and opened his eyes. 'You're having a bad dream,' she said, licking his face. 'I thought I'd never wake you!'

Rasci was panting. Wolves do not sweat under their thick coats, and as his heart beat fast and his tongue hung out in the cool night air to aid his cooling system, he let Zelda lick him until his metabolism rallied. 'Phew!' He stood up and shook himself. 'I'm sorry Gran. I didn't mean to disturb you.'

'Disturb me? You weren't disturbing me. I have nothing to do but sleep all day.' She paused and picked her words. 'But I was concerned. There's something up and I don't know what it is.'

Rasci sighed, stretched and looked around, but there was still no light from outside the mouth of the cave. He sniffed the cool air then, relaxing a little, he sat back down next to Zelda. 'I'm not sure,' he said eventually. 'I keep dreaming all sorts of weird things.'

'Well, I can tell that! You were kicking and barking and snapping in your sleep. If I hadn't known you were lying next to me I would have sworn you were fighting for your life!'

Rasci sat and thought for a long minute. 'I think I was,' he replied eventually. 'Only I was there, watching, and barking and snarling, but they couldn't see me. Nobody could! It was as if I were invisible!'

'That's dreams for you.' Zelda shuffled closer to him. 'Come on, my young hero, tell me. Tell me everything you saw. I want to know every detail.'

Rasci was still panting heavily. 'Well, it's odd really,' he said, broken by yet another round of heavy breathing. He tilted his head and contemplated what he was about to tell her. 'It's really strange. I've been having dreams like this for a while now.' He paused and panted some more. 'And it's always Rhamin, Yeltsa and me fighting other wolves,' he continued, 'but I can't make out what we are fighting about or where we are. It's as if it hadn't happened yet but it was going to happen, if you see my meaning.'

Zelda nodded. She knew exactly what he meant. Dreaming of the present was one thing. You knew where you were, you knew what was happening. But she had been a seer for as long as she could recall, and dreams that were prophetic were always shrouded in mystery. There were seldom any sharp edges of clarity. All one usually saw were shards of detail cutting through a velvet curtain of blackness, a murky mire of ideas and thoughts mixed and mingled, poking out of the kind of infinite and unclear shadow that you only get in dreams and nightmares. 'And you have had this dream before?' There was deep concern in her voice now.

'Yes, several times; four, perhaps five now.'

'Then you must tell me whenever you have it again, do you hear?'

Rasci seemed relieved to have shared his doubts and troubles with his old mentor. Then he spoke again. 'I had a different dream earlier today.'

'Oh?' said Zelda, still very interested, but now a little remote. Rasci had been watching her; she was deep in thought. He could tell her mind was churning over what he had been saying; analysing and trying to make sense of it all. But, as he spoke, her mind snapped back to receiver mode. 'And what was that about?'

'Well that's just it, I don't understand it really. This one was a clear as sunlight. Once again, it's as if I were there but, this time, everything, every detail is understandable. There is nothing mysterious about it.'

'Then I suspect,' Zelda said encouragingly, 'that this was a dream about the present rather than the future; two quite different things!'

Rasci regarded the old wolf. He admired her wisdom. 'I think you might be right,' he said. He gathered his thoughts for a moment and then explained, 'There I was, at the farmer's home. You know the one, the man whose farm we raided, the one that we saved from the bears?'

Zelda nodded in the darkness. 'Yes, I know the one.'

'And I was there!'

'In your dream?'

'Well yes. But somehow it seemed more than that. It seemed like I was there, but I know I wasn't, because when I woke up, I was lying where I'd fallen asleep!'

'So what did you see?'

'Everything.' Rasci shrugged. 'I tell you, it's uncanny. I was there!' I saw the farmer asleep at the front of his home. I saw his mate talking to another man and giving him instructions. I saw Ben playing…'

'Ben?'

Rasci sounded startled. 'Yes.' He leaned his head to one side and thought for a moment. 'Yes, that's his name, Ben.'

'And how do you know that, young wolf?'

'Well, that's just it, I didn't know I knew!' He considered what he had just said and then went on, 'I just know.' He shook his head. 'And what's more, I can understand everything they are saying. It's as if, because they are in my dream, then they speak my language! It's… I don't really understand it, but it's as if I am one of them. But what I do know is that, although I am there, they cannot see me.'

'I know just what you are saying, Rasci. I have had dreams like that. It's all part of being able to see things.' She thought for a moment. 'Although, I am not sure I ever saw anything with such clarity.' She paused again. 'Or, perhaps I did, but I can't remember.' She shook her head and sighed deeply. 'I'm getting too old. I'm a blind, decrepit, useless old fart! I'm certainly too old to be of any use anymore.'

'Nonsense!' Then he added, 'Well, you're not useless, anyway.' He chuckled and Zelda gave him a reproachful nudge with her nose. 'You've taught me everything I know, Gran.'

'Huh, well, perhaps so. Anyway, you were saying?'

'What? Oh, yes. Hmm, I was saying… what was I saying Gran?'

'Oh deary me! I thought it was me that was losing my memory! You were saying that you were there and you were watching what they were doing, and…'

'Oh, right. Yes, that's what.' He paused and thought again. 'Yes, Ben… that's the young boy's name… boys are young men you know?'

'Really?' Zelda sounded interested. 'No, I didn't know,' she said, shaking her head.

'Well that's true, or at least that's what young men are called when I hear men folk speak in my dreams. I am not at all sure if I would understand any of the words they say if I were awake.'

'Go on. I understand.'

'And young females are called girls.'

Zelda nodded. A new day was beginning to creep slowly into the mouth of the cave.

'And well, I saw the girl; they call her Margo. She was mixing stuff with Smokey's food!'

'Smokey?'

'The dog.'

Zelda nodded. 'Right. The dog. You mean…'

'Yes, that dog, Lexa's natural mother. And you know what?'

'What?'

'If it hadn't been a dream, I'd have sworn it was Lexa herself. You'd not believe it, you know! The resemblance is remarkable.'

'Really? Now that does surprise me; a creature that looks like its mother!'

Rasci caught the irony in her voice. 'Well, it… it's just a bit of a shock, that's all, Gran. You know, Lexa is Lexa. She's a wolf.'

'Yes, but she looks like a dog.' Zelda nodded patiently. 'Carry on, it's a new day and I have all of it.'

Rasci looked at the old wolf's face. He was sure she was smiling. But it was a well concealed smile. It was the sightless eyes that gave it away. They changed ever so slightly, perhaps crinkling at the edges a little. But perhaps the light wasn't all that good yet. 'Yes, I know you have. Great, isn't it? I can talk all day and you can't escape. You're perfect for my purpose.'

'I had gathered that in the past.'

Rasci chuckled again. 'And the dog… Smokey, she was playing at finding a rabbit with Ben.'

'Oh, sounds like a well balanced family then.'

'Yes.' Rasci shuffled awkwardly. 'Oh, I see. Well, to cut a long story short, this thing flew over the farm and the farmer awoke with a start, cursing and waving his arms, and…'

'Thing?'

'The big bird machine thing and its beating wings. They are ever so noisy, you know?'

Zelda nodded again. 'Yes I do know. I know very well, in

fact. It flew over the Darin yesterday afternoon.'

'Right. Well, it flew over the farm. And there were several men inside it. I could see them inside it just the same as I could see inside the farmer's home. And one of those men was the one that was with the farmer, hunting deer, when we fought off the bears.'

'Really?' Now Zelda pricked up her ears. 'Are you sure about that?' She shuffled uncomfortably and winced as her hip bones creaked. 'Are you really sure about that?' she asked again. 'This might be very important.'

Rasci took his time to answer. He nodded and said, 'Yes, I'm absolutely sure.'

Zelda thought for a moment, and then asked, 'So what happened then?'

'Well, I don't think the farmer knew who it was. He carried on cursing and the machine flew off. Yes, it was heading straight towards the Darin, now, I recall.'

'So the end to this tale is?'

Rasci shrugged. 'I don't know, Gran. That's what's bothering me. I woke up, you see.'

'So you don't remember anything else, anything at all?'

'Nope. That's it,' said Rasci, shaking his head. 'Except when I woke up a voice was saying something… what was it?' He strained through the dregs of his memory. 'Something about birds don't land in trees, I think… I'm not sure. Or was it, *some* birds don't land in trees? Yes, that might be it.'

They both remained silent for a while. Then Zelda asked, 'Is it daylight outside yet?'

Rasci turned his head to the mouth of the cave. The air above the rocks outside was already beginning to shimmer as the sun heated them. 'Bright and sunny. Why? Do you fancy a walk?'

'Good idea,' Zelda said encouragingly. 'And while we're at it, you can call for the rest of the pack again. I think there is something we all need to discuss.'

'That's what I thought. But what?'

'I'm as much in the dark as you are Rasci.'

'More really.'

'Huh. Watch your lip.'

CHAPTER FOURTEEN

It was late on in the day when Rasci heard from Silvah again. She sounded no closer than she had been the previous evening, and her voice seemed different somehow. Natan and his group, who had been further away in the morning, arrived back at the Darin, in the middle of the night, tired and thirsty, but they still greeted Rasci in the normal way. But there was still no sign of Silvah by morning.

The dappled early morning sunlight speckled their coats with sovereigns of gold as it broke through the leafy branches of a nearby scrub thorn bush. Natan padded over to Rasci, who was sitting in the shadow by the base of the podium rock. He, too, seemed concerned. 'Where is everybody?' he asked Rasci. 'Where's Rhamin?'

Rasci shrugged. 'I don't know, young wolf,' replied Rasci, anxiously. 'But I'm worried. Did any of you hear him calling?'

Natan shook his head. 'We called for him, but only Silvah replied.'

'I still don't understand,' said Rasci. 'He was closest to the Darin when I last heard from him. He was with Silvah, Lexa, Ramusan, Yeltsa and the cubs.'

'Then they are probably still all together,' Natan suggested.

But it didn't allay Rasci's fears. He got more and more irritable as he waited for them. Eventually, however, to Rasci's sheer relief, he heard Silvah call again, only this time, she was telling him she was coming home.

It took another twelve hours before Silvah finally appeared from a cloud of dust, loping out of the red disk that was settling on the horizon behind her. As she came towards the Darin, they saw that she was with two other wolves and the three cubs from this year's litter. Lexa was there and so was Ramusan, but Rhamin and his mate Yeltsa were missing.

Silvah didn't say anything at first. Her group were also tired and thirsty. None spoke, and they omitted any of the usual greetings. Natan managed to get a cursory lick on the chin from Silvah as she and the others with her shook the dust off their coats before they passed through into the cave. All took their time taking on water. They packed the cubs into their small den inside the cave and made sure they were settled. Then, sombrely, they returned to the gathering place at the base of the rock by the mouth of the cave. All three were visibly distressed. The rest of the wolves watched them and waited, no one speaking until Silvah was ready.

'Rhamin is dead,' she said in a matter of fact tone, a tone that only a battle worn soldier would use when her comrade had been killed. There was no emotion, no tears; just anger and fatigue.

Everyone gasped.

'Dead! But how?' asked Natan.

'Men!'

'Men?' he parroted.

'That's what I said.' She shook her head as she tried to come to terms with the thought of her beloved Rhamin being no more. From the time his mother had been killed, when he was a small pup, she had looked after him. She hadn't given birth to him but she felt he was her son.

'How?' Rasci was speaking now. He hadn't foreseen this.

Silvah curled her lips back. Rage was her only emotion. 'The one we saved!' she snarled, then broke down and sobbed uncontrollably.

A stunned silence cloaked the pack. Others joined in, crying, howling; wearing their grief openly. No one spoke until, eventually, Silvah lifted her head, sniffled loudly and said, 'We have no leader now. Until we do, we cannot do anything to avenge the death of Rhamin and Yeltsa. We must act soon.'

'Revenge is not the answer,' stated Zelda. Her sightless eyes, too, had been weeping. 'Why, oh why did I not see this?' she chuntered, half to herself, half to her comrades.

'But I didn't see this either,' consoled Rasci. 'I was seeing all sorts of things, but I didn't see this!'

'Perhaps you weren't meant to,' Silvah stated in response. 'It could be that fate's intention had already been designed.'

'Possibly,' Zelda grunted. 'I know what you mean. Sometimes, when nothing can be done to change the future, then even I cannot get an inkling of what is going to happen. But I think we had better hear what happened before we draw any conclusions.'

Silvah looked at Lexa and Ramusan. 'We were all out on the plain,' Lexa began. 'We weren't hunting, just travelling along, letting the cubs play fight, you know, just being happy.'

'And then we heard it,' Ramusan came in. 'At first we only heard a faint drumming sound, far away. Then, as it got louder, Rhamin said: '"It's one of those men's flying machines. They are like mechanical birds. It's nothing to worry about. I've seen them lots of times before. Men use them for travelling."'

Rasci nodded. 'We heard it,' he confirmed.

'It flew past us several times,' Lexa said. 'It flew down low and I could hear the men shouting over the noise of its beating wings. They were pointing at us.'

'Pointing? What with,' asked Rasci.

'Just their paws at first,' said Ramusan. They were pointing at Rhamin and then they saw Lexa and started pointing at her.'

'And then What?' Rasci was shocked. 'Carry on,' he ordered, eager to determine the reason behind the attack.

'And then, they started pointing their long weapons at us,' Lexa stated.

'Just one weapon,' Silvah corrected. 'But when Rhamin saw it, he told us all to run. He told us to head for the trees. He said that this kind of bird could not land in the trees and it would eventually have to leave because, if it landed there, it would break its wings.'

'So we ran.' Lexa took up the story. 'But however hard we ran, there was no way to shake off the bird. And the trees seemed so far away. Eventually, Rhamin told us to split up. The cubs were too big to carry so Ramusan and I went with them and Silvah stayed with Rhamin and Yeltsa.'

'And the bird followed Rhamin,' Silvah continued. 'I was with him. It was as if the man was aiming his weapon at Rhamin all the time. He didn't seem to be concerned with any of us; only Rhamin.

'Then, as we ran for our lives, we heard the noise from the weapon. It cracked like the sound made by snapping a dry twig, and nothing happened at first. But as we ran, Rhamin began to breathe heavily. He slowed down so much that Yeltsa and I had to turn back to urge him on. But as we got close to him, Rhamin went down. There was nothing we could do. We both turned around again and ran for our lives. Yeltsa veered off to the right and I went left. Neither of us looked back. I heard another shot as I reached the cover of the trees. I didn't know they had killed Yeltsa at that time. When I looked around, she was nowhere to be seen. I thought she might have escaped. From the edge of the woods, I watched as the giant bird landed, throwing up clouds of dust as it came down to earth. Then, all I could see was the men heading into the trees on foot. But soon my worst fears were confirmed; they came out carrying Yeltsa. They lifted her into the bird and I watched hoping they had not killed Rhamin, but then they took off again and landed further away. I presume they were collecting Rhamin's body because, as soon as they had done what they were doing, the bird took off again towards the east and I never saw it or our wolves again. We searched for hours, but found nothing. No trace of Rhamin or Yeltsa.'

Already, darkness had cloaked the rocky escarpment. A thin moon shone on the rocks, casting long shadows that meandered along the ground and disappeared into the darkness. It was a good night for hunting game, but no wolf felt like hunting this night.

By morning, the sense of despair within all the wolves had turned to anger. None had slept well; Lexa and Silvah not at all. The others slept off their fatigue fitfully, stirring and strolling about until, finally, wearily, they dropped down on the ground and tried to continue their troubled sleep.

It was a cool cloudy start to the day. The rain clouds were piling up in the west, and although motionless, they had secretly crept a little closer every time Silvah lifted her head and looked towards them. As the senior member of the pack, she took charge of convening a meeting. It wasn't difficult. All the wolves present were expecting it anyway. Despite some of the pack being absent, leadership had to be resolved.

When all the wolves were assembled, Silvah lost no time explaining that the pack had to have a new leader. 'I know some of us are still missing,' she began. 'But of those, Powla, Rowan and Charka are females and Fatz is only a yearling. I know I am the most senior wolf here except for Zelda. But the pack leader will inevitably be a male, and we have to have that leader before we can go any further.'

Of those present, Bamar was still limping badly from his injuries last year. He had fought with the bears and showed his courage, but he was not prepared to challenge any of his comrades. 'I propose that either Natan or Rasci take the leadership,' he said. 'I know the newcomers, Vela and Goma are tough, but I would ask them to respect our predicament. We need a leader that is no stranger to the pack.'

'I'm all right with that,' Vela replied straight away. He was still only two years old and, although he was a lean, fit and tough male wolf, he was in no hurry to take on a leadership with little experience.

'I'm no stranger to the pack.' The voice came from behind the circle of wolves. Instantly, all eyes turned towards it.

'Solin!' gasped Vela. 'I thought you were…'

'Dead?' Solin grinned. 'Indeed, so did I! But alas, Rhamin was too soft for his own good.'

'What would you know about this matter?' Zelda

demanded. 'Why are you here?'

'Well, I heard you had lost your leader.' Solin smirked.

They all looked at him. He seemed to be a shadow of his former self. He wasn't noticeably thinner, but his grey coat exhibited a dullness that was not just caused by dust. But what made the rest of the wolves stare, was his ears. They were torn to ribbons and hung in tatters by the side of his face. 'I know,' he said, amused by their looks, 'You're thinking I look like that dog.' He looked straight at Lexa.

'My ears might be floppy, but they are not torn to pieces,' retorted Lexa with a snarl. 'Obviously Rhamin had a sense of humour.' She stood up and faced Solin toe to toe.

'I might be able to help you with that,' Solin responded.

'I would like you to try.' Lexa curled her lips back and barred her razor sharp teeth.

Solin casually turned his head away. 'Do any of you really think you are a match for me?'

'You over estimate yourself,' Lexa said without hesitating. 'If I don't defeat you, then I am sure someone in this pack will. None of us will be led by you. We would all prefer to die first.'

'That's your problem. You are all too soft for your own good. That's the mark of your lost leader. His ways have dulled all your instincts. It's made you all soft. He was soft. Strong, yes; tough, no doubt about it. But he was too soft on the inside. If I had beaten him, do you think I would have spared him?'

'There was never any chance of that,' Natan came in. 'You were and still are a runt compared with Rhamin.'

'Well, well! The new heir apparent, I take it?' Solin stepped over to Natan. The young wolf stood his ground.

'The leader of the pack is expected to have a mate,'

Rasci put in. 'Do you seriously think there is any female here that wants to even look at you? Have you seen your face in the water lately?'

'Indeed I have, Rasci. And since you and I are brothers of the same age, then perhaps you are my challenger?'

'Same father, different mother,' Rasci corrected. I inherited the good from Anval as did Rhamin. Unfortunately, you seem to have taken your mother's side; the bad blood.'

Solin shuddered but checked his anger. He grinned, his teeth pointed and as sharp as Rasci had ever seen them. 'Oh yes, I was forgetting my father had a bit on the side. What was her name?'

'Father obviously didn't need a vicious bitch like your mother to keep him company.'

'My, my!' The worm has popped its head up from its hole!' Solin gesticulated. 'The clown has lost his sense of humour. Now that could be dangerous!' he said mockingly.

'But not for me,' Rasci stated, undeterred by the menacing behaviour of his half brother. 'I might have a sense of humour, but I am not a fool. You are not taking charge of my pack and I suggest you leave before I do what Rhamin should have done. And believe me, I will not just leave you with a damaged pride.'

'What are you saying, idiot one? Are you trying to tell me that we might all split our sides and die laughing?'

'One thing for sure, you will die sooner than you think.'

Silvah had never before seen this side to Rasci. He was the clown of the pack. But although he was not as big as Rhamin, he was as big if not bigger than any of the other wolves. It seemed that because he had always behaved like a jester, none of the wolves had really noticed his physique.

Solin looked around at the others and then swung his gaze

back to Rasci. 'So who would take you as a mate?' he asked, mischievously. He looked at some of the females present. 'Who would like idiots for babies?'

Rasci barred his teeth. 'You have two choices, Solin. Fight or leave.'

Solin shrugged. With a look of resignation and a dismissive shake of the head, he turned to leave. Rasci didn't see the slick smile on his face. Suddenly and without warning, Solin spun around and, with mouth wide and teeth barred, he lunged at Rasci. Rasci had been half expecting a challenge, but even Solin's action caught him off guard. As he parried the attack the best he could, turning his head and neck away from the onslaught, the aggressor's teeth sunk into the thick coat of guard hairs on his shoulder. But that left Rasci's head and neck free to swivel around and bring his jaws level with Solin's neck. Solin was fast to realise he had missed his target. Yanking his clenched teeth free with a mouthful of guard hairs, he spun around and landed on all fours, spitting fur. He was free and stable ready to make another attack, but he hadn't expected Rasci to come back at him. He had expected the fear of combat to make Rasci fight a defensive battle. That way he would be able to attack again and again until he eventually got the right hold to defeat his opponent. But Rasci showed not the slightest particle of fear. The joker was transformed. He was a wild and aggressive animal; and he was determined to win. He went at Solin with everything he had, all his skill, all his strength, and most of all, all his determination. And so the fight continued, on and on, attack and counter as both wolves tried to gain an advantage, watched by all, but interrupted by none.

Many creatures fight when they are afraid. And many

win despite their trepidation. But fear weakens their resolve when faced with a strong opponent. And since many battles are won or lost purely on the mental attitude of the combatant, confidence is an extra weapon that strengthens the will and sharpens reactions. Solin saw that Rasci had that weapon and, realising now that Rasci was no more the fool, he made a desperate lunge at his opponent's head. Once again, Rasci reacted quickly and instinctively and bounced backwards to avoid the attack. Then, as Rasci adjusted his balance, as suddenly as he had started the fight, Solin turned away, casually it appeared to Rasci. 'Just testing,' he said, grinning, as he strode away, head turned to ensure Rasci wasn't retaliating with another attack.

'Wait!' Rasci's voice was loud and determined. 'Don't think you can walk out as easily as you walked in here.'

Solin turned back to face him. 'Neither of us has won, Rasci. Let's leave it at that, shall we?'

'Remember that you are an outsider now. You are not challenging for leadership from within the pack. You are a trespasser in Rhamin territory. If you don't want me to order the rest of the pack to join me to finish you off, you'll tell me how you know about Rhamin.'

Solin's grin widened. 'You're not the only wolf that has spies.' With that, and with large droplets of rain beginning to fall from the sky and exploding in the dust, he turned and sidled out of the camp, broke into a trot and loped casually into the distance, ribbons that were once his ears, flapping in the rain as he bounded away.

'Well done my young cub!' Zelda shouted at the top of her voice as she got to her feet and wagged her tail triumphantly. 'Well done my lovely!'

'All right, Gran. I'm trying to look tough here.'

Silvah laughed. 'You are tough, Rasci. You are a deserving leader. I'm with you Rasci.' She looked at the rest of the assembly. Some showed amazement, but most showed pride.

'I think I can speak for us all here,' Natan said, happily. 'We will be proud to have Rasci lead us.'

'Er… I was only joking. I just didn't want that prairie rat poking his nose in.' Rasci looked around at the pack. As the rain began to attack with blasts of blustery, wind propelled droplets he turned to the cave. 'Honest!'

CHAPTER FIFTEEN

'What are we to do about these men?' Natan asked Rasci after they had all retreated to the shelter of the cave. The sky had gone darker than the night as the rocks outside were lashed by squally rain. 'They have killed wolves for no reason. What are we going to do about it?' His mood was as black as the weather.

Rasci shook his head. 'Honestly Natan, I really don't know. I'm going to have to think about it.'

'But they've already killed Rhamin and Yeltsa. None of us are going to be safe. We must do something to stop them attacking us again.'

Rasci's face was grave. 'One thing I do know,' he said, pacing the dry rock floor, 'is that we can never win a battle against men.'

'But we must do something.'

'Rhamin taught all of us one important rule. Wolves have to live and exist alongside men, whatever they do. Over the years, we have had to adapt to whatever men do. But men do not have to live alongside wolves. Do you remember the story of what happened to Rhamin when he was a cub? I was lucky. I wasn't born until the following year, but when

Rhamin was a young cub, men hunted down and killed his mother as well as two other wolves. It was Silvah who saved Rhamin that day. But the wolf pack could do nothing to retaliate. They all had to accept the fact that the men had hunted and killed some of the pack. They had to accept it and just get on with their lives.'

'So we just let them kill us, do we?' Natan asked bitterly.

Rasci shrugged. 'That's the way of the world, I'm afraid. Everything is hunted by something. We have few real predators, but men are one of them.'

'But we fought back against the bears. Why can we not fight back against the men?'

Rasci sighed. 'Look, Natan, men do not hunt like we do. They don't hunt just for food. They kill other creatures just for fun. They even kill their own kind just for fun, Zelda will tell you that. That's how she first came upon men.'

'That's true,' Zelda said from somewhere in the darkness.

'Rhamin taught us that we have to show men that we are no threat to them,' Rasci continued. 'That's why he stopped Solin from killing the farmer's children. That's why we all helped to save the farmer from the bears. And by helping the farmer and his friend, Rhamin saved us from his wrath.'

'That's not exactly true,' Lexa, argued. 'It was one of the men we saved that was in the mechanical bird. I know; I saw him. They were chasing us and, as I glanced up, he was pointing at me. I thought I had seen my last rabbit. I'm not kidding; I was scared stupid.'

'But why would he do that?'

'I really don't know, but it was him, I swear!'

'Have men kind got no sense of honour?' Natan asked, shaking his head in disbelief. He slumped dejectedly onto the hard rock floor.

'Some of them, apparently not,' Ramusan remarked. 'But it wasn't the farmer. I'm sure, it was the other one. On the mountain, the farmer stopped him killing Rhamin. I saw him push the other man's weapon aside. It made the invisible claw miss Rhamin. It passed harmlessly through the branches above our heads, remember?'

'I know.' said Rasci, contemplating the situation. 'I know the farmer is a good man.' He thought again, recalling his dream and the farmer's reaction to the mechanical bird. He was some time forming his words in his mind. 'And besides that,' he said eventually, 'I know the farmer never left his home.' He knew the others would wonder how he knew that. The statement was going to require an explanation. Many of the pack were used to Zelda and her predictions. But he knew that some of the pack, especially the newcomers from the north, would think that dreams were something that should remain firmly lodged in your sleep. 'He is still crippled after the bear attack,' Rasci added quickly.

'But that doesn't mean anything,' argued Natan.

Rasci gave out more information that would take a lot of explaining. 'He was sleeping on his veranda when the metal bird passed over his home. It woke him with a shock and he was very angry.'

'Oh, was he? And just how do you know that? Were you there? Did you see it?' asked Ramusan sceptically.

'In a way, he was there, Ramusan,' Zelda remarked, coming to Rasci's aid. She nodded. 'Yes, in a way he was there.'

Rasci wanted to avoid the questions. What he needed now was time; time to think; time for the pack to cool off; time to work out what to do. Somehow he just felt that there was something he could do, but about what, he had no idea. At this very moment in time he felt like a stone that was rolling down a mountain. He couldn't say where he was going or where he would end up. He was in a free fall situation. He was being carried along by a sequence of events, and only time would bring him to his final destination along with the answers.

Outside, the initial flurry of rain had abated to a calmer steady but persistent downpour. They all made their way back outside.

Without the gusty, squally winds that head up the front belt of a storm, hunting would be easier. Rasci saw this as an opportunity to take the pack members' minds off the loss of Rhamin. Despite anything he said they were all looking to him for leadership. 'I think it best if we all go out and find some food. When we've eaten then we should sleep.' Realising they were all still waiting for his command, he said, 'I will let you all know what we shall do when I know the answer myself.'

'I wonder if what Solin said was true,' Rasci remarked to Zelda, as they rested. The rains had slackened off a little. An elderly buffalo had provided them with a good meal and they were doing what all wolves do after a heavy meal. Some wolves slept, others rested; others, to keep their minds off the previous day's events, played with sticks and small rocks, tossing them away and chasing after them. They were all a little more reassured than the previous night, but they were still restless. As things stood, they didn't know what the man's intention was. They didn't know if they were to be hunted down like Rhamin and his mate, and they didn't know what to do to stop the man if that were the case. Neither did they know how to avenge the missing members of their family. For most of the wolves, it was good to have a new leader; someone to rely upon; someone to make the decisions; someone who could come up with the answers to their questions. But Rasci had no answers.

'You mean about the spies?' said Zelda. 'Oh yes, I think so. After all, there are lots of birds in the sky.'

'But it couldn't be Corvak, surely.' Rasci frowned.

'No, it would not be our old friend the raven; that I do know.' Zelda put her paw comfortingly on Rasci's. 'Now is not the time to doubt your friends, young wolf. Corvak and his family are as much behind you as we are. Just because he has not visited you lately, doesn't mean he has abandoned you.'

A short distance away, resting by the water hole, Silvah lifted her head. 'Corvak knows,' she called to Rasci. 'He was with us when the mechanical bird came over. He left for safety. The wings of that bird would kill any creature that gets in the way. But he didn't return whilst I was there. I hunted for hours and travelled miles to try and trace Rhamin but during that time Corvak never returned.' She sighed sadly. 'Rhamin's gone. Gone for ever,' she added in a whisper. Then raising her voice she added, 'But Corvak will return; I know that much.'

With that, Rasci felt a little easier.

'I wonder why Solin hated Rhamin so much,' Rasci said as he settled down for the night.

Zelda grunted. She gave a big sigh and rested her chin on her paws. 'Sibling rivalry,' she said eventually.

Rasci lifted his head and looked at her. Her eyes were closed and she was speaking as if having a vision. But she was just recalling the past.

'You were all siblings,' she continued. 'You and Solin were

born the year after Rhamin, but you and Solin were from different mothers. When your father, Anval, lost his mate that day when Rhamin was saved by Silvah, it was as if he had lost a part of himself. He was still the leader of the pack, but until he took another mate, he seemed to lose interest in leadership. It was Solin's mother, Rhiana who brought his will back. But she was an ambitious and determined mate, and with that determination, came a certain anger and ruthlessness. She never tolerated any other wolves, male or female near her den. Anval was lucky to hold the pack together. But, by showing kindness and consideration, the rest of the pack remained loyal to him despite Rhiana. And despite Rhiana, he had a bit of a fling with Celion, a young female who had comforted him when he was at his lowest ebb. She was a kind creature. She gave birth to you and three other pups the same year that Solin was born, but died shortly after. Something burst inside her and she bled to death. But you were the only one of Celion's pups to survive. Rhiana had asked Anval to fetch her some food and, while he was out of the away, she killed three of the pups. She would have killed Celion, only the other senior wolves in the pack, especially Silvah and Seth, gathered around her and saved her. You were snuggled beneath your mother. Rhiana never saw you. But by the time Anval returned, Celion had already passed away. He was very sad. He seemed to give up somehow. He was killed soon after that. It was just sheer carelessness. He didn't care about himself any more.

'But, although he wasn't himself, while he was still around he insisted that Silvah and I reared you. You have no idea how difficult that was.' She stopped and thought for a moment. 'You know, you never left our sides. One lapse in concentration and that bitch, Rhiana, would have killed you!'

'So Solin was brought up to hate me then?'

'Not so much that,' Zelda replied. 'but Solin was brought up by Rhiana as the next in line to take over as leader. Then, Anval' was badly wounded. He later died from his injuries but, when he passed away, there was no leadership contest. Rhiana was a vicious and dominating wolf and she asserted her position. She wasn't going to be demoted just because her mate had died. In fact, Anval's death seemed to release an even more dominant streak in her. Without Anval around she had absolute power and was not prepared to relinquish any of it. She took over leadership on her own. She didn't take another mate and her plan was to raise her son as the leader. That's all she seemed to live for. And she kept to it as well. She kept Solin and his three litter siblings, close to her. It was hell, I can tell you!'

'So what changed?'

'It was Rhamin. He was less than two years old, but he was big. Soon, he was big enough and strong enough to challenge her. He made Rhiana stand down and, despite his inexperience, the pack welcomed his taking over as leader. He was very popular with them. He was already so much bigger and stronger than any wolf by that time.

'But the move dismayed Solin. He was racked with jealousy. He had always been jealous of Rhamin, but now, still only a year old, and unable to defeat him, he became rebellious. He always had something to criticise or complain about.'

'So why didn't he leave when Rhiana did?'

'Because he had a dream. His mother had instilled it into him from the day he opened his eyes. And because, despite himself, his big brother still loved him. Rhamin spent a lot of time with you and Solin, but he was never together with you both at the same time. Rhiana saw to that.' She paused to think. 'It was like he had two separate lives with two separate families while Rhiana was the leader. But it didn't seem to bother Rhamin. Even when he was a year old, when you were born, he was too big for anybody to stop him doing what he liked. Rhiana became wary of attacking him. And, after he deposed her as leader, she just up and left the pack with the other three cubs. Nobody knows where she went. She just left on a hunting trip and we never saw her again.' She thought again and shrugged. 'There were rumours.'

'Rumours?' asked Rasci.

'Yes, there were a few stories going around. One was that they had been killed by a mountain lion.' She paused again and gazed sightlessly at the sky. 'Perhaps they are still alive, who knows? We never heard anything about them after that.'

As the darkness drew in, Rasci settled down to another night of fitful sleep. At first he couldn't clear his mind at all. Try as he may, sleep slipped away each time he began to capture it. Something was preying on his mind; something had to be done. But what? If he knew that, then he'd know how to do it. He began to question his motives for taking over the leadership. Why had he done it? Until Solin had appeared, he had had no intention of taking control. Young Natan would have been his first choice. But then, Natan would not have been able to stand up against Solin as he had. Rasci knew that. Damn Solin! All Rasci wanted was a quiet life. He wanted to hunt and play and act the fool. That was his way; it always had been. Now it was all changing. He had always felt free. Now he felt trapped in another life, one that was totally alien to him. Now he was making decisions for himself; making decisions for the others; being responsible for their safety. Where would it all end?

Weary with thought, he sighed. Before he could sleep he had to stop his mind from galloping from one thought to another. To do that, he had to make a decision. And this was it: In the morning he was going to resign his leadership. Suddenly he felt much better. A heavy rock lifted from his soul. So now he could relax. He fell into the sleep of the drained and weary.

All sleep is interspersed with dreams. It is a time when the mind recalls events, formulates ideas, processes data. Dreaming is essential for animals and humans alike. It is a period marked by rapid eye movement. And more often than not the body moves and jerks about as well. It wasn't long before Rasci began to dream. Old Zelda couldn't see him, but she sat nearby; near enough to feel the twitching and the jerking and to hear the whimpers and the woofs. She knew Rasci was solving a problem in some way, so she didn't wake him.

'Damn' the man had said. 'Why in hell did you do that, Raymond?'

The men on the mountain were the first images that came into Rasci's dream. He was right there, beside them, watching, listening to them, but they looked straight through him. At the same time, as he watched the scene, like in any dream he could see himself down the slope behind Rhamin, watching what was happening from the cover of the heavy leaf laden branches of a tree. He'd watched as the farmer pushed the other man's gun up in the air when he shot at Rhamin. It had provoked an angry response from his friend and now the farmer was explaining why he had stopped him killing the black wolf. Once again, in his vision, the words were clear to Rasci.

'I know that black wolf, the one with white ears,' said the farmer 'He saved my family from an attack by another wolf.'

'That seems a bit far fetched to me. Just look at him. What a magnificent trophy!'

'I don't do trophies,' Raymond replied brashly. 'I do guided tracking for deer hunters like you, Petersen. I don't shoot all the wild life willy-nilly.'

Something was going through Petersen's mind. Rasci suddenly saw a vision of a dead bear. It had been killed with what the men called a gun and it was being skinned, and then he saw its skin had been filled to make it look alive again. It was standing motionless in the front passage leading to a room in the home of the man. Petersen had put it there to look at and admire. It was there for his friends to see. Rasci understood now what the man meant by a trophy.

His mind flicked back to the mountain.

'But nobody will believe me when I tell them about the size of this animal!' Petersen exclaimed. He shook his head. 'Raymond Rozalski, I'm really disappointed in you.'

'Be that as it may, these wolves deserve a life as much as we do.' And then, the farmer smiled. Not at the companion. It was a smile aimed directly at Rhamin. The farmer said something to the black wolf, but it made no sense to Rhamin at all, and then the farmer gave him a wave of acknowledgement; a wave that Rhamin did understand. Rhamin lifted his head slightly as if to let the farmer know that he had understood. There was a long silence as both looked into each other's eyes. Then, still held in the farmer's gaze, Rhamin turned slowly and hopped down from the ledge into the cover of the dark undergrowth.

Raymond looked down at his own gun that lay on the rocks beside him. Giving out a big sigh, he went on, 'I did shoot a couple of wolves last year,' he confessed. 'But that black wolf was with them. I didn't know it at the time, but I know now that he wouldn't attack a human being, man or child, even if he were starving. I know that for a fact because he and his pack *were* starving. The wolves I shot were thinner than I had seen an animal for a long time. They were just looking for food. When they started worrying my sheep, I just reacted automatically and started shooting.'

'But there are plenty of them about Ray! You shouldn't beat yourself up over a couple of dead wolves for goodness sake!'

'There are plenty of humans about, but it doesn't give us a right to shoot them for pleasure. We kill deer for the meat. *You* hang stuffed animals on a wall!'

'I didn't mean it that way. What I mean is, dead is dead. You can't undo what's already been done.'

'I know, but it's not that. It's because that black wolf stopped one of the pack killing my kids. All right, it stole one of Smokey's puppies, but I think he only did that to divert attention. I really do! He's a clever one that black wolf, mark my words.'

'Too clever,' Rasci thought he heard the man say under his breath, but he wasn't sure. The look in the man's eyes made Rasci give a sudden shudder in his sleep. With that, the picture that had appeared so real started to dissolve away like all dreams do.

Zelda just watched as Rasci stirred and turned in his sleep. She knew not to wake him, and after a long while, he stopped twitching, fell back into a deeper sleep, and dreamt no more. She was still awake when he eventually woke.

He felt better for his sleep, but the dream still haunted him. Silvah was already up and about washing herself and making her coat spotless as usual. Eventually, she saw Rasci had awakened and came over and lay beside him and Zelda.

'Are you all right, my young wolf?' she asked, as Rasci stretched.

'I will be,' he replied and went over to the water hole to drink. Having taken his fill he returned to Silvah and Zelda and sat beside them.

'I don't think I'm a leader,' he stated plainly. 'I think I am more suited to being a hanger on.'

Silvah chuckled. 'Yeah! Well that's not the impression you gave us all yesterday, Rasci.'

'But I'm…'

'A clown?'

'Precisely!'

'And a good leader,' said Zelda crossly. She could tell Rasci was having second thoughts.

'That's what I want to talk to you about, Gran. I don't think I can do it.'

'Huh! It's already done!' Silvah said firmly. 'You're the wolf! You are the chosen one. You fought and you won!'

'I wouldn't have fought any of my own pack,' Rasci stated firmly. 'I could never have done that.'

'Rasci, you young dope,' Zelda said, 'You didn't need to. The pack needed a leader and they saw one. They saw you and they're all proud of you. They look up to you. You can't let them down now!'

'But I… I…'

'I, nothing,' Zelda snapped crossly. 'This isn't about you. It isn't about me. It's about the pack. The pack is the pack because it has a good leader. Without that we are all doomed to wander off by ourselves or in little groups. The pack needs you Rasci. And believe me, you need them!'

Rasci sighed. His resolve had just been systematically dismantled piece by piece. 'So what do I do now?' he asked.

'You do what you believe is right for the pack, of course.'

'Right,' he replied as if everything had suddenly become crystal clear.

Some time later that day, whilst the rest of the wolves were away hunting, Rasci, Silvah and Zelda discussed the situation some more. Once again they went over what Rasci had described in his dream.

'If that is right,' Silvah commented, 'then it sounds like that man, Petersen, intended to kill Rhamin from the very moment he saw him.'

Silvah suggested that it might be a good idea if they met regularly to discuss the situation. They were keen to offer their willing ears if he was prepared to discuss his thoughts and dreams with them. But Rasci was still troubled. It still worried him that the other wolves might think he was still acting the fool. Dreams were not reality. But Silvah and Zelda promised to keep everything they discussed, secret. No other wolf need ever know that what he was doing was directly as a result of things he was seeing in his mind.

But Rasci still wasn't settled. There was something bothering him, preying on his mind. There was something he should be doing, but whatever that was, he was unable to pluck it from the air and form it into a firm proposal. Somewhere, an idea or thought was trapped and couldn't get out. That thought or message needed processing. It was there, tickling and turning, trapped in the depths of his mind. He just hoped that he could discover what it was before it was too late.

CHAPTER SIXTEEN

Just thinking about leading the pack, gave Rasci a head ache. He was used to being alone much of the time and it had always given him time to think and day dream, without the pressures of following the hunting pack. But being alone was even more essential now. If he was to come up with any answers to the problem that he believed existed, he was going to have to use all his resources to find out what the problem was in the first place.

It was fortunate in some respects that the pack knew Rasci so well. The next few days seemed like any other, with wolves wandering off alone or in small groups, hunting, playing, keeping themselves occupied. They didn't ask Rasci for anything, and they didn't do anything out of the ordinary.

Except worry. They all worried.

But they kept it to themselves. Fear of being caught out in the open made the wolves spend most of their time hunting at night or, if hunting during daylight, they confined themselves to the forest. Whilst crossing the plain, they would be continually listening for the subsonic noise of the beating rotors and looking up into the air for the hidden and deadly danger that they feared would swoop down and continue the killing. At any time the metal bird could reappear, and at any time the man could point at any one of them again, only the next time he would not be distracted by the black wolf. They had seen what the man's weapon could do and he would keep pointing at them and then kill them.

Each day Rasci returned to the Darin with no further idea of what to do. He had hoped that the answer to all his problems would come to him in his dreams, but his dreams were the usual dreams of wolves. Some of them were about Rhamin and Yeltsa; some were about the farmer hunting on the mountain with his companion; some were totally incoherent with strange wolves and big cats; and some of the dreams disturbed him deeply, but still he couldn't fathom any of them out. The more he thought about it all, the deeper the fog became that engulfed his thoughts. There was no clarity, no solution, no idea what it was that was eating away at him, day after day, night after night.

Zelda had been concentrating on the events that had happened, thinking about them, just like Rasci. But she was old, and she did not have the worry of having just inherited the title of pack leader. She could relax more than Rasci, and when she thought of Rhamin, in her mind she saw him as if he were still alive. Several days passed before she discussed this with the young leader, for she too was confused. She had no idea why she thought that Rhamin might have survived, but she felt it, and seeing Rasci's deep concern, she decided to tell him what she had been feeling.

Gradually, Rasci began to piece bits of his muddled thoughts together, and somehow, some of those pieces formed the same thought as Zelda's. Rhamin might have survived. Neither he nor Zelda could explain why they thought this, nor was there any solution springing forward that would answer the question for sure. Was Rhamin still alive? They just didn't know. But one thing for sure, this must have been the question that had long been lodged deep in some fissure in Rasci's mind, for suddenly he had given up seeking the problem and all he needed now was the answer.

Perhaps this was the turning point that made him relax. He used to always relax, and enjoy life. He enjoyed being part of the pack with his companions, but also he enjoyed being alone. It was a kind of freedom. For a while, it had all seemed to have been snatched away from him. Now that he was relaxing again, he could, even though he didn't know it, begin to work things out. That night, he slept well.

Raymond Rozalski was a hard worker. His leg was almost completely healed now, and he had discarded the crutch that made him feel like an old man. Now he was itching to get back to work on the farm, which had been neglected somewhat, despite the efforts of his wife and the hired man who had worked none stop to keep things running smoothly. The farm was a huge sprawling enclosure that bordered on a region of scrub land to the west and nestled against the leading edge of several other larger and more productive farming ranges that lead up to and bordered the high snow peaked mountains a hundred miles or so to the east. The income from the farm was supplemented in the spring by taking clients hunting in the forests that sprawled along the foothills and up to the mountains in the north. This spring, Petersen had been his last client. The attack by the bears had seen to that. Since then, Raymond had been recovering from his wounds. The little money he had earned from taking

Petersen hunting would soon be spent and now he had to sell some cattle in order for his family to buy the essentials of modern living.

He was up early in the morning. With the hired worker and his wife, they gathered six well fattened cattle together in a small pen inside the yard. He hitched a cattle trailer to the station wagon and together the three of them loaded the livestock. By seven thirty, with Ben for company, he was on his way to the cattle market, in town, eleven miles away.

The town would not stand up to that description in most parts of the world. There were white, timber board houses and a small, grey, timber framed building that doubled as school house and a dance hall, a general store and a bar that was combined with a café for hunters coming up north in the hunting season. There was a church with a modestly peaked roof, topped by a large white cross and a cattle market that was a large wooden railed corral with a small wooden stand under a three sided hut that served as an auctioneer's podium. Cattle sales were held at monthly intervals except during the winter and, somehow, it attracted buyers from hundreds of miles away. Huge articulated lorries with cattle trailers, filed in and out of the town from the day before the sale, until the day after the last lot was sold. Beyond the town, towards the cities and beyond, thousand acre arable farms ranged toward an even bigger arable area which seemed to have little in the way of definitive borders. To birds like Corvak and from the men's metal flying machine, just as the city looked like an endless forest of grey tall rock built structures towering into the sky, the arable areas looked like a sea of flat green endless landscape, rippling in the wind like waves on a lake. And, as the crops grew, just like the water in the lakes, the rippling waves turned the area to a moving, living organism, inhabited by submerged wildlife.

To Raymond Rozalski, the town was a place to meet old friends and catch up on the news. The general store advertised his services as a tracker and guide, and it was through such an advertisement that he had met and hunted with Petersen. The store keeper had a young daughter called May who was about the same age as Ben, and after the sale Raymond left Ben to play with her. They had played together on previous visits and were good company for each other. Ben would soon be joining May at the school. He knew his son would be safe with her and, giving Ben a little wave, he limped over to the bar.

Ben talked to May almost none stop for at least ten minutes. He wasn't used to having a playmate of his own age. Little Margo was still a little small to play with. She was still under the strict supervision of her mother. Margo knew right from wrong in terms of children versus mother, but she still chose the 'wrong' most of the time. And after all, she was only four years old, so, while he could, Ben enjoyed May's company. Even though she was a girl they had plenty to talk about. Ben explained that he played with Smokey a lot. Smokey wasn't just a dog, she was his friend. He asked if May had a dog. She said she hadn't. Ben explained that he also had another friend, or so he thought. This friend was hard to describe and he wondered if he should be telling anybody. But May seemed very interested, so he told her about his ghostly wolf friend. This friend was like a shadow. The first time he saw it, he couldn't be sure what it was, but every time he saw it, the spirit form became a little clearer, and now he was sure it was a wolf. The ghostly shadow watched him and Smokey when they were playing in the fields, or in the garden. It wasn't always there, but today he had seen it. Once again it was watching him. He asked May if she could see it. Wide eyed, she shook her head, making her pigtails swing wildly. She thought that perhaps she, too, could invent an imaginary friend for when she was lonely.

During the sale, several acquaintances had spoken to Raymond, all smiling as if they knew a secret. 'Good to see you've recovered,' and 'Sorry to hear about the bear attack,' and 'Are you well now?' were all things said by people, some who he hardly knew apart from the nod of visual recognition he usually gave and received. It gave him a nice feeling that he was better known than he had thought and, after the sale, many of the cattle sellers were eager to talk to him. There was no shortage of people offering to buy him a drink, and he accepted one gracefully and settled on a bar stool. It was a dusty day and a beer would just wet his throat before driving back to the farm.

Word had spread about his exploits. Not just that, but for some reason, there was a tale going around that he had helped the millionaire's son capture the giant black wolf; the one with white ears.

'Black wolf?' Raymond asked, perplexed. 'I hunt deer, you all know that.' He removed his hat and wiped his sleeve across his brow. 'We did see a black wolf once, but we didn't hunt for it,' he added.

'Well, Petersen said it was your wolf! He said you had led him to it,' an acquaintance by the name of Jethro Poulson replied, slapping him on the back and chuckling.

'He didn't say that I had taken him out hunting deer then?'

Poulson shook his head and rubbed his stubbly chin with the ends of his chunky fingers. 'No, he just bragged that you had led him to The Black Wolf. He called it Rozalski's wolf.

He told us that you tracked it for him. Done your reputation no end of good, I should think. You certainly kept that a closed secret, Raymond. Rubbing shoulders with the rich and famous. I bet that earned you a pretty penny!'

Raymond's face hardened. 'So what was he telling you exactly?'

'That you showed him The Black Wolf. He couldn't believe it was so friendly!'

'I showed him the wolf?'

'Yep.'

'He didn't mention anything about it saving his damned life or anything like that then?'

Poulson removed his hat and put it on the bar. He scratched his head. 'Well he did tell us that it had helped you fight off three grizzlies.'

'And?'

'And it's in his father's safari park or something now. Drawing in customers right left and centre, by all accounts. Until he got The Black Wolf, his father had seriously considered selling the whole shebang, animals, parkland and all.'

Raymond just nodded silently as he sipped his beer. It was warming up. He had lost his thirst. The conversation carried on in the background, but he hardly heard a word. Something had struck him hard in the gut; a feeling of defeat, a feeling of betrayal; not just of him but by him. Without another word, and watched by all the men around him, he drank up and left.

Ben was outside, playing with May and a couple of other children that had come into town with their families. His father walked over to him, picked him up in his arms, and gave him a big hug.

'What's the matter, daddy?' asked Ben, seeing his father

had a tear in his eye. He put the palm of his little hand against his father's face.

Raymond sighed. 'Oh, nothing my son.' He squeezed him again. Then he said goodbye to May and carried Ben to the station wagon. He spoke very little on the way home.

Back at the farm, as they got out of the station wagon, Ben thought he saw the shadow in the corner of the yard, the same shadow that had been watching him in the street outside the bar in town. But when he turned his head, the shadow wasn't there.

Rasci woofed and kicked in his sleep. Once again he was dreaming. Zelda was asleep when he woke but Lexa was awake in the corner of the cave, guarding the cubs. He nodded to her in a way that told her she was doing a good job; after a long drink he left without waking the old wolf.

'There has to be an explanation,' Rasci said to himself, as he broke into his usual loping stride. He wondered if his dreams were capturing something real, or were they just comforting him, creating something he longed for? His life wasn't getting any easier. Just as he had established that there was one big question that needed an answer, namely, was Rhamin alive? It had opened a passage to a flood of other questions. He was hoping that Zelda would be able to explain to him what his dreams were about. Why was he dreaming of men? Why was the dream so real that even the language was clear and understandable? How could he watch Ben and his father in two different places at the same time? At least, spending the day alone had helped him identify the questions, but he wondered just how many more there remained to be asked. For the time being, however, all he needed were the answers to the questions he had already formulated, and on his own, he was at least able to think about them without any of the distractions of responsibility.

As the day drew to an end, and the dark clouds from the west began to smother the sky he felt an urgent need to talk to Zelda. He loped on, skirting the edge of the trees that led to the forests and the mountains. Above him two vultures hovered on a thermal, watching, waiting for some sign of death. Rasci looked up at them. There would be no carcass for them today. What little Rasci had caught, he had eaten. Now he had no time to hunt. He was anxious. Feeling angry that the world had suddenly changed and become a complicated place, he needed to get back to the Darin.

But he did stop for a while. Holding his head in the air, he howled. He howled to let those back at the Darin know he was coming. He howled, because if there were vultures about, then his old friend Corvak might be somewhere near. Then, hearing a distant howl from the direction of the Darin, he headed home well before the sun began to set.

Outside the cave, Rasci passed Lexa. She was teaching the cubs how to hunt mice. They greeted each other gladly, then, leaving them play hunting, Rasci, with his mind distracted by other things, strode on towards the cave. Zelda was lying down beside the opening. Silvah had fed her and her sightless eyes were closed. But hearing Rasci approaching, she lifted her head, opened her glazed eyes and woofed. Rasci woofed back, prompting the old wolf to push herself up onto her feet. Her long thin legs seemed to wobble for a moment and then, wagging her tail, she squeaked a delighted greeting to Rasci and trotted unsteadily towards him.

'Zelda has been thinking about you,' Silvah said as she joined them from the back of cave where she had been busy washing herself at the water hole. 'She says that you are troubled.'

'Troubled?' He thought for a moment. 'Yes, you might say that. Troubled with what has happened to Rhamin and Yeltsa; troubled by opening my big mouth and saying I was leading the pack. Yes, troubled is perhaps about right, considering I am not too tired and not too hungry.' He paused again. 'Perhaps it is slightly understating the fact, however,' he suddenly snapped, 'considering that I can't sleep properly; I keep dreaming things that I don't understand; I'm already worried that I am useless as a leader and on top of that, I keep worrying about getting the feeling that I haven't begun to get seriously worried yet.' He calmed himself down a little and thought introspectively. 'But worried about what, I haven't got the faintest idea?' he added quietly, this time, more to himself than to the others.

'I have been feeling things too,' Zelda said reassuringly.

'Oh, well at last!'

'Now don't be cheeky. I'm only trying to help you here.'

'Well I wish you could do all the worrying and foretelling and whatever else we have relied on you for, for the past umpteen years, because, honestly Gran, I don't think I'm cut out for this seeing lark any more than I'm suited to leading a pack.'

'It all depends what you are seeing.'

'Not what you used to say you were seeing, that's for sure. I don't see anything that is going to happen. I see things in my dreams that we have done in the past, only with so much more clarity that I feel I am back there again reliving the experience for the benefit of getting it right this time.'

'That is normal,' Silvah came in. 'Everybody has dreams about things that have already happened. We even have dreams about what we would like to happen.'

'But I also get the feeling that what I see in my dreams at the moment is happening right now, at the very present, and somehow I am there watching. I am not really there, nor have I been there, but my dreams are taking me there. I'm for ever dreaming about that farmer and his young ones. There's no way I could have been there with them. Yet it is as if I can project my mind to another place. I can see the people, I can listen to them, I can walk right up to them without them seeing me, and it matters not one jot where I am.'

'Then you certainly have a gift, my young wolf,' said Zelda.

'A gift? It's a curse Gran. I don't want to be around men and their offspring. I just want to be a wolf.'

'You are a wolf,' came a voice from behind him as two wings paddled at the rapidly darkening night air. 'Mind if I stay the night?'

'Corvak!' Rasci gasped as the bird alighted on a bendy branch of the nearby scrub bush. 'Where have you been?'

'Oh, here and there,' the old raven said dismissively, as he folded his wings and checked for something up the feathers on the front of his chest. All three wolves waited for him to speak again. Eventually, lifting his head, he looked along the line of expectant faces and said, 'What?'

Silvah couldn't mask her delight. She chuckled. 'You just don't get it, do you?'

Corvak looked around as if to see if she was talking to some other bird behind him. Then, swivelling his head back to his wolf friend, he said, 'You haven't missed me have you?'

'Pah!' said Rasci.

Silvah gave Rasci a withering glance. 'Of course we've missed you. For goodness sake, Corvak, we were beginning to think you had died on us or something.'

'Yes,' Rasci nodded. 'We are always concerned about having somebody to clean up the carcasss after us.'

'Died?' Corvak replied to Silvah, ignoring his friend. 'No, no. I've been away.'

'Away?' asked Rasci. 'That's why we haven't seen you then!'

'Let's say having a little break from the daily routine.'

'Break!' exclaimed Rasci. 'Daily routine?' His eyes bored into Corvak. 'Wolves don't take breaks. Daily routine is our life! We hunt, we sleep, we wake up and we hunt again.'

'Or get hunted,' added Corvak. 'You missed that one.'

'That's not routine,' Rasci stated, as he recalled how Silvah had returned without their leader. 'That was a one off.'

'Was it?' Corvak shook his head.

'Well, wasn't it?'

'I think not.'

'What do you mean?' asked Zelda, speaking for all, for none truly understood what the old raven was getting at.

Corvak shook his feathers into a fluffy cushion and settled onto his heels. 'Well, it came to me at first from my two young ones, Crufus and Betrix. They were out exploring for new territory.' Then he added, 'besides scouting for potential partners.'

'And?' asked Rasci impatiently.

'And it seems like hunting wolves from the air is becoming commonplace.' He moved sideways along the flexi branch and resettled on a spot where it was a bit firmer, springing it a little with his weight to test for optimum weight-resistance-to-spring-take-off ratio.

'Go on,' Rasci urged, now suddenly more serious.

'Well,' Corvak replied when he had settled again. 'I saw what happened to Rhamin and Yeltsa. I was there, Silvah, remember?'

Silvah nodded silently.

'And I flew off, if you recall.'

'Yes.'

'And when I saw my youngsters a few days later and told them what had happened to Rhamin, Crufus said he had seen the men's giant bird doing the same thing in the territory of the Pagin Pack.'

Rasci suddenly felt a surge of adrenalin. It was as if he was about to start a chase or get ready to attack. It was a feeling of expectancy as his senses suddenly peaked. There was something in what Corvak had just said that, in his mind, suddenly, somehow, began to form a bigger picture. 'Is... that... so...' he said slowly, and then, 'The Pagin Pack heh?'

'That's right,' Corvak confirmed, 'The Pagin Pack.'

'And just how many of them did the men in the bird kill and take away that time?'

'Kill? Did I say kill?'

'You said "doing the same thing,"' Zelda remarked.

'Right. That's what I thought I'd said. For a moment I thought I had said something else. It's old age you know.'

'Corvak!' Rasci's surge of adrenalin was turning to anger. There was nowhere else to channel it. He needed answers. He needed the fuller picture. He began to tremble a little, impatient to hear Corvak's news. He just wanted him to get on with his report while his mind was in the right frame to analyse it.

'Calm down now Mr. Wolf,' Corvak said, soothingly. The raven seemed to be jesting the jester.

'Just what are you saying here?' Silvah broke in to calm down the mounting tension.

Corvak cleared his throat. 'Well,' he said, 'what I am saying is that the men's big bird has been around a bit. It's been here and it's been there.' He cleared his throat again, this time for effect. 'And it might well have been elsewhere.'

'Elsewhere?' the three wolves parroted. Rasci fidgeted. He was wondering if he leapt up as high as he could, whether he could swipe Corvak.

'In other wolf territories.'

'Killing wolves?' asked Rasci.

'Well, no, that's the point. Not killing.'

'No?' Three voices said, again in unison.

'No. The wolves were knocked unconscious somehow, but they weren't dead.'

'Not dead?' Three voices again.

'No. The men fired at them with the hollow stick things they use as weapons, but they didn't kill the wolves they took from the Pagin pack.'

'And Crufus saw this?' asked Rasci.

'Crufus tells me he didn't fly away. The men were only interested in the wolves. And anyway, Crufus is a brave young bird,' Corvak stated proudly. 'He just hung around and watched. After all, dead is dead. He thought perhaps there was a meal in it for him.'

Rasci gave a little shiver, knowing that his friends would eat wolf meat if it was available. But then wolves will do the same. If their young pups die, then the mother will eat them. 'And what did he see exactly?' Rasci urged, desperately trying not to think about ravens eating dead wolves.

'He saw the men hit four wolves in total with their invisible claws. Each one fell over and looked dead. But as the bird landed by each one, he saw the men get out of the bird and lift the wolves back into the creature. And each time, before the bird took to flight again, one of the men poked each wolf with something and almost immediately, as if it had been asleep, the wolf came back to life. Each one was still limp, but they were alive. Crufus would swear to it.'

'And then what?'

'And then, each one was placed in a cage inside the bird.'

'For what purpose?' asked Rasci.

Corvak shrugged.

Rasci thought for a while and then said, 'Perhaps I know why, my weightless friend. Perhaps I know why!'

CHAPTER SEVENTEEN

'My dream about the farmer and his son seems to make sense now,' said Rasci.

Silvah and Zelda listened patiently as he explained how he had seen the farmer in a wooden building in the town talking to men about a black wolf. It had to be Rhamin, and if it was, then he must still be alive. But then Rasci shook his head as he recalled what he had heard the men on the mountain say in the other dream. "What a magnificent trophy," the man had said; "I don't do trophies," the farmer had said; "But nobody will believe me," the other man had said; "You hang stuffed animals on a wall," the farmer had said. The more he explained it, the more the conflict of information seemed to point to Rhamin's demise. 'Oh, I really don't know,' he said dejectedly. 'Perhaps he is de…' He stopped himself from saying it. Something in Silvah's eyes seemed to warn him not to even go there. She thought she had seen Rhamin killed and now there was just the slightest chance he had survived, she didn't want that tiny particle of hope dashed against the rocks.

'I don't know what to think either,' Zelda said, closing her eyes. She fell silent and concentrated, watched expectantly by the other two. Eventually she spoke. 'Do we know where they have taken the Pagin wolves?'

Rasci shook his head. It was beginning to ache. He looked over to where Corvak had perched. As darkness had finally closed in, the old raven had fallen asleep in the bush. The night was light to the keen eyes of the wolves, but they dare not wake Corvak in the darkness. The old raven would feel disorientated. Not until dawn, could they question him again.

'I suggest we all do the same as Corvak,' Rasci said, resigned to waiting. He was glad the others agreed. He found all this thinking very tiring. Running; chasing; loping along; sleeping; even fighting, that was wolf business. This leadership thing was something all together different. A pulse throbbed above his right eye sending a pain deep inside his head. With a sigh, he settled down where he was, folded his tail around his face, and fell into a deep sleep.

'Is he always like this?' Rasci could hear Corvak's voice in the background.

'What?' He struggled to pry his eyelids open, but his unconscious mind was still driving him to sleep on. He was sitting in front of Ben. Smokey had been with him, but she had barked at a shadow and then run off into the house. But this time, Ben was able to see Rasci properly. He had spotted him almost straight away, and now, somehow, they were talking. Ben was saying how his father had told him he was glad The Black Wolf hadn't killed the dog pup that he had stolen that night the wolves raided the farm, and he was describing to Rasci how The Black Wolf had saved him and his little sister, Margo, from being attacked by the dark grey wolf that accompanied him.

'That was Solin,' Rasci had explained. 'He's a bad wolf. But Rhamin, the Black Wolf is a good wolf.'

'I know,' Ben replied. 'The Black Wolf and his pack saved my daddy.'

'Yes,' Rasci said proudly as he recalled the fight with the bears. 'I was there.'

'Really!'

'Yes, really. I was one of Rhamin's pack.'

'Aren't you any more?'

'Rhamin, is dead,' Rasci was explaining, sadly.

Ben studied what Rasci had said. 'Oh, Daddy doesn't think so,' he said, his little eyes suddenly wide with excitement as he realised he could help his wolf friend. 'Daddy says that the man Petersen has got him.'

'Is Petersen the one that we saved on the mountain with your father?'

'Yes, he has been taking animals to his father's safari park.'

'What's a safari park?'

Ben looked at Rasci, trying to read his face. 'It's a place where they keep animals as if they are in the wild. But they are not in the wild. Daddy says it's like our farm, only it's not for cattle and sheep.'

'And just where would that be?'

Ben shrugged. 'Daddy hasn't said.' Then he added. 'He's very angry. The men at the cattle market think he was the one who caught The Black Wolf for Petersen because Petersen had told everybody that Daddy had tracked the wolf for him, but it's not true. He only tracks deer. Daddy says that The Black Wolf appeared when he was hunting deer and he came back and saved him when the bears attacked.'

'But your father didn't do any of the things that Petersen

says he did?'

'Oh no. He's really angry about it!'

'Can you find out…?' Rasci stopped speaking. There was a voice behind him.

'Who are you talking to?' Ben's mother came over and gave her son a big hug.

He shrugged her off. 'Not in front of my friend, Mummy!'

'Oh, right.' She smiled at him and patted him on the head. 'Are you coming in for breakfast now?'

'In a minute, Mummy.'

She walked away, completely oblivious to Rasci. It was as if he wasn't there. It seemed to puzzle Ben. 'This is my friend, Rasci,' he shouted after her.

'Hello, Rasci,' she said without turning to look as she marched on.

'She can't see me,' said Rasci. He knew he was a ghost in the bright morning light. He realised he was invisible, except to Ben.

Ben scowled. 'Why?' he asked.

'I'm not sure yet,' Rasci replied honestly. 'In fact I'm not sure why I am here at all.'

'Was it to tell me about the puppy?'

'What, Lexa, you mean?'

'Lexa? Is that her name?'

'Yes.'

'That's a nice name.'

'I'm glad you think so,' Rasci was saying, when he began to feel something tugging at his coat. 'But it's Rhamin, The Black Wolf, I want to ask you about. Are you sure about the safari park?'

He turned but saw nothing behind him. He could feel his whole body now, being drawn away from the boy. He locked eyes with Ben and tried to resist the force that was becoming stronger every second, but a voice said, 'Is he always like this?'

Ben waved. 'Bye-bye,' he shouted softly after him.

'What?' he shouted hearing the voice, and then, 'Are you sure the men didn't say that he had been skinned and stuffed to look like he was living,' Rasci called desperately to Ben as his gaze snapped away from that of his young companion. Suddenly he felt his body dissolving. Frantically he called to Ben but the child began to disappear backwards into a hazy mist.

'He dreams all the time now,' said Silvah, as Rasci's eyes burst open.

He blinked as the bright morning light danced upon his eyes.

'Skinned and stuffed?' asked Silvah.

'What?' Rasci lifted his head and looked at those around him.

'You said that he might be skinned and stuffed.'

'Er…' Rasci thought for a moment. He thought about the bear that he had seen in Petersen's house. He thought about Rhamin. Next to Yeltsa, Silvah was the closest to Rhamin. Like Rasci and the other wolves, she loved him. It was an emotion that flowed so deep within her, it was part of her soul. She had saved him as a pup when his mother had been killed, and lately she had seen her Rhamin shot and carried away in the helicopter. If there was a seed of hope, he didn't want to crush it. 'The man who took Rhamin,' he said, trying to think. 'He may have him in a prison.'

'But you said…'

'I was dreaming about the bear.' He stood up and shook himself awake. He looked up at Corvak who hadn't moved from where he was in the night. 'What do you know about safari parks?' he asked, looking at his friend intently.

Corvak tilted his head on one side, his eyes fixed on a butterfly that was fluttering across the mouth of the cave. 'Never heard of them,' he said eventually as the insect alighted on a warm rock. The wolves followed his line of vision and momentarily became entranced by the gossamer wings lifting and falling as they absorbed the warm rays of sunlight. 'What are they?' the raven eventually asked.

'Yes, what are they?' asked Silvah.

Rasci realised he was talking about things only described to him by Ben. He tried to explain the best he could, that just as the farmer enclosed his cattle inside large areas of fenced off pasture and scrubland, so he had been told by the little boy, some men, and he was referring to Petersen in particular, make similar enclosures to keep in naturally free and wild animals.

'But why would they do that?' asked Corvak.

'I really don't know,' said Rasci. 'But then,' he said on reflection, 'Why do they kill wolves and other creatures for fun?'

'It wasn't always so,' Zelda stated, as the others listened and wondered how any of her knowledge had been acquired. 'Men were once very much alike with wolves. They hunted for food like we do. But then, they changed.' She shrugged. 'They began to kill with impunity. And they don't just kill other creatures; they kill their own kind all the time.' She thought back to when she had met her mate, Romax. 'Some are bad, but some are good. Wolves are not so dissimilar, really.'

'But we don't kill for fun,' Rasci said, saddened by the implication.

'Huh, you forget your half brother,' said Zelda.

Zelda had suggested that if Safari parks were as big as Rasci had surmised, as big as the sprawling farms that men fenced in, then the wily raven might be able to spot one easily from the air. Corvak was willing to help them find it, but he told them he didn't hold out too much hope. Even from the sky, the world as he and the wolves knew it was a vast place. Unless he flew in the right direction, then no matter how long he looked, he would never find the safari park. But he told them he would see what he could do. He had relatives down in the region to the south, who might be able to help, but the area bordered on a large man made forest of tall buildings and there was nobody he knew in the area that lay beyond that. However, he assured the wolves he would make some enquiries, and after stretching his wings and inspecting and admiring them from every angle, using the branch of the bush as a spring board, he eventually set out to the far south east to see if he could find out what exactly a safari park looked like.

After seeing off his friend, Rasci returned to where Silvah and Zelda lay just outside the entrance to the cave. He still needed to discuss what he had seen in his head. Somehow, it just seemed too true to be anything but real. But he couldn't understand how it could be real. He was in one place. At the same time, his mind and even his body appeared in another place, but wasn't really there. He was discovering something about an unknown world. He was discovering something about himself, and it just didn't seem to fit in with being a wolf.

'Do you know if Ben was dreaming like yourself?' Silvah asked him as he sat beside them.

'I have a feeling that Ben wasn't dreaming,' said Rasci pensively. 'It's as if I am seeing him in real life. And I saw the farmer as well, remember. They can't all be dreaming. It's me that is travelling to them in *my* dream.'

'There is one way to find out if your meeting with the boy was real,' Zelda suggested.

Rasci knew what she meant. Zelda was thinking that if Ben was so friendly in a dream then he might be friendly with the real live wolf.

'No,' Silvah interrupted, also understanding what Zelda was going to say. 'It's far too dangerous.'

'Not at all,' Zelda insisted. 'What you need to do the next time you visit Ben in your dream is to tell him you intend to visit him in real life, fur and all!'

'No, it's still too dangerous,' Silvah argued. 'Even Ben will know a real wolf from a vision of one. He is bound to be frightened.'

'But Zelda's right, Silvah,' Rasci said. He paused while he formed in his mind what he wanted to say. 'If Rhamin is still alive,' he continued, 'then he is likely to be a prisoner of that man. And if he's a prisoner, then I can't see any way another wolf will be able to free him. Except…' He paused again. 'Silvah, do you remember what Solin did?'

'That desert rat did more than I like to recall. He's the lowest of the low,' Silvah stated intractably. 'There's nothing but a scheming rat inside that wolf's fur of his.'

'Well, scheming, perhaps. But he was clever. He used the man to try and get what he wanted.'

'Hmm,' Zelda grunted. 'I see what you are getting at. You reckon that we can get the farmer to find Rhamin?'

'Right!'

'But only if your dreams are true.' Silvah shook her head. 'On the basis of that, are you prepared to risk your life? You have dreamt that he is upset about Rhamin being struck down by that man. You have dreamt that Ben, as you call him, has told you that Rhamin is alive. You have even dreamt that Ben tells his mother you are his friend, but we just don't know if any of it is really true. I saw Rhamin being struck down by that evil man, the friend of the farmer, remember. He looked dead to me. We have lost one leader. We can't afford to lose another.'

'As I am feeling at the moment,' argued Rasci, 'I don't think that would be any great loss.'

'Oh, for goodness sake!' Zelda interjected. 'Will you two stop it?' Her hips were aching. She shuffled to make herself more comfortable. 'I think Rasci is right about Rhamin. We have to try and do something. And I think Rasci was right about Solin.'

'Puh,' Silvah whispered angrily for them both to hear, as she got up and walked away to the cave. It was time for her morning wash.

While they were alone, Rasci broached another question that had been on his mind.

'Hmm, how old are you Gran?' he asked.

'What on earth do you want to know that for?' she gasped, giving Rasci a strange look.

'I don't know really, but I seem to have some sort of mental ability and I can't work out if it's just wishful thinking.

'And?'

'Well, I was just wondering what relation am I to you. Are you really my grandmother or is it just an affectionate title? I've grown up calling you Gran, but perhaps if I knew you really were, then it would be easier to believe I can do some of the things you can do.'

'Oh, you can do them, Rasci, believe me. And more! You have abilities that even I don't have. It's all about bringing you up to believe in them. We are all born with some degree of psychic ability but it fades as realities of living and surviving take over. So many youngsters nowadays are steered away from using these natural and inbred gifts. The problem is none of the pack ever had their abilities nurtured beyond the ability to hunt. It's so wrong.' She looked at Rasci with her sightless eyes. 'When your mother died, you were reared by Silvah and me.'

Rasci considered what Zelda had said. 'So I didn't inherit any of this dream stuff from you then.' He gave out a sigh.

Zelda could tell he was a little saddened. 'Well, that's not exactly the case,' she consoled. 'You could well have inherited some of your ability from me. But who you get the rest from, I'm not so sure.'

'So you are my Gran?' Rasci said excitedly.

'Not exactly.'

'Not exactly? What do you mean?'

'Well, I'm older than your Gran,' Zelda admitted.

'Meaning?'

'Meaning that I am your great, great Gran.'

'Well I know you're great Gran.'

'No! Great, great Gran,' she corrected as Rasci lifted one eyebrow sceptically. 'It means I am the Gran of your Gran.'

'Right,' said Rasci, not sure if he should have broached the subject at all. She would always be great to him.

'Let me explain,' Zelda said patiently. 'Generations are often attributed to different litters of pups from the same parents in successive years. But that is wrong; that is not a generation gap. That is simply a sibling gap. Pups born the year after or the year before are simply brothers and sisters.'

'And?'

'And a generation is where one family is born from the

last family. A son or daughter is born from a son or daughter. That is a generation.

'Right, got it,' said Rasci patiently.

'And Anval was your father and Celion was your mother.'

'Yes, I know that.'

'Well Celion was a cub whose mother, Eva, joined from another pack from the far west.'

'So Eva was my Gran?'

'That's right,' said Zelda, with a fond smile. 'And her father was a wolf called Rufus.'

'And just who was Rufus then?'

'Rufus,' Zelda said with a fond smile, 'was my first born male cub,'

Rasci studied the picture that had been drawn in his mind. 'So how come you are in Rhamin's pack?'

'Well I joined at the same time as Eva. We were two of six survivors from a pack that was hunted down by the same men that killed Dori, Rhamin's mother, only that time they not only had horses to carry them along, they had a pack of big dogs that seemed to be trained just for hunting Wolves.' There was more to that story, of course, but, feeling tired Zelda didn't want to go into that at this time.

But it pleased Rasci that she had explained, and it delighted him that he was actually related to her, somehow. It gave some kind of authenticity to the feelings and experiences he had been going through. His gift had been inherited from Zelda. It gave him a reason for being there; not just because he had been raised by her, but because he was carrying on her psychic gift. And now he really could call her Gran, and that suddenly meant something completely different. Before their discussion, he had called her Gran through a mixture of affection and fun. Now his affection was given a seal of approval, like a certificate of authenticity gives a human a proof of identity, a proof of provenance, something substantial that gives owning something or belonging to something a completely different meaning.

'I might be right, then' Rasci said quietly to himself after deliberating. But Zelda heard it and smiled to herself.

'I think so,' she said proudly.

CHAPTER EIGHTEEN

The next day, as golden fingers lifted the black clouds off the mountains to the east, Rasci set off alone in the direction of Raymond Rozalski's farm. He was impatient for news of Rhamin and he had decided that the quickest way to find out was to see Ben, to confirm that his dreams and visions were taking him into reality and not to some place in his mind; a place he was inventing to prevent the pain of certain truth.

The trip was a relief in some ways. Alone, he felt no pressure to either lead the pack or report to his Gran or Silvah what he was thinking or dreaming. In fact, he had purposely withheld information from them. He had dreams but he sometimes felt it better not to speak of them. In particular, he kept having a recurring dream that he and Rhamin were fighting some strange wolf pack. But that was too unsettling to discuss at this time. He knew for a fact that if it were a dream of the future then Rhamin must be alive, but how could Rasci be with his great leader unless he, too, had been shot and taken to the giant prison camp called a safari park? Or was there a possibility that Rhamin was to escape and Rasci was seeing events that followed? Either way, he didn't feel that upsetting his companions would help matters. They certainly would have tried to insist that he stay in the cave if they thought there was any chance of their new leader following the first.

So he loped along, almost care free, for hour after hour, day dreaming, with hardly a care in the world. This was how he liked his life; uncomplicated. First he thought of the hunt upon which they would all be soon embarking as the great herds of buffalo migrated in the autumn months. That would give weeks of easy living for the whole pack and an excellent training period for the young cubs.

The young cubs! He had hardly set eyes on them since the demise of his leader. Since Yeltsa's death, they had been cared for by Lexa. They had hardly missed their mother and father, because they had been kept busy in their young lives, learning their hunting skills, play fighting, eating and sleeping. Rasci wondered if he shouldn't have been with them. It sounded to be just his kind of life really. But perhaps it would have been another disruption to divert him from his appointed task. The pack had been good in that respect. They were so good that he wondered why they even needed a leader. They all got on together so well and they seemed to manage in their small groups whenever they were away from the Darin. So why did they need Rasci to tell them what to do? In fact, Rasci hadn't told them what to do. They had just done what they usually do. And really, Rasci decided, that is also what they did when Rhamin was leader. Perhaps leadership was not what he had really expected. It seems the job of leading the pack was just a matter of being a necessary figure head for the other wolves. Yes, that was probably it. He was just a figure head, a uniting blob of sticky tar that held the pack together as a whole when unity was essential. His sticky tendrils of authority drew the individual wolves back to the centre of their universe. So this was what power was about, he thought. He wielded a gummy, rubbery gravity that tugged them from their distant wanderings, back into one congealed pack.

Comforted by his deliberations, he loped on. It was such a relief to be alone again and to have fathomed out his duties. He didn't have any. All this leadership stuff! It was an image, a shadow of responsibility. It was just in the minds of the other wolves in the pack. When he got back, he was going to explain to them that his honorary position could be vacated with no ill effect on the functioning properties of his beloved friends or their kinship. He wasn't necessary. He was just an easy going, simple living, hunting, eating, sleeping clown of a wolf. He would resign!

He skipped along, lighter than the dewy evening air. His excitement mounted as he anticipated his resignation. It gave him such a good feeling. He relaxed so much that, as night time closed in, he had forgotten just what it was he had in mind to do when he set off. But eventually, as his subconscious, automatic guidance system brought him upon the first of the outer fences of Raymond Rozalski's farm, he was suddenly jerked back to reality. He stopped for a moment and regarded the fence. He had travelled sixty odd miles and couldn't remember a single stride. For a moment, he had to think hard to get back into the picture that he had sketched in his mind on departure from the Darin. 'Oh bollocks!' he grunted to himself as he remembered.

In the powdery earth, he dug himself a shallow hollow by the fence and then settled in it to rest. So now what? He sighed. He wasn't sure if he had ever had any idea what he was going to do when he got here. He certainly didn't have any idea now. He blew out a heavy breath and rested his head on his front feet, feeling tired and a little deflated. What was it he intended to do? He thought about Raymond Rozalski, wondering if that really was his name, or just what he had imagined in a dream in order to put a tag of identification on him. And what about Ben? Was that a proper name? It didn't sound wolfish. In fact it didn't sound any more wolfish than Raymond, although, the name Rozalski had a certain ring to it. And Smokey? Did that name have a meaning to it in human language? The word he was hearing in his language meant the colour of the air on top of the orange flames of bush fires that often ravished the dry plains. He shook his head. Already it was beginning to hurt and he hadn't even started thinking hard yet. The pulse above his right eye began to throb. His eyes closed with the pain.

The fight with the other wolves seemed so real. Both Rhamin and Yeltsa were thwarting attack after attack from at least ten other wolves. The other wolves were total strangers. He knew he had never seen them before. For a moment, Rasci couldn't see himself there. He woofed to try and get them to see him. He thought he could distract some of them, but none of them took any notice. For some reason, he couldn't get Rhamin to see him either. 'Rhamin,' he called out. 'Rhamin! I'll take this one!' But it passed right through him.

Panting heavily, he jerked himself awake. He shook his head as he stood up, making the wave of the shaking action, ripple through his body right to the end of his tale. 'Phew! Another damned dream,' he muttered. He was beginning to hate the dreams; in fact he was beginning to hate sleeping.

He had always loved sleeping, but now all he wanted to do was keep awake as long as possible to put off the inevitable.

He began to contemplate what he was going to do. He couldn't go to the farm during the night. Humans sleep at night. Wolves sleep at night also, but not all the time. Sometimes, in really hot weather, they hunt at night when the air is cooler, and then they sleep during the day. But, at the moment, it wasn't that kind of weather. The problem was, during the day, the farmer and Ben would be with their dog, Smokey. And Smokey hated wolves. Rasci wasn't afraid of the dog. But he knew what a lethal combination the man and the dog made together. He couldn't rely on the farmer recognising him. Raymond Rozalski had never seen any of the wolves close up on the mountain. And, anyway, apart from Rhamin, most wolves would look the same to a human, the same as most humans looked the same to a wolf. The only thing that distinguished wolves from humans in that respect was that wolves had the extra advantage of an extremely sensitive sense of smell which gave every man and every animal a distinct and separate identification tag. The farmer might think Rasci was Solin. That could be a lethal mistake. Although he strongly believed that the farmer was wolf friendly, and would treat any wolf with respect, Rasci was sure that Raymond Rozalski would gladly make an exception in the case of the killer, Solin. And Smokey was the next problem. Even on his own, it was possible that the dog would not take kindly to her territory being invaded by even a single wolf.

Rasci began to contemplate the options. His plan when he left the Darin was simple. Approach the young man, Ben, and get him to introduce Rasci to his father and his dog. Brilliant!

He looked at the fencing and slumped back down into his hollow. There had to be a way of befriending the only human ally he was likely to gain. 'What am I doing here?' he muttered to himself. 'What good is making friends with them, anyway?' he chuntered. It wouldn't advance things much further than they were at the moment. Rhamin was still either dead or in a prison compound.

What was the brilliant plan that Solin was supposed to have put in place? Oh, yes, kill some cattle and get the farmer to kill Rhamin. Another sparkling conclusion to an even more dazzling chain of thought. So, based on those criteria, all Rasci had to do was provoke Raymond Rozalski into welcoming him into the circle of friendship. "Welcome to my family, Mr. Wolf. I trust you implacably! Make yourself at home. Smokey, you are instructed to love your wolfish friend!" That should do it. Easy really. Just like getting a hare to jump into your mouth. They do it all the time.

Rasci's head thumped.

Once again, troubled sleep engulfed the tired brain of the well meaning wolf, and for a while the pain in his head retreated to a tiny throbbing pulse above his eye. For the time being, without the pain, it was almost a relief to sleep, to dream.

Little Ben was in his own room in the farmhouse, lying on a frame made of wood, and was covered by a light sheet of woven fabric, the same stuff from which humans make coats to cover their naked hairless bodies. The room was light for an enclosed space. Through an open window, a strong shaft of moonlight was gradually panning the room as the earth slowly turned. Eventually, as the hour passed, the light fell across Ben's little face. He was smiling and talking in his sleep. 'What are you doing here?' he asked.

Rasci couldn't see anybody there, but to the boy his

dream seemed real as he continued to chat to his friend. 'What's your name?'

Rasci heard him repeat the name. 'Rasci? That's an unusual name.'

The boy listened to something the imaginary wolf was saying to him in his sleep. Rasci strained to hear, but he heard nothing. 'I need to talk to you,' Rasci called out.

Ben carried on chatting in his sleep.

'I need your help,' Rasci called again.

Ben stirred.

'I need to talk to you and your father.'

Ben's eyelids fluttered.

'Ben, can you hear me?'

Ben's eyes opened and he lifted his head. 'Rasci, is that really you?' he asked, looking to the side of the bed.

'Yes,' Rasci replied. 'It really is me.'

'Why do you keep disappearing?' Ben's little voice asked as he rubbed his eyes.

Rasci understood what he meant. 'I can only visit you in a spirit form for the time being.'

'What does that mean?'

'What it means, is that we are connected by our thoughts,' Rasci tried to explain. 'And when we are connected by our thoughts, we see each other as if we were together. Do you understand?'

Ben nodded. It was a universal signal of understanding, but he confirmed it with a, 'Yes.'

Rasci was about to speak again, when Ben said, 'Will we meet in real life then?'

'Well, that's what I wanted to talk to you about,' explained Rasci. 'I would like to visit you in person. Wolf to wolf as it were.'

'Wolf to Wolf?'

'Yes, Ben. You are an honorary wolf you know.'

'Am I?'

'Yes, you are. You have been an honorary wolf ever since your father saved Rhamin from being shot by that man on the mountain.'

'Petersen, you mean?'

'That's the one.'

'He's got Rhamin, you know? I asked Daddy the last time I had seen you. He says Petersen has definitely got The Black Wolf.'

'Yes, I believe that is so, my young friend. Rhamin was my leader, and I want to save him, but I don't know how I can do it.'

Ben thought for a moment. 'I don't think there is any way to save him,' he said eventually. 'But Daddy says Rhamin is supposed to be happy with plenty of other wolves to be friends with.'

'It's not as simple as that Ben. Freedom is precious. Neither wolves nor men were put on this earth to be kept prisoner against their will.'

'My friend May's mother is locked up all day in an office, but she is let out to go home at night.'

'There are many kinds of prison, Ben. That "office" as you call it will be a prison of her own choosing. Even wolves can live their lives in a self made a prison.' He thought about the mental strings that were binding him to the dark oppressive prison of leadership. 'But that man, Petersen as you call him, has taken Rhamin and his mate against their will. Wolves are born to be free. They travel thousands of miles a year, seeing different things every step of the way. They hunt when they are hungry. I expect that Petersen feeds his captives regularly?'

'I expect so,' Ben replied, frowning.

'But wolves don't eat regularly. We eat and then sleep for days. We enjoy the chase and the hunt. We enjoy being part of a community that relies on each member for survival. There is none of that in a prison. Their survival will depend on doing exactly what the man wants, looking like a wolf, but behaving like a dog.'

Rasci suddenly realised what he had said. 'I didn't mean to criticise Smokey, Ben. But she was brought up to be a man's companion. We wolves are brought up to be companions not only to other wolves, but to the animals we kill. Those animals benefit from our killing their weakest ones. And they seem to realise that we do not kill needlessly.'

'That bad wolf killed Daddy's cattle needlessly last spring.'

'That is exactly right, Ben. We have bad wolves just as there are bad men.'

'Is Petersen a bad man?'

Rasci was careful to answer. 'In a way he is, Ben. He may think he is doing something good, but what he is doing is for his own fun or to please other people. He isn't concerned about the happiness of the animals he locks up, nor about their families. That is behaving badly.'

Ben rubbed his eyes again. 'Are you going to disappear again?' he asked innocently, aware of the fragile connection.

'Soon,' Rasci replied.

'But I don't want you to go.'

'Perhaps... perhaps we can do something about that,' Rasci said, suddenly getting a flash of inspiration. 'Perhaps we can actually meet in real life. Perhaps I can come to your home and talk to you as a real wolf.'

'Can you do that?' Ben asked, excitedly.

Rasci thought for a moment. 'Well, perhaps you could tell your father and your dog that I am coming to visit.'

'When?'

'In the morning.'

'What, tomorrow?'

'If I can.'

'How?'

'Well, that's the problem. I'm not sure I can just walk up to your house.'

Ben fidgeted eagerly. 'I could tell Mummy and Daddy that you are coming to visit.'

'What about Smokey?'

'I can ask Daddy to keep her under control.'

'Look, Ben,' Rasci said seriously. 'It's not only my life that depends on your managing to persuade them that I come in friendship. Rhamin's life too could well depend on it. Can you tell your father that the life of Rhamin, The Black Wolf that saved him from the bears, depends on our friendship? Do you understand?'

Ben nodded. 'Yes, I understand Rasci.'

Rasci watched him for a moment. 'I'm going to go now, Ben. I'll see you in the morning.'

'You're my best friend next to Smokey,' Ben called after the evaporating vision.

CHAPTER NINETEEN

Rasci squeaked and turned his weight onto his other side.

'I could kill you and you wouldn't even know about it,' a voice said in the background.

'What?' Rasci's eyes sprung open.

'You don't exactly hide from danger.'

Rasci's eyes focussed. As he came to his senses, he realised he was looking at a wolf who he had never seen before. She was smaller than he was, but then most female wolves are smaller than males. She was dark grey with a lighter grey chest. Her eyes, like all wolves, were amber, but they carried a light that Rasci hadn't noticed in the eyes of other wolves. It would be hard to explain it, but he felt there was something magnetic, something that impelled him to gaze into them. 'Who… who are you?' he said, tentatively.

'I could have killed you, you know that?'

'No you couldn't.'

'You were giving your position away. I could hear you for miles.'

'No you couldn't.'

'So why are you lurking here in a hollow in the shadows?'

'I'm resting, not lurking.'

'Well, I can't argue with that. You were certainly resting! Not a light sleeper though, I can confirm that much.'

Rasci didn't want to explain. 'Who are you, anyway?'

'I asked you first.'

'No you didn't.'

'Sleep where you drop heh? Not a good example to set for your pack. You were totally exposed to attack.'

'I wasn't trying to set an example.'

'No, just trying to get killed. There is danger in this area. Be warned.'

'What danger?'

The unfamiliar wolf smiled. It was a rather becoming smile actually, Rasci thought. She avoided the question. 'That's why wolves don't snore like some other animals. We don't make a noise, so that predators don't know where we are.'

'I don't snore.'

'No, you don't talk and shout and kick at the sides of your hollow and stir up lots of dust, either, do you?'

'Hollow?' Rasci realised he was peeping up at the newcomer from his sleeping place, and jumped up quickly. 'Oh, it's not *my* hollow.' He didn't know what else to say.

'No, I can see that. You share it with that big bear.'

Rasci swivelled around. 'What big bear?'

The visitor laughed. 'So what's your name?'

'I think I just asked you that,' Rasci complained.

'Really?'

'Well I'm Rasci, anyway.'

'Roxana, pleased to meet you.'

'No, Rasci.'

She laughed again. 'No, *I'm* Roxana.'

'Oh, right. Er… er, pleased to meet you then,' he shrugged.

'Glad to hear it, Rasci Anyway'

Rasci smiled. 'Just Rasci.' The smile broadened to a grin. He was looking at a wolf with a good sense of humour. He suddenly felt more at ease. 'So what are you doing around here?'

'Around here? Oh, I am just passing through.'

He looked past her into the distance. 'You haven't seen any other wolves around or bears or anything?'

'No. Why should I have?'

'Oh, no. It's just that sometimes I get the feeling I'm being followed.'

'Well, I can say I haven't seen anybody.'

'You're alone then?'

'Yes, now that I've squeezed through this crowd behind me.'

Rasci laughed when he realised he had begun to glance past her shoulder again. She tilted her head and scrutinised Rasci's face. 'And you?'

'Me? Oh, I live here.'

'In a hole, by a man made wire hedge?'

'Not *here*,' said Rasci, looking down at the hollow. He scanned the area with his eyes. 'All around,' he said. 'This is Rha… this is my pack's territory.'

'And who's your leader?'

'Why?' The question had been a little too direct. It caught him off balance.

'Well, I might think of joining.'

Rasci considered his options. Here he was in the middle of nowhere and along comes an attractive young female, probably a couple of years younger than himself. He was cautious. 'Our leader is away at the moment,' he said convincingly. 'He's coming back soon.'

'Oh, how fascinating! Where has he gone? Is it important?'

'Well, since he's a pack leader, I should have thought

so,' Rasci answered evasively. 'So where is your pack?' he countered, to change the subject.

'I left. I had a problem with the leading female.'

'Really?'

Roxana smiled. 'I didn't like being second in line. I want to be a mate to a pack leader.'

'Really? Got ambitions then?'

She looked at Rasci charmingly. He looked back at her enchanted. She was indeed a beautiful wolf. Her coat was clean and smooth; her amber eyes glinted in the starlight. Her dark grey coat, though not as dark as that of his leader, in the night light, reminded him of Rhamin. 'Where are you heading?' she asked eventually.

'Er…' Rasci shrugged. He had no idea whether to trust this wolf, and he had no idea if she would believe him if he did trust her. He certainly couldn't discuss his plan to see the farmer with her. He hadn't even discussed it with his own pack. 'I was on my way to the northern hills,' he lied.

'Is it far?'

'Not really. I trust you came from the south then?'

'Yes,' Roxana nodded.

'I'll have to be going soon,' said Rasci trying to make his excuse and leave. He didn't want to give his true mission away. But more than that, he just didn't feel he could explain it.

'Oh, can I come with you?'

Taken aback, Rasci fumbled for words. 'Is that where you're going then?'

Roxana nodded eagerly.

'Oh, right. Hmm, the thing is…'

'You'd rather be alone?'

'It's nothing personal. It's just that I am used to being on my own, that's all.'

'Oh, don't worry. I understand.' Roxana didn't seem a bit upset. 'Thought I'd ask, though. Might have been interesting.' She threw Rasci a glance that seemed to say something more. He couldn't speak. She turned to leave. 'You know where to find me,' she called over her shoulder as she broke into a light trot.

Rasci watched her disappear into the night. He still hadn't had an answer to his question. How did Roxana happen to be where he was sleeping? In all the thousands of square miles of territory, in the middle of the night, she happened along at just the same place and at the same time. The lone wolf had unsettled him now. Roxana seemed to know more than just Rasci's whereabouts. She seemed to know about some kind of danger. Just what that danger was, Rasci had yet to discover, but for the time being, he was going to stay awake.

Shafts of light forced their way through holes in the thick grey clouds to brighten another dull morning. A cold northerly wind was making waves in the dry, brown tussock grass. In the distance, a pair of vultures hovered on a thermal, waiting for the spoils of the wolf's day. But Rasci didn't feel like hunting. He felt nothing but trepidation at the thought of going into the heart of the farm. He had only a dream upon which to rely for calming his raw nerves. And in the reasoning of full consciousness it seemed far less likely to work. The idea that he could just walk into the farm was not backed by any solid fact or incident. 'It was just a dream,' he muttered to himself, incoherently. 'Ben is probably not Ben. He's probably a Zoglan or Sumplinck or some other un-pronounceable human name I've never heard of.'

Dejected by the way his whole life had turned around, he slumped back down into the hollow and wound his tail around his face. The cold wind from the north was picking up dust and gritty sand particles and, with a mind of its own, and with the singular purpose of demoralising Rasci, it was slinging them at his eyes. He closed them and began to think of a way he could just turn around and head back to the Darin.

Suddenly, he was with Rhamin again. Only, this time, he wasn't seeing the events as a spectator. This time, he could clearly see himself. He was alongside his leader, fighting some more unfamiliar wolves, but they were not the same that he had seen before. Yet, this time, although Yeltsa was there, she had a white leg. It was Rhamin, Yeltsa and Rasci against the rest. It was another time, another place, another dream.

Then he saw himself walking alongside a dark grey wolf. He recognised her. It was Roxana. They trotted along, side by side, chatting and being good friends.

The distant sound of cattle lowing for their young ones broke him out of his trance. Turning with the wind to his back, he considered his options. He could go back to the Darin, but then he would be no further forward in finding Rhamin. And what would he tell Zelda and Silvah and the rest of the pack? He could go into the centre of this farm and get killed. Then he wouldn't have to explain anything to his comrades. He could stay there and think about it a bit more. Yes, that seemed like a reasonable course of action. He would settle down and rest a bit more and daydream.

Ben was up and about early. Even his father, who was usually the first to rise, was still sleeping soundly beside

Ben's mother, in the next room. As he looked out of the open window towards the distant plain, a wisp of blond feathery hair fell over his eyes and he brushed it aside with his tiny fingers. He leaned on the sill with his elbows and rested his chin on the palms of his hands and patiently waited. Not once, in the next hour and a half did the young child move from the window. Not once did he doubt that he was going to receive a visitor.

Eventually, Ben was distracted by movement in the adjacent room. A cough and the sound of his father clearing his throat, made Ben turn away. He rushed over to the door and turned the handle. Pulling his bedroom door wide open, he waited on the landing for his father to emerge from his room. He knew he must wait. He had always been told never to disturb his mother and father while they were asleep; though that didn't seem to stop his little sister Margo from disturbing them. He had often seen her heading towards his parent's room, toy bear under her arm, sleepily wiping her eyes with the back of her fist. She would just turn the handle and walk in. He wasn't allowed to do that. But he forgave Margo. She was still very young.

Eventually, the door handle turned and the door opened. His father looked down at Ben. 'Good morning, my little Action Man,' he said and bent down and lifted Ben up to his chest. 'And what gets you up so bright and early on a cold morning like this?'

'Daddy...' Ben put his hand against his father's cheek.

'Yes my boy?'

'Daddy, I'm glad the wolf saved you from the bears.'

Raymond chuckled. 'So am I my little boy.' He nodded and smiled, giving Ben an affectionate squeeze. 'So am I.'

'Daddy...'

'Yes, Poppet, what is it?'

'Daddy, can my friend come to visit me?'

'Well of course she can.'

'No, not May, Daddy. I mean, well she can come, but what I mean is my other friend.'

'Your other friend?' his father said jokingly. 'And just who might that be?'

'His name's Rasci.'

Raymond screwed up his face. 'This is your imaginary friend, I take it?' He had been told the full story of how Ben had been talking to his invisible friend, Rasci, by Ben's mother. She had been a little worried, but Raymond had said that he thought it was perfectly natural for a child who was playing by himself to make up imaginary friends and places and all sorts of other things to make his games more realistic.

'Yes, but he's not imaginary.'

'Oh, isn't he?'

'No, Daddy. He's real. He's a real live wolf.'

'Oh, well I think your mother would have a thing or two to say about that,' Raymond said, tweaking Ben's nose and carrying him down the stairs into the kitchen.

'But it's important, Daddy.'

'Oh, is it now? What do you want for breakfast?'

Ben didn't answer. 'He's a friend of Rhamin.'

'Oh, and just who is Rhamin? Is he another imaginary friend?'

'They aren't imaginary, Daddy,' Ben insisted.

'Benjamin, you can invite as many of your friends as you like so long as they aren't wild wolves.'

'Good.' Ben turned to leave. 'They're not wild.'

'Hoy! Hold on a minute Buster. You have to have some breakfast before you go out to play. Your Mummy is taking you to school remember.'

But Ben wasn't hungry. 'I'll have it later when Margo gets up,' he shouted as he ran out of the kitchen. He opened the front door and skipped out into the yard.

Rasci smiled to himself, now that he knew Ben was waiting for him. Slowly, he came out of his trance, stood up, stretched, gave a big yawn that showed all his teeth, and then scrambled under the fencing.

It was still some way to the next boundary fence and by the time Rasci reached it, he was ready for a drink from the water troughs that dotted the perimeter. As he drank, he couldn't help recalling the night the pack raided the farm. He remembered how, in the drought, the farmer had still got a plentiful supply of water. He wondered how that had come about, how the farmer had filled the troughs so far away from the farmstead. He realised then, for the first time, just how remarkable and mysterious some men were. He wondered if he would ever learn the secrets of the farmer.

Then, his mind flashed back to that awful night again, and how the farmer's dog had attacked the wolves and how the farmer had made the dog drop to the ground with a single command, leaving the wolf exposed to that terrible invisible hot tooth of death that the farmer's weapon dispatched. He thought of Seth and Fayli who died that fateful night He gave a shudder, licked his lips and, determined not to be a coward, he bounded on.

The last fence was within sight of the farm buildings; those tall buildings that the pack had seen on the night of the raid; they were threatening buildings, unfriendly and stark as they loomed up head.

Rasci stopped by the corner of the first of the structures that formed one of the sides to a perfectly square, big yard that stretched to the right. There was a vehicle there like those he had seen on the land of another enclosed farm far to the east. It had huge black wheels with big lumpy ridges that made an impressive footprint, even bigger than that of a wolf. He looked around it to the left and saw the farmhouse. At the other side of the farmhouse, he could see the paddock where he had seen Ben playing with his dog. (Well, he reminded himself, where he had seen Ben with his dog in a daydream). But it looked familiar somehow, even from a distance. He looked around, seeing no movement of man or machinery. The wind had dropped. Everything around him seemed quiet and calm; too calm for his liking; eerily calm. Not even the sound of cattle or sheep broke through the deafening silence that filled his head. The pulse above his eye throbbed. His head was thumping as if some creature was banging on the inside to get out.

He took a deep breath and trotted as casually as he could across the yard towards the paddock. In the distance he could see Ben. He had seen Rasci and was starting to run towards him; a broad smile lighting up his little face. Still, Rasci's head was filled with a booming throb that raced through his ears with every heart beat. It seemed like everything had been slowed down. Every stride seemed to carry him through the air for endless seconds. Little Ben moved the same, springing forward, one stride at a time, each one so slow that Rasci could see the tiny muscles in Bens knees flexing as his legs bent and straightened.

'Raymond!' a voice broke through the silence. The farmer had rushed out through the farmhouse door and was running towards the paddock.

Rasci only heard it in the background. His head was still choked with noises from the inside.

'Raymond! Quickly! There's a wolf in the yard. It's heading towards the garden!'

Somewhere, a dog barked. The sound got through to Rasci. He turned his head. In the distance, he could see a face at a bedroom window. He could see a woman, dressed in white, with a very pink face. She was yelling and screaming. She was saying things to Rasci but he didn't understand them. The language was foreign to him. But then, suddenly, he understood. It was the body language; a universal language that, with only a little understanding, can be interpreted by all species; like the warning bark, the welcoming look in the eyes, the aggressive snarl. This woman was threatening him; he had no doubt in his mind about it. She was waving something at him. Or was she pointing it? Rasci's head was still pounding. He couldn't focus his eyes properly. He was still drawn towards Ben and the small paddock at the side of the house.

'It's after Ben. Oh Raymond! Stop it! Stop it!'

But the words just sounded like a moderately pitched screech of varying syllables. 'aicy ahhhuum!'

Then he heard Raymond's voice. 'Ben!' the man called. 'Ben, where are you? Come inside now!' Rasci recognised the word. *Ben*. It was Ben! His dream hadn't been just wishful thinking. He had told Zelda and Silvah that the boy's name was Ben. A warm feeling of relief began to flow through Rasci from the toes up. He realised that his conversations with Ben had been real.

Again, the farmer called out. 'Ben, come to me.'

Ben didn't answer. He was running up the paddock

towards Rasci.

'Ben, come here now!' his father shouted, sternly.

'It's Rasci, Daddy! It's Rasci!'

'No it isn't,' Raymond shouted angrily. 'Come here now!' His voice was harsh and stern.

Ben stopped and turned towards his father. 'Daddy, it is Rasci, my friend!'

Raymond was running towards his son. 'This is a real wolf Ben!' he shouted as he scooped up his son and faced the wolf broadside on. 'Come on you bastard!' he called to Rasci. 'Get a mouth full of my foot!'

'No, Daddy, it really is my friend. I told you he was coming! Don't hurt him!'

His father ignored him. Holding Ben under his left arm, he stooped down and picked up a piece of rock with his right hand and threw it with all his force.

Rasci had stopped. He was trying to tell the farmer that he was there to see his son. He was woofing words that the farmer didn't seem to understand. Neither did the words of the farmer make any sense to him. The rock hit Rasci square in the chest.

'Oomph!' he gasped as the rock bounced off his thick coat. Another rock glanced off the side of his leg. He howled with the pain.

'That'll teach the bugger!' the farmer said to Ben.

'It's not who you think it is Daddy! It's my friend Rasci.'

'It's that damned killer wolf! Maria, get my gun!'

'I've got it!' Rasci heard the woman shout, but still none of the words made any sense to him.

A shot rang out, filling the air with the sound of thunder. The inevitable, invisible tooth cut into Rasci's outer fur, the thick guard hairs that overlie the softer inner coat, and travelled on past the top of his shoulder blade. He could feel the heat as it sliced his skin on its way to the fur on the other side of his shoulder. He ran. He swerved. Another invisible tooth cut into the ground beside him as he dodged and weaved his way around a tractor. There was another loud crack followed immediately by a thud and a loud hissing, blowing sound as another invisible tooth cut into the rubber tractor tyre. Amidst a flurry of dust, the wounded tractor slumped down to one side

'Bloody hell Maria!' Rasci could hear the farmer shouting as he disappeared behind the shelter of the corner of the vast building that lay alongside the yard. He could hear words escaping from the farmer's lungs that sounded expletive.

The feeling of safety was short lived as the pain in his leg began to make it throb. Behind him, beyond the corner of the building, he could hear another familiar sound; a growling, deep throaty sound like he often heard back at the Darin. It wasn't the sound of a wolf. It was the sound that Lexa made when she was play fighting with Ramusan. For a second, his heart lifted, but then he realised it wasn't his own wolf dog, his beloved pack comrade, it must be her mother. He limped on. The growling sound emerged from the cover of the building. He had a fifty yard start on the dog but he was limping badly. Wolves have long thin legs. Their limbs carry little flesh. The rock that had hit his leg had hit the bone. There was a trickle of blood running from the wound. It dripped from his knee in slow motion, each droplet sending up a corona of dust as it hit the dry ground.

Limping so badly, he knew he couldn't outrun the dog. It was like a nightmare, fleeing from an ever approaching enemy through thick tar. He glanced over his shoulder. Smokey floated over the ground, unimpeded. As she closed in on him, he spun on his heels and faced her. 'I came to talk to you and Ben,' Rasci shouted desperately, hoping the dog had not become so close to man kind that it had forgotten the basic language that bound dogs and wolves from way back in their common ancestry. The big dog skidded to a halt. 'I need your help,' Rasci said again, this time more calmly, but desperate on the inside to say something to temper the dog's attack.

'What are you doing on my territory?' the dog demanded, racing forward, hair bristling on her back and shoulders.

Rasci suddenly felt a surge of relief as he realised that, despite a strong dialect, the dog spoke reasonable wolfish, but he hadn't prepared any answers. He hadn't expected to have to explain himself to a dog. 'I know Ben. I know he calls you Smokey. I am a friend of The Black Wolf,' he rattled out, one statement following rapidly after another.

'The Black Wolf?' She skidded to a halt.

'We were on the mountain and fought the bears with you.'

There was a flicker of recognition in Smokey's eyes. 'You were there?' she demanded.

Rasci nodded. 'We saved Ben's father. But he thinks I am another wolf called Solin, the one that attacked your cattle.'

Smokey's coat unbristled. She came closer to Rasci and sniffed at his coat. 'You're not him,' she said, lifting her head and looking Rasci straight in the eyes. 'I remember that wolf.'

'Well he looks different now,' Rasci explained. 'His ears have been torn to shreds.'

'Really?'

'Yes,' Rasci went on, trying to keep Smokey talking. 'You'll definitely recognise him at a distance, if you see him again.'

'So why are you here? I've no more pups to steal. The bad wolf saw to that.'

Rasci looked over Smokey's shoulder. Soon, the farmer would be appearing. If he had his weapon, Rasci knew that he wouldn't miss. He thought quickly and spoke faster. 'Look, Smokey, I have to go or else your master will kill me. I didn't come here to steal anything, to kill anybody or anything like that. I came to ask you and Ben for help.' He turned and began to limp away. 'I'm not going to fight you,' he said as Smokey trotted alongside him. Her head was up and her ears, even though they were flopped over, were pricked forward. 'I am leaving in peace.'

'I reckon I owe you one,' Smokey panted. They were running faster now, side by side. 'Those bears would have killed us all if hadn't been for you.'

'Smokey,' Raymond Rozalski called. 'Smokey, come!'

They were a good three hundred yards away from him. 'I'd better go back,' Smokey said, slowing.

Rasci stopped and looked back, thankful to rest his painful leg. The farmer was standing with his hands on his hips. 'Smokey,' he called again. 'Come, girl.'

'It was my leader Rhamin that led us to save you,' Rasci said.

'Rhamin?'

'The Black Wolf.'

'I see.'

Rasci sighed. He watched as he saw the farmer walking briskly towards them. But, he wasn't carrying his weapon. 'And it's Rhamin that needs your help. He needs Ben's and your master's help.'

'Why?' Smokey glanced back at her master. He called her again. She lowered her head. 'I'll have to go,' she said.

'Wait!'

But Smokey turned and headed back to Raymond Rozalski.

Rasci sat there for a minute while she trotted towards him. Raymond scratched his head and spoke to Smokey. He pointed at Rasci. Smokey looked back at the wolf and then looked up at her master. Raymond spoke again and then bent over and patted Smokey on the shoulder. He straightened up and looked towards Rasci. Rasci stood up, gave the farmer one last glance and limped away.

CHAPTER TWENTY

It was going to take him days to get back to the Darin. He stopped more times than he could count, each step a struggle, and each stride getting harder as he limped on. His leg was badly bruised, but his ego was pulped. As the day progressed, he considered what he was going to tell the pack? 'I went to the farm and got stoned and shot!' or 'I went to the farm but they weren't in.' That sounded better, but how did he get his injuries? He had a deep cut in his front upper leg, a badly swollen knee, a gash across his shoulder blades in the skin on his back and a groove in his fur where the woman's invisible tooth cut its way into his coat at one side and carried on, unimpeded, out at the other. 'I was walking through the forest when…' No. that wasn't right. 'I was visiting the farm to talk to Ben…' That sounded like he knew the farmer's son personally. None of the pack would believe that. Besides, he had never met Ben. He got within thirty or so yards of him, that's all. 'Well, the idea was to get help to save Rhamin…' Only, they didn't know that there was a good chance that Rhamin was still alive. He wished now he had told them about his dreams. But, then they wouldn't have believed that either! 'I was passing by the farm, you know, the one that we raided, and I happened to come upon the farmer who threw rocks at me…'

Phew. This was going to be a nightmare, never mind a dream. He blew out his cheeks as he settled down to sleep. The first night of his journey home was about to begin. The dreadful day was behind him and a night's sleep would make it easier to think. His pounding headache had been replaced by sheer fatigue. He found a covered hollow beneath the roots of an old stag headed oak tree. He felt safe there. What Roxana had said was still rattling about somewhere in his head. 'There is danger about,' she had said. It made Rasci uncomfortable, and whatever the danger, he was in no fit state to fight. Even Solin would make little work of him if he were to challenge him. And the feeling of being watched seemed stronger somehow.

'It was Rasci, Daddy, not the bad wolf.' Ben was crying. 'You hurt Rasci!'

Ben was sitting at the kitchen table. His father sat beside him, his arm around his son's shoulder. His mother was sitting opposite, face flushed and still rather breathless. 'You nearly got yourself killed today, do you realise?'

'He's not going to kill me. He's a friendly wolf.' He wiped a tear from his cheek and looked up at his father's face. 'Like the ones that saved you Daddy.'

'He was a grey wolf, Ben,' his father responded 'He looked like the one that killed the cattle. For all we know, he was the same wolf.'

'But he wasn't. He'd come to see me.'

'We were afraid for you. Whichever wolf he was, he had

no business lurking about in our yard.'

'But I told you… this morning, I told you…'

'It's no good, Ben,' his mother broke in. 'A wolf's a wolf,' she said crossly. 'We would no sooner let you near a wolf than we would let you near a stray dog. They can't be trusted. You hear? They can't be trusted young man. Pretend that you have a wolf friend by all means, but we will not let you go near a live one.'

'But I have a proper wolf friend Mummy. I'm not pretending.'

'If you don't stop this now, then you'll have to go to your room. It's already too late to take you into school. You will be made to sit in your room all day. Do you hear me?'

'But…'

'I'll keep him with me,' Raymond said, getting up from the table and taking a hold of Ben's hand. 'He'll be all right in a while.'

'I don't know where he gets it from. I really don't!' She shook her head and picked up a tea towel from the table. Busily, she wiped the table top, standing as she reached to the furthest side. 'I really don't know,' she muttered.

Raymond ushered his son out of the door and into the front garden. It wasn't a busy garden, with lots of flowers and neat little borders. It was just a square of wild pasture, with a few climbing roses propped against an old criss-cross trellis that was attached to the wall at each side of the door of the house, and some golden marigolds in a patch by a crazy stone pathway that led to an old oak plank bench. The rest was long wispy grass that seldom got mowed. It made a good place for Ben and Margo to play safely away from tractor wheels and dangerous farm machinery. It was a good place to talk. 'Now then Ben,' Raymond said, lifting Ben up to his chest and walking over to the bench. He slid his son down to the ground and sat on the planks. Holding both of his son's hands, he looked him in the eyes. 'I realise now that the wolf that came today was not the bad wolf.'

Ben looked back at the kitchen door. His mother was nowhere in sight. He looked back at his father. 'Rasci isn't a pretend wolf, Daddy.'

'I could see that.'

'But you tried to kill him!'

'No, Ben. Your mother tried to kill him!' Remember my tractor tyre?'

Ben smiled. 'She's not as good a shot as you, is she Daddy?'

Raymond smiled back and shook his head. 'Perhaps it's just as well.'

'But you threw a stone at him.'

'Your mother's shouting panicked me a little, I think.' He straightened Ben's shirt collar. He was still dressed in his school clothes. 'All I could do was think about saving you…' He paused and then said slowly in a deep voice, 'from the big… bad… wolf!'

Ben chuckled.

'So, my biggest bestest son, we're going to have to forego the pleasure of meeting your wolf friend. There is no way your mother will allow any wolf near you.'

'But…'

'No 'Buts' Ben. Your mother has been frightened by wolves too many times; when they came into the house that night, remember? And when that bad wolf went for her after killing the cattle?'

'But you said that The Black Wolf saved her like he saved us in the house.'

'He did. And not just that. That wolf was the one that brought his pack to the mountain and if it weren't for him,

I'd be bear food now. But grey wolves are not all that easy to tell apart. Oh, I know they have different markings, but it takes time to get to know one from another.'

'So what if he comes back?'

'I don't think he will come back now, Ben.'

Rasci could see them as if he were there. And, it wasn't like the shouting he heard that morning, when none of it made sense. Then, he couldn't understand a single word; except for the names of the boy and the dog. But, as before, now, in his dream, he could understand everything. It was as if they were speaking wolfish. In his dreams, he had an overview that would never have been possible in reality.

He stirred in his sleep and began to awaken. His hiding place was small but comfortable. As he opened his eyes and stretched, pushing his big feet against the sides of the hollow, he felt safe. For the time being he was free from worries. He had covered little ground that day, and limping slowly, he had many hours travelling ahead of him to get back to the Darin, and when he got back there he was expected to be a leader. A leader! That word! Suddenly, his head was aching again. The thump, thump, thumping was back with a vengeance every time he thought of it. He was beginning to hate being the leader. In fact he was even beginning to hate the thought of having to go back, and what's more, he hated himself for being so weak. At the moment, being killed didn't seem so unattractive.

For the time being, however, there was nothing he could do about it. He had to accept the status quo. A spark of determination lit his eyes as he gazed out of the hollow into the cloud swept night. He had made a decision. There was no alternative now. Fate had placed him where he was. It had given him his gift of seeing the unseen and was carrying him through a process that would eventually end one way or the other. He knew he wasn't cut out for the life that had been cast upon him, and he knew that he would eventually let the whole pack down. He couldn't carry on as he was. If Rhamin returned, then all his worries would end. His mind was made up. He would save Rhamin or he would die trying.

His headache suddenly subsided. The hole gave him a sense of well being, a sense of security. He snuggled back down inside it, wrapped his tail around his face, relaxed into a deep sleep and dreamt of Rhamin. 'Don't worry Rhamin,' he heard his voice saying, 'your pack is waiting for your return.'

Rasci awakened to the sound of barking; not dog barking, wolf barking. Cautiously, he lifted his nose above the edge of the hole and looked out. At first he saw nothing. A morning mist clung to the ground, clouding his vision like a veil in one of his dreams. He turned his head, searching for the source of the sound, but his head wasn't clear and his eyes seemed to be playing tricks on him. He swore he saw the dim figure of a wolf disappearing ahead of him, but the vision had evaporated before he could form it into a picture in his mind. He shook his head to discard the pangs of sleep.

'Woof, woof,' he heard it again, but the sound wasn't ahead of him. It was coming from behind the tree. The voice seemed familiar, but it was agitated. Quickly, he jumped out from beneath the roots and sprang around to the other side of the tree. He could see the back of a dark grey wolf, but in the murky light it looked as black as Rhamin's coat. He shook his head again, even harder this time. The wolf, hair bristling at the shoulders, was standing facing away from him, fifty or more strides away.

'Rhamin?' he muttered. Then, as he stepped closer, through the mist, he could make out the form of another wolf. It was not his leader. What he was seeing was the smooth, dark coat of the stranger he had met the evening before. It was Roxana.

'What is it?' Rasci called, but she didn't answer. She was still facing away from him.

She barked again and parried to one side. It was then that Rasci saw it. He knew immediately what it was. With its short, coarse, brown coat, its muscular, supple limbs and long, black-tipped tail; its pointy ears and long retractable claws protruding from its large feet, as it swiped at Roxana, there was no mistaking a mountain lion. Its creamy white underside looked grey in the diminished light and its white throat and chest looked equally grey until he got closer. Its pink nose in a striped black muzzle seemed deceptively harmless until the face that held it wrinkled in an aggressive snarl. It swiped out again at Roxana, with its front paw, but she lightly hopped to one side as the razor sharp claws breezed past her face. She squatted down on her front paws and snarled back, feinting a lunge that made the big cat spring to one side and circle around her, evasively.

A male mountain lion can weigh as much as, if not more than a full grown male wolf. At around 70 kilograms, it is bigger than most female wolves. Roxana was a big wolf, but Rasci reckoned that the big cat had a definite weight advantage. But mountain lions, like all cats, have extremely fast reflexes. Wolves have reaction times faster than a human being or a domestic dog, but that is still slower than the reflex time of most members of the cat family. As the big cat jumped backwards to avoid the expected lunge of its adversary, it sprung forwards again, instantly, with another, lethal, claw filled swipe at Roxana. But she hadn't lunged. It was just a manoeuvre. She had merely made the cat think that she was attacking, so the vicious claws, once again cut through the cool morning air inches from her face.

Circling around, the cat attacked again, only Roxana was expecting it and raced to one side, pursued by the flailing arms of the cat. Once again she stopped and then lunged forward with her long canine teeth lashing at the air and then retreating. Suddenly, from the corner of its eye, the mountain lion saw Rasci who, despite his limp, had already gained an advantage. He was upon the lion from the rear, and even though, in the cat's eyes, Rasci was moving relatively slowly, he had caught the mountain lion on its rump with his teeth. Seeing this second adversary, the big cat swung around and with a reflexive, lightning strike, landed its claws against the thick impenetrable coat on Rasci's shoulder. Rasci yelped as the impact compressed his wound where the man's bullet had cut past his shoulder blades. He lunged sideways to avoid another swipe by the ambidextrous cat, which seemed to brandish each front paw with the same cutting, punching, swiping agility.

But, mountain lions do not have thick coats like wolves. The sudden attack from the rear had left it with an open stab wound where Rasci's canine tooth had landed on its rump. Instead of continuing the attack, it scuttled off into the mist. Rasci watched it disappear and then, stretching his neck to ease the pain in his shoulder, he turned to Roxana.

'Good job I was around,' he said, looking at the face of his new companion, proudly.

Roxana shook her head. 'Tut. Males!'

'What? Whaaat?'

'You think you saved me, do you?' she asked, her face

showing anger, not gratitude.

'Well, didn't I?'

She waited a moment before answering. She sighed heavily and then said, 'No.'

'So what did I just do?' Rasci asked, surprised at her reaction.

'You helped me save your skin,' Roxana said firmly.

'My skin?'

She nodded. 'That's right, your skin.'

'But…'

'But your backside!' she said and started to walk away.

'Wait!' He hadn't approached this just right, he could tell.

Roxana turned, tilted her head, and waited.

'I… I thought you were in danger. I thought…' He walked closer to her. He could smell her. She smelt very agreeable.

'You thought!' she said angrily. 'Can you think?'

'Well, yes, I think so.'

She shook her head. 'It was stalking you, you idiot!'

Somehow the description didn't upset Rasci. After all, that's how most of the pack used to regard him before his lapse into leadership. The word 'idiot', in fact seemed to have a warm comforting sound to his ears. 'I didn't think they bothered with wolves,' he said, perplexed.

'Not when they are in a group, they don't; but a single wolf that is obviously wounded, then that is an entirely different matter.'

'Wounded?' Rasci had forgotten his injuries.

'Yes,' Roxana said, with as deep a sigh as Rasci had heard in a long time. It was a nice sigh, though he wasn't sure why. He wasn't unduly upset by it. 'A wounded wolf is good prey. We hunt wounded animals all the time.'

Rasci turned his head and looked at the dried blood on his shoulder. A trickle of fresh blood was running over it.

'Oh. Well, yes, I have got a slight cut on my…'

'Slight cut my bum!'

Hmm, nice bum though, Rasci felt the thought trickling through his brain. 'Well, I must admit…' He paused for a moment and then, discarding the thought, he said, 'How do you know, anyway?'

'How do I know? I saw you hobbling along like a cripple. That's how I know.'

'Well I was limping a bit, but…'

'You were limping a lot.'

'I was limping a lot,' Rasci agreed with a nod.

'I told you it was dangerous out here!'

'I thought you were kidding me. I travel around on my own all the time. I don't recall ever getting eaten by some mad, vicious cat at any time.'

'There's always a first time.'

He nodded. 'Hmm. Well what was it doing in my territory, anyway?' He stopped and thought about what he had just said. 'What are you doing, still in my territory, come to that?'

Roxana seemed a little unsettled. 'Oh, looking for you,' she said. Rasci felt she was straining to be casual.

'For me? Looking for me?' He lifted his head and gazed into space for a second. 'Right,' he said as if he suddenly understood; which he didn't. He waited for her to explain, but she just shrugged. 'Er, why?' he asked her, eventually.

'Oh, a little bird told me you were really a pack leader. As you said, I have ambitions.'

'Ambitions? Did I? Oh, well yes, but… a little bird? You don't know Corvak do you?'

'Corvak?'

'A bird.'

'It's a saying, stupid.'

'Stupid? Oh, yes, that's me. I… I'm not really a pack leader,' he fumbled with his words. 'No, I am more your, how shall I put it?'

'The following type?'

'Yes!' He thought again for a moment and then asked; 'So who told you I was a pack leader?'

'Some lone wolf I met up in the forests.'

'One of my pack, no doubt,' Rasci nodded.

'Not that I could make out, he wasn't'

'Oh?'

'No. This one seemed a little bitter. Had badly torn ears.'

'Solin!' Rasci gasped. 'I see.'

'You see?'

'Oh, Solin was hoping to be a pack leader. He just messed things up a bit, that's all,' Rasci said with a sigh. He realised that, had Solin not betrayed the pack, he would now have been the new leader. But then, would Solin have wanted to save Rhamin? Rasci thought not.

'You don't sound like you dislike him.' Roxana looked puzzled. 'He said you hated him.'

'No, that's not true. He just did the wrong thing at the wrong time. Perhaps he was born at the wrong time, I don't know. Solin is just Solin, that's all.'

'So what about your pack?' Roxana asked, coming closer to him. 'How come you don't have them around you? How come you didn't tell me you were a pack leader?'

'I felt a bit embarrassed,' Rasci said, shrugging sheepishly. 'It's all a bit new to me.'

'Embarrassed?'

'Well, I don't feel like… I don't think other wolves see me like that.'

'Well, obviously, your pack does.'

'Yes,' Rasci said, suddenly realising the significance of what Roxana had just said.

'You're not frightened of me are you?'

'Me! Frightened? I've never been frightened of anything in my life,' Rasci stated truthfully. He was a courageous wolf. He just didn't feel the need to be courageous all the time. Being a leader meant he had to be on top of the job. He had to show a certain strength all the time. But perhaps, with more thought, he wasn't as courageous as he would have liked to be. He was afraid he would never see Rhamin again, and he was afraid that even if Rhamin was alive he would not get the chance to save him. On top of that he was afraid that if he went back to the farm, the farmer would be just as intransigent as before.

'I'm sorry, I didn't mean it that way,' Roxana assured him. 'You seem, well, a bit shy.'

Rasci knew what she meant. 'I'm not what you think I am,' he said earnestly. 'If you are looking for a leader to... to have babies with and things...'

Roxana smiled. 'I am.'

'Well, it's just that, I am not really the leader of the pack.'

'That's not what I've heard. That wolf Solin seemed to think you were.'

'Did he?' asked Rasci, suddenly feeling rather proud of himself.

'Yes, he said that you were the new leader now that Rhamin is dead.'

The words cut deep into Rasci's soul. 'Hmm, well I...' He was going to explain what he felt, but thought better of it. 'So he told you about Rhamin then?'

Roxana nodded. 'He told me that Rhamin was his brother, and so are you.'

'Did he, now?'

'Isn't that true then?'

Rasci thought for a while. Explanations, explanations, explanations. When would he be able to just get back to being his old self; just following the leader? No explanations, no responsibilities, no wolves wanting to be the alpha female matched with the alpha male. He tried to picture himself with Roxana.

'Rasci?'

Rasci snapped back to consciousness. 'What? Oh, yes, he… they are… were. I mean he is and Rhamin was.'

'Brothers?'

'Yes.'

'And what he says is true then?'

'Er, what did he say?' Rasci's mind was beginning to somersault.

'That you took over from your brother Rhamin when he died?'

'Yes, that's right.' It seemed a simple explanation to a complicated question. The pulse was beginning to throb above his right eye again.

'So how did Solin get his torn ears?'

'Oh, I'm not sure,' Rasci lied. 'Perhaps we had better travel together,' he said, changing the subject. 'After all, there is a dangerous cat about.'

Roxana smiled. 'Do I take it that you are warming to me a little?'

Rasci couldn't deny it. He hadn't really cooled to her in the first place. But he still felt uncomfortable. He was not leadership material, and usually it was only leaders that took a mate. And besides, Roxana made him have feelings he didn't know existed before he met her, and was still trying to come to terms with them. He thought about being the pack leader and wasn't sure if he wanted to prolong a friendship which was based on a false premise. But was it a false premise? Now, suddenly, for some reason, he wasn't sure if he wanted to give up being a leader. But why was he thinking that? He wasn't sure. In fact he wasn't sure about anything any more. 'Look,' he said finally, 'we'll walk together for a while. That way I won't attract predators. You know,' he said, after giving the subject some thought, 'even the vultures seem to have been taking a strong interest in me lately.'

'Really? Vultures?'

'Yes, there's a pair that seem to be waiting for leftovers all the time now.' He considered them for a while as he walked beside her. His brush with the farmer had been unsettling but, although he didn't feel particularly good, he didn't think he looked at all like dropping dead. Maybe he looked worse than he thought. 'Perhaps you are right, even the vultures are waiting for me to keel over.'

'Oh, I'm sure they know you're all right,' Roxana replied with a comforting smile that made him feel better instantly.

Eventually, a hot morning sun burnt away the cool, lingering mist and the pair walked silently together, heading towards the Darin.

'So how did you get your injuries,' Roxana asked later, as they circled a clump of trees and instinctively peered into the thicket in search of prey.

Rasci walked over to the cover of the shade, and slumped down to rest. He didn't want to say anything to Roxana about how he got hurt. He didn't want to tell anybody. A swarm of flies buzzed enthusiastically around his head, making him feel rather dizzy, and his leg ached so badly that he needed to rest. Roxana came over and licked the gash on his shoulder. It had to be cleaned or else the flies would start to lay their eggs in the open wound. Her closeness to him made his head spin even more, but with Roxana's attention to the cut, he almost immediately began to feel better. More than that, her attention to his shoulder relieved the pain in his leg. He found that quite remarkable. 'You are very quiet,' she commented as Rasci began to feel the tension drain from his body.

'Sorry, I was thinking,' Rasci replied truthfully. His eyes began to close as he relaxed.

'Oh? What about?'

'About… about.' Rasci lapsed into sleep mode, turning off all his senses to the things around him. He could still feel Roxana's tongue gently cleaning his wound as he slid out of reality.

For the first time since his elevation to pack leader, he slept more soundly than he had for days; no dreaming of Rhamin and Yeltsa fighting, no dreaming about the farmer or his son, no complicated matters of leadership, or at least none he would remember. Instead, Roxana was in his head, talking to him with her velvet voice, looking at him with her magnetic eyes. 'What you need to do, is stop worrying about the old and start thinking about the new,' she was saying. Then they were playing in the sun, nowhere in particular, just a place with bright, warm light all around them as they threw sticks in the air and chased after them. They ran together, walked together, lay together.

The sun was high in the sky when he woke again, but he felt so much better. Somehow, his problems had been solved for him. In his sleep, everything had seemed to fall into place. He knew now what he was going to do, what he was going to say. He had to get back to his pack.

He was so refreshed that, at first, he didn't remember his injuries. But, as soon as he pushed himself up into a standing position, he remembered his damaged leg. Then he remembered Roxana. He swung his head around to see where she was, but she was nowhere to be seen. Careful not to catch his sore leg, he wandered through the copse, from one side to the other and then around it looking in. No, there was no female wolf. Perhaps he had dreamed it all, he thought. Perhaps the dark grey female wolf was a figment of his imagination. He stopped and looked down at the ground while he thought. Perhaps that was what he really wanted, a female that would lead the pack with him. What was the saying? "Behind every successful male wolf..." He tried to think. Was she real? Or was it a deeply rooted desire?

As he looked down at the ground, he saw a paw mark, not unlike his own, only slightly smaller. He bent his head forward and sniffed at the print. With his remarkable sense of smell, it wasn't difficult to recognise the scent of a female wolf. It was Roxana's scent. It was Roxana's footprint. Ergo, he was not dreaming. He was almost overcome by the sense of relief, chuckling to himself, feeling lighter on his feet than he had since Raymond Rozalski's rock had hit his fore leg. Then, without any idea as to the practical use of his behaviour, and holding his injured leg up out of harm's way, he stooped forwards and rolled on the ground where the footprint had lain.

Eventually he stood up and shook the dust from his coat, looking around, to see if Roxana had returned from wherever she had gone. She was nowhere to be seen, and after a final search of the area, he lifted his head and gave out a high pitched howl. He tilted his head for a minute or so and listened intently, but no response came. He was about to howl again when, seeing the vultures circling high on a thermal, he thought better of it, and with a final shake of his coat, and favouring his damage leg, he set off once more towards home and the Darin.

CHAPTER TWENTY ONE

Although it took a further two days of slow, painful walking to reach the Darin, Rasci didn't see Roxana again. Each time he stopped to rest, he howled, but as he got closer to the Darin, the only response was from his own pack members who seemed overjoyed to hear from him.

'We were getting worried,' Lexa said as she ran to greet her leader, her stump of a tail wriggling ecstatically while the other wolves happily wagged their long brush tails. There was no sign that any of them thought less of him for returning with a bruised leg and a cut along his shoulder blade. In fact their devotion to their new leader seamed to have been even more cemented. There was such a lot of squeaking and tail wagging that, for a time, Rasci forgot what had been on his mind for the last three days and nights. Somehow, he thought that Roxana may have gone ahead to meet him at the Darin, but then, as a stranger, she didn't know where it was. And besides that, the other wolves would not have taken kindly to an outsider without some kind of introduction. So he'd travelled alone and had arrived alone. Nothing different; everything back to normal, he thought, as he went to the water hole in the rear of the cave.

After some time, he emerged into the daylight and came and sat beside Zelda. Silvah carried over some food that had been brought back from their latest kill and left it for Rasci to eat while he talked to Zelda. He had been in no condition to hunt, and it was now more than five days since he had eaten anything. They just lay beside him and waited for him to finish his meal, unhurried; and then, when he was ready, they listened to how he had been to the farm, once in his dream and then once in person. He had decided to tell them the whole story, no excuses, no exaggerations. Meticulously, he explained what had happened, and how the farmer's wife had shot at him, and how Raymond Rozalski had thrown rocks at him just as he was about to talk to their child. He left nothing out. But he never mentioned Roxana.

'You tried,' Silvah comforted Rasci. She licked his leg gently. While he had been away, the whole pack had gathered at the Darin, but Corvak had failed to return, and without the intelligence gathering skills of his feathered friend, Rasci could not see any way of confirming the answers to his questions. Was Rhamin still alive? If he was, then where was he? Was he a prisoner, and how far away was the prison? If he was a prisoner, what escape routes were there?

'I didn't try hard enough,' Rasci said, shaking his head. 'But, it was an important trip. I know now what I have to do next time.'

'Next time?' exclaimed Silvah. 'You're not going back!'

'Of course he is,' Zelda said emphatically. 'He has no choice. We have no choice, unless we want to leave Rhamin rotting in a prison for the rest of his life.'

'That's all very courageous,' Silvah countered. 'But we have already lost one leader. And now, Rasci almost got himself killed.'

'Perhaps we should ask the rest of the pack,' Zelda said in a critical tone.

'We can, if we get positive news that Rhamin is alive,' Silvah argued. 'But until we know for sure, then how are we going to explain anything about Rasci's visit to the farmer, and how are we going to suggest any plan involving the pack if they don't know what the aim of the plan is?'

'I don't need the help of the pack,' Rasci intervened.

'I see,' Silvah said in a sarcastic tone. 'So you are going to find where Rhamin is being held, kill all his prison guards, rescue him and Yeltsa and just walk off into the sunset!'

'Something like that,' Rasci said with a confident smile. 'Except for all that killing stuff. Ugh! That bit sounds…' A glint filled his eyes… 'too enjoyable!'

'Silly wolf!' Zelda scolded. 'Behave yourself and talk properly.'

'Sorry Gran.' He licked her on the face. 'No, I am angry with the men who I believe have taken Rhamin, but I'm not that angry.'

'Glad to hear it.'

'But you can't do anything on your own,' Silvah insisted. 'What can one wolf do?'

'I won't be alone,' he replied.

'But you said you didn't need any help.'

'I said I didn't need the pack. But I will need the help of one wolf.'

'Oh?'

'Yes.'

'And who might that be, pray tell?

Rasci smiled. 'Lexa,' he said.

'Lexa!' Silvah exclaimed. Then she paused to form her words. 'Lexa, our wolf dog !'

'I think we might have the makings of a plan, if I am not very much mistaken,' said Zelda.

By the time Corvak returned four days later, Rasci was well on the way to recovery. He, too, had just about given up on the idea of gaining any intelligence from his aerial spy, but Corvak's appearance was a joyous event when it happened. He glided in from a great height, croaked half a dozen times to let his friends know that he had returned, did a couple of fly overs and then tried a somersault which nearly made him stall and tumble to the ground, only he corrected his flight path just in the nick of time and swooped upwards from within inches of the floor as if it were all part of his aerodynamic display. Eventually he glided faultlessly into his favourite bush, landed on his favourite branch and shook himself to adjust all his feathers as he folded his wings.

None were more pleased to see Corvak than Rasci, not for the information he might be able to impart, but just for the sheer joy of seeing him return alive and well. And the old raven knew it. When all the wolves in the greeting pack had calmed down, Corvak took up his usual position. He bobbed up and down on his branch, croaking and giving out an occasional husky whistle. 'I can see you're glad to be back,' Lexa said to her friend as she passed on the way to join the others. She and Ramusan had arrived too late to see Corvak's splendid entrance. 'Did you find out any news?' she asked.

'I certainly did,' Corvak boasted, fluffing out the feathers on his chest and burying his beak in them for a brief spell of preening.

Lexa looked at Silvah who translated.

'Well aren't you going to tell us?' asked Lexa.

'He will, when all the wolves are gathered,' said Silvah. 'I think that what Corvak has to say concerns us all.'

'Absolutely!' called Corvak lifting his beak so that it pointed upwards in an important looking stance. 'Absolutely. What I have to say concerns all my friends.'

Once again Silvah interpreted.

'But not all the wolves understand ravenish!' said Lexa.

'Quite so,' said Silvah, 'but I shall interpret for the benefit of those that don't understand.'

So, eventually, as the meeting was convened and all the wolves took their place forming a semi circle next to the bush, Silvah instructed Corvak to proceed. She positioned herself under the bush, facing out towards the convened assembly.

'Well,' Corvak began, his beak still pointing upwards importantly. 'I flew for many days…'

'We know you did, Corvak, get on with it,' Rasci heckled 'We've all been sitting around waiting for you, remember?'

'Well some of us were,' Zelda stated, nudging Rasci to silence him.

'I'll ignore that, Rasci,' Corvak chirped cheerily. He knew his friend well.

All the wolves laughed as Silvah did a running translation.

'As I was saying,' continued Corvak, 'before I was so rudely interrupted, I flew for many miles.'

Rasci fidgeted but remained silent.

'And I flew for many miles more!'

Rasci grunted. He wasn't sure he could stand the suspense without grabbing his friend and shaking the news out of him.

'I'd have asked questions amongst the birds that are friendly towards ravens.' He paused for effect. 'But there aren't any!' He chuckled to himself. 'And eventually, I flew to a place beyond the man's forest of rock buildings.' He glanced around at all the faces while Silvah continued with her translation. 'That, for those of you who have never seen it from the air…' Silvah looked up at Corvak, tutted and shook her head, but carried on translating, much to the amusement of the pack. 'As I was saying, the forest of rock buildings is a man made area so big that it would take you a whole day to travel across it on foot.' He paused again and then added, 'Wolves that is. It would take me about a year on foot!' The listening wolves burst out laughing.

'Anyway,' he went on, 'there are tall structures that the men folk use for living in or something. They stretch as far as the eye can see.'

Rasci shuffled impatiently. He was beginning to regret that he hadn't asked Corvak to go to one side and tell him first.

'Well, I flew all over the area to the south of the man made forest of rock. There was no sign of Rhamin there. In fact there was no sign of Rhamin anywhere I went in the first two days. None of the other ravens in the area knew anything about him either.' Corvak side stepped along the branch and tested it for springiness. 'But then I decided to fly out beyond the man's forest,' he continued, after seemingly satisfying himself the branch was still strong enough to take his weight. All the wolves sat and waited patiently, all silent, all expectant, except one.

'Go on,' Silvah urged quietly. She sensed Corvak's need to dramatise, but she knew he needed to tell the story through from beginning to end.

'I don't think I have flown so far and so high for years, not since I was a youngster. But I had to. I flew out and back. Not just a few miles; but for half a day each way. I was determined to find Rhamin and I didn't want to have cut my search short before I was sure I had been far enough. But the task seemed fruitless.' He paused again while he recalled what happened. 'But then, I stopped near a wooded area for the night, and I met another pair of ravens. They were a bit hostile at first, of course. We ravens are very territorial, you know,' he said, looking down at the assembly. 'Just like you wolves. But I explained that I was only passing through and that my real motive for being there was to find a friend that had gone missing. They were very interested, for when I explained, it turned out that they too were friends with a wolf from a distant wolf pack.' He raised his voice triumphantly. 'And then! And then they told me! They told me that one of the wolves from that pack had been taken prisoner as well, by a man in a giant bird. And guess what! They knew where the man had taken her!'

As Silvah translated, all eyes widened in anticipation.

'They showed me! They took me right there and showed me, can you believe my luck?'

All the heads shook as Silvah finished speaking.

'And guess what! I saw Rhamin. I spoke to him. He recognised me and I spoke to him!'

'So he's alive?' asked Lexa.

'He certainly is,' came back the reply. Silvah's voice couldn't conceal her joy. 'He certainly is! He is. He is. He is,' she chanted over and over again. A ripple of conversation passed between all the other wolves as they looked at each other in surprise.

'Silvah!' Rasci called. 'Please?'

'Oh, sorry folks, I didn't mean to interrupt.'

Corvak cleared his throat and, when the rest of the pack had settled again, he continued. 'The place is enclosed by high man made barriers. Some of them carry lightning. They would kill you if you so much as tried to climb over them.' He shook his head. 'Yes,' he continued, but in a sadder voice. 'Rhamin is alive, but there is no way he can escape. There is no way for any of the animals to escape.'

'Any of the animals?' Rasci queried.

Corvak sprang on his branch like a human using a diving board, his feet leaving the branch on the upswing and landing on it again on the way down. 'That's right, all sorts of animals. Animals I have never seen before in my life. Animals I have never even heard tales of!'

'Go on,' Silvah encouraged him.

'There were immensely tall brown creatures with huge lumps on their back, and even taller creatures with blotches all over them and necks that reach into the clouds!'

A sound of awe washed through the gathering.

'And grey creatures with horns on their noses and bigger ones with great noses and huge ears. One ear would make a shelter for all of you!'

'Ooh!' came from the crowd.

'And then there were big cats, like the mountain lions, but different. Some were bigger with more hair on their shoulders. Some were much bigger still with black and orange stripes that made them look like the flames of the grass fires that wash through the plains every now and then.' He cleared his throat again. 'Er, is there any food, by the way?' he looked at all the transfixed faces.

'Soon,' Rasci snapped immediately, not giving Silvah time to interpret. 'And what else? What else was there?'

'Well there were animals I did recognise, of course; buffalo, and deer. But most of them were completely strange to me.'

'And what did Rhamin say?' Zelda called from the front.

'When you talked to him, what did he say?'

Corvak sighed. 'Well, unfortunately, I didn't have long. There were men about, you see. And they looked dangerous. They had their long weapons and I was fri… I was…'

'Cautious,' Rasci said immediately.

'Exactly! I was careful not to get killed. But, despite only staying a short time,' he continued, now unperturbed by his own embarrassment of being afraid, 'Rhamin was glad to see me. Well, you know Rhamin doesn't understand ravenish very well, but I told him, best I could, that I had come looking for him. Whatever he understood, he was absolutely amazed that I had come to call on him at all. But he seemed resigned to his fate. He explained everything he could to me in the short time I was there. He gets food every day, and has sorted out the other wolves that attacked him and Yeltsa when they were first put in the enclosure with them. Yeltsa had been quite badly hurt, but Rhamin was so proud of her. He told me they had repelled an attack by fourteen fully grown wolves! That's remarkable! Yeltsa killed one that had grabbed her leg, by turning on it and grabbing its throat; and Rhamin would have killed some as well, only the men broke up the fight. They hit Yeltsa with a heavy shaft of wood to make her leave go of the wolf she was fighting, but it was already too late to save it. But they didn't hit Rhamin. He said he didn't think it was because they were afraid of him. The men had helped Rhamin to see the other wolves off. They seemed to have been less worried about the other wolves, being hurt, but seemed to be protecting Rhamin. He's rather pampered compared with the other wolves. He said he is some kind of attraction. But that makes the other wolves even more aggressive. They are jealous of him as well as threatened by his size.'

Silvah was having trouble keeping up with Corvak; his words were getting quicker and quicker as his excitement rose. She could tell by the look in his eyes that he too was so proud of Rhamin.

'Eventually, I had to leave. It is very dangerous there. But Rhamin asked me to tell you all he is thinking about you. He said he will never forget any of you and he told me to tell you not to worry about him and get on with your lives because there was no way for him to escape.' Corvak paused a moment. From where Rasci stood, his eyes seemed wet. Corvak sniffed loudly and swallowed and then, quietly, he said, 'He seemed sad to see me leave. Perhaps I will go back and visit him again.' Silvah didn't translate that last part. She knew he was speaking to himself.

With the knowledge that Rhamin was definitely alive, Rasci's confidence grew. Although he had doubted himself, and had suspected his dreams had been wishful thinking, he had been right all the time. Now he believed in himself again and with that, he was sure he could save Rhamin. He knew for sure how he was going to do it. He had one more dangerous task to complete before he could embark on the most perilous adventure of his life.

He knew he might be killed, but it mattered no more. Without Rhamin reinstated as leader, his life was not going to return to normal anyway and he wanted his old life back. It wouldn't be exactly the same of course; nothing ever is. Zelda had told him that experiences become part of us all and we are part of every experience. We are part of everyone we meet and everything we touch, and by his reckoning,

Rasci's mistakes made him the most learned wolf in history. He knew that the experiences of the last few weeks had boosted his standing in that respect, and, more than likely, his experiences in the weeks to come would not only add to his knowledge but would also have a profound effect on his life from there on. They were risks worth taking.

Following the talk by Corvak, Rasci took up a position facing his pack. He called for all the wolves to listen to him carefully. For his plan to succeed, he needed the support of all his wolves. Up to now, he had kept all his dreams and feelings secret from all but Silvah and Zelda. Now he needed to explain to the rest of the pack what he was doing and why he was doing it.

'We're are all very pleased to hear that Rhamin and Yeltsa are alive and well,' he began. 'But are we going to accept that? Are we going to say our last goodbyes to our leader?'

'But you are our leader now,' called Jual. 'We can't have two leaders.'

'Exactly! I am so glad you understand that! If Rhamin were here, who would be leader?'

'Rhamin,' she replied.

'That's why I am going to do my best to get him back home.'

'But how?'

'To tell you how is not so important. All I want is for you all to trust me when I tell you that, like Gran,' he said, nodding towards Zelda, 'I too, have some sort of ability to see into the distance with my mind.'

'I must say something here,' Zelda interrupted. All heads turned towards her, some wolves expecting her to refute what Rasci had said. 'Rasci is gifted in more ways that I ever was! He has gifts that we should all accept. He told me, when Rhamin first disappeared, and Silvah thought he was dead, that our leader was alive. But Rasci didn't want to raise your hopes, because he knew you would all want something more definite than just his visions. Well, now you have it. And I for one want to give him the chance to do what we all would like to do; save Rhamin.'

'We can all help,' Ramusan shouted out.

'Perhaps we can,' Zelda agreed, 'but I think Rasci has an idea that he wants to put to you all first.'

Rasci nodded. He looked at all the expectant faces in front of him. 'It's a pleasure being your leader,' he said, looking at each wolf in turn. 'However, it will be just as great a pleasure for me to be one of the pack, led by Rhamin.' All the wolves listened in silence. 'The one problem is, you may have to pick yet another leader, for if my plan goes wrong, then you will not only have lost Rhamin, the greatest leader that any pack could have, you will have lost me, Rasci, the next best leader.' He lifted his head proudly and chuckled aloud.

All the wolves laughed with him.

'I want you all to agree to what I am going to do, and I want you all to be prepared for the worst.'

'The worst?' asked Ramusan.

'I may not succeed. But the prize is worth the risk, don't you think? And it would be nice if I knew that you were all behind me.'

'We always have been, Rasci,' Lexa stated. 'And without Rhamin here, you are the best.'

Rasci smiled at his wolf dog. His fondness of her made him dread what he was about to say. He cleared his throat and looked at Lexa with warm eyes. 'It's you that holds the key to solving our dilemma,' he started by saying. 'You, Lexa, are the one wolf here that has a natural affinity to the farmer, for he too has a wolf dog in his own pack. His dog is part of his family as you and all the other wolves here are part of ours.'

Lexa just looked at Rasci with her folded ears forward and her brow wrinkled with interest and curiosity. She said nothing.

'You know by now, Lexa, that you were not born a wolf, although you are wolf at heart. You think like a wolf and you act like one, but you have a body like that dog back at the farm.'

Lexa nodded. She had seen the dog in the mountain side when they fought the bears and had seen her own reflection in the still waters of the lake when she was drinking. 'I know I look like a dog,' she said, resigned to the fact.

'But we only noticed that when you were next to the farmer's dog. Any other time, we see a wolf.'

'Well, I am a wolf,' Lexa stated proudly.

'Indeed, you are; and an excellent one at that. But you have to know something and I think it is time to tell you.' He hesitated for a moment, wondering if he was doing the right thing. 'You are the... the...'

'Daughter of that dog,' Lexa prompted.

'Yes,' Rasci said. 'And that gives...' He stopped speaking and tilted his head at Lexa. 'You knew?' he asked, totally perplexed.

Lexa nodded. 'I worked it out last winter, when everybody was being so good to me because I wasn't able to stand the cold like the rest of you. It made me wonder. Then, in the spring, I saw the man's dog on the mountain. I had seen my own reflection in the water and at first I thought there was something wrong. But then I realised that the rest of you were looking at me and then at the dog. I realised that you too could see the resemblance. So I asked Rhamin.'

'You asked Rhamin?' Rasci asked, still surprised.

'Yes, and he told me the whole story.'

'The whole story?'

'Yes, about how he found me and brought me back, you know?'

'Found you? Right, he found you, yes, that's it!'

'Only, he didn't find you,' Zelda broke in. She glanced at Rasci with a silencing look. 'It's about time we told her the whole truth, Rasci.'

'The whole truth?' He didn't sound so certain.

'The whole truth.' She waited for a response, and then said, 'Are you going to tell her or am I?'

'Er, well, perhaps you can explain it best,' he said, feeling rather afraid that he might say the wrong thing. Our leader, Rhamin kidnapped you. Or, Rhamin took you for food, but Yeltsa slapped him about a bit and made him hand you over to rear as a baby wolf. Or, Rhamin stole you just to distract the dog. No, Zelda could do it much better.

Zelda looked at Lexa. 'Lexa, our lovely wolf dog,' she said fondly. 'If you are to help Rasci save Rhamin, then you will have to meet your mother. If we don't tell you the truth, she surely will. So, young one, I am going to tell you a little story.'

Lexa nodded excitedly. The rest of the pack shuffled in their places to make themselves more comfortable. They hadn't listened to one of Zelda's stories for quite some time.

She thought for a moment, before speaking. All the wolves waited silently, and then, 'Smokey,' she said suddenly. 'That is what Rasci tells me the farmer calls his dog.'

'Smokey?' gasped Lexa.

'Oh, it's a man's name, Lexa. You can't blame her for that!'

'Smokey,' Lexa said quietly, trying to get a feel to the

sound. She nodded approvingly. 'Sounds like a wolf's name really,' she said eventually, quite proudly.

'Well, Smokey is your birth mother; you'll have already gathered that.'

Lexa nodded. So did all the other wolves, for they too were enthralled.

'And one day,' Zelda began, now sure she knew what to say, 'only a few days after you were born, Solin burst into the farmer's house to kill the farmer's young ones.'

'Ooh,' gasped Fatz.

'But Rhamin stopped him. He made Solin leave the home of the farmer.' She paused to give her next words more effect. 'But!' she said, her glazed eyes crinkling at the sides as she smiled and looked up to the sky, 'But, Rhamin saw a bundle of baby dog pups in a nest in the corner of the room.' She paused again and looked sightlessly at the gathered wolves before turning back to Lexa. 'Now, Rhamin had been worried about Yeltsa, for she too had been expecting babies, but she was much later than she should have been in giving birth, and Rhamin was worried that she might lose them.' The pack remained silent. Zelda sensed that some of the wolves who were at the farm when Rhamin stole the dog pup were curious what she was going to say next.

'Now Rhamin needed to distract Smokey, for at that particular time, she and the farmer were enemies of the pack. Smokey worked so well as a team with the farmer, in fact, that between them, they killed two of our strongest wolves.'

Another gasp came from some more of the younger pack members. Depni and Floss looked at each other and then at Lexa, approvingly.

'And that's when Rhamin decided he would steal one of Smokey's babies. He stole two really, but, as the big dog broke off its task with the farmer, he dropped one to try and make her stop chasing after him.'

'Absolutely true,' called Natan, who had been there.

'Rhamin had no intention to hurt either you or the pup he left behind. But, as you lay in a ball in his mouth, something inside him told him not to leave you. He could have done, and the big dog would have given up the chase much more easily, but he didn't, because, when he tasted your fur in his mouth, when he smelt your little body, he knew he wanted you, and he wanted this tiny baby for his mate and the rest of the pack.'

Lexa smiled.

'However, when he returned to the Darin,' she said kindly to Lexa, 'he found to his relief that Yeltsa had managed to give birth. But she had lost one of the babies, so Yeltsa willingly took his new gift and placed you, Lexa, along side your brothers and sisters.'

Depni, Floss, Fatz and Ramusan all looked at their sister, proudly. 'And that's how the pack has its very own wolf dog. You were reared as a wolf and loved as a wolf.'

'I know,' Lexa said with a nod.

'So my little one,' Zelda said with a toothless grin, for Lexa was now bigger than most of the other wolves, 'that is the story of how Smokey's daughter became a wolf.'

'And Lexa is our secret weapon,' Rasci said proudly. 'Lexa is the one wolf that can gain the friendship of the farmer now that Rhamin has gone, for although Rhamin and the farmer eventually became friends, he knows none of us as well as he knew Rhamin. In fact, he still remembers Solin, and that makes him very protective of his family. That's why I have had a bad leg. He thought I was Solin. In fact,' Rasci said with a grin, 'I really don't think he can tell one wolf from another!'

'Incredible!' muttered Natan, unable to understand how a creature so lacking in sensory ability could become so powerful on the earth.

'And because of that disability,' Rasci continued, 'we need to befriend Smokey, his dog. I have already started that process,' he said, proudly. 'and have already spoken to Smokey. But with Lexa's help, I hope to gain the farmer's trust the way that Rhamin did.'

'And then what?' asked Natan.

'And then I intend to put my plan into action.'

Rasci left Silvah and Zelda to explain in more detail to the rest of the pack just how he had known about Rhamin and what had triggered the request to Corvak to go in search of their leader. He was sure, now that the proof of Rhamin's survival had been delivered, that the pack would not think him to be a weird and rather stupid leader. Strong as he was, prior to Corvak's revelation, they could well have thought that they had made the wrong choice, for even Rasci had thought that.

Rasci wasn't far away and the explanation by his two female elders drew a few chuckles, despite the overwhelming evidence that Rasci's dreams were something substantial; something that they could rely on. But overall, the pack seemed willing to accept what Zelda and Silvah were saying, so Rasci silently stepped away into the cave, where he could settle down and meditate. In the last few days, determined to isolate the good dreams from the bad dreams, he had discovered that he could open his mind to his remote visions by deep concentration in a trance-like state, rather than relying on the right type of dream passing through his mind when he was asleep. He knew he would have to contact Ben, but until he had a definite appointment with his young man friend, there was no time frame in which to bring the plan to maturity.

CHAPTER TWENTY TWO

Ben was in his class at school. The elementary school, a little wooden building at the edge of the town, only had three classrooms each capable of holding around twenty children. Mrs. Steadman was Ben's teacher. As it happens, only a few children of Ben's age attended the school. It was only his second week there. May, his best friend, had been there a little longer. Like Ben, May had golden blonde hair. Hers was not cut short like Ben's, it was plaited into long pigtails at either side of her face.

Rasci sat beside Ben and watched the class as Mrs. Steadman explained something complex that he didn't understand. Looking at the faces of the children, he thought that they were no wiser than he was. A little child called Sophie was still chatting to May and Ben was making pictures of wolves on a sheet of something white and flexible, with something that looked like a wooden stick.

It was a strange feeling being amongst so many humans but none of them saw Rasci, of course; only Ben. He turned his head as soon as Rasci appeared, and his eyes widened with delight. 'You're alive!' he exclaimed, mouth open with surprise.

'What was that Benjamin?' asked Mrs Steadman.

'Oh, nothing Miss.' He knew she couldn't see Rasci.

'But you said something about being alive. Are you going to tell the class to whom you were referring?'

'To whom…? Oh, yes Miss. Who I was talking to, you mean?'

Mrs Steadman sighed and nodded.

'It's my friend, Rasci. He comes to visit me sometimes.'

Mrs. Steadman looked around, examining every corner of the class room. She looked directly at Ben and shook her head. 'You'll have to do better than that, Ben,' she stated among a chorus of giggles.

Ben knew he was the only one there that could see Rasci, so he decided on diplomacy. 'Sorry, Miss. What I meant is that I have an imaginary friend called Rasci. He visits me and we talk together.'

'An imaginary friend?' She shook her head again and wagged her finger under Ben's nose. 'Benjamin, if you don't concentrate, then you will be sent home with a letter for your parents. Do you understand me?'

Ben understood all right. On his first day at school, he had seen another boy, Mark departing from the classroom with a letter in hand. It was a serious matter indeed. Unfortunately, Mark accidentally lost the letter under the car seat on his way home. If Mrs. Steadman hadn't followed it up with a phone call, the plan might have worked, but it had not been particularly well thought out. It seemed a good idea at the time, especially as it was the idea of a bright newcomer called Ben, who had suggested losing the letter in the first place. Ben wasn't sure what punishment Mark's father had meted out, but he behaved himself in class for the next four days, and Ben wasn't his friend after that.

Rasci just watched patiently.

When Mrs. Steadman turned to go back to the front of the classroom, Ben turned to one side and smiled at Rasci. 'See you outside,' he mouthed silently, nodding towards the back door. 'Play time soon.'

Rasci was enthralled by the fact that, like wolves, other members of the human pack helped to rear and to teach the young ones. It fascinated him to watch how humans lived and learned and played and communicated. It fascinated him just how alike, wolves and men kind were.

Eventually, he watched as Ben and the others left the school house to play outside in an open area at the back of the building. Leaving the other children behind, Ben walked over to a little swing and sat on it, pushing himself backwards and forwards gently with the tips of his toes. Rasci was sitting in front of it, waiting for him. 'Thanks for waiting,' he said, squinting at Rasci as the sun shone into his eyes. Rasci went around to the other side of the swing and Ben got off and changed sides so that the sun and the school house were behind him. Now facing the school house, Rasci had a good view of the other children and, as he looked beyond them, he noticed that Mrs. Steadman was watching through a small window that looked out onto the play area. She watched Ben nodding and chatting to his imaginary friend with a definite and noticeable look of concern on her face. Even though the child was not her own, she still watched over Ben the in the same way that unrelated wolves watch over the youngsters of the pack. Rasci liked that.

'Who was the grown up in the room?' Rasci asked Ben, watching her with interest.

'My teacher,' Ben replied, glancing back over his shoulder to see what exactly it was that Rasci was looking at so concertedly.

'Teacher, heh? I suppose she teaches you how to hunt and things like that?'

Ben laughed out loud and shook his head. 'No!' he said, trying to contain the bubble of laughter that kept welling up from his tummy. 'Daddy's doing that.'

'So what does she teach you then?'

'I'm learning to read and write,' Ben said, expecting Rasci to understand. 'Although, Mummy has started to teach me that already.' He paused and then said, 'And I'm learning to add up and all that stuff.'

'Add up?'

'Yes, I can add numbers. Two wolves plus two wolves are…'

'Four wolves,' Rasci said proudly.

Ben's eyes widened. 'Gosh, you know this stuff as well!'

Rasci tried to grasp the reason why Ben should spend much of his life learning to count wolves, but something inside him prompted him to think better of asking for any further information. 'But… but what's reading and writing?' he asked instead.

Ben chuckled again. 'You don't know much about humans, do you?'

Rasci shook his head. 'No, but I'd like you to teach me.'

'What, to read and write?'

'What does that mean?'

Ben was pensive for quite a while. 'Well,' he said eventually, 'it's like… like putting words down on paper…'

'Paper?'

'You know, that stuff I had on my desk. I can say something

and you can hear it. But just imagine you are not here when I say it. Then you won't know what I've said.'

'Obviously!' Rasci said, confused.

'But if I put what I am saying down on paper,' Ben continued, 'then you can see that paper and know what I've said, even if you are not there when I say it, you know...' He got off the swing, bent down and wrote his name in the sandy dirt with his finger. 'That says "Ben",' he said proudly, standing back up and pushing his bottom back onto the seat of the swing, which was a fraction too high to sit on without standing on tiptoe in the first place. 'My mummy showed me how to write that.'

Rasci still looked puzzled.

'It says "Ben", but when I can write better, I could write "Ben needs help"and you would know that from the writing, even if I were not here to read it for you, because if you can read, you know what it says. Understand?'

Rasci was overwhelmed with admiration for the cleverness of this young man. He nodded. 'Yes, I understand very well now, thank you. You explain things very cleverly.'

Ben smiled, appreciative of Rasci's praise.

'And when you want to know something, it is easy to learn if somebody has already said it and put it in writing. That way, they can speak to you without being there. And you can hear it over and over again, every time you read it.'

'Fascinating,' Rasci said, approvingly, wondering why wolves hadn't thought of teaching their cubs how to leave messages like that.

'Do you want me to teach you to read, Rasci?'

'What? Oh, perhaps, one day! One day I would like you to teach me about yourself and your kind. But at the moment, Ben, I have something very important to ask you.'

'And what is that?'

'Well, first of all, would you like to see Smokey's pup that Rhamin stole?'

Ben's eyes widened. 'Smokey's puppy?'

'Yes. You know that Rhamin stopped a wolf called Solin from attacking you, remember?' Rasci knew that the tale Rhamin had told of what happened inside the farmer's house was true. He and Solin had argued about it days later.

And Ben remembered well the night that a wolf, he now knew as Solin, had entered his home and Rhamin, The Black Wolf, had followed and stopped Solin from killing Ben and his baby sister. And then, Rhamin had stolen two of Smokey's pups, but later, Smokey returned with one of them. 'You mean that the dog Daddy saw on the mountain is Smokey's puppy, don't you?'

'Yes, I do.'

'Daddy thought it was.' His eyes lit up with excitement. 'Oh, yes I'd love to see her.' He seemed excited at first, but then his mood changed. 'But I know Daddy would as well. That bad wolf came back with some other wolves and killed the other pups, you know,' he said, looking down at his feet, sadly.

'Yes, I know,' Rasci said despondently, 'and I'm sorry about that.'

'Oh, it wasn't your fault, Rasci. I know that.'

'The pup that Rhamin stole; her name is Lexa.'

'Lexa, wow!' His little face lit up again.

'And would you be able to tell your mummy and daddy that she is coming to visit you?'

'Oh, yes,' Ben said eagerly.

'And would you be able to tell them that I need your father's help to rescue Rhamin, the wolf that saved his life?'

'How?' Ben was beginning to get excited.

'Well, I have a plan, but I haven't worked out all the details yet. That's why I need your father's help. But I'm bringing Lexa, so that he'll know that you really are talking to me. Unless he knows that we are able to talk to each other, then he'll never believe what you say. I carry the scars to prove it. That invisible tooth cut my shoulder.'

'Invisible tooth?'

'From the fire stick that your mother used,' Rasci explained.

Ben chuckled again. 'That's Daddy's gun,' he explained. 'It fires bullets.'

'Gun? Bullets? Right,' Rasci said, as he began to understand more of man's language.

'I'm really sorry about them attacking you, Rasci. Mummy doesn't believe me at all, when I tell her about you, but I think Daddy does, now,' he said and then added, 'A little.'

'Then I shall fetch Lexa, and then he'll believe you a lot, won't he?'

A broad grin cracked Bens face. 'He sure will!' he said excitedly. He paused for a moment. 'When are you coming?' he asked, his eyes lighting up in anticipation.

'In a few days. Perhaps when you are not away from home.'

'Well, I don't go to school at the weekends,' Ben said eagerly.

'Weekends?'

'Oh, we go to school for five days and have two days off. Those two days are called the weekend. Seven days all together in a week.'

'How interesting,' Rasci said, gazing at the teacher. She was watching every nod and gesture that Ben made.

'When is your weekend?' asked Rasci.

'In three more days,' Ben said, fidgeting with anticipation. A little bell tinkled in the background. 'I have to go in now,'

Ben said, with a shrug of his shoulders. 'Are you coming?'

'No,' Rasci said, with a smile. 'But I'll see you again very soon.'

Ben pushed himself off the swing and turned to go back to the school house. Mrs. Steadman was still watching him, but from the doorway now.

'Don't forget to tell your Daddy, that Lexa is coming to visit.'

Ben turned back to Rasci for a moment and shook his head. 'No, I won't,' he said and with that, he skipped off back to join the other children who had already begun to go up the steps by the school house door and were being ushered inside by Mrs. Steadman, who's gaze still remained fixed firmly on Rasci's little friend as he ran to catch them up. Rasci watched on as May looked around and said something to him and then, they both went inside together. As the door closed behind them, Rasci could see the face of Mrs. Steadman as she took one last glance towards the swing.

Rasci's meditation had lapsed into sleep and he slept through the rest of the day. But he dreamt no more about Ben. His dreams seemed more jumbled and imprecise, at first, bearing on nothing in particular, but just flicking from one part of his mind to another. Then, eventually, his mind turned to the stranger he had met on the plains. There was something about Roxana that had intrigued him. Momentarily, he thought about the mountain lion that had stalked him, and then, through a thick misty fog, he saw Solin, talking to Roxana. She had explained that it was he who had told her about Rasci but, with the passing of the mist cloud, the vision faded before he could establish what had been said, or whether it was the past or the present and, as quickly as it came, in front of his eyes, the scene was transmuting into a picture of another wolf, one he thought he recognised, only the thick mist, once again, drifted across his line of vision, obscuring everything.

When Rasci awoke, it was dark outside the cave. He could hear Zelda's heavy breathing as she slept beside him. There was no sign of Silvah. She would be out hunting. Slowly, Rasci stood up and stretched, putting a little weight on his injured leg to test it for pain. It was healing fast and, as he strode over to the water hole for a drink, he let his full weight fall on his bruised leg. It still hurt, but he knew that in three days time he would be well enough to travel at his usual loping stride to the farm once more. In the meantime, as a result of his restless, dream filled sleep, he had something he felt compelled to do. He would let Zelda sleep for now. In the days to come, he would tell her of his dream about Ben, but the thought of talking about Roxana troubled him. He didn't know how to tell either Silvah or Zelda about the young wolf that he had met out by the perimeter of Raymond Rozalski's farm, or how they had met. He wasn't sure how any of the other members of the pack would take it either, if he said he wanted to introduce her into the pack. He wasn't even sure if Roxana wanted to join, nor was he sure why he was even considering it. She had suddenly appeared in his life and then, just as suddenly disappeared. He wondered to himself if being a leader meant that he should have all the answers, but then thought how difficult it was for Rhamin, sometimes, to decide what was the best thing to do. Rhamin relied a great deal on Zelda's wisdom. Perhaps, if he told Zelda about everything that had happened to him, she would be able to advise him too. Looking down at the frail old wolf once more, he was determined that he would broach the subject before he left on his mission but, until then, he was going out where he always felt best; alone, in the forest.

Still favouring his right leg a little, he headed slowly northwards. In the distance, he could hear some of the pack calling to each other, but he didn't call out. He was listening for a specific call, but it never came. Or perhaps Roxana was too far away to be heard. Perhaps she was calling him right now. But then, as he thought about it, that wasn't likely. Even if she wanted to call to him, she wouldn't do so in the territory of another wolf pack, for even though it was Rasci's pack, none of the other wolves knew her. To them she would be a stranger, an intruder. No, she wouldn't call, that's for sure.

He knew exactly what he was looking for, but he had no idea why. Nor did he know where to look. He trotted on, letting his feelings and his instincts lead him. Roxana had said that she was heading up into the mountains. 'You know where to find me,' she had said, so he was heading the same way.

The ground was beginning to rise towards the tree line of the foothills as the day broke through a thick heavy cloud that hung over the mountains, crowning the tree lined slopes just like the guard hairs enveloped his tender shoulder blades, thicker at the top and thinning at the bottom. The first trees on the lower slopes looked like so many legs supporting the coat of mist like a canopy.

The heavy vapour deadened the sounds of the morning. What birds there were, chanting their morning shrills, sounded close and muffled. He soon reached the legs of the canopy and settled for a rest beneath the first line of trees.

From his resting place he could still see the plains clearly beneath him, stretching into the distance. The thick rain clouds blocked out every bit of white sunlight. Even the trees and rocks below looked grey and colourless.

He turned his head towards the forest and listened. Soon, his keen ears picked up noises of moving deer as they grazed upon the rich green foliage, belching and cudding and generally moving in their unperturbed manner though the undergrowth. He wasn't hungry enough to hunt them and neither was he intending to return to the Darin that day, so the deer were safe for now. He would wait until he came upon something small and which he need not waste or leave for the vultures that seemed, even now, to have sensed his presence.

To Rasci, the vultures were just pests, creatures that persistently waited for him to leave his kill after taking his fill. They waited and, more often than not, there was something left for the scavengers. He knew that Corvak was the same kind of predator but, being a friend and companion on many of his trips, Corvak was never seen in the same light. He was invited to join in. He was an honorary wolf, a honour bestowed upon him for the many times he had helped the pack. The vultures were not part of Rasci's family. They just presumed that they could come in after the kill. It was their way. But he had to admire them for their persistence. He watched them circling up above, appearing from the dark cloud and then disappearing once again as they followed the rising air currents.

Slowly, Rasci headed up into the forest and into the veiling mist. He could still hear the deer and the ultrasonic chatter of the small mice that travelled, otherwise undetected, through the lush grass beneath his feet. He let them be. He was on a mission and food was immaterial. The problem was; he wasn't sure why he was looking for the mysterious female wolf. Neither was he sure exactly where to find her.

Gradually the fog became so thick that he could barely see from one tree to another, but he still strode on, forwards and upwards until, suddenly, his leisurely stroll halted abruptly. There was a commotion up ahead, a crashing of undergrowth and a squealing of an animal in flight. He could hear one of the vultures calling out above the cloud. It unsettled him. They were normally silent birds, never wanting to draw attention to themselves. Then there was silence.

Rasci quietly moved forward. The fog was wrapped like a belt around the waist of the mountains. It was thinning a little as he climbed higher up the slope, but it was still too thick to see far. He stopped and waited. The vulture called out again. Even though the fog was thinning, he couldn't see the bird, but he could hear it descending, brushing through the air above him. There was a flutter and flapping of wings as it alighted somewhere further up the mountain, perhaps a minute or so, in walking distance, away. Rasci crept on forward, careful not to tread on any brittle sticks, as he ascended from the thick mist into a clear day beneath dark cloud cover. The other vulture called from high in the sky. Rasci stopped. Then silence again. Then, suddenly, he thought he could hear voices, faint murmurings, but even his keen ears were unable to make out what the sounds were distinctly. The flapping of wings and the brushing of leaves told him that the large bird was taking to flight again.

Rasci lay in some thick moss by the base of a tree and waited. He lifted his head and sniffed the air, but there was no air movement, no scent drifting either to him or from him, but he still waited. He looked up through the trees. The vultures were circling, high in the sky, directly above his head. Then he heard it; at first, just an almost imperceptible foot fall; then another and another. The vulture screeched again, cutting through the silence. The foot falls were heading away from him. He remained as still as a stone. He could have sworn the first steps were coming towards him, but that wasn't the case now. They fell silent for a while, and then, he heard them again, once more heading back towards him, getting closer and closer. He hunkered down in the moss, head forward, his back legs beneath him, tensed, ready to pounce, ready to react. Then, silence again for several moments until a humming sound suddenly broke the stillness. It was a voice, the sound of a happy animal, the sound of a happy wolf. The voice was instantly recognisable. It was Roxana. As the recognition dawned on him, the body behind the cheery voice broke into the gap between the trees. She hadn't seen him. She almost walked past before he spoke.

'Roxana?'

The female wolf swung around, astonished at hearing his voice. 'Rasci! What are you doing here? I hadn't seen you.'

'I gathered that,' Rasci commented. 'Unless you were ignoring me.'

'Ignoring you? Why would I do that?'

Rasci stood up from his resting place. 'Oh, I get the feeling you don't want to see me.'

Roxana laughed. 'Whatever do you mean? I love seeing you!' She came over to him, wagging her tail, and gave him a lick on the nose. 'You're looking much better now.'

'Yes, I think I've just about recovered from my small mishap.'

'You haven't told me about that yet.'

'I didn't have the chance. You disappeared before I could tell you.'

'You might recall that you fell asleep before that.'

'Well, whose fault was that?' Rasci said with a grin.

'That'll teach me to be nice to strangers then.'

'Yes,' Rasci said, reflecting on the day they had met for the second time. 'It was rather nice.'

Roxana looked at him with her wide amber eyes. He couldn't help thinking she looked even better than he had remembered. Still, when they had last met, she had just had a scrap with a mountain lion. Her dark grey coat was dusty and ruffled then, but not now. Now she was sleek and clean. She looked in perfect health. He could understand her desire to become the alpha female of a pack. 'I enjoyed it too,' she stated in her soft voice. Their gazes met. 'You're staring,' she said, abruptly.

'Heh? Oh, sorry, I… well I don't know what to say quite honestly. I rather like looking at you.' He shrugged as if to indicate that it was something he was likely to do again and then looked away. 'I thought I heard you talking,' he said, to change the subject.

'Oh,' Roxana said, smiling gently, 'when I'm alone, I talk to myself. Or, rather, I mutter to myself. I've often been told that I give my position away too easily.'

'Did you have some food up there?' asked Rasci, looking up the mountain from where she had come. The fog, lower down the mountain was beginning to thin and disperse as the day warmed.

'No. Why, did you want some? We can hunt together if you like.'

'Well, I'm not over hungry, really. It's just that I heard one of those stupid vultures land near here. I thought, perhaps he had come to finish off your meal.'

'Oh, I heard it come near, but I didn't see it. Perhaps it was after some live food for a change, or perhaps it has its young somewhere near.'

'Probably.' Rasci started to stare again. 'I never really thought of them having families. They seem to be for ever hung above us in the sky.' He blinked. 'Let's walk together,' he said, to break the trance. 'See what we come across.'

Roxana gave him the best smile yet. 'That sounds okay to me,' she said. 'What are you doing up here anyway?' she asked, as she led the way along the side of the mountain.

'I don't know; I just happened to be passing. I come up here often.' He paused and then asked, 'What are you doing up here then?'

'Hunting of course.'

There was a brief silence. 'I tried to call you,' Rasci stated eventually.

'Yes, I heard,' Roxana replied.

'Why didn't you reply?'

'I wasn't sure I was doing the right thing,' she said quickly. 'It's not my own territory, remember.' She looked away and started humming lightly to herself. Rasci found it very distracting. His head suddenly seemed like it was going to float away. 'I could leave the pack,' he stated suddenly. It dispersed the light headedness. He looked away and thought about what he had just said. He wasn't sure why he had said it.

'You look surprised,' Roxana said, a smile turning on her lips.

'I... I don't know what made me say that,' Rasci said, remorsefully. 'I know I am not the right wolf for you.'

'Who told you that? I didn't say that you were the wrong

wolf. I just said that that I have ambitions to be with a leader of a pack. You are a leader, Rasci. And anyway, it's the sort of thing I might have said to any stranger.'

'To put them off, you mean?'

'To keep my space, I'd say. Until I knew them better.'

'But you left so suddenly. You didn't want to know me better, then?'

They wandered into a small clearing where the grass was growing long in a dappled shade. She stopped and turned to him. 'Look, Rasci, I just don't want to see you get hurt. It's a bad world out there. You seem to have a lot on your shoulders and I didn't want to add to your problems.'

'My problems?' It made Rasci think. He certainly had problems, and Roxana knew it. She had seen him one day perfectly all right. The next time they met, she had seen him injured and being stalked by a wolf eating cat. He reckoned he had problems all right, and she didn't even know the half of it. He had the problem of not only finding Rhamin but of getting him away from his captors. He had the problem that he might be killed doing it. And now he had the problem that he might want to be the leader of the pack after all. The pulse above his right eye throbbed.

'Why don't you share them with me? You know what they say.'

Rasci tried to concentrate on something other than his own troubles. 'What? Oh, the weight of a problem is halved when it is carried by two, you mean?'

'Something like that.'

Rasci shook his head. 'You wouldn't want to know, trust me.'

'How can I know that? When you say it like that, it clearly shows *you* don't trust me. You obviously aren't confident enough to let me try and help you.' Her eyes seemed angry.

'It's not something you can help with, Roxana. It's… well it's not really anything any other wolf can help me with.' He stepped close to her and muzzled her neck. 'I'm sorry.'

She pulled away. 'No, you aren't,' she said crossly. 'You say you're sorry, but you really don't want me to know anything about you, do you?'

Rasci wasn't sure. At this very moment he wanted to tell her everything about himself, about how Rhamin disappeared, about how he became leader of the pack, about how he had dreams that took him to places far away where he could talk in another language and see things more clearly than actually being there. But how could he do that without making her think he was some kind of nut case? Even his own pack members had a chuckle or two when it was explained to them, and they had known Rasci for years. It certainly wasn't a recipe to impress the females!

'Look, Roxana, I like you very much, but I am about to embark on a task that at the very least will cost me the leadership of the pack, and might, more than likely get me killed.' He looked at her with saddened eyes. 'And the problem is; I think I would like to see what life with you is like.'

'Oh, would you now,' she said, mischievously. 'Well, Rasci, you are going to have to impress me by telling me then, just what this adventure of yours is all about.' She stepped closer to him. 'And I'm going to lie down here and wait until you have told me.'

Rasci breathed a sigh of resignation. At this particular moment, he didn't have much to lose. If he told her something that put her off him, then what would it cost him? He was going to reinstate Rhamin, or die trying. So, bang goes his chance of setting up a happy pack with the wolf of his dreams. 'Well, you know about Rhamin?' he began.

'Yes, he was killed.'

Rasci realised Roxana hadn't heard the news that Rhamin was still alive, and hitherto, he hadn't even told her of his suspicions that Rhamin was still in this world.

'When we last spoke about him,' Roxana continued, 'you didn't seem to think that you could live up to his memory. You seemed to be saying that you were not the new leader of the pack.'

'Er, I… I'm not sure that I will be leader for all that long.'

'Why not, for goodness sake? With a strong mate, you could be an outstanding leader. You could hold your own against any other wolf. With a strong mate you could do what you liked and no other wolf would be able to object or try to take over.'

'It's not all that simple,' Rasci stuttered. 'I… I believe Rhamin is still alive.'

'Alive?' Roxana's forehead wrinkled as she frowned with curiosity. 'You think Rhamin is alive?'

'Well, he is definitely alive. That's what I meant to say.'

'Definitely alive!' Roxana looked disturbed. She got up and paced around. 'Well, he's not exactly doing a brilliant job of leading your pack, is he?'

'No, but…'

'Why don't you just admit it, you don't like me.'

'No, I like you very much.' He stopped what he was saying and thought about what he should have said. 'I mean, you are a good and ambitious young wolf. I have no doubt that if Rhamin were not alive, we could have something going for us.'

'So where is this leader of yours? Why isn't he with your pack?'

Rasci tried to be as precise as he could. 'He's been captured.'

'Captured? Who by?'

'By a man of course. They are the only creatures that

capture animals.'

'Well, of course, I know that,' Roxana retorted, settling down beside Rasci again. 'But what man?'

'Oh, it's a long story.'

'I've got time.'

Rasci tried to explain as simply as he could, how Rhamin had led the pack to save the farmer and the other man when they had been attacked by bears. He explained that the other man had seen Rhamin and wanted him for his own animal enclosure that men kind called a safari park. He didn't try to explain how he knew all this for sure.

'So is there a chance the man might free him, then?'

'No, not exactly,'

'So what is going to change? Is he coming back, or isn't he?'

'I… I am… I'm going to try and help him escape, yes.'

'So where does that leave me? If you succeed, I have no leader, no pack. If you fail, well, are you going to be back to tell the tale, I wonder?'

Rasci felt like he was going to faint. His head thumped and his eyes seemed only to see Roxana. The vultures were calling out again, unseen, somewhere above their heads. He could feel their eyes on him; he could sense the feeling of being watched.

'Look,' he said eventually. 'I don't know why I came out here. In all the territory that I could have travelled today, I had an urge to come up here. Perhaps we were meant to meet. Perhaps we are meant to be together, I don't know. All I know is that I have to do something for myself. I have to do something for Rhamin. The two things are inextricably linked. I know that if I don't do what I feel I want to do, then I will never be the leader I should be.'

'If what you say is right, you'll never be a leader, anyway!'

'I could leave the pack. We could start our own pack. I know plenty of territories that could stand being farmed by wolves. There are plenty of deer and plenty of buffalo. We needn't be in the same pack as Rhamin. And perhaps some of my… I mean Rhamin's pack would come with me.'

'Is there any point, Rasci? You are going to try and save your leader, and as far as I can see, you will probably end up being killed or locked away in that safari park thing with him. If the men kind have got him, then there is no way you can rescue him, believe me.'

'I think I can do it.'

'How?'

Rasci was already regretting the conversation. Telling her about his remote viewing capability wasn't going to enhance his argument at this particular time. His heart had already fallen through his chest. 'Oh, never mind Roxana. It was just a dream. I'm sorry. I shouldn't have bothered you with any of this.'

'But that's where you're wrong. If Rhamin is alive then you have to come to terms with the fact that you are not going to be able to rescue him. It just isn't possible. Men are so inferior to wolves in so many respects, but they have other abilities that keep us in our place; beneath them. They have a unique capability to kill without using their puny teeth or their puny claws. They can build enclosures to encage wolves and other animals; and they can guard them with weapons that will kill a wolf at two thousand paces.'

'I know,' Rasci said, nodding his head. 'I have seen their weapons. I was hit by one the day you found me hobbling home.'

'So that was a wound from one of their invisible teeth then?'

Rasci nodded. 'Yes', he said quietly.

'And I suppose you were trying to rescue Rhamin then, were you?'

'Well, not exactly, no' He didn't expand on the statement.

'Oh, so that was somebody who had no interest in stopping you rescuing their prize!' She threw her head in the air. 'Well, saving Rhamin will be easy then! Do you really think they won't try to kill you?'

Rasci grimaced. 'I really don't know what else I can do. I have said I am going to do it, and now, I am not going to back down. My mind is made up.'

'Then, count me out,' Roxana snapped as she stood up and walked away. 'Don't bother following me. I don't want to get any more attached to you. I don't like losing friends I care about.'

With that, she ran off up the steep bank and disappeared amongst the trees. Rasci knew it was no use following. He had told her that his mind was made up, and she had made her point of view perfectly clear. He watched the moving branches that she had brushed past in her haste to get away. They had stopped swaying a long time before he turned down the mountain and, with a leaden heart, and the two vultures still orbiting high in the sky above him, he headed down to the plains.

CHAPTER TWENTY THREE

The trip to the mountain had done nothing to ease Rasci's mind, but his return to the Darin that evening and the praise and affection from his pack lifted his spirits once again. The mounting excitement, however, failed to raise his confidence. He was tired from his journey, and it was early in the night when he left the pack playing and talking. He went to the darkest corner of the cave to settle down to a troubled sleep.

Half way through the night he awoke, panting. His dreams, once more, had been a congealed mixture of tangled visions, bringing back all the events of recent days and liquidising them with a mixture of the fears and nightmares that had long troubled him. First he had seen Roxana, through the fog, smiling at him, shaking her head, gesturing for him to follow her into the mist, but then Solin broke through the cloudy veil laughing at him, and telling him that no female would want the fool of all wolves, before disappearing into the mist again, in the opposite direction. Then, as he had seen in other dreams, he saw Rhamin. The Black Wolf and Yeltsa were fighting for their lives, only once again, in his dream, Rasci was with them. There were other wolves milling around, and then the mountain lion sprang on him and tore at his throat. Two vultures landed by his side and began to eat him while he was alive. He shook them off only to find himself shaking off Zelda who was tugging at his fur to wake him. 'Rasci, wake up. Rasci, wake up,' she repeated over and over again until eventually, snarling and lashing at her, he exploded back to consciousness. At first he wondered if he was still dreaming. With his eyes open he was still engulfed in total darkness. But then he remembered where he had settled down to sleep.

'Gran? Is that you?' he asked, weakly, trying to catch his breath, and sniffing her comforting smell.

'Yes, my young wolf. You were dreaming again. But this time I had to wake you. I was frightened.'

'Frightened Gran? You mean for me?'

'Yes Rasci. I have never heard you so troubled. You are going to have to talk about your problems. You can't keep them gathered up inside your head. You'll make yourself ill.'

Rasci slumped back down on the hard floor. 'Oh, Gran, I don't know what is becoming of me. Ever since Rhamin disappeared, I have had nothing but dream after dream. Some of them are like seeing things from a distance. Those don't bother me so much. But others are so mixed up that I don't know if I am going out of my mind.' He looked at her in the darkness, not seeing her, but feeling her presence. 'What's happening to me Gran? What is to become of me?'

'You are just trying to sort out all the events that have happened to you lately,' she reassured. 'You are just getting rid of all your fears and all your inhibitions, dreaming like all wolves do, only you have had too much to cope with and your mind has gone into a state of over activity.'

Zelda lifted her head and prompted him. 'Come,' she

said gently, 'Silvah is waiting near the cave entrance. Come and join us and tell us all your news.'

Rasci did as he was asked, calling at the water hole on the way past, to take on some refreshment. He settled down beside his two companions and began to relate everything he had done, and dreamt. For the first time, he told them about Roxana and how they had met.

'So, when are you inviting Roxana back to meet the pack?' asked Silvah, eagerly.

'She's not interested in me,' Rasci stated bluntly. 'She is looking to be the alpha female running a pack with her own alpha male. She isn't interested in a would-be leader who dreams all the time.'

'Did she tell you that?'

'More or less.'

'More or less? You mean you told yourself that,' said Zelda.

'I am not a leader, Gran, and whatever the pack says, it won't make me one.'

'Only because you never had aspirations to be a leader. But you have all the qualities of a brave leader. You're a strong wolf and you're not afraid to hold your territory or fight for your pack.'

'That's what she said, Gran.'

'There's no betrayal by wanting a pack of your own, Rasci. How do you think Romax and I got started?'

Rasci looked at his old companion. 'Of course! You must have had your own pack! I never thought!'

'Well, there you are then. Problem solved. We save Rhamin and then we talk to him about you and a new pack. He loves you Rasci. He's not going to be worried by your turning out to be strong like him.'

'I'll never be as strong as Rhamin, Gran. I don't think any

wolf ever will!'

Suddenly, Rasci felt sad. 'The problem is, Gran, I don't have a chance of saving Rhamin, really. It's just a dream; something we all want to happen. I'll never be able to do it.'

Rasci had finally realised the futility of the whole project. What Roxana had said was absolutely true. But even worse, he realised now that dreams were one thing. But meeting Ben and his father in real life was another. It wasn't going to be a remote viewing; it was going to be a real meeting, face to face. Other than in his dreams, there was no way he could converse with them in their own language. There was no way to talk them into helping him.

'You can't give up before you've tried,' Silvah said crossly. 'Rhamin means as much to me as he does to you. If I had your gift, I would at least have a try. I would go to the farm and try and get through to the farmer. Somehow, we have to get him to help us.'

'It's worth going that far, Rasci,' Zelda said in support. 'At least, give it a try.'

'Is it worth a try, though?' asked Rasci.

'Well, you have to go back to the farm, anyway,' Silvah said angrily, 'because Lexa has already made plans to go with you. You can't let her down now, can you?'

Rasci smiled. In his panic to work out his own worries, he had forgotten about his wolf dog. He loved her like the rest of the pack and would die for her the same as he would for any other member of the family. The least he could do for her was to take her to meet her biological mother.

That day, more relaxed and sure of his motives, Rasci

meditated for several hours. He saw Ben again, only this time, he watched the young boy and his sister Margo from a distance. Instead of being there at one particular time, it was as if Rasci was just seeing snippets of what had been happening during the time that he had been away.

Ben hadn't heard from his wolf spirit since the visit to his school, but Rasci could see that he wasn't worried. He watched as Ben told his father that Rasci was bringing Lexa to see him, and that they wanted to see him about saving Rhamin. This time, his father realised that his son wasn't just day dreaming. There was something in Raymond Rozalski's face that showed more understanding.

Rasci saw Mrs. Steadman give Ben a letter to take home to his mother and father. Ben didn't know why she would want to write to his parents. He hadn't been misbehaving like his friend had been. He was very nervous when his father picked him up from school in the station wagon and Ben carried the letter in his pocket, his hand on it all the time, until his father dropped him off at the front door of the farm house. Although the thought had crossed his mind, he dare not lose it. 'Daddy,' he said eventually, as he was getting out of the station wagon. His father turned to look at him. 'I have this for you.' He pulled the folded, sweaty envelope from his trouser pocket and thrust it forward, a look of apprehension on his face. 'Mrs. Steadman says I must give this to you,' he said meekly.

His father took the letter but didn't read it immediately. Instead, he waited until they were all together in the kitchen. Ben tried to busy himself, playing at throwing biscuits to Smokey and letting her catch them one at a time. He didn't want to let his father and mother know how nervous he was, and had decided that he would act normally and play, pretending he wasn't listening.

Raymond stood by the table. Maria was sitting down. Ben watched as his father opened the envelope but, to Ben's relief, his father just laughed when he read the letter. He had felt for a while that Ben was seeing something that others couldn't see. Whether it was real or imaginary, he didn't know for sure, but he knew there was more to it than a disturbed child. Smokey had shown that. Smokey had no hang ups about attacking wolves, yet she virtually stopped and greeted Rasci when she caught him up. That had really made him stop and think.

Rasci watched as the farmer read the letter. Now he realised a little more clearly about writing and how what you say can be stored and kept till later. Wolves had to relate their messages with their voices or by scent marking, but here Raymond was receiving a message from Mrs. Steadman and she wasn't even there, she wasn't even speaking. He couldn't help feeling a spark of admiration for the frail, physically inferior men kind. He watched as the farmer read it alone. He could tell Raymond was being careful not to upset the balance he had achieved between accepting Ben's psychic gift and increasing his wife Maria's scepticism. Raymond turned to his wife. 'Mrs. Steadman says that, at first, she thought Ben was badly disturbed. But now, after watching him closely over the past few days, she reckons he's a sensitive,' he said, putting the letter down on the kitchen table.

'A what?' Maria asked, looking for clarification.

'She reckons he can see ghosts or something,' he chuckled.

'Well, I've got to be honest, Ray, he's got me a bit worried.'

Raymond hadn't yet broached the subject of Ben meeting Lexa. 'Wait till Mrs. Steadman hears that I am meeting a wolf and a dog based on a conversation that Ben had with a wolf spirit, then!' he said out of the blue.

'What!'

'Ben reckons that the wolf that came by here the other day is a friend of The Black Wolf, the one that saved me on the mountain. You know?'

'It happened to save me as well, don't forget,' said Maria. 'And don't forget the children, that night, right here, in the kitchen.'

Raymond nodded. 'Then you won't go panicking me again this next time, will you darling?'

'This next time?'

'Er, well, the wolf is coming back on Saturday, according to Ben.'

'Oh, is it now?' Her voice was raised. 'Now look here…'

'Calm down, Maria. I won't let anything happen to him or Margo, you know that.'

'It's all getting a little too far fetched for my liking. You'll be talking to the damned things next. You're bad enough with your blinking dog!'

Raymond gave a dry, throaty chuckle.

'Mrs. Steadman'll probably think you're as daft as I do,' she continued unperturbed.

'Ah, but what if the wolf brings Smokey's pup along with it? What if it really is the pup that The Black Wolf stole?'

'It'll be as wild as the other wolves, then,' Maria countered. 'It's not going to come and sit by your feet, or anything.'

Raymond thought about what she had just said. 'No, you are absolutely right, dear,' he said eventually. 'But if it comes on Saturday, wouldn't that say something? Wouldn't we know then, that Ben can get messages from a wolf spirit?' He settled on a chair and faced his wife. She brushed some crumbs off the table, agitatedly, and scooped them into her hand. 'You're not going to like what I am going to say next,' he said gently. Maria just looked at him with her handful of crumbs in an upturned fist. 'You know the man Petersen?'

She nodded. Her lips were tightly compressed.

'You know he went back and captured The Black Wolf?'

'For his father's safari park; yes, you told me. I never did like the man. What right has he to go taking our wolves anyway?'

'Our wolves?' Raymond smiled. 'Yes, I reckon they are,' he said, nodding his agreement.

'And what right has he to take animals from the wild?'

'Well, I suppose he'll argue that they are an endangered species.'

'In some places I suppose they are,' Maria said strongly, 'but that doesn't mean they are around here. He's taken that wolf away from his family, do you realise that?'

'Yes, that is what I think. If they really were endangered in this area, then it would be a different matter. But he's taking animals because he wants them, not because he's helping them. There's a difference.' Raymond scratched his head. He leaned back in his chair and then said, 'Ben reckons that the wolf that came the other day wants my help to release Rhamin.'

'Who's Rhamin?'

'The Black Wolf.'

'Since when did it acquire a name, for goodness sake?'

'That is what Ben says it is called.'

'Oh, Ben says it's called Rhamin? Right,' said Maria, a note of sarcasm creeping into her voice. She re-compressed her lips, but her manner changed. 'Well, Petersen won't want to release anything,' she said, eventually. 'No matter what you say to him, he won't budge. He's got too much invested in that animal now. I've heard he's advertising the fact that his wolf is the main attraction at that park.'

'And do you think that's fair? Do you think the giant wolf that helped us and became our friend should be rewarded like that?'

Her lips relaxed. 'Of course not! But, I'll bet you your last penny, there's precious little we can do about it!'

'Ben reckons the wolf thinks there is. He says the wolf reckons we can help him escape.'

'Ben? The wolf? Just when did wolves think up escape plans for goodness sake, Raymond? Can you hear yourself? Do you realise what you sound like? Do you realise what people would say if they caught us seriously saying that our Ben could talk to wolves? They lock people in padded cells for less than that. Worse still, they might think we were a danger to the little mite and take *him* away instead!' She relaxed her grip on the crumbs and studied them as she let her exasperation subside. She gave a big sigh and then, lost in thought, she scattered the crumbs back on the table. She studied them for quite some time. 'My mother used to read the tea leaves, you know,' she said eventually.

'Really?' Raymond gasped, letting her talk.

'She was good at it. She was quite well known for it, in fact.'

'Was she?'

'Somehow, concentrating on the tea leaves makes the mind see into other dimensions, other worlds,' she said, her gaze still fixed firmly on the table top.

Raymond remained silent

'I don't have that gift.'

Raymond still remained silent.

'Perhaps our Ben has inherited it,' she said eventually.

'Perhaps.'

Eventually Maria prized her gaze from the table and

shook her head. 'Well, I can't read bread crumbs; that's for sure!' She looked up at Raymond and they both laughed.

Raymond stood up and went round to the other side of the table. Bending over, he put his arm around her shoulder and kissed his wife tenderly on the cheek. 'We'll see what happens tomorrow, shall we?' he said, squeezing her gently.

With a resigned look on her face, she nodded and leaned her head against his chest.

Rasci felt more relaxed now that he knew that the farmer was expecting him. The last thing he needed was another invisible bullet cutting through his skin or a rock on the knee, or even worse, getting a rock tossed on his head or being shot through the heart. Reassured, his vision faded and he melted into a deep, undisturbed sleep. He was awakened by Lexa.

'Rasci,' she whispered in his ear, 'We ought to be getting ready to go. If we're to arrive by the morning, then we must travel through the night.'

CHAPTER TWENTY FOUR

What uncertainties and misgivings Rasci had about the meeting with the Rozalskis were dispelled when he saw them. His trip overnight with Lexa, had been straight forward, but he had brought Ramusan, Silvah and Natan with him as far as the perimeter fence. His experiences of the last week were still haunting him, and there was still something niggling away in the back of his mind; some thought or suspicion that made him wary. His encounter with the mountain lion hadn't increased his confidence either. The last thing they needed at this stage was to be held up or even injured in a scrap with a savage cat and, after relating his story to her, Silvah had insisted that Rasci had a body guard at all times now. The pack had too much to lose. Corvak had travelled on behind them at first light and had caught them up well before they reached the fence. From now on, Silvah insisted on aerial reconnaissance as well, but the trip had been uneventful.

It had been light for several hours when Rasci and Lexa departed from their escort and made their way to the centre of the farmstead. Corvak stayed close by in the air above, until Rasci and Lexa crossed the final fence and headed towards the farmhouse.

Rasci could hear Lexa's heart thumping in her chest. Her anticipation was mounting. His heart thumped the same except the tension and fear that the day may turn sour began to make the pounding reach the pulse above his eye. It throbbed.

As they came around the corner of the huge farm building, there, in the distance, off to the side of the door of the house, they first saw Ben and Smokey, Ben sitting on the wooden bench on the veranda, and Smokey lying at his feet, head up, ears forward and with a crinkled brow of curiosity as she watched Ben looking out expectantly towards the corner of the building. Smokey saw them first and, jumping to her feet, gave out a short, sharp warning bark 'They're here,' Ben shouted elatedly, jumping to his feet. Even at that distance, Rasci could see his blue eyes widen with excitement. He ran to the door and, jumping on the spot, unable to contain his exhilaration, he shouted, 'Mummy, Daddy, Margo. They're here! They're here! Quickly!'

Rasci could sense Lexa's tenseness; but her nerves could not have been jangling any more than his as he took the first uneasy step towards them. The words that Ben had called out had been in some language foreign to Rasci. They walked together, slowly, heads high in a non-threatening posture. Up above he heard an encouraging caw from their friend, Corvak. Within seconds, Raymond was at the door, looking out towards them. Then, slightly behind him was Maria, looking rather nervous, holding Margo tightly to her breast. Smokey barked again, but she didn't attack. She tilted her head on one side, her curiosity changing her whole face as she studied the two visitors who still walked slowly, side by side, towards them. Rasci thought he saw her bottom move the same way that Lexa's did when she wagged her stumpy, non-existent tail, but he couldn't be sure. Lexa let out an ultrasonic whine; a combination of excitement and greeting; then another, lower pitched and audible to human ears. But they were still too far away for the humans to hear her. Smokey did the same, returning the greeting. Somehow, she knew this was her only surviving baby. She squealed for all to hear and strained against Raymond's fist as he restrained her with a shiny metal collar. But she was a big animal. If he hadn't let go, then she would have dragged him forward with her. As the chain collar broke loose from Raymond's hand, she bounded towards the visitors, mouth wide, and tongue out; panting wildly.

'Stay,' Raymond called after her. 'Stay!'

As if a switch had been turned off, Smokey skidded to a halt, still panting, still with a total look of excitement on her face. Now, unable to contain her excitement, she turned and looked pleadingly back at Raymond and then back towards the visitors who were getting closer.

Rasci noticed that Lexa's hair on her shoulders had bristled. 'It's okay, Lexa,' he said gently. 'She looks glad to see you.'

Lexa didn't speak. Her eyes were fixed on the big dog, thirty or so yards in front of her. This was not a wolf she was facing. She lowered her head and put back her ears.

'No,' Rasci commanded. 'Relax! Lexa, you must control your emotions. You must. Do you hear me?'

Lexa lifted her head and let out a quiet whine of frustration. All her instincts told her that this was an enemy, but as she looked on, and as she relaxed as Rasci had instructed, the vision turned to one of something else. She had set off on this journey with only a natural mother in mind; someone she was eager to meet. But in reality, her wolf instincts were trying to get the better of her. Slowly, as step by step, she moved closer to Smokey, her hackles smoothed and her head rose. She remembered that she had intended to speak to the dog. She squeaked a greeting, 'I'm Lexa,' she said nervously, almost too quiet to hear.

But Smokey had heard. She was treading ground with her front paws. Unable any more to restrain her feelings, the invisible leash that had been holding her snapped. She bounced forward, startling Lexa, squealing as she ran towards her. 'My baby!'

Rasci stopped and watched as the big dog greeted Lexa. Judging the size of Smokey, next to his wolf dog, it was clear that Lexa still had some growing to do. He watched as they circled around each other, stumpy tails wriggling, sniffing, squeaking in ultrasonic tones; a true greeting of friendship. He sighed with sheer relief as tension drained to his feet and through into the ground beneath him. He almost laughed out loud with the sudden release of anxiety. The throbbing pulse above his right eye gave way to euphoria of endorphins almost making him float off the ground like the spirit in one of his dreams. He looked past them and, now only thirty yards or so from the Rozalskis, their faces were a sight to behold. Their mouths had dropped open; their eyes were wide with surprise and pleasure and Raymond was grinning. Ben was laughing and jumping on the spot. Maria had one hand to her mouth as she spoke.

'I can't believe it,' she said, lowering her hand from her face and pointing towards the group of animals. 'Who'd have believed it?'

'Er, Ben did,' Raymond said, ruffling his son's hair.

'I like that wolf, Mummy,' Margo said, pointing with her little hand towards Rasci.

'Hello Rasci,' Ben called to his wolf friend.

Rasci heard Ben call his name. But nothing else they had been saying seemed to make sense. The noise Lexa and Smokey were making had perhaps obscured their words. He trotted towards the family, leaving the dogs, sniffing around each other, in raptures. Stopping a few yards in front of them, he sat down, looked at Ben and spoke. 'It's good to see you in person my young friend,' he began. 'I'm so glad you were able to understand me.'

Ben frowned. He tilted his head on one side as his mouth dropped open.

'That is Lexa,' Rasci said, turning his head back towards the happy pair.

Ben still frowned. He shook his head. The woofing sounds the wolf was making made no sense to him. 'I… I don't understand,' he said, turning his face up to his father. 'I thought…'

'You thought that you could understand what the noises he is making meant, didn't you?' his father said with a resigned nod.

Ben nodded back. He looked saddened. The wolf was making woofing throaty sounds and squeaking; and to Rasci, Ben and his father were making similar noises. Rasci's heart sank. His absolute worst and suppressed fears had, like a bubble trapped under a deep rock in the lake, escaped and sped to the surface, expanding as it burst into reality. He spoke again. 'Ben, I don't know how we are going to talk together.' He looked at Ben sadly. His whole idea of getting help from the farmer was beginning to crumble like the crust on a sun dried pond. He lowered his eyes to the ground in despair. 'I'm sorry,' he said sadly, then looking back at all the faces, 'I can't even tell you how happy I am, that we are all friends.'

Four faces looked down at him. There was a long silence

while they all looked from one to the other. Ben's face showed utter confusion. Raymond looked at him, shook his head and shrugged his shoulders.

'I'm happy too,' a little voice broke the silence.

All heads turned to Margo. 'What?' her mother asked. 'What did you say?'

'I'm happy to meet Rasci too,' she said, placing her tiny arms around her mother's neck and looking her straight in the eyes.

Her mother squeezed her affectionately. 'We're all glad to meet Ben's friendly wolf,' she said.

Margo looked back at Rasci. He had fallen silent, knowing now that all he said was in vain. Their eyes met and for a long moment they interlocked. Once again her little voice broke the silence. 'He's happy that we are all friends.'

Rasci looked up to Margo's little face. Could she understand what he was thinking? He studied her eyes again for several seconds. Silently, she gazed back at him. Sensing that there was some kind of connection, he thought, 'I need your father's help.'

Margo still gazed at Rasci's eyes.

'I need your father's help,' Rasci thought hard again; this time, concentrating on getting the message into Margo's mind. For a long moment he thought he had lost the connection. Was there just a fleeting chance that their minds had been brought together or was it just coincidental thoughts?

Suddenly she spoke again. 'Ben has asked daddy to help you.' Her mother and father and Ben all looked on, bemused, not sure if Margo was communicating with the silent wolf or just talking to him. Although he couldn't understand the sounds Margo was making, he was sure that, with his mind, he was actually communicating with Ben's little sister. What was it Zelda had said? We are all born with some degree of psychic ability but it fades as realities of living and survival take over. Perhaps young men kind are the same as young wolves, he thought. Like Ben, little Margo was still young enough to capture those elusive wave lengths.

'Will he help me?' his mind pleaded, still sceptical.

He could see Margo was concentrating hard. There was clearly some difficulty, but eventually she looked across to her father. 'Are we going to help him, Daddy?'

Raymond nodded, an astonished smile still cracking his face. 'If I can.'

'He says yes, if he can,' Ben and his parents heard Margo say, looking into Rasci's amber eyes.

Again, he wasn't sure of her response, but then he saw her nodding. He knew what nodding meant. His heart leapt. He jumped in the air, spun around and raced around in a circle, sliding to a halt in front of the family again. He couldn't stop himself. Something inside of him had snapped and sent him into an uncontrollable fit of behaviour. He suppressed it enough to look at the family again. They were smiling at him totally dumbfounded by his performance. A crazy wolf was dancing in their yard.

Lexa and Smokey trotted over towards them, their tongues hanging out and their chests sucking in air as they panted uncontrollably. 'How's it going?' Lexa asked, unsure of the silence.

'You're not going to believe it,' Rasci said turning to his wolf dog.

CHAPTER TWENTY FIVE

The transfer of thoughts between Rasci and Margo was not fluent. Even if she could tell what he was thinking, he still wasn't sure he could tell what was in her mind. Eventually, while the family were all engrossed in getting to know Lexa, he went out of sight of them to a quiet corner of the garden, where Corvak stood on an old post, cawing softly. With a sigh, he lay down beneath his friend. 'I think they are going to help me,' he said, 'but I can't understand what they are saying.'

Corvak hopped down between his front paws. 'Then communicate the only way you know how,' he said bluntly. 'You must do what you have been doing.'

Rasci lowered his head onto his paws. Corvak was a wise old bird. With his friend's light body resting gently against his muzzle he was able to relax a little. The whole morning had been too intense, the excitement too great, but Corvak's presence was reassuringly soothing. Gradually Rasci began to relax enough to try and meditate. The whole Rozalski family was just as excited, but if he could confirm things with Ben then the plan could still work.

Eventually, Ben caught sight of his spirit wolf watching them, trying to catch his attention as he and Margo had snacks, and Raymond provided treats for Smokey; tasty things that were not really to Lexa's palate, and by the end of the morning a simple and very rudimentary plan was formed; one that everybody understood. Rasci should return in a week's time. They would go to the safari park together.

Much would have to be left now to Raymond and it would take him time to get ready. He was going to have to make enquiries about the safari park. If possible, he was going to have to go and do a reconnaissance. Although he had agreed to help to rescue Rhamin, he would need to know what it was that he was up against. But all he made clear to Ben on the day was that it would be essential to take Rasci with him in order that The Black Wolf would know his intention was to help him escape. Rasci had to be back at the farm by first light in seven days.

The following week seemed to drag on and on. The pack needed to get the whole dangerous scheme behind them. None were expected to join Rasci, because the plan had been devised with the inclusion of the only wolf that could communicate with the farmer through his children. But they had all been warned; there was a good chance the rescue would fail and there was no knowing if Rasci would end up being a captive as well. None wanted to lose a second leader and they were desperate to show their support in whatever way they could.

For a whole week, all the wolves had to just get on with life and Rasci was no exception. At first, he decided to keep clear of the mountain forests. His last trip up there had been too harrowing to repeat. Every time he thought about Roxana he felt as if a lead weight was swinging on his insides. He thought about her constantly, wondering if she would still be interested in him after the mission. If he survived, that was. He thought about the things Zelda had said, that she had been a leader's mate, and how Rhamin would be pleased for Rasci if he wanted to form his own pack. But everything he knew and with which he was familiar, was around the Darin. Every one he knew was around the Darin. He had been right; his life was changing. He would never be able to be the old Rasci again. He was happy that he was learning so much; things no ordinary wolf would even dream about. No ordinary wolf. That said it all. He wasn't ever going to be ordinary. Even as a clown, he wasn't ordinary. He had been and still was a magnificent hunter and fighter. He still had some of Zelda's psychic talent, though now, it seemed to have channelled mainly into the ability to remote view other places and the wolves or people in them. But he knew so much more about life now. Zelda had, for years, told him about men, but he had learned even more in the last few weeks. And there was Roxana. That was an experience he had *felt*. He had felt it every time she looked at him with her big amber eyes. He had felt it when she brushed close to him. He had felt it with every word of her soft, velvet voice. Would she want him after he returned from his rescue mission? Would he return safely to her, he wondered? For Roxana, he desperately wanted to return.

Every day, he went hunting with Natan and Lexa for deer, but he was only with them in body. His mind and soul were elsewhere. They were never very far from the Darin, and were well within calling distance. They went to the foothills and the first belt of trees. But he wasn't really hunting. Not for food, anyway. He just wandered aimlessly through forest, following his companions around the slopes, thinking what he would say if he came across Roxana. But she never appeared. The vultures did. They started to follow him by the fourth day and would remain above until they left for the farm.

Natan and Lexa knew Rasci had a great deal on his mind, so they didn't mind his aimlessness. Hunting was easy and when they did chase a deer, it broke their leader out of his sombre mood, if only for a short while.

The fourth night was the first time since leaving the farm that Rasci communicated with Ben. He went to a quiet corner of the cave, where he knew he would not be disturbed, and started his meditation. He soon located Ben in his room, preparing to go to bed. The boy shouted with delight when he saw his wolf spirit appear. 'Rasci! I've been thinking about you.' He ran over to his bed and jumped on it, turning around and swinging his legs back over the side.

'And me about you,' Rasci lied convincingly as Ben settled in a comfortable sitting position. He didn't know how to explain that his mind had been elsewhere. 'I've come to see what plans have been made if any,' Rasci said, determined that he was going to make no mistakes.

Ben explained everything that his father had done during the week. It was a longer trip to the safari park than he had expected, taking more than seven hours on the road to get there in the station wagon. So, because of that, they were going to set off on the first day of the weekend, called Saturday, and travel to the safari park ready to enter it on the next day called Sunday. Rasci had to come along because he was the only one that could communicate with the incarcerated wolves, and Ben and Margo were going in order to make the visit to the safari park look like an authentic family event. The rest of the very basic rescue plan remained unchanged.

'Thank your father for doing this for Rhamin and me, won't you?' Rasci said gratefully to his little friend.

Ben got up off the bed and ran to the bedroom door. He opened it. 'Daddy,' he shouted down the stairs, 'Rasci wants to thank you for helping him!'

'Tell him he's welcome,' Raymond replied with a chuckle of disbelief that he was really doing any of this.

As Rasci came out of his trance, he realized how much more reliable and informative his dream visits to Ben were now; how easy it was to get the full picture of the plan this way. The system of thought transference with Margo, if indeed that is what it was, had not been reliable enough to communicate at anything but the most basic level and back at the farm his close proximity seemed to get in the way of good communication. Now, after talking to Ben in his spirit form, he felt much more reassured.

On the day before the weekend, the day the Rozalski's called Friday, Rasci hunted and fed well. Corvak, who was still with him, did the same. Once again, the vultures were ready to take over when the other predators had left. But before they departed and left the carcass to the birds, the wolves rested and then ate again. There would be no time for food once they set off to rescue Rhamin.

There had been no sign of the female wolf that had infatuated him. The sense of disappointment was mingled with relief. Let's get this over with first, he thought. He had plenty of time to make up with Roxana, afterwards. Once she saw him alive and well, he'd tell her he was going to leave the Rhamin pack and form another pack of his own.

In the early evening, as the sun was setting in a crimson sky, Rasci, Silvah, Ramusan, Natan and Lexa began their journey back to the farm. It was a familiar trek by now, and time seemed to pass quickly as they all loped along, silently thinking their own thoughts, not really noticing anything around them. It wasn't until halfway through the journey that Silvah suddenly stopped in her tracks. 'There's something behind us,' she warned, as the others slowed down, turned back and returned to where she was standing. Her ears were pricked forward as she faced the way they had come. They all listened intently. Sure enough, they were being followed. Rasci was the first to recognise their pursuer long before she came within sight. Although it was a calm night with the very slightest of breezes, they were all travelling slightly down wind and, once they had stopped, the scent of Roxana reached him only seconds later. Silvah picked up the scent too. 'Is that Roxana?' she asked quietly.

Rasci nodded, and they all waited. Only the moonlight in her amber eyes stood out in the blackness until she came very close. Then, like a dark shadow in the night, she came panting her way towards them. 'Oh, Rasci,' she panted. 'I'm so glad I caught you.' She trotted to a stop and then took a breath. 'I heard you were setting off on that trip tonight,' she said, still quite breathless.

'That's right,' Rasci replied, trying to keep a strong will. He knew she would try to bend it.

'How did you find that out?' asked Lexa, her look of mistrust rather than that of curiosity, cutting a cold advance.

'I met one of the wolves from your pack. He asked who I was and what I was doing in your territory, and when I told him I was Roxana, he seemed to know who I was.' She took another couple of deep breaths. 'It seems like you have told them about me!'

'Yes,' Rasci replied simply. He looked at Silvah quizzically. He wondered just what Silvah and Zelda had told the rest of his wolves. He wasn't sure what to say to Roxana either, and he wasn't even sure if she had wanted him to tell any of his pack about her.

'I'm glad you did,' she said quickly. Her eyes seemed to glint in the moonlight.

Rasci just nodded.

'Well aren't you going to introduce me?' Roxana asked, smiling.

'What? Oh, er, this is Roxana, everybody.'

Silvah chuckled, dryly. 'We gathered that much.'

'Hmm, this is Silvah,' he nodded towards his elder companion. 'This is Ramusan and this is Natan. And this is Lexa,' he said, nodding to his wolf dog, proudly.

Roxana considered Lexa carefully. 'Hmm, yes, I have heard a lot about you.'

'Oh, where?' Lexa asked, rather sharply Rasci thought. Her curiosity seemed more than just casual.

'Oh, well the other packs around, you know. They all know about Rhamin and his pack. You are all quite well known, really.'

'Oh,' Lexa said, slowly. 'Rasci never mentioned you to me.'

Roxana smiled at her, but it seemed to Rasci that the smile didn't put the usual light in her eyes. She turned her head towards him. 'Rasci, I need to talk to you.' She looked at the others tentatively.

'Come, we'll go ahead a little,' Silvah said to them. 'Rasci will catch us up in a minute.' She turned back to Rasci. 'Don't be too long, will you?'

'I'll be right there,' Rasci said, and with a nod of

acknowledgement, Silvah led the others away.

'How are you?' Roxana asked.

'Fine, thanks. And you?'

Roxana smiled warmly. It was a better smile than she had given Lexa. It lit up her whole face. 'I'm fine,' she said softly. 'I was hoping to catch you.'

'I thought you had left the territory,' Rasci stated, honestly.

'Why would I do that? What I want is here.'

'Here? Oh, you mean...'

She smiled again. This time her eyes seemed to take on a different look; a look that said more than her words. 'Look Rasci, isn't there anything I can do to persuade you not to go on this crazy mission? It can only end in disaster, you know that.'

Rasci took his time answering. Her eyes were still drawing his will power from him, sapping his resolve. 'It's too late to go back now,' he struggled to say. 'We are on our way.'

'I know, but...' She tilted her head and looked at him in a way that made his thin legs turn to slush.

Rasci struggled against the magnetism. 'I'm sorry Roxana. I have to go. If you wait for me I'll call for you as soon as I get back.'

'Get back? Where exactly are you going, Rasci?'

'Oh, it's a long way to the safari park. I can't explain now, but I have to go there. I have to try and get Rhamin and Yeltsa out, and I have to get back. Each part of the mission seems more impossible every time I think about it,' he said, trying and hoping to gain her support. 'I'm only going to find out just how impossible when I try them.'

'I thought impossible was totally impossible. There's no such thing as nearly impossible!'

Rasci muzzled her shoulder. 'We'll have to see,' he said,

maintaining his steel. 'I'm going now. Promise you'll wait.'

'Rasci, don't do it!'

Rasci shook his head. 'It's too late; my mind's made up.' He turned to go.

'Don't, Rasci. You could have so much. We…' She hesitated. 'We could have so much.' Her warm eyes looked at him pleadingly. 'You can't do this, Rasci. You mustn't do this!'

Something heavy was tugging at Rasci's insides. He felt the weight begin to draw him towards her. He put his face close to hers and breathed her in. She responded by pushing her face against his. For a few seconds, Rasci felt like he had never felt before. It was a feeling of discovery, of understanding; a realisation of what he wanted to do. He felt a wave of elation blanking out everything else from his mind. He wanted the feeling to last for ever.

'Rasci, we need to be going,' Silvah's voice broke into the moment. She was standing behind him. Rasci turned and looked at her, wanting to say something, but couldn't. She looked at Roxana. 'Rhamin needs him now,' she said plainly. 'He'll be back.' There was something in her look that surprised Rasci, a look of determination, but more than that, it revealed an unbending resolve to finish what they had all started. 'We need to do this,' she said, looking back at Rasci. 'Rhamin needs you to do this.'

'Rhamin?' Rasci's vision was blurred. 'Yes, of course,' he said, suddenly surprised. He looked around and, realising where he was, he shook himself and took a deep breath. He steeled himself for what he was about to say.

'Rasci?' Roxana's soft voice still pleaded.

He turned towards her. 'I'll be back,' he said, his head suddenly clearing. 'You'll wait for me, won't you?'

Roxana gave a resigned nod. She breathed out heavily.

Her eyes looked very sad in the grey darkness. Without another word, Rasci turned and joined his companions, and together, they loped off into the night.

The group reached the outer perimeter fence of the farm before dawn and settled down to rest until the sun came up. The outer fence seemed to make Rasci a bit uneasy, probably because that is where he first met Roxana. The hollow where he slept was still there. It brought back memories that he would rather not think about at this particular moment in time. At first light, he said his farewells to his companions. They assured him they would be there to greet both him and Rhamin when he got back, and he set off loping towards the farm house.

He hadn't expected any of the Rozalskis to be up and about when he arrived but, as he approached the farmhouse in the semi light of early morning, the door opened and the farmer walked out to meet him. Without a word, he waved him inside, turned and went in. Rasci followed. Maria, Margo and Ben were all waiting to greet him.

It was easy to see why Smokey liked being part of the Rozalski family. The farmer made a good leader. He immediately set to the task of loading items into the vehicle they called the station wagon. The back opened up like a magic door, holding itself up in the air without any help. He loaded a large container made from sticks, later to be called a basket, which smelt of some kind of food; a large container of water; a set of metal implements which Rasci could neither recognise nor describe; several thick sheets made from the fur off a sheep, which Rasci was later to learn were called blankets; and then he opened the side doors and let Ben and Margo into the seating area behind the part where, later, Rasci learned Raymond was to be seated for an enormous length of time, holding and turning things that made the vehicle go where he wanted it to.

Rasci was directed into the back of the vehicle. The door was pulled down and was closed behind him. A feeling of panic fleeted through his insides as he suddenly became enclosed. The sides of the vehicle were covered with sections filled with a hard substance that was clearer than water. He looked around, wildly, and through the sides, he could see Maria bending her head and looking at her children. Ben was to later tell him that the clear sides were called windows. The back door and the front of the vehicle too, were covered the same. Without further delay, Raymond pressed his face against that of Maria and then said something to her before sitting inside the vehicle. There was a frightening roar, the vehicle vibrated and gave out a cacophony of sonic and infra sonic sounds, a door slammed, the vehicle jerked, making Rasci splay his legs to keep his balance, and then, gaining speed, it moved forward towards an opening in the fence and onwards to the road.

Rasci firmly believed that the trip was going to kill him before he got to the safari park. The noise made his head thump. It penetrated his sensitive ear drums and buffeted the inside of his head. Besides the sounds, something inside his ears felt strange as well. He began to pant uncontrollably as a feeling of nausea swept over him. As if expecting it, Raymond realised that Rasci was not travelling well. He opened all the windows and let the cooling, early morning air wash through the inside of the vehicle. It seemed to help Rasci regain his composure; a little.

Unlike Rasci, Margo and Ben seemed well adapted to travelling in this way. Ben leaned over the back seat and, grabbing a hand full of Rasci's thick coat, pulled downwards. Rasci did as he signalled. He lay down, facing the front of the vehicle, resting his head on the back of the seat between Ben and Margo, letting the cooling breeze take away his angst. He watched the two children as they played and chatted in their own little world. For a while, his mind was distracted from the nauseous feeling running through his body but soon the fatigue of travelling all through the night to get to the farm, and constant drone of the vehicle for hour upon hour, eventually drove him into a deep sleep.

The fight seemed real. Rhamin was protecting Yeltsa. As before in his dreams, one of her front legs was white. Then his dream switched to the mountain lion, and once again, he saw himself attacking it. Then the dream switched again and he saw more wolves. He had seen them all before but he couldn't recall their faces. Everything seemed mixed up. First there was Rhamin's face; then Roxana; then Solin; then the wide mouthed spitting fangs of a big cat. Yeltsa appeared; then Roxana once again, pleading with him. Over and over the images appeared, each time, the sequence, more jumbled than the time before. Then everything went dark.

Feeling that he was pinned down under a great weight, the trauma subsided and then he was sitting next to Ben. They were enjoying the trip, watching everything flash by at a speed that Rasci couldn't have ever thought possible. There were lots of other vehicles, some passing going the same way, some passing like lightning, travelling in the opposite direction; there one second, gone the next. 'Hi Rasci,' Ben said, looking over his shoulder and seeing the real Rasci fast asleep.

The wolf spirit chuckled.

Raymond looked in his rear view mirror and smiled as he watched Ben chatting away to his invisible friend. 'The world is definitely a complicated place,' he said to himself as he shook his head. 'Mrs. Steadman wouldn't believe this even if she were here!' he said, to Ben.

Ben smiled proudly. 'I'm explaining things to him Daddy. He wants to know EVERYTHING! And he's asking me!' His eyes were wide with pleasure and pride.

Eventually, Rasci's dream subsided and Ben lapsed into silence before snuggling up to Margo and sleeping through part of the journey. When Rasci awoke, he remembered everything Ben had told him. Refreshed, and with a cool breeze still running past his face, he had got over the queasiness of travelling in the farmer's vehicle and was beginning to enjoy it. He realised he was enjoying being with Ben and his family. There was so much to learn. He thought of Zelda and her many stories, and smiled to himself. He was going to have enough stories to tell the pack till he grew old like his Gran.

Eventually the vehicle slowed down and Raymond steered it into a place where there were lots of cars and lots of other men kind. The children stretched and stirred to consciousness while Raymond got out of the vehicle and did something out of view. There was a smell of fumes, a chemical smell that made Rasci's head spin, and a clunk as the farmer did something else. He walked over to a building and, after a little while, returned. Without a word, he got in, started the vehicle again and drove slowly for several minutes until eventually he reached another area which was covered with short green grass and tables like the one the farmer had in his home. He stopped the station wagon. It went quiet. He spoke to the children and Ben turned and spoke to Rasci, but he could tell that his wolf friend didn't understand.

Raymond got out and went around to the back of the station wagon and Rasci could see lots of other people going about their own business. As the farmer looked around, some of them began to stare, making noises of surprise and pointing towards Rasci. Raymond just ignored them. He lifted up the back door amidst a chorus of 'Oohs' from the spectators who, by now, were more interested in the farmer and his family than they were about their own business. Rasci just looked out in awe. Never had he been so close to so many people. Some put their arms around their young ones and ushered them away to their own vehicles. Others gathered together like buffalo, feeling more secure as one of a herd.

Raymond took out the basket and, resting it by the back door he opened it up and took out items of food that he handed to Margo and Ben. He took out a gadget and twisted off its top. Hot steam came from it as he tilted it into a container and poured out its contents. He passed it to Ben who took a sip and placed it down by his side. Then he passed some more food to Ben and Margo, which they both ate in silence. He offered some to Rasci, but Rasci wasn't hungry. He was used to going without food for days, but his nerves made his stomach too tight to contemplate eating at this time. Anticipation of the possible dangers ahead, like before a hunt, increased the adrenalin and reduced any pangs of hunger, keeping the body unencumbered until the task was accomplished.

The farmer understood. He poured some water out of a big bottle and into a metal bowl. Rasci watched him, tilting his head with interest. As Raymond pushed it towards him, he licked his hand; then, slowly he lapped at the water until it was all gone. Raymond left him to it, closing the back of the station wagon, and opening the side doors to let the children out amidst a round of chatter from the spectators. He closed the doors again and, together, Raymond and the children walked over to a building. They were gone for some time, but Rasci just lay and watched as strangers ventured closer for a better look inside. They were all making speaking noises. He found it all very amusing, but he felt safe inside the vehicle and eventually Raymond and his children returned, opened the doors and got in. With that, he started up the engine and they went on their way.

The journey lasted all day and was interspersed by more stops, one just for Rasci, when he became fidgety and whined so much that his companions guessed what he wanted. They stopped where there was no one about and plenty of bush cover for him to get out and tend, unseen, to the call of nature.

They eventually came to an area in the countryside where they were to camp for the night. Raymond seemed to know where he was heading, and his reconnaissance had obviously taken in all the stages of the trip and all the requirements of himself, his children and his wolf. It was just a feeling that Rasci got; that Raymond was proud to have Rasci with him. He laughed and smiled whenever people seemed concerned or afraid, or just curious. For the time being, Rasci was *his* wolf.

At first, the children were given the blanket to cover them as they lay across the rear seat to sleep but, somehow, during the night, they both ended up lying on or across Rasci in the back of the vehicle. Raymond slept soundly on the front seat which went all the way across the station wagon just like the seat in the rear, used by the children.

By two hours after dawn, they were all awake, fed, reasonably well rested, and ready to undertake the day's task. Rasci hadn't eaten, although he did taste one of the pieces of white substance, proffered by Ben. It wasn't to his liking, and Ben didn't seem too bothered when Rasci turned his head away uninterested. There was a certain tension in the air, a sense of anticipation, a period when the adrenalin in their bodies was preparing them for fight or flight, for none of them knew exactly what was going to happen to them on this fateful day.

CHAPTER TWENTY SIX

The safari park wasn't what Rasci had expected. From the outside, there was little sign that there was, somewhere in the area, a prison or enclosure that detained Rhamin. There were rolling hills covered with trees, and vast areas of lush grassland that were greener than any that Rasci had ever seen. The road led under a giant man made archway with what Rasci realised was writing on it. It was the entrance to the park, and the writing announced it to be "Petersen's Wild and Wonderful Animal Experience." The description didn't make sense to either Margo, Ben or Rasci, but Raymond explained the gist of it to his children. From the archway, a long road continued through vast tracts of countryside. Rasci took in all the scenery.

Eventually, on Raymond's instruction, Margo and Ben climbed into the back of the station wagon with Rasci and together they pulled one of the blankets over him. Rasci realised what was happening. From now on, he had not to be seen, for wolves were not allowed in the visitors' vehicles. In fact the sight of a wolf in any vehicle would have aroused suspicion immediately; a suspicion that he had been stolen. The last thing any of them wanted at this stage was for them to be stopped as thieves and Rasci "rescued" and returned to his proper place, inside the wolf compound. So Rasci hid beneath the blanket, his nose poking out from a tunnel of cloth facing forwards above the back seat so that he could see through the front window.

They were not alone by the time they arrived at a huge fence. More vehicles were in front of them and several more were behind. The fence was many times higher than Rasci. He considered it carefully. It was made from the same metal substance that the farmer used for his fences; only this stuff was shiny silver in colour and was woven into an impenetrable wall with spaces through which nothing bigger than a sparrow could pass. Along the top of the fence were some single strands of metal, held facing inwards to the enclosed area by struts that looked to be coated in some other substance. Rasci knew immediately that these were the parts that carried the lightning that Corvak had described. He could hear the sub-sonic buzz of death as the electricity paced backwards and forwards, like a caged animal, along the strands, waiting to be released when something reached up and touched it.

A man emerged from a small wooden building by the side of the road, and stood nearby. He pushed at the fence and a huge section of it slid to one side. All the vehicles moved on. It wasn't far to another building, this time made of rock. Another man emerged and spoke to Raymond. Something small was exchanged and, as the man outside looked through the windows into the back of the vehicle, Raymond casually drove on.

Corvak had been right. From the next gate on there were animals that defied description. It enthralled Rasci. The children were spellbound. Both stood up against the back of their father's seat and gazed out in amazement at animals which had brown patches all over them. Although they were not as tall as Corvak had described them, the creatures were as tall as trees. They strode past, totally unfazed by the presence of traffic, bending their enormous necks and waiting for tit bits of food to be passed through the open windows of the vehicles

Raymond drove on amidst a queue of trailing vehicles. They passed more tall animals, only these were hairy and had two enormous lumps on their back that flopped over to one side. They too were impervious to the presence of people and cars. They wandered close to the vehicles in search of some tit bit or treat.

Then, beyond another fence, Rasci spotted some buffalo bunched together, grazing on the lush green grass, and to the side of them were some strange kind of deer with long thick, straight horns, lying and cudding lazily in the morning sun. But no people wandered amongst them; for Rasci knew how dangerous the male buffalo could be, and obviously the men kind and their children knew also. In fact, from this stage on, nobody seemed to have the windows of their cars open. A sensible precaution, Rasci thought. There was another large enclosed section where horses roamed. But these were not ordinary horses. They were white with black stripes.

The vehicles just drove slowly and in line through each enclosure. Each time a new enclosure loomed, there was another tall fence and a sliding gate to go through. Eventually, however, they reached a different kind of gate system. Now, as they approached the sections which Rasci was to discover contained the most dangerous animals, the carnivores, there were double gates. Each time, an attendant waited for several vehicles to accumulate. The first gate would close behind them and then, only when it was clear that there were no animals in that fenced section did the second gate open in front of them to let the cars proceed.

Once again, the enclosure was vast but now Rasci spotted some strange vehicles, not moving, but waiting, like a wolf waits for its prey. He could see a man inside each one. And most strange of all was the fact that the vehicles were white with black stripes, just like the striped horses they had passed earlier. After passing some in every enclosure, Rasci worked out that they were most likely the prison guards. They were there to make sure that none of the animals escaped and at the same time to check that nobody got out of their cars for it was obvious that some of the bigger animals could and would attack if someone was unprotected. At least once Rasci saw the occupant of one of the patrol vehicles drive over to a car and unmistakably instruct the visitor, with a winding motion of his arm, to close the window. Clearly, the underlying principle of the safari park, must certainly have been to entertain men kind and their offspring, and not to feed them and their youngsters to the animals. Rasci noticed that each man in his patrol vehicles was armed with one of the deadly stick weapons that, at the school, Ben had called a gun, but he was baffled as to how they worked. Keeping his head well covered as they went by the patrol vehicles, he was just thinking that puny men were vulnerable to attack from animals that wouldn't even attempt to attack a wolf, when suddenly the hair on the back of his neck bristled. Raymond had stopped the station wagon. There, in the middle of the road, right in front of their vehicle, and stopping all the traffic, was a cat so big it would have dwarfed two of Rhamin. It was the colour of the flames that sometimes wash over the dry grassy plains just as Corvak had described, but it was bigger than he could have imagined. It strolled casually around to the side of the station wagon, sniffed at the glass window and looked inside. Its face was wider than the window; its amber eyes many times bigger than those of a wolf.

With an instinctive reaction, Rasci barred his teeth. At first, the big cat picked up its ears as it picked up the ultrasonic noise from Rasci's throat. Then it lay them down flat against its head, placed a huge paw against the glass, opened its mouth, rolled back its lips and snarled. Raymond revved his engine and drove away as quickly as he could.

Needless to say, it wasn't long before, and with a sense of relief that, they reached the next set of gates. 'This is it,' Raymond said to his passengers as he read the sign "Wolf Enclosure."

Rasci could feel both the tension and the anticipation in his companions. He too was tense. He knew it wouldn't be long now before he saw his brother Rhamin again.

CHAPTER TWENTY SEVEN

Rasci didn't recognise Rhamin as first. The wolf he was watching was very thin, and this wolf should have been black, but his coat was stark and the guard hairs on his back were tinged at the ends with brown. Even his white ears had turned a dull grey. This wolf looked ill. If it was Rhamin, then he looked to be a whittled down version of his former self, unsteady on his feet, glancing around warily at all the cars that were filing past. Something about his manner was diminished as if a large ember had fallen off his previously blazing fire. It seemed that the energy to take control was no longer there. He was no longer driven by determination. Instead, there was a resigned disregard for either himself or the other wolves that were milling around.

Rhamin watched as vehicle after vehicle slowly grumbled past, the windless heat doing nothing to disperse the choking fumes of their breath. The occupants of each vehicle were observing the spectacle of the giant black wolf. It was one of the things they had come to see, and he was the centre of attraction. None of the other wolves that were wandering around the compound seemed to draw such interest. But he was getting used to it. He stood in the middle of the hard road and watched as a gap appeared in the line of traffic. One vehicle was holding back. Eventually it started to move forward again and drew alongside him.

'Want a ride?'

Rhamin looked around. The station wagon had eased to a standstill in the shade of the trees on the left hand side of the concrete road. It had stopped a few feet from the black wolf. The voice had seemed familiar but was muffled. It definitely came from the man's vehicle. He looked again at the man. This time, instead of looking about furtively, he turned to face Rhamin. It was a face that Rhamin would never forget. But he didn't know whether to be pleased or angry. This was the farmer who had led the man, Petersen, to him, the farmer whose eyes he had met in the forest and thought he'd understood what he was feeling. This was the farmer who had almost been killed by Bortag the bear and, had it not been for Rhamin and his pack, would surely have perished that day on the mountain along with his companion. Was this farmer here then, as part of the conspiracy? Was he here to gloat? What did he want? Had he planned it all? Rhamin couldn't tell.

'Psst. Want a ride?'

The voice seemed to come from behind the farmer, but the sound was coming from the other side of the vehicle? Slowly, still without any real purpose, but perhaps now curious, Rhamin stepped around to the other side, only to see just a grassy bank that led away to the adjacent monkey compound.

Another vehicle behind drew nearer for its occupants to look at this black wolf, the focal point of the safari park. It stopped alongside Raymond's station wagon waiting for the celebrity wolf to emerge from behind it. Raymond remained where he was and Rasci could sense the farmer was anxious. Beads of sweat bubbled up on his cheeks and forehead. He slipped the vehicle into gear.

'Wait dad,' cried Ben.

Raymond's hand hovered over the hand brake. 'Damn these sight seers!' He relaxed a little. 'What do you think, Ben?'

Ben shrugged. But his father couldn't see him. His eyes were fixed on the people in the other car. 'They can't make us move, can they Daddy?'

'Like to see them get out and try,' Raymond said with a dry crackling chuckle. He took his hand off the brake and picked up his bottle of water. He slowly unscrewed the cap and took a long swig. Rasci squeaked and the wolf outside pricked up his ears. Rhamin remained at the verge side of the station wagon. Stepping a little closer he sniffed at the glass.

'Rhamin. It's me.'

Rhamin lifted his head. There, inside the vehicle, was the little boy from the farm; the courageous young man kind that had pushed Rhamin away from his little sibling that night in the farmhouse when the wolf had reached past him to pick up the dog pups. The boy's eyes were wide, but not with fear. Rhamin tried to read the look. The boy seemed excited, perhaps a little anxious. His little lips were parted as he looked around at the vehicle outside. Slowly, still watching what was going on outside, the little boy lifted the edge of a blanket. Rhamin was perplexed. But then, slowly, from beneath the edge of the sheet, a black button nose poked out at the end of a grey snout. Two long canine teeth showed as the figure spoke again. 'Rhamin, it's me!'

'Rasci?' Rhamin leaned his head to one side. This was not what he had been conditioned to expect. 'Rasci, is that you? Is it really you?'

The adjacent car pulled forward and stopped a little

ahead to try and get a better view. The occupants could no longer see inside the back of the station wagon. The blanket lifted a little more as a face appeared behind the nose.'

'Well who else do I look like for goodness sake?'

Rhamin couldn't speak. Instead, his ears went forward, and his tail began to wag uncontrollably. But his head began to shake as his pleasure was overtaken by despair.

'But what are you doing here? I'm in a prison. Don't you realise? You are in a prison!'

'So, do you want a ride or not,' Rasci repeated.

A small flame rekindled in Rhamin's eyes. 'Oh, Rasci. You fabulous little brother of mine! It's so good to see your ugly face!'

'Right.'

Rhamin looked around. The spark of hope in his eyes suddenly dulled. 'It's impossible, Rasci. There's no way out. I know. I've looked at every corner of this pen.'

'But we can get out. You can come with us.'

Rhamin backed away as another two cars pulled closer. Rasci dropped down beneath the blanket again as Rhamin spoke. 'I can't, not without Yeltsa.'

'Yeltsa? Is she here?' But the other cars had stopped. They too seemed to want their money's worth. It was early in the day, but already the drive through traffic was building up.

'She's not very well,' Rhamin said as he stepped away from the vehicle.

Rasci's face disappeared. A zebra-painted patrol vehicle drove closer from across the grass.

'You'll have to move on,' the driver stated.

'I've paid to look at the wolves,' Raymond shouted back, remaining exactly where he was.

'So have the others,' replied the patrolman.

Raymond took another swig of his water. 'Give us a minute,' he said as he fumbled with a camera.

The patrolman nodded and drove away.

'It's too busy,' Raymond stated dejectedly. 'We'll never do it.'

Margo looked towards her father. 'Daddy, we can drive through again can't we?'

Raymond turned his head and looked at his little daughter. 'That's a good idea. Why not?' he said with a determined grin. Ben and Margo looked down at Rasci who was trying to remain below the edge of the back windows. For a moment, Ben slipped the blanket to one side and patted him. Nobody saw Rasci. He was too low down. And Ben thought that even if Rasci had sat up in the back, nobody would have seen him because all eyes were on Rhamin, standing so close to the station wagon.

'There will be fewer vehicles just before the park closes for the night,' Raymond stated, as he began to move slowly away.

Rasci thought their opportunity to save Rhamin had passed as the station wagon left the compound. Whining, and noticeably distressed, he lifted his head and looked back as his friend disappeared from view.

'Don't worry,' Ben said, patting him confidently. 'We're going back.'

But Rasci didn't understand and a sense of despair began to overtake him.

Steadily, Raymond drove through the remainder of the park, stopping in the animal locks and waiting for the gates to close behind him before the ones up ahead opened to let them through. The lion enclosure was next. Ben and Margo's preoccupation trying to calm Rasci prevented them from noticing anything. The drive through the lion enclosure took seventeen minutes. All the time Ben and

Margo spoke soothingly to their companion. What Raymond didn't want, was for Rasci to see the lions or the lions to see Rasci. The wolf's reaction to the tiger had been provocative to say the least, and he knew that the lions were used to seeing humans behind their glass windows of their vehicles but he wasn't sure if that would stop them noticing another animal. Consequently, with Ben and Margo in charge of the unenviable situation in the back of the station wagon, there were strict instructions not to let Rasci lift his head under any circumstances.

Eventually, they left the last enclosure and arrived at a large open green where many cars were already stopping for their occupants to enjoy a picnic or simply to enjoy sitting in the sun. Raymond picked a remote corner, under the shade of the branches of a big spruce tree. Nobody seemed to want to be in the shade, so by being there, they maintained a respectable distance between the station wagon and the nearest vehicle; and that must have been over fifty yards away.

Calmed a little now, realising that they had not completely abandoned their mission, Rasci settled down to wait and see what was happening. Raymond lifted the back door slightly, to enable air to circulate, and Ben opened all the windows, got out a sandwich box and a flask, and shared out some food. There was little else to do on a hot mid-day in August. The group dined, slept and waited. They offered to share some of their sandwiches with Rasci, but he couldn't eat. His mind was not turned towards food.

Margo was the first to drop into a deep slumber. Later, Raymond managed to get half an hour's sleep, but Ben stayed wide awake and fidgeted constantly. Rasci, although too stressed at first, relaxed enough to go into one of his trances. It was then, reassured by Ben that they were returning to the wolf enclosure, that he realised that the mission had only just begun.

It was a long wait. Raymond knew that Rasci was a liability if anyone saw him in the back of the Station wagon, and he wouldn't exactly class as a pet. But he needed to keep Ben and Margo occupied. It was still only eleven thirty in the morning. The safari park accepted last vehicles to drive through an hour before closure. But, with a definite plan in mind, now it seemed a little more of an adventure and less like grand larceny. Ben fidgeted when Rasci awoke. Margo had not emerged from her deep sleep. Raymond tapped his fingers, hummed and was clearly having trouble relaxing and Rasci, who had no urge to give the plot away, now he knew they were returning to the wolf enclosure, and who was used to spending long hours resting and sleeping in the shade, of all the station wagon's occupants, was the coolest and the calmest.

But they all began to feel the rush of adrenalin as the sun began to drop from its highest point. Each one seemed to be counting the minutes and the seconds. Rasci, somewhat in the dark regarding the time that their mission was to commence, began to lift his head and peer at Ben with questioning eyes. 'Won't be long now,' Ben kept saying soothingly, stroking Rasci's head, for he too was not yet able to tell the time by the station wagon clock, and was just waiting for something to happen; waiting for a sign from his father.

As closing time approached, Raymond started the engine, let off his parking brake and slipped the vehicle into gear. 'Are we ready then?' he asked with a final look at his watch. No one answered. They were all too nervous. Slowly he drove past the remaining picnickers and headed to the massive mesh gate that led to the enclosures. The first enclosure they had to go through was inhabited by water buffalo, grazing beside a large man made lake. Rasci thought that if circumstances had been different, the animals would not have been so calm. Slowly, they approached the next big mesh gate, letting cars pass them as they drove through the compound at a leisurely pace. Then they came to the next enclosure, the first with a double gate lock. As the second gate closed behind them, Raymond drove slowly forward, but the enclosure seemed empty the second time around. The huge tiger that they had seen in the morning was now nowhere to be seen, nor were any other similar animals, if there had been any others in there in the first place.

At the next set of gates, leading to the wolf enclosure, they were next to last in the line of traffic. The first gate closed behind them, and nervously, they watched the gate up ahead. A minute or so passed while the guard lit a cigarette. Finally, the front gate rolled sideways. This was the moment they had been waiting for and Rasci could sense that they were all nervous, no one more than he. If this didn't work then there probably would be no other chance. Raymond held back and let the one car that was behind them pass them by. He slowed almost to a standstill to let the other cars drift off ahead up a slope towards the main denning area of the wolves. Once again those people in the vehicles stopped to try and get a view of the wolves, but only six grey wolves wandered about, none with any particular purpose.

Rasci was watching now, his head poking up above the window ledge. He thought how pointless the lives of these captives were. They had food, and plenty of it, but their lives had ended. Hunting in the wild needed cunning and courage, but there was none needed here. Rasci recalled a story that Zelda had told him a couple of years ago about a wolf pack that killed all the members of a trespassing pack, all except one. That one wolf they just left and they walked away. She had fought fearlessly and with courage. Rasci hoped that he would be fearless if the time came for him to fight for his life. That's why he loved his leader. He had never once seen Rhamin show fear of anything. That's why it saddened Rasci now. He had seen his leader broken and wilted; the fire of life now only embers glimmering dimly within him.

Raymond still held back, and soon, the drivers of the cars in front drove off around a bend, and disappeared behind the tall oak trees that overhung the road, while the farmer pulled up close to the spot where he had stopped before.

Rasci's heart began to thump now. Where was his friend? Still there were only six grey wolves loping around. Surely Rhamin had understood that he was coming back. If he didn't appear soon, a patrol vehicle was most likely to arrive. They would check that all the vehicles were out of the enclosure before locking the gates for the night.

'Come on, Black Wolf,' Raymond said aloud. 'Come on boy. Where are you?'

As if hearing the plea, a black face poked out from behind a thick, rotting tree stump. It looked each way, time being of no urgency to it. Then, slowly, Rhamin raised his body into view and turned around. He was speaking to another wolf, urging Yeltsa to come out from deep inside a hollow.

Rasci couldn't hold his nerve any longer. He threw off the blanket and barked at his leader. 'Rhamin, be quick!' But, although Rhamin must have heard him, his back remained turned towards the station wagon.

'Open the back door, Ben,' Rasci instructed. 'Quickly!'

But Ben didn't understand.

Rasci scratched frantically at the glass.

Precious moments passed, while Margo and Ben considered

the situation. 'You have to open the back door, Ben,' Rasci exclaimed, scratching now at the crack at the base of the door. His actions told the message. Without losing another second, Ben pushed past Rasci, pulled a lever and pushed. The back door swung open and upwards.

'Come, Rhamin. Come quickly,' Rasci pleaded. But Rhamin still had his back turned towards them. 'Rhamin!'

'Quiet!' Rhamin called back softly. In the distance he could hear the patrol vehicle coming though the lock. So could Rasci; he heard it too. But Rhamin still hadn't budged. With every nerve in his body tingling, Rasci pushed past Ben, leapt out of the back of the station wagon and loped towards Rhamin.

'Rhamin! We must go now or we will all be prisoners.' He looked down at Yeltsa, and his heart sank. She was unbelievably thin, her eyes were dull and she could hardly push herself up into a standing position. 'Yeltsa!' Rasci exclaimed. 'You're not going to let those few yards be the end of you, are you?' He watched as she lifted her head, fresh spirit lifting her to her feet as she heard the sound of Rasci's voice. 'All the pack are waiting for you,' he went on. 'Your new cubs are expecting you!'

It was the mention of her latest litter that gave her the surge of energy she had lacked.

'Are they still alive?' she asked, her drawn face showing total incredulity.

'You had better believe it,' Rasci said, getting down into the hollow. He pushed her with his muzzle.

Only yards away, Raymond waited, tapping his fingers nervously on the steering wheel, looking and watching for the patrol vehicle. He couldn't hear it like the wolves could; they could hear it slowly coming around the bend beyond the trees. Soon it would come into full view. It would see the station wagon, and the game would be up.

The other wolves were running towards them having spotted the stranger. 'Quickly,' Rhamin said to Yeltsa. 'They are spoiling for another fight.' There were more of them than before.

Slowly, Yeltsa staggered forward, each step a laboured effort. One of her front legs hung loosely in front of her. She swayed but two wolves at her sides supported her. 'Just don't go down!' Rhamin said to her, as he urged her forward.

Up ahead, the patrol vehicle would soon appear. The sound was getting closer. Raymond could hear it now. Impatient, he got out of the driver's door. He knew the patrol vehicle would appear, and he had seen the other wolves bounding towards them. Trusting Rhamin, without a second thought, he snatched Yeltsa up in his strong arms, and lifted her into the back of his vehicle. She yelped with pain as he let her down onto the floor of the station wagon. Quickly, he ran to the driver's door to get back in, but the first of the other wolves were almost upon him. He stopped, ready to repel an attack, when Rasci came around from behind his legs to face them. These wolves were well fed, but no wolf in captivity can compare in fitness and strength to one that hunts and eats well in the wild. Rasci looked intimidating. And thin as he was, Rhamin was still bigger than any other wolf. Suddenly, he appeared at the other side of the vehicle. The thirteen attacking wolves skidded to a halt, none wanting to be first in the front line of attack. Raymond ducked inside and pulled the door closed behind him. He couldn't be seen out of his vehicle, nor could he be seen fighting off the wolves. The patrol vehicle had stopped just before the brow of the hill; the top of its cab was clearly visible now. Had the driver seen Raymond?

None of them knew, but they didn't have chance to think of the consequences.

Regaining their courage with the man out of the way, the other wolves went for Rasci. Rhamin ran between them. They must have fought with Rhamin before, because, once again they halted in their tracks. 'Get going,' Rhamin said as he turned his head to Rasci. 'I'll keep them off you. You can get away.'

Rasci, of course, didn't obey. He bounded past Rhamin's shoulder and went for the throat of the leading attacker. It yelped and bounced out of the way. The other wolves scattered. 'You are no match for the Rhamin wolves,' Rasci barked as the fragmented pack began to reassemble, each waiting for another to take the lead. He bounded at them again, lashing at the wolves on each side and once again they dispersed. He turned to Rhamin. 'Well, are you coming or not?'

Rhamin didn't speak. He looked at Rasci in admiration. His brother was magnificent. He obeyed. Shakily, he went around to the back of the station wagon and jumped in to join Yeltsa.

Rasci bounded back around the vehicle and jumped in after him bouncing on top of Yeltsa as she lay panting. Ben squeezed past them and reached for the strap that he could use to pull down the door. His fingers slipped past it, unable to grasp. He looked down at the angry pack that was now searching around the back of the station wagon.

The patrol vehicle was moving forward again, and was in full view now as Raymond released the hand brake and selected his gear. He let out the clutch too fast and stalled the engine, halting the station wagon with a jerk. The jerk made the back door oscillate and as it moved downwards, Ben caught the strap, but the momentum of the door returning up to its open position pulled him forward and made him lose his balance. He was falling head first towards the angry pack of resident wolves. Raymond spun his head around and watched helplessly as a huge mouth closed around Ben's waist. It dragged him backwards as he clung desperately to the strap. The door closed with a thud at the little boy's feet. Rhamin let him go and as he tumbled backwards over Rasci's head, Rhamin lifted his face level with Ben's and licked it with a damp shammy-leather tongue.

The patrol vehicle was coming down the slope towards them. Desperately, Raymond turned the ignition key, the engine fired and he gunned it as the patrol vehicle drew up alongside.

'Anything the matter?' the patrolman asked through his half open window. He was watching the milling wolves at the back of Raymond's station wagon.

Raymond wound his window halfway down. 'Had a little engine trouble. Flooded it,' he said coolly, fearing that the patrolman would look through the back windows. The patrolman hadn't seen what Ben, Margo and the wolves were doing. His attention was drawn to the activity of the angry pack of wolves, still milling about by the back door of the station wagon.

Neither had Raymond seen what his son and daughter were doing. Nerves shredding rapidly, he was too busy getting ready to panic. The station wagon was large, but with three big wolves under the blankets, there was little room for Ben and Margo. Their little legs were tucked underneath them as they both sat astride Rasci. They had hastily tugged at the blankets, but Yeltsa was lying on them and they had only managed to hide her and Rhamin. Rasci's back and head were still exposed. If the patrolman looked into the back he would see a five and half year old boy sitting on a wolf's head and a four and a half year old girl riding the same wolf, bare back; not what is normally expected to be happening inside an average family car, even in a safari park. Not the normal activity of the average family.

'Do you need any help?' The patrolman's eyes flicked from the pack outside to look at Raymond.

'Nope,' Raymond said cheerily, a bead of sweat trickling down in front of his ear. He wound his window back up. 'The problem seems to have cleared itself now,' he called as the gap above the glass disappeared.

'I'll lead you out,' the friendly patrolman shouted as he drew forwards and, honking his horn to disperse the pack of wolves that were now in front of his vehicle, he began to swing his jeep around on the grass. As he passed, his face was within two feet of the children and their contraband. Ben pressed his face against the glass and smiled cheerily. Margo, her blond hair sticking to her face, swept it to one side with one hand as she waved at the patrolman with the other.

The patrolman gave them both a friendly wave and, swinging his vehicle around on the grassy field, he headed away back up the hill.

'Are you all covered?' Raymond asked, now that there was no one watching them.

Ben and Margo busied themselves adjusting the wolves. Without any fear or effort they got them to move just where they wanted them. As Ben drew the blanket level over the last wolf, a warm, appreciative tongue caressed his little hand. He responded automatically with a light pat on the wolf's head and then he and Margo climbed over into the rear car seat.

As they approached the gates, the first one rolled back and they followed the patrol vehicle into the lock. Patiently they waited as its driver paced past the side windows. He operated the lever and closed the gate behind them and then, passing the station wagon again, he glanced inside. Ben gave him another wave and the broadest of smiles. Grinning and waving back at them, the patrolman went and opened the next gate. He got in his jeep and drove forward, leaving room for Raymond to pull in behind him, and then he closed the gate, got in his vehicle and led them through to the next enclosure. The lions were still there, but no one took much notice as they proceeded to the next set of gates.

Once again, they travelled through the animal lock one gate at a time. Each time Ben smiled at the man and got a smile in return. 'You're steaming up,' he said to Raymond as he passed his window. 'You can put your windows down now if you want.'

They waved to the friendly patrolman one last time as they drove off, following the signs towards the exit. Raymond was very quiet. Margo was whispering to the wolves. Ben stood against his father's seat with his hand on his shoulder. Rasci and the other wolves remained concealed beneath the heavy woollen blankets. He was later to learn what happened. At this moment, however, everything around him sounded jumbled and unclear.

'We've done it, Daddy!' Ben whispered in his father's ear.

'I don't know if we have, yet,' his father replied. Up ahead was some kind of checkpoint. There were only two other cars heading that way, and they had already been stopped and set off again by the time Raymond drew up to the small kiosk that stood by a long pole barrier. The barrier was up. Raymond resisted the urge to drive straight through, and wound down his window. A man handed him a leaflet.

'Hope you enjoyed your visit, sir,' he said.

'Very exciting. Quite an adventure,' Raymond said truthfully, wiping his forehead with his handkerchief and smiling the best he could, his heart still pounding inside his chest.

'It is, isn't it, sir? Have a good day.'

'And you.' With a cursory wave, Raymond drove off without looking back.

Once away from the main gates of the safari park, Raymond opened the windows at the front and told Ben to do the same at the back. The station wagon had become a boiling pan. The wolves were panting desperately as Ben pulled the covers off them. He pushed the blankets into the back seat and stood back while the three wolves expanded into the extra space and lifted their heads so that the cooling breeze could wash over their faces.

It was some time before, Raymond stopped. He pulled off the busy road, and followed a timber cutters track that cut an avenue through the trees, past some fields of corn and, eventually, came to a stop in a wooded area. Here, they were well away from the road and out of sight or sound of any traffic. Rasci thought that Raymond seemed to know exactly where he was going. Clearly, this man had reconnoitred the area better that Rasci had at first thought. He was focussed and seemed to be working to a pre-designed plan. Raymond stopped the engine, got out and went around to the back of the station wagon. He clicked the catch, lifted the back door and shook his head. 'You'll be hot there,' he said, to his cargo. He was right of course. The three wolves were panting rapidly. Their coats were damp with condensation, but the late afternoon air was cooler now and it was a relief for the wolves to be able to breathe the fresh, cool air. Raymond took the basket that was buried beneath the blankets on the back seat, opened it and took out the water bowl. He pulled out the water container from under the blankets and poured the last of the water into the dish and let the wolves all take a drink. Yeltsa was the thirstiest. She had been lying partially underneath the other two. Raymond helped her to move to one side, totally confident that she would allow it, and she let him, watching him with her amber eyes, for this was the first time she had actually seen the farmer from the mountain, the man that Rhamin and Rasci had spoken about so often; the farmer that, during their incarceration, Rhamin had sworn had betrayed them. But now she knew differently.

The sense of relief and the feeling of freedom were not just felt by Rhamin and Yeltsa. It was clear that Rasci and his human friends felt the same. Until they had finally escaped from the enclosed fences, they had all been trapped inside a prison.

CHAPTER TWENTY EIGHT

None of the wolves spoke until the station wagon was on the road again. Even in the shelter of the wooded glade, there was a sense of unease. They felt free, but there was still danger in the air. Raymond sensed it also, but he kept his nerve. Instead of driving off as fast as he could go, he stayed in the copse, letting the wolves recover, letting them breathe the free air of liberation. Even with the back door open, none of the wolves ventured out of the station wagon. They knew that this vehicle, this man made, roaring, noisy metal horse of a thing, something they would normally walk a mile around to avoid, was now their saviour. They knew they were many miles away from the farm and the Darin. There was no temptation whatsoever to try and make their bid for freedom on their own. They lay, facing the open door, ears pricked forward, not speaking, or even communicating. Their company, the closeness of their bodies and their mere presence seemed more than enough. The sense of belonging seeped back into their aura, as they listened and watched silently for any sign of danger.

The sun had set long before Raymond told his children to sit back inside the station wagon. He took his time, glanced once more back along the track towards the road, closed all the doors and, as the daylight began to fade, he set off to drive through the night without stopping.

It was only then that the wolves began to relax, no longer looking out for danger.

'Well,' Rasci began suddenly, his mood gradually lightening, as if they had been talking for hours, 'you don't exactly look like you've been receiving special treatment, Rhamin. In fact, you look like… how can I put it? Er…'

'Like?' Rhamin asked with a smile.

'Like a pile of bird poo,'

'Worse!' Yeltsa said as Rhamin chuckled. Yeltsa was usually the most serious wolf in the whole pack.

Rasci looked at her.

'I fear she has a broken leg,' said Rhamin serious once more. 'The patrolmen beat her with a stick when we were fighting the other wolves.'

'But why? If she was defending herself…'

'She had one by the throat,' Rhamin explained, sitting up and scratching vigorously at his neck.

'No more than it deserved,' said Yeltsa.

'She wouldn't let go. They were attacking both of us because we were in their territory. She defended herself the only way we free wolves know how. But those wolves in the prison camp didn't behave like us. Some of them are new, from their own territory outside the park, but the rest seem to have always been there. It was their territory. The other wolves, that had once been free, accepted that and fell into line, following the established leader. But I don't think that the resident wolves have ever hunted and killed. It was like they belonged there; you know, dependent on men for their food. Even with some wild wolves amongst them, they were no match for us; you saw that yourself when they confronted us. We weren't prepared to follow their leader.'

'Yes, I did notice. Even looking half the wolf you should be, they backed off.'

'When Yeltsa and I first confronted them, we were both much stronger. We were still free in our minds. But back there, I think they were backing away from you, Rasci. You can look quite fierce when you have to.'

'Thank you, Bro,' Rasci said, lifting his head proudly.

Rhamin looked at the face of his brother. 'What on earth were you doing here, anyway? I'd have thought the pack would have got itself a new leader by now and forgotten about us.'

'It has,' said Rasci. 'Not forgotten about you… I mean got a new leader.'

'Oh, who is it then?'

'Well, it's… er… well it's me, actually.'

Rhamin laughed. Come on Rasci, stop playing the fool. Tell me, who really is the leader.'

Rasci sniffed and looked over the edge of the window at some fleeting light beams as cars passed on the other side of the road. 'It's me, Rhamin.'

'Seriously?'

'Well it was,' Rasci said, a little sadness creeping into his voice. He thought of Roxana. Would she still be there when he got back? She never really answered him when he asked her to wait. Perhaps he didn't wait for the answer because he feared she would say no. He wasn't sure. 'We don't need two leaders, do we?' he said philosophically.

'That sounds like you enjoy being the leader of the pack, Rasci.'

'Not really, brother. I don't think I ever meant to be leader, it just happened.' He told Rhamin how Solin had appeared as if from nowhere, and how he had stood up to him and how, by some fluke of fate, by seeing Solin off, he had assumed the role of leader without actually putting his name forward for the position.

'But why the sadness then?'

Rasci had tried hard not to show it. He considered what he had done over the past weeks and how his life was changing. He explained that he had met a young female by the name of Roxana and how she was ambitious and wanted to be the alpha female of a pack leader. Rhamin wanted to know all about her. Rasci didn't tell him that she had begged him not to risk his life trying to save Rhamin. He didn't tell Rhamin just how hopeless she thought the rescue attempt was, nor did he tell him just how close he had come to believing it himself. Without the strength and the will of the pack behind him, especially Silvah, Zelda and Lexa, Rasci realised he would have let Roxana talk him out of completing the planned rescue mission.

'Healthy packs increase,' Rhamin said eventually. 'They evolve. The Rhamin pack isn't a single wolf or a set group. It's growing like a tree.' He looked at Rasci affectionately. 'I have no doubt that the pack think of you as a great leader. Some may want to stay with me, but some will choose to go with you. You've told us that, by some miracle of fate, our babies are safe and alive. Well then, the pack is already renewing itself. It has room for a few deserters.'

'Deserters?'

'I'm joking Rasci. Where's your sense of humour gone?'

'Oh, I see. Oh, well I've had rather a lot on my mind lately.' He nodded towards the human occupants of the station wagon, two of whom were fast asleep. 'Developing relationships and all that.' He went on to explain how he was first sure that Rhamin was alive and how eventually he turned up at the safari park. Corvak had been the key to convincing him that all the visits to the different places in his dreams and trances had been for real.

'Yes,' Rhamin said with a look of affection in his eyes, 'Corvak did come to visit me.'

'I know,' said Rasci, 'I asked him to find you. If there's anybody in this world that could find you if you were alive, it's Corvak.'

'Yes, he is quite a remarkable little bird, isn't he?'

Rhamin thought for a long time. When he spoke again, he looked at Yeltsa. 'You know, Rasci, Yeltsa and I are really grateful. There isn't any other wolf that I know who could have brought off such a daring escape, or got the help that you did. We thought we were there to stay. Neither of us thought we would ever see you or the pack again.' He paused and looked Rasci in the eye. 'But you need to think about your own life now and we'll understand if you want to leave.'

'But I'm not sure if that is what I want. I was never happier than when I was following you.'

'There's nothing to stop you developing another relationship, then seeing how you feel, is there?'

Rasci shook his head. He breathed a heavy sigh of relief. 'Whatever happens, I hope we'll always remain friends,' he said as he lowered his head onto his front paws. He was weary of it all and somehow, a great weight had lifted from his mind. He was beginning, at last, to feel free again.

'You can count on it.' Rhamin said quietly, as he watched his friend slowly doze and then eventually sink into a deep, trouble free sleep.

Raymond didn't stop once. The children slept, the wolves

dozed and he drove and drove and drove. Rasci knew that this man and his young ones had done more than any friend could have been asked to do. They had entered the world of the wolf, without question and had risked their own liberty in so doing. He realised that the rescue mission had meant that Raymond was breaking the rules of men, and breaking those rules has consequences. Whatever they were, they hadn't happened during the rescue. From this time on, even Raymond Rozalski's life had changed.

He pulled the station wagon into the farm yard as the grey light of the next day was beginning to creep over the horizon. Maria was there to greet him. She came hurrying from the house followed by Smokey. Maria was fully dressed and looked like she had had no more sleep than her husband. He got out of the vehicle, brushed her hair from her face with his fingers and kissed her on the lips. They hugged for a moment or two and then, breaking away, Raymond went to the back of the station wagon. As he opened up the door, Maria saw the eyes of three big wolves looking out at her. Their ears were forward. Two of their faces showed definite curiosity. The third, Rasci's, panted with a wide smile that even humans recognise as happiness. She spoke to Raymond in words that Rasci didn't understand. 'I was so worried,' she said with a trembling voice.

'You were not the only one,' he said, taking off his jacket and throwing it to the ground. 'We have an injured wolf here,' he said in a business like manner and then, putting his arms underneath Yeltsa, hoisted her up to his chest and carried her to the kitchen. Rasci could tell that, not for one moment, did he fear Yeltsa or the other wolves. Rhamin watched, ears forward, a concerned look in his eyes, but did nothing to impede the farmer. He knew his life had been changed by the farmer's actions and trusted him completely.

So did Yeltsa. She was thin and weak. He laid her on the large pine kitchen table and pressed his hand on her shoulder to indicate that she was to stay there, while the other wolves stood inside the door, watching. Raymond spoke again to Maria and she disappeared into another part of the house. He took up Smokey's bowl and filled it from a tap with cool water and placed it in front of Yeltsa. She waited a moment and then, as he spoke some words in an encouraging tone, lapped at it gratefully. He just stood and waited patiently. Eventually, with the bowl almost empty, he removed it and refilled it once more, placing it down in front of the other two wolves, and said something to Smokey, who was watching everything with interest. She went to a basket in the corner and sat down while Rhamin and Rasci drank.

Soon, Maria returned with two bags which she handed to Raymond. From the first, he pulled out some fresh beef and placed it on the floor in front of the two male wolves but they just stood and watched him, oblivious to the food. From the second bag, he took out some rolls of white material. He fiddled with the first one and it began to unwind into a long tape. He placed his hand in the bag again and took out a short flat piece of wood. Carefully, he placed it against Yeltsa's broken fore leg, straightened the break as gently as he could and began to wind the tape around both the stick and the leg. Yeltsa never moved. She just watched him, bearing the pain without any audible sound. Rasci and Rhamin could hear her cries, of course, but still she remained totally motionless while Raymond continued to gently bind the leg.

When he had finished, he stroked her head with such

emotion that even Rasci and Rhamin could feel it. When he gave his affection to an animal, it was clear that Raymond Rozalski held nothing back and, as Maria watched him, it was clear also that she knew he was like that. Her eyes were soft, the way that Yeltsa looked at Rhamin. Rasci thought that perhaps, that was the way that Roxana had looked at him, only he had not recognised the look for what it was. He wasn't sure.

Raymond helped Yeltsa to her feet and lifted her down to the floor. She stood quite firmly; seemingly stronger than she had been when he lifted her into the station wagon back at the safari park. He coaxed her over to the meat that still lay on the floor. She sniffed at it, looked up at him, then grabbed a piece between her jaws and hobbled out of the open doorway. Rasci looked at Raymond. The farmer smiled and nodded to him. Taking his cue, Rasci took up a second piece of meat and carried it outside and Rhamin followed suit.

Raymond watched them from the doorway for a short while, and then he called Maria. Together, they walked over to the station wagon and, careful not to wake them, carried their children inside the house.

Rasci introduced Smokey to Rhamin and Yeltsa. It was a rather strained meeting without Lexa there, but the dog and the wolves were no longer arch enemies. Smokey watched them as they rested, some way away from her. Rasci promised that he would return again soon with Lexa. He knew that Lexa would be waiting for him at the perimeter fence, but he said nothing to Smokey. There would be too many other wolves there, and there would be a better time and place for them to meet again.

They slept and rested all through the day, occasionally watching the two vultures hovering high on a thermal, looking for some carrion, something to plunder. And, as the sun was falling from its highest point over the tree tops, nearing the end of another day, Raymond and Maria returned to the front door. Rasci thought that perhaps the farmer had been asleep also. Raymond and Maria watched the wolves resting for a while longer, and then watched as Rasci stood up, stretched his legs, and squeaked at the other wolves.

'Time to go. We have family waiting for us,' he said.

Smokey understood. She barked softly and wagged the stump on her bottom. The three wolves turned ready to leave. Rhamin gave Raymond a final look of appreciation, lifting his head and gently woofing a message of thanks. Yeltsa just looked around and gave a final glance at the two people, eager now to get back to her pack and her young cubs. Rasci didn't look back. He still sensed that the adventure had yet to run its course. Walking steadily beside Yeltsa, they left the farmstead behind and headed to meet Silvah and the others by the boundary fence.

CHAPTER TWENTY NINE

Yeltsa's strength was returning as they walked, but it was going to be a slow journey home. The wolves would not be able to lope along like they usually did.

As they reached the outer perimeter fence of the farm they all looked around but the company they were to meet were not at the rendezvous point. 'They've probably gone to find some food,' Rhamin said, as Rasci began to show his annoyance. He couldn't set off towards the Darin and let the others return to the fence, thinking that he had still not arrived. He put his head in the air and called. They would be within earshot and would return his call. But as Rasci waited, no reply came.

He called again. Yet once again there was no reply.

'There's someone coming from the south,' Rhamin said, straining his eyes to see in the fading daylight. There were two wolves as far as he could make out. 'And there are some vultures hovering over there,' he said, facing slightly further west.

'They seem to follow our pack wherever we go nowadays,' Rasci complained.

'There's some more of our pack!' Yeltsa said, excitedly, pointing her nose to the north as she spotted a small rising cloud of dust.

Feeling happier now, Rhamin and Yeltsa lay down and waited patiently. They were still experiencing the sense of new found freedom, smelling the air and listening to the sounds around them. Even the sky looked better than it had ever looked. The first star could be seen now that the sun had disappeared from sight. It was the first in the canopy that was to cover their homeland instead of the first in the cover over their prison. It was a different sky, a sky of liberty and freedom of will, a freedom that had been given back to them by this miraculous wolf that lay there beside them. And yet Rasci looked no different to them than he had ever looked. Except that, this evening, he was not the usual happy wolf that they knew. Clearly agitated, he got up and paced around them impatiently. 'We'll have to go,' he said suddenly, looking at the movement to the north.

'Settle down, Rasci,' Rhamin said soothingly. 'We're safe again now, thanks to you. We're not in a hurry.'

'Those are not our friends approaching!' Rasci's voice was strong and authoritative.

Rhamin and Yeltsa lifted their heads and followed Rasci's gaze. They saw several animals moving towards them but they were not wolves. At first it was hard to make out the figures. But Rasci knew what they were. 'It's five mountain lions,' he stated with a sense of urgency. 'It looks like two adults with some younger ones.'

'Better see what they want then,' Rhamin said, wryly. 'We can't outrun them. Yeltsa is too badly injured. The lions will not stay when they see us or the other wolves. They don't attack healthy wolves,' he insisted.

'Healthy?' Rasci's mind was thrown back to the time he had been injured. 'You're not healthy, Rhamin. I've seen more meat on a dead rabbit. And Yeltsa! She would hardly pass a fitness test if we had to make a run for it.'

Rhamin sighed. 'Huh, perhaps you're right, Rasci,' he said in a resigned voice. 'But I still can't understand what they want.'

'Well, we're going to find out, that's a fact,' Rasci said, shrugging and watching the big cats coming nearer. He could see them clearly now. He recognised the male cat that he and Roxana had fought. It still carried the marks of their last encounter. With it were a female and three cubs. Up above, Rasci heard his friend Corvak shouting loudly. He lifted his head and saw that their raven friend was trying to warn them, but it was already too late.

Rasci brought his gaze back down to earth. 'Well, what are we waiting for?' he called as he set off to meet them.

Rhamin instructed Yeltsa to stay where she was and bounded after his brother. The mountain lions seemed to be coming at them with a definite intent to attack, for normally, predators take detours to avoid coming face to face with other predators. The two big cats were at the front now, low to the ground, starting to break into a run. Behind them were three younger ones, at least three quarters the size of the female cat. Rasci could see them holding back, clearly not as confident as their parents. He met the male mountain lion, head on. Its right paw swung out to meet him, claws out and flashing at him like a striking snake, but he had seen how cats fight before. He had seen how Roxana had parried similar blows. It crossed his mind that she must have fought mountain lions before, because she was adept at it. He did the same as she had, ramming his front paws into the ground, suddenly slowing in his tracks for a split second and then, with the weight of his body still carrying momentum, he followed through as the cat's claws swung past his face. Rasci's teeth hit the mountain lion's skull as its other paw flashed around, ripping at his thick coat. With the force of Rasci's solid body still moving forward and the pressure of its own paw hitting Rasci, the big cat was thrown sideways, stunned, blood gushing from a wound above its eye as it skidded away on its side in a cloud of dust.

The female cat was going for Rhamin, but he simply side stepped as the mountain lion, leaping at him and leaving the ground, was unable to correct its trajectory. He spun around ready to take on the next strike. Now looking southwards along the fence, he could see several wolves approaching.

With its companion injured, the female cat carefully circled round until she was in front of the male lion. The three younger lions came forward nervously behind them. Rasci made another lunge at the whole group, and they all sprung backwards, the injured male, low, ears back against its skull, hugging the ground and spitting wildly as it backed away.

'We have company,' Yeltsa's voice called, as she came up behind Rhamin. With their backs to the fence, he and Rasci looked around. Two hundred yards away, four wolves were loping towards them.

'About time,' Rhamin said dryly.

'They aren't ours,' Yeltsa said, suddenly. The wolves had come well into view. They were coming along the perimeter fence and were approaching them rapidly.

'No, it's all right,' Rasci said, reassuringly, 'I know one of them.'

As the strangers came towards them, he glanced around. The mountain lions had backed off. He thought it unusual that they should attack like they did. Mountain lions seldom hunt during the day; they usually wait until darkness has engulfed their prey and then spring out of the blackness of the night. And their attack on a group of wolves seemed totally out of character. On top of that, male mountain lions don't often stay around to look after the family. It was all a bit bizarre. They milled around but maintained their distance. The two adults faced Rasci and Rhamin, and crouched down, tails flicking angrily. Their ears were back and their noses wrinkled as they spat and snarled aggressively. That seemed a good sign to Rasci. If they were going to pounce, then their ears would be forward, their faces pictures of pure concentration.

Rasci turned back to face the visiting wolves. 'Gosh,' he said, his eyes lighting up at the sight of Roxana. 'Are we glad to see you!'

But Roxana's eyes didn't reflect the same light. Her face was serious; her manner dour. She didn't speak.

'Have we met before?' Rhamin said to an older wolf. She was dark grey with a muzzle that was turning white with age. Rasci estimated she was about the same age as Silvah.

The stranger smiled. 'Surprised, are you Rhamin?'

Rhamin studied the wolf for a second or two. 'Yes,' he said, slowly. 'Yes, you could say that.'

'Thought I was dead?' she asked.

'Well as a matter of fact, I did,' Rhamin replied. 'There was a rumour that you had been killed by…'

'A mountain lion?' she asked, now grinning broadly.

'A mountain lion,' Rhamin nodded as he turned and watched the pride of mountain lions, sinisterly watching and waiting. It was all becoming clear to him.

'Tell me this is a coincidence,' Rasci said satirically. He

was already aware that there was more movement out to the west. He hoped it was his own pack.

'I doubt there is any coincidence where this wolf is concerned,' Rhamin said. 'You know who this is, don't you?' he asked turning to both Rasci and Yeltsa.

'Can't say that I do,' Rasci admitted.

'You were only young when she left.'

Yeltsa didn't speak. 'When she left?' Rasci said, more to himself than to Rhamin. Then suddenly he realised who the older wolf was. 'Rhiana? Is that really you?' he asked, surprised. She had aged, but now he recognised the wolf that had once dominated the pack and had killed his baby siblings.

Still grinning, she nodded. 'And these are my daughters, Caysha and Jyan. Don't you remember them?'

Rhamin nodded. 'You had another son, as well, I recall.'

'Indeed, I have. Brenlin. He's on his way as we speak.' She turned her head towards Rasci. 'You've already met Roxana, I believe?'

'So I've been told,' Rhamin said, before Rasci could speak. 'So, to what do we owe the pleasure?' he asked, pointedly.

'You don't remember, do you?' Rhiana's smile disappeared. Rhamin said nothing.

'Remember what?' Rasci asked. 'What should we remember?' His mind was racing now. Besides trying to work out what Roxana was doing there, he was struggling to recall what had happened when he was only a year old. As far as he knew, Rhiana had left when Rhamin took over as leader of the pack, and with her she had taken all her cubs except Solin.

'You took what my son should have had,' she said bitterly to Rhamin.

'Oh, that old song again,' Rasci put in. 'When will they ever learn, Rhamin. There is and always will be a better leader than Solin.'

Rhamin chuckled. He looked at Rasci, who was talking about Rhamin, but could just have easily been talking about himself. As he looked at his younger brother, he saw a magnificent leader.

Somewhere in the fading daylight, he could hear a vulture squawking from its night perch in some nearby tree; though at what, he didn't know.

'They sense that there's a meal in the offing,' Rhiana remarked.

'Really?' Rhamin looked back to see where the lions were. They were stalking forward again, slower this time. Yeltsa was facing them, hackles risen, ears back, head low. Rhamin moved across in front of her, keeping her protected against the fence, and then turned back to Rhiana.

'You have your mangy black spy, the raven,' Rhiana said to him with a sneer that made her yellow teeth look even more pointed. 'The vultures are my spies,' she said proudly. 'I'd introduce you to Kara and Lutz, only they don't like to come too close to their food until the meal is dead and ready to eat. They'll be along at first daylight though, to pick your bones.'

'Really?' Rhamin's posture didn't alter. 'We'll try not to disappoint them, shall we, Rasci?' Rasci thought his brother was remaining unusually calm. But that was the thing about Rhamin. He had never seen his brother show any kind of fear. His confidence was entire; no worries, no hang ups, no fear.

'They told me every move your weakling substitute has made,' Rhiana swanked, looking towards Rasci. 'He really is pathetic, you know.'

'Really?' sighed Rhamin. He sounded bored. 'So where is your other magnificent son? Don't tell me! Solin's staying out of harm's way as usual?'

'Oh, he'll be here. He's been carrying out the first part of his plan.'

'His plan?' Rasci asked, sensing that she was dying to tell them. Keeping her talking gave them time; time to think, time for Silvah and the rest of the pack to arrive.

'The decoy? You know, where Solin attacks the Darin and your stupid pack leave to assist.'

Rasci's heart sank.

'Another of his weak plans then,' Rhamin chided, still unruffled.

'Solin is twice the wolf you are, Rhamin,' Rhiana bragged.

'I hardly think so,' Rasci said, his voice becoming grave. Even in his weakened state of health, Rhamin was always going to look magnificent to Rasci. He turned to Roxana. Until now he had hoped there was a way to avoid the question. 'What are you doing with this wolf?' he asked. He wasn't sure if he wanted to know the answer.

Roxana's face was still grim. 'I tried to tell you but you wouldn't listen. You had to go on your silly rescue mission, didn't you? You couldn't just stay your stupid, silly self and be happy with that, could you?'

'Stupid?' Rasci's face saddened. 'That's what you thought of me?'

Roxana grinned bitterly. It was a face Rasci hadn't seen before. It wasn't so attractive as the smile she had given him in days gone by. Her eyes showed no pleasure now. 'We would have killed you the second time I saw you, if we had known for sure,' she hissed, nodding towards the male mountain lion. 'You thought we were fighting, didn't you?'

she laughed. Her voice cracked bitterly. 'We'd have killed you in your sleep, only you were bleating away like a crazy sheep.'

'Bleating?' Rasci felt as if he had been hit in the stomach by another of Raymond Rozalski's rocks. Suddenly his head ache had come back.

'You were dreaming, saying things about Rhamin; that he was alive and how you were waiting for him to return.'

'But you were fighting that stupid cat over there,' Rasci protested. 'I helped you send it off.'

'It was an act, you idiot wolf; a complete and utter sham!' she cackled.

'Why, for goodness sake?' He turned his head towards the mountain lions who had stopped moving forward and were reconsidering their approach.

'Because, until then, we thought Rhamin was dead and gone. But by talking in your sleep, you warned us that he might still come back. We needed to know for sure. But, it wasn't until later that we realised he was out of the way for good.'

'I thought you and I… well I thought…' Rasci didn't know what he thought any more. At this moment, nothing seemed to be real. His head was spinning.

'I made a mistake,' Rhiana broke in. 'It was I who persuaded her to make friends with you instead of killing you.'

'You were there?' He thought about the morning he had poked his nose out of the hollow into the mist; the morning that Roxana fought the mountain lion; or at least pretended to. 'I thought I'd seen another wolf!'

'Bravo!' Rhiana said, her eyes widening with delight. 'Your survival skills are sorely limited,' she sniped. 'I was sure you would have seen me before you crept out of your hole.'

'Yes, it was a mistake,' Roxana said, bitterly. She looked at Rhiana reproachfully. Somehow, to Rasci, the old wolf didn't seem so dominant now. 'Except for your interference,' she said, turning to Rasci, 'Rhamin would have remained where he was. But hearing you chuntering to yourself, my grandmother thought there was a chance that he would return. I wasn't so convinced. I wish we had killed you then, it would have saved me the trouble of having to persuade you not to go in search of your leader.' She shrugged. 'And I really thought I'd succeeded until that old wolf, Silvah butted in.' She tossed her head in the air defiantly. 'I'm impressed though,' she added. 'I really didn't think you had the brains to be able to find Rhamin let alone help him to escape from that man's prison.'

'You said "grandmother?"' Rasci said crinkling his brow as he looked at Rhiana.

'Oh, sorry!' Roxana said, bitter sarcasm in her voice. 'This is my grandmother, I'm the daughter of Brenlin, the brother of Solin,' she announced proudly, nodding to the west. From the distance, two more wolves had come much closer. 'Here comes my father and Solin, now,' she said, grinning savagely again.

'That's enough talking,' Rhiana snapped, 'Kara and Lutz are waiting for their meal. Solin will take his rightful place as ruler over this territory,' she announced, no emotion in her voice. 'We are going to end this, once and for all.' With that, she looked towards the mountain lions. 'Kill them!' she shrieked. 'Kill them all!'

As if released from a sling, the mountain lions took their cue and bounded forwards. The male, now recovered, but still bleeding, went for Rasci, but his confidence had gone and Rasci repelled him back towards the younger ones which, although they were doing a lot of spitting, threatening and posturing, hadn't swung a claw between them. The female mountain lion went straight for Rhamin. He didn't move. The female cat was smaller than her mate and Rhamin was bigger and heavier than any wolf. Her size matched his well. Yeltsa was behind him again, against the fence, in the right position so that he could protect her. Rhamin's thick coat seemed impervious to the mountain lion's ripping claws which swiped at him from both sides as her jaws of needle teeth headed towards him.

But, on three legs and with her splinted leg poking out in front of her, Yeltsa pushed past her mate and went for the tender underside of the big cat as it leapt for Rhamin's throat. As Rhamin's strong jaws contacted with the cat's face, Yeltsa grabbed the feline's underbelly. It rolled over, thrashing with its claws as Yeltsa stood over it. Using every ounce of her strength, she pinned it down, keeping her head and face close to its body while it clawed at her and snarled and spat. But she didn't let go until Rhamin was clear of its fangs. He was moving to repel three of the enemy wolves that were bounding towards him. When he was well clear of the cat, she released the mountain lion. It reeled away sideways, spitting and snarling. Regaining its balance, and struggling to run, it staggered off towards her mate.

Rhiana and her daughters attacked together. Rhamin caught Caysha's front leg and, whipping his head up, he heard something snap as she plummeted into Jyan. But, as Rhamin did that, it gave Rhiana a chance to grab a hold of the top of his fore leg. She ripped at it, pulling Rhamin off balance.

Rasci was about to grab hold of Rhiana, when Roxana, now accompanied by Brenlin and Solin, threw herself at him, lips curling, teeth lashing. Rasci fended her off, not sure that he could hurt her. But the attack gave Brenlin the chance to get in beneath her. He darted in and ripped at the flesh on Rasci's side, pulling him sideways. As Rasci moved with the motion of his attacker's head to prevent serious damage to the flesh on his rib cage, he toppled to one side. He was going down, and as he did so, Roxana grabbed his leg to prevent him regaining his balance while Solin grabbed a hold of his throat.

It would have been a fatal move for Rasci, but for Yeltsa. Running on three legs she came from behind him and clenched her jaws hard on Solin's muzzle, preventing him from closing his jaws, covering his nostrils so that he had to let go of his grip on Rasci's wind-pipe in order to breathe himself.

But Rhamin was also down, and now there were two wolves, Rhiana and Jyan, on top of him, trying to get at his throat. Prevented only by his huge mouth full of lashing teeth, they began to bite at his underbelly. What strength he had built up in the last few hours, was rapidly beginning to diminish.

From the corner of his eye, Rasci could see the female mountain lion stalking forwards once again. Now she was concentrating on Rasci. He could tell she was waiting for the chance to flash in with her sharp teeth when his neck was exposed. But he too was still down, held by Roxana who retained a firm hold of his leg, and by Brenlin who stood astride him, his jaws locked on the flesh on Rasci's side.

Now Yeltsa too had succumbed to Solin's superior strength. She had used up every drop of energy that she had recovered during her few hours of freedom and now she was at his mercy. Solin showed none. His mouth closed on Yeltsa' throat. But then, as sure as death was to follow, Solin let go. There was a cracking sound as he travelled sideways and landed squarely against Brenlin's back legs. Some force had hit Solin and had taken his body in an arcing trajectory towards his brother.

Rasci could only watch as Lexa's hot, growling, snarling form impacted with the wolf at a speed that he thought would surely break her neck. With her teeth heading up the onslaught, she impacted with the side of Solin's chest, the momentum of her thick set body and neck, knocking him in the air harder than a kick by a buffalo. He heard the crack, but it wasn't Lexa's neck. It was Solin's ribs.

Brenlin's legs buckled, but he still struggled to keep his grip on Rasci's side. Rasci's head swung upwards as Brenlin's balance changed. His teeth grabbed at Brenlin's throat but only managed to grip the loose fur beneath his windpipe. As he tugged at the flesh to draw Brenlin closer Rasci could see the female mountain lion charging towards him. She was in mid air when Lexa intercepted her, her own jaws against the mountain lion's jaws. But Lexa didn't have the thick coat of a wolf. The cat's claws ripped at her left shoulder, tearing it like a leaf. Holding onto the mountain lion's face with her clenched jaws, Lexa tried to spin out of the way of the flailing claws. Again her skin was torn, this time on her face. Blood ran into her eyes as she jerked her head from side to side, trying to worry the cat like a terrier shakes a rat. But she was going to have to let go, and if she did, then blinded by blood, she would be at the cat's mercy. The claws came around again, but unable to see them, she maintained her grip and fell sideways with the impact, dragging the growling cat with her.

Rhamin's strength was failing. He was on his back.

Rhiana had a strong hold of the flesh on his rib cage and Jyan had managed to grab a hold of his neck. Using every ounce of remaining energy, he twisted over onto his belly, dragging Rhiana around and underneath him. Jyan was also now beneath him but still holding tight onto his neck close to his throat but she dare not leave go and get a better hold. He was twisting his head to one side and lashing his teeth only inches from her own jugular.

Unlike Rhamin, Rasci was well fed and well built. He was in his prime and his energy was nowhere near depleted. He used all his strength to push himself upright with his free front leg and shook hard at Brenlin's neck. He could feel Brenlin's grip on his side weakening, but Rasci's eyes were still turned towards the lion. Its eyes were red with Lexa's blood, and wide with rage, but the enraged creature was unable to turn on his wolf dog. She was determined not to let go. Again she shook the big cat's head viciously from side to side. It was beginning to lose consciousness when the male lion came to its help. In mid air, leaping towards Lexa, its claws cut into her right shoulder, spinning her onto her back. Anchored by its claws, it landed squarely on top of her. Its jaws were already open as its teeth flashed towards her throat.

The three lion cubs had not gained their courage but they were desperate to help their mother. They had seen their father go to her aid but they could also tell that Rhamin was breaking free from his attackers and that his next move would surely be to wade in and help the dog. Together they ran at Rhamin. Now they would find out if their play fighting had only been a game or if it had taught them to survive in a real fight.

Rasci watched helplessly. He saw the lion cubs taking

off, leaping towards Rhamin as if they were one. He saw the male lion's mouthful of deadly teeth closing on Lexa's throat. Desperately he swung his head ferociously from side to side, let go of Brenlin's fur and, with his teeth barred and ready to strike anything in their way, he curled his body and pushed with his back legs against Roxana. It was all he could do to lunge in an attempt to get in between the male cat and Lexa. But Brenlin who was on the ground had grabbed at Rasci again and once again latched onto his fur, this time from beneath him, biting at the skin beneath his chest. The thrust with his legs had not been enough to put Rasci between the male lion's jaws and his wolf dog. Still pinned down, his leap fell short by inches. There was nothing Rasci could do to save his Lexa now.

But then, suddenly, a dark shadow passed over the male lion. As it glided past, it took hold of the lion's neck and carried it off to the side like a strong wind catching a leaf. The male cat crashed to the ground, legs sprawling and dust flying as it turned over and over, entwined with the black angry figure. But then Rasci recognised Smokey as the whole area was bathed in bright sunlight. Smokey had left the male lion lying wounded and was heading towards the female lion. Lexa hadn't let go of it but she needed help desperately.

Yeltsa had seen what was happening and had to think quickly. Rhamin was between her and her beloved Lexa. There was no way she could reach her but she could help Rhamin. As she jumped towards the lion cubs, the furthest of the three was thrown to the ground as Rhamin grabbed its whole head in his massive jaws and flicked it to one side. It landed next to its father, howling and spitting. Yeltsa grabbed the nearest one's neck and swung it backwards over her head. Her strength seemed to come from nowhere. One moment she was weak, the next she was unstoppable. Nothing was going to part her from her mate. She was filled with the same determination and aggression that had overtaken her in the prison camp.

The third and final lion cub was on Rhamin's back and had just closed its jaws on the back of his neck when the light came on; a dazzling unstoppable beam that made every one of the combatants freeze. Except for Smokey. She was going to kill the female lion; her anger was volcanic. It saw her anger in her eyes and in her snarling teeth and in her massive muscled body that was careering towards it like a deadly avalanche. But its face was still pinned in Lexa's jaws.

Lexa shook the female cat's head to one side yet again. Blinded by her own flowing blood, she couldn't see but she had heard the deep throaty growl of her natural mother as her black, shadowy form carried the male lion away from her body. Knocked away, the big male cat's jaws had closed a hairs breadth from her throat, but he still tore at Lexa's face with his claws, as he was spun off into the darkness. When it came, through a fog of blood Lexa couldn't tell what the light source was or from where it was coming. Then the female cat howled in surrender as Smokey's strong jaws closed on its spine. Lexa could tell it was no longer attacking her. Its claws had retraced and it was struggling against her jaws to turn its head. Amidst a chilling howl from the cat, she relaxed her grip on its face, and let her head sink to the blood soaked earth.

The male lion was going to help its mate when a crack like thunder opened the air above their heads; then again and once again. But this time, the invisible tooth of Raymond's gun cut through the air between the male mountain lion's ears. His interest in the wolf battle had suddenly wilted. The cat looked up and then, ducking his head down in case of more stray bullets, he jerked away and disappeared out of the light beam and into the night.

In the light, Rasci could see clearly what was happening. Smokey had the female lion at her mercy, her jaws locked on its backbone beneath its shoulder blades. There was no way it could reach her with its teeth or claws. It howled again as she shook it viciously. But then a call from Raymond made her leave go instantly. The lion howled again and then, dragging its back legs behind it in a trail of dust, it scrambled away after its mate and sidled off on its belly, into the black shadows.

The third lion cub sprung off Rhamin's back and followed as fast as it could.

Brenlin and Roxana followed suit and backed off. Eyes wide and stunned by the intense light, they turned and galloped away into the safety of the night.

Rhiana was last to let go of Rhamin. Jyan had already decided to retreat and fight another day, but Rhiana too, had to give way eventually to the superiority of Raymond's gun. She knew too well what it could do if he pointed it directly at her.

When Rasci regained his feet and looked around, he saw Rhamin getting up and shaking himself. He looked weak, but apart from that, he seemed no worse for his ordeal. He just sat down and scratched himself behind the neck as if it had all simply been a tumble with the cubs. Yeltsa lay on the ground. Finally spent of all her energy, she rolled over onto one side and lay panting incessantly.

Rasci went over to Lexa. Despite her exertions, her breathing was becoming shallow. He licked her face helplessly wondering what he could do to stop the blood pumping from her wounds. She was bleeding to death. As a hunter, he had seen animals wounded as badly as this before. They never lived.

Lexa raised her head the best she could and turned her eyes to him. 'I'm sorry,' she said weakly. 'Solin drew us away.' She heaved to take another breath. 'It was a siege. They attacked the Darin. Corvak warned us and we went...'

'Save your strength,' Rhamin said as he listened from Rasci's shoulder. 'Don't talk.'

But Lexa knew how badly she had been wounded and, in the time she had left, wanted to explain to Rasci why they had not been there to protect the returning wolves. 'Roxana,' she whispered. 'Silvah and I knew she had lied. I was in the back of the cave with the cubs when you told Silvah and Zelda about her. None of us ever told any of the other wolves.' Again she took a deep breath. Her voice was suddenly much fainter. 'When Solin stopped heading the attacks Silvah asked Corvak to go back to the farm to warn you. But I broke through their lines.' Closing her eyes now, she lay her head back on the blood sodden ground. 'I'm sorry we let you down,' she said, her voice trailing off to silence. She took another deep breath and fighting unconsciousness, she spoke again. 'Thanks Smokey,' she whispered.

'We're all so proud of you,' Rasci said, licking the blood from Lexa's eyes. 'You saved all our lives.' He turned to Smokey. He didn't need to say anything. He just licked her on her nose. Her big, sad, brown eyes just looked back at him from her crumpled face.

He looked towards the bright lights of the station wagon. Raymond Rozalski was silhouetted in front of them, casting a long shadow past and beyond them. He had taken off his shirt and was walking towards Lexa.

Rasci looked up at him. 'If you can understand anything we say,' he woofed, 'please don't leave her here for the buzzards.'

As if he understood, Raymond knelt beside Lexa and wiped the blood from her face, talking to her in comforting tones while he tried to stem the flow of blood from the deeply gouged flesh. Quickly, he ripped his shirt into broad strips. Then, wrapping the pieces around Lexa's chest, he folded the largest flap of skin back into place on her shoulder and pinning it tightly with his knee to stop the flow of blood, he tied it securely. He bound another length of the material tightly around her head and jaw and then, carefully, and without so much as a whimper from his patient, he lifted her limp body into the back of his station wagon, laid her on a blanket, and turned to look at the others. He just stood over the three wolves and the dead stranger and shook his head. How he had arrived there just in time, nobody knew.

Except Corvak.

But Corvak would have to wait to tell his tale. Without another word, Raymond stood to one side. The three wolves knew what his gesture meant. They were all wounded and needed attention. And without their escort of wolves back to the Darin, safety lay back at the farm. With no sign of the rest of the pack, Rhamin turned to Rasci and said, 'Looks like we've got a ride again. What do you think?'

'I think we had better take it,' Rasci suggested, and sprang up into the back of the vehicle.

Recovering slightly, Yeltsa struggled to raise her head off the ground. Seeing how weak she was, once again, Raymond lifted her up in his arms and placed her in the back of the station wagon. As soon as he had seen his mate safely inside, Rhamin followed.

Raymond took some time examining Caysha, but she showed no sign of life. It was obvious, the way the other wolves ignored her, that she wasn't one of their pack. Eventually, realising there was nothing he could do for her, he stood up straight. He walked over to the station wagon and let Smokey jump into the passenger seat, then, closing the doors, he went around to the front, got in and drove off.

Back at the farmhouse, Raymond opened the back of the station wagon and lifted Yeltsa out. Although she was still weak, she was strong enough to stand. Rhamin and Rasci jumped out beside her and then watched as Raymond lifted Lexa up in his arms and, led by Smokey, carried her through to the kitchen. Yeltsa wobbled slightly as she followed the other two wolves and Raymond through the kitchen door. They were all worried about their wolf dog. She showed no sign of life.

'Oh dear!' Maria said when she saw the state of Lexa. 'Can you save her?' she asked. Maria had been waiting for Raymond to return from the moment Corvak had noisily alerted them. They knew that Corvak was a friend of the wolves and when he landed outside the farmhouse a short time after the wolves had departed, and had danced about on the veranda first going away and then croaking as he fluttered back to their feet, refusing to go away until Raymond followed him, they had both realised that something had gone wrong.

'Can't say,' Raymond replied curtly. 'I think she's lost too much blood.'

He lay Lexa on the kitchen table and the wolves and Smokey watched as he did things with a tool sharper than the mountain lion's claw, pulling a long hair-like strand gently through the flesh and binding together the edges of Lexa's wounds while Maria pressed hard against them. When he'd finished, both Maria and he washed her carefully, dried her with a soft blue towel and then bound the injuries best they could with the same kind of white tape that he had used for Yeltsa's leg. Still the patient showed no sign of life. Raymond checked all the dressings once again and, satisfied with his work, he carefully lifted up her limp body and placed it on a blanket in the corner next to Smokey who had watched with the same unbending curiosity as her companions.

'We've done all we can.' He took hold of Maria's hand. 'We'll have to just wait and see now,' he said, shaking his head wearily.

Nobody except the children slept at the farmstead that night. Raymond and Maria checked Lexa constantly, and the door was left open so that the wolves could enter if they wished. In the middle of the night, well before daylight had broken, a stranger drove up to the farmstead in a large black truck. The three wolves watched as the driver got out, looked at them curiously in the light cast from the farmhouse door, just as they, keeping their distance, similarly watched her, and then she disappeared inside.

She was there a long time, and after she had gone, Rasci ventured into the kitchen through the still open door. Smokey came to greet him and he licked her on the nose. There was something hanging above Lexa's prone body that looked to contain liquid, and from it a tube ran down to her foreleg where it was bound to her with another white bandage.

'They took some of my blood,' said Smokey, her face strained with worry, 'and they gave it to Lexa.'

Rasci just listened to her fascinated as she explained

what had happened. He was greatly impressed. Everyone in the Rozalski household was doing what they could to save his wolf dog.

None of the wolves felt like eating that night but over the next two days Raymond offered Rhamin, Yeltsa and Rasci plenty of raw meat. Knowing that pining for their comrade would not help them recover, the wolves eventually began to eat. They took only a little food on the first day but then, on the second, they ate well for they knew they needed to build up their strength. Rhamin and Yeltsa in particular were badly under-nourished and they needed to put on some weight to even attempt the journey back home to the Darin.

Corvak had flown in and joined them on the first day. Unlike his wolf friends, he ate well and then flew off in the direction of the Darin.

Not until the third day after the fight did the wolves show any desire to leave the garden of the farmstead. It was early in that morning when Rhamin replied to a wolf call from Silvah. She had told him that, after a few skirmishes, the remainder of the renegade pack had disappeared. Rhamin was back; their enemies all knew that, and with the backing of their man friend, Roxana and her followers seriously feared retribution.

Raymond was already awake. He knew then that Rhamin's pack members awaited them. His guests had suddenly become restless and ill at ease. They needed to join their pack.

But even then, it was hard for the wolves to leave without their wolf dog Lexa. Although she had opened her eyes for just a few seconds on the second day, she was still gravely ill and had taken no food or water. They knew that in the wild open spaces of their territory, the chances of a wolf surviving such wounds would have been nil. She would have died within hours from loss of blood, or she would have been finished off by predators. The vultures would have started feeding on her open wounds even before she had taken her last breath.

The only thought that consoled them was that now she was in the one place where she had the best chance of survival.

CHAPTER THIRTY

But the life of the pack had to go on and when the wolves reunited, it was with a sense of exuberance that even though tainted with sadness, Rasci had never experienced before.

Celebrations took up a great part of the afternoon as all the wolves rejoiced. Rasci was welcomed back as a hero and he, Rhamin and Yeltsa, despite their injuries, joined in the celebration too.

Deep down, Rasci's heart wasn't in revelry, but he put on a brave face and joined in the merriment best he could, despite feeling like he would rather go away somewhere and die. It wasn't his wounds that made him feel like that. It was his heart and soul. They had been ripped out and trampled by a buffalo.

He had left Lexa dying, still no better than when Raymond had carried her from his vehicle and placed the limp body on his table. The farmer had stitched up all of Lexa's gaping wounds, but what good had it done? She had lost more blood than Rasci thought she could have ever carried in her veins. Lexa in good health would surely have cheered his spirit, but now he may have even lost her.

However, she had still been breathing when they left the

farmstead and that gave him hope. But, Lexa apart, his heart was still broken. He had believed in Roxana but now he had no idea if he had just been unlucky to be betrayed by a particularly clever and cunning wolf, or if he was really as stupid as she had said he was. The feeling lasted for days while the pack rallied around both leaders, waiting for decisions to be made, but although he showed them how much he appreciated their loyalty, Rasci's heart wasn't in any way inclined towards leadership. Several wolves, including Natan, offered to go with Rasci if he wanted to start a new pack, and Rhamin told him he could take over any part of the territory he wanted. But it was an offer that Rasci could not accept. Since Rhamin's return his headaches had completely disappeared. He hadn't had to make a single decision and, despite his sadness, he had, for a short time at least, acted the fool, playing with the cubs and all the young wolves.

As each day passed into night, his thoughts drew more and more to Lexa. He went to the back of the cave and meditated for the first time since Rhamin had returned. Why hadn't he done it recently, he wondered? It was as if he didn't need to remote view any more. His responsibilities had been handed back over to the old leader. Or was it that his mind had, for too long now, been drawn away to some other light in his life, a burning flame that had rapidly began to burn so brightly that he had begun to see nothing else around him. But it was a light that, when he reached out to grasp it, had caused him to be very badly burned. Then suddenly it had blinked out as if it had never been there in the first place. He thought about Roxana, constantly trying to work out if it had all been about power and domination rather than love and affection. Well now, despite the embers of that firestorm still smouldering inside him, he knew that this night he needed to go to see his wolf dog. She had put her life on the line to save his, as any wolf in the pack would have done, he knew that. But he couldn't help feeling there was more to it than that. Why did he think of Lexa as his wolf dog? He suddenly felt compelled to see her.

Sure enough, she was where he expected to find her. She was lying next to Smokey who was fast asleep. When they had left the farmstead his wolf dog was lying on her side, her rib cage rising and falling so slowly that he couldn't tell if she had already stopped breathing. Now she lay on her stomach and dozed with her head on her paws, breathing steadily but not really sleeping. She still had huge scars on her body with crimpled lines where the edges of her skin had been sewn together. The wounds were open to the air but had been coloured with something purple, a die that stained not only the edges of the wounds but the dark coat around them. Rasci's heart was lifted as he stood beside her and realised that, through some miracle worked by Raymond Rozalski, she was going to survive. And somehow, just like Ben had done, she noticed Rasci's ghostly figure. She lifted her head. Her floppy ears turned forward and her brow creased with the same old curious look she used when asking a question.

'Hello Lexa,' Rasci said in his mind. Lexa tilted her head on one side. She was definitely stronger. Her stump of a tail moved from one side to another ever so slightly. But she didn't make a sound. Rasci was sure she knew he was there. Then suddenly he realised they were not alone.

'Hello Rasci,' Ben's small voice said happily. 'You've come to see us again! I thought perhaps you had forgotten us now.' He had come down stairs in the night, as he often did, for a drink of milk. He looked as surprised to see his wolf friend as Rasci was to see him.

'That will never happen,' Rasci said affectionately. And he knew that was the truth.

'Lexa is getting better,' Ben said excitedly. He went over to the dog and stroked her muzzle. 'The lady vet gave her some of Smokey's blood and some salty water. She said it was her only chance.'

Lexa looked at her little friend and licked his hand, a kiss of a lick, like wolves of the pack give to each other when they meet.

Rasci's heart soared, lifted high on wings of relief. He still had his ability to visit his friends. He had established that Lexa was going to be all right. And he was positive that his wolf dog, like Ben, could see into another dimension. Now that was something to think about!

'Talking to Rasci, I suppose?' came the voice of Raymond Rozalski from the stairs.

'He's here, daddy! He's come to see how Lexa is.'

Raymond nodded. 'I know,' he said, looking at the way both his son and Lexa were looking at a point in the air a few feet from their faces.

Smokey heard the voices and finally awoke. She too could sense Rasci's presence, although she couldn't see him. She stood up and went over to where the vision of Rasci was standing and sniffed around, trying to locate him. Then she looked at Lexa and Ben with a look of puzzlement on her face before returning to her basket in the corner.

'I'll see you soon,' Rasci said to them as he turned to go. This time Lexa squeaked, not an audible sound that Ben or the farmer and his family could hear, but nevertheless one that Rasci heard.

As the days passed, Rasci still thought about his encounter with Roxana. How could he forget? Zelda had once said to him, "you are a part of everyone you meet," and so, inevitably, Roxana was a part of him. And understanding that, he was not so bitter now. But since then, all the stress of life had dissipated. The past weeks had just been a cauldron of nightmarish events, which he wanted to forget, and although he knew that total amnesia would never happen, he knew the challenges and worries that had dragged at his whole being were finally over. Now, daydreaming about unimportant things, once more there was peace and tranquillity in his life. Now, despite the dull ache of disappointment that tugged heavily at his soul, he was the old Rasci again and was discovering that, despite the past, his life hadn't changed all that much at all. He slept when he liked, played the fool when he liked and generally reverted to being his old self. And for Rhamin, Yeltsa and the rest of the pack too, life had settled back to a happy, easy going existence with plenty of game to hunt and plenty of time to sleep.

The only real worry any of them had was their concern for their wolf dog, Lexa. Rasci had explained to the rest of the pack that he had seen her and that she was getting better. They all knew he was right. None would ever doubt his psychic abilities again. Lexa still remained at the farm, however, and was to do so, it turned out, until she could regain all of her strength. She was still weak and needed more care than the pack could ever have given her; and Raymond Rozalski was the only creature that could make sure she was given the attention she needed.

It was Corvak that, more than three weeks later, brought the good news that Lexa was about to return. He had been to visit her several times and always brought back news that, spun into one of his narratives, enchanted the whole pack in the late hours of the evening. Escorted and guided by the black raven and met by a pack of excited wolves, the farmer himself, along with his children and Maria and Smokey, drove Lexa as near as was possible to the Darin to meet her pack once again. Although he would have liked her to remain at the farm as a companion for Smokey, he knew that her home would always be with the wolves.

The celebrations that took place when Lexa returned lasted as long as they had done for the leaders' arrival, the whole pack displaying their fondest affection for their heroine. The wolves all milled around the Rozalskis, not one remotely afraid. Yeltsa went over to Raymond and let him rub her broad head. Then, he bent down and looked at her bandaged leg. Though badly soiled the splint and its wrapping were still in tact. He took a sharp tool from his pocket and gently cut away the grubby binding. Yeltsa lost no time in going to showing Rhamin that her leg was completely healed. He was getting particular attention from Maria. She would never forget how he had saved her.

On her feeble legs, Zelda wobbled precariously towards Ben and Margo, and spent some time licking their faces and hands to thank them for what they and their father had done for Lexa, Rhamin and the pack. She had, for a long time, wanted to meet Rasci's little friends. The farmer and his family stood and watched the wolves' celebrations for a good half hour while Smokey seemed to get special attention from the wolves who had, no doubt, all been told of her part in the ending the battle.

Eventually, they all watched as Raymond and his family drove off into the distance and then they danced and played and squeaked their greetings to Lexa over and over again. Some of the wolves brought food from the cave and the pack ate until, having feasted until they could eat no more, their excitement abated. Eventually, tired and feeling happy that it was good to be alive, they all retired from the blazing sunshine into the cool depth of the cave to sleep.

Rhamin rested his head on his front paws and leaned his body against Yeltsa as they dozed off into their restoring sleep. Rasci went to his usual place at the rear of the cave, not far from Silvah and old Zelda. They had long ago left the party and had already succumbed to deep dreamless sleep. Lexa had also retired to the back of the cave. For a long time now she had been thinking of her two older companions whose thick coats next to her had saved her life so many times during the bitter cold winter. It was her turn to watch over them now.

Wearily, Rasci lay down next to them and thought that the day really couldn't have been any more perfect. His eyes closed, his head sunk slowly onto his feet and he began to dream.

Suddenly, he lifted his head. His ears pricked forward. Had he heard something? Was it just a wolf stirring in its sleep?

Nothing.

The subsonic vibrations were still so far away they were almost inaudible. He rested his head back on his paws and, tiredness creeping over him, he settled down to sleep and dream again.

— THE END —

The mid twentieth century was a time when wolf populations were decreasing rapidly due to many factors including farm expansion, deforestation and in particular a paranoia that drove the human species to hunt wolves to virtual extinction. It was brought about possibly by a dislike of the wolf for being more than co-incidentally comparable to the human species in its social and hunting behaviour. Long ago when man hunted for his food the wolf co-existed in great numbers. Then, when agriculture and domestication of animals developed with the consequent enclosure of those creatures, man began to take away the hunting grounds of the wolf and naturally the wolf preyed to some extent on the farm stock. The hunting of wolves that preyed on domestic animals was a natural reaction. But it did not end there. During the late 19th century early and mid 20th century the human species killed, tortured and bragged about their slaughter of wolves. They hunted them professionally and for sport and, although wolves have rarely been known to attack humans, they were hunted down in the name of self preservation. The almost overwhelming pathological hatred of wolves resulted in government financed extermination programs, especially in the USA.

There are few recorded and confirmed reports of wolves attacking humans in the USA. In Europe, there were a few incidents where wolves preyed on human beings, and in those cases their prey was mainly children (hence the depiction of wolves as savage beasts in many fairy stories). One pair of wolves killed over sixty children in France in the mid 18th century and that resulted in thousands of wolves being killed in an attempt to kill the pair responsible. But as a rule, wolves and man co-existed. The North American Indians and the Eskimos admired wolves for their hunting skills and many tribes named their members after the wolf. Compared with the savagery of man, the wolf is a social and relatively harmless animal.

Throughout many parts of the world, in the last thirty years, there have been attempts to repatriate wolves to their original homelands, although these are much smaller areas than the total geographical coverage in the northern hemisphere that wolves dominated two or three hundred years ago. The legislature of the USA in particular, (after passing laws in the earlier part of the century offering bounty on wolves to eradicate them) has taken steps in the US Endangered Species Act of 1976 to protect wolves, although even today wolves (including those wearing tracking collars) are still killed.